Revelation

Part I

J.B. Vosler

The New Atlantian Library

Habent Sua Fata Libelli

The New Atlantian Library

Manhanset House
Shelter Island Hts., New York 11965-0342

bricktower@aol.com • tech@absolutelyamazingebooks.com
• absolutelyamazingebooks.com

Library of Congress Cataloging-in-Publication Data
Vosler, j.b.
Revelation, The Sons of Jacob Series, Book VIII. Part I
p. cm.

1. FICTION / Thrillers / Psychological. 2. FICTION / Romance / Suspense.
3. FICTION / Mystery & Detective / International Mystery & Crime
Fiction, I. Title.
Part I, ISBN: 978-1-955036-53-5, Trade Paper
Part II, ISBN: 978-1-955036-54-2, Trade Paper

November 2023

Revelation

Part I

Sons of Jacob

Book VIII

J.B. Vosler

Contents

END OF PART I

THE SONS OF JACOB Saga

BOOK I: "Shadow of the Phoenix"

This novel introduces MARTIN HENDERSON, who has survived a deadly fire only to return three-and-a-half years later as an assassin for EDWARD MORNINGSTAR, a Pentagon aide who sees himself as a Biblical Jacob. Henderson, once a brilliant entrepreneur, is now compelled to do whatever Morningstar asks – including murder – as a result of Morningstar's threat against a notable little girl, LILI PLATACIS. Henderson had sworn to protect Lili, and, when she is then taken, Henderson vows to bring down not only Morningstar, but his entire operation. In the meantime, Henderson's former lover, Senator Cynthia Madison – MADDI – has also become a Morningstar target, and it's up to Henderson to save her.

BOOK II: "The Maker's Prophecy"

The delusional Morningstar, who thinks he is Jacob, is well on his way to world domination. He has "adopted" twelve sons, who are his soldiers and will do whatever he asks. Henderson has made it his goal to stop Morningstar, and is doing what he can to undermine his efforts. Meanwhile, a deadly virus has been unleashed in Columbia, South Carolina, and Maddi's brother, ANDREW, as Medical Director of a downtown clinic, is the first to see its effects. When a more aggressive strain of the same virus shows up in Chicago, L.A., and Texas, Henderson knows Morningstar is somehow behind it. Maddi is once again threatened, and he must figure out a way to keep her safe from Morningstar's relentless pursuit.

BOOK III: "The Rise of the Avenger"

An entire village is massacred outside the town of Bariloche, Argentina, and Maddi is pulled into action at the request of one of her dearest friends, SIR ARTHUR KAUFFOLD, a former ambassador. She puts together a coalition to travel to the region. Morningstar learns of it, and sends two 'sons' to Bariloche to stop her. She succeeds not only in defending the coalition, but in averting a war with Argentina, thanks to the intervention of her former lover, HANK CLARKSON, the Deputy Director of Homeland Security. Meanwhile, Henderson has gone to Russia to undergo a revolutionary surgery designed to give him a completely new face. He then vows to seek revenge against Morningstar.

BOOK IV: "Strike of the Cobra"

A vicious assassin, COBRA, has killed a former IRA operative outside Donegal, which has thrown the Irish Republic into chaos. Cobra, also known as Dan, is one of the sons of Jacob, and has been instructed by Morningstar to carry out multiple killings in an effort to disrupt the UK and France. Maddi discovers that she is being stalked by someone from the UK, and insists on flying to London to find him. Henderson, who has undergone surgery and has changed his name to MATT, goes to D.C. to introduce himself to Maddi as Martin's cousin. He learns she has gone to the UK, and – when he learns why – follows her there. Hank does the same, and the two men are forced to work together to keep her safe.

BOOK V: "A Battle for Justice"

MARK JUSTICE, a British Private Inquiry Agent, seeks help for debilitating headaches, only to learn that he has an evil alter ego. Maddi had sought his help to find her stalker, and he has now become obsessed with her. She has left London to meet up with Henderson at his Latvian estate, their first reunion after four long, desperate years. Hank follows them, but then sees Maddi's devotion to Henderson, and decides to leave. But before he can, he learns that his CIA agent son, ROGER CLARKSON, has been taken by Cobra. He and Henderson are again forced to work together to try to not only keep Maddi safe from Morningstar, but to find Roger and save him from Cobra. It is then that Hank learns a terrible secret about Henderson.

BOOK VI: "The Morning Star"

A Nazi-era warship has been under the protection of a small group of families since its discovery in the late 1940's. Calling themselves "The Morning Star," a translation of the vessel's name, the group's mission is twofold: to understand its technology, and to keep it from falling into the wrong hands. When a powerful neo-Nazi threatens them and tries to steal the warship, the group is called into action. Led by Henderson's father, WALTER, they must do all they can to protect the vessel. Morningstar learns of the group, and assigns his son, SIMEON, to infiltrate their organization, which is about to meet in Paris. Meanwhile, Henderson and Hank arrive in Paris to save Roger from Cobra, and are led on a deadly game of cat-and-mouse. Maddi follows them, and saves Roger, but is devastated to learn that Henderson has been taken by the infamous killer.

BOOK VII: "The Vesper Bell"

Both Walter and Maddi have been lured to Lyon, expecting to meet Henderson in the town square. Instead, they are kidnapped by Cobra and taken to a remote dungeon, where they find Henderson close to death. Cobra travels to Scotland, stumbles upon an exact replica of his childhood school, and decides to bring his prisoners there. They are soon joined by Inspector Pritchard, Walter's wife Dora, his mistress Nenita, and psychiatrist James Samuels. When a fire begins to consume the old school, Cobra is prepared to leave them to die. Through the heroic efforts of Maddi's brother Andrew, and CIA agent Roger Clarkson, all seven are saved. Cobra escapes, however, and Henderson falls into a coma. As Maddi is about to go with him to the hospital, she reveals to Hank the stunning truth that Matt Henderson is actually Martin.

"The truth is rarely pure and never simple."

~ Oscar Wilde ~

PROLOGUE

December 1982, Indianapolis, Indiana

Harold Madison ran a hand through his thin gray hair, sighing as he waited for the 747 to taxi to the terminal. *I'm too old for this,* he thought, as he folded his novel and tucked it in his bag. Though flying in the 1980's was quicker and far more comfortable than it had been a decade ago, he still found it to be long and tedious. He looked to the seat next to him, where his financial advisor was stowing his ledger into his briefcase. Peter, who had been with him for nearly thirty years, also looked a bit ragged from the journey. Oh, that they could both be settling in quietly for an afternoon brandy by a fire in the hearth. But there would be no fire, and there would most certainly be no brandy… not on this trip. This flight across the pond had been predicated on need, and, though Harold had yet to learn what it was that was needed, he could tell by the tone of his daughter-in-law's voice that something terrible had happened.

Nonetheless, he was glad that Jeannie had called him. She hadn't been willing to tell him over the phone what had happened, but one thing was clear: there would be a mess to clean up. And, though he would soon be 78 years old, with his memory fading in ways he hated to admit, one thing still held true: Harold knew how to clean up a mess.

He and Peter stepped off the plane, each with a small carryon. They walked from the overseas terminal toward Customs. They had no luggage to retrieve; they weren't going to be there long. As a matter of fact, if things went as hoped, Harold would handle whatever thorny problem had occurred, check in on his grandchildren, then leave on the last flight out. *Back to England by tomorrow's sunrise.*

3

They got through Customs with little fanfare and walked to the front of the terminal. They stepped outside, and were met with the biting chill of an early December morning. Harold hiked his collar and lowered his hat. Though the air was cold, it wasn't entirely unpleasant. *Perfect for growing Christmas roses,* he thought absently, as he buttoned his coat to his neck.

They walked several yards to the taxi queue. He had refused to let Jeannie pick him up. For one thing, even at nine in the morning it was quite possible that she had been drinking. For another, it was imperative that Harold control every step of the agenda…including when and where he traveled.

The phone call from Jeannie had surprised him. He and his daughter-in-law weren't exactly close. Though he and his wife Gloria had done their best to stay in touch with the grandchildren over the years, they hadn't done the same with Jeannie. Gloria had done a far better job of it, as she was more compassionate toward the situation, and had made a point of calling Jeannie at least once a month. As for Harold, he and Jeannie had barely spoken since the funeral of her husband – Harold's only son – ten years ago. It wasn't out of animosity, but out of a keen understanding that their strongest point of commonality had been laid to rest. Harold flinched as he recalled that painful day in this painful place. A memorial service, followed by a burial, and that was the end of it. There had been no viewing; his son's face had been shattered by a felon's bullet.

A stiff breeze forced him to lower the brim of his hat even further. Gloria had made several visits to America since the funeral, and had made a point of inviting the children to England at least twice a year. Harold, on the other hand, had crossed the Atlantic only three times since then, and never for more than a day or two, and he had hated every minute of it. Not that he hated America, or even Indianapolis, he just hated what had happened to his son. He had never approved of Stewart becoming a cop. *"What sort of occupation is that for the son of a British nobleman?"* But Stewart had insisted. His best friend Colon, who had flown over as part of a university exchange program, had gone missing from a small college in Indianapolis the year before and Stewart had been bound and determined to find him. *"What better way than by becoming an agent of the law in the region where he disappeared?"* Harold had felt that

Colon had vanished by choice – he had always been an unhappy boy filled with the wanderlust – but Stewart had been convinced that something sinister had happened. *"His last letter just wasn't right, Father."* Regardless, there had been no talking him out of it, and, once Stewart had been accepted into the Indianapolis Police Academy, that was the end of it. But the final straw had come when he had chosen to marry the charming but rather common Jeannie Cantrell from McCordsville. It was then that Harold knew that he no longer had a say – or a stake – in what happened to his son.

Though he might have disregarded the call from his estranged, alcoholic daughter-in-law, there were two reasons he had chosen to respond. The first was Gloria's insistence that he do so, *"She is the mother of your grandchildren, Harold…it is your duty."* The second was the nature of Jeannie's request. *"We need your help, Harold."* Not only had she used the plural "we" instead of the singular "I," but her request for help was uncharacteristic. In spite of the fact that he had never approved of Jeannie, she did possess one quality that he admired greatly: she never asked for help.

"Where to?" the cabby asked as Harold and his aide slid into the back seat.

Harold frowned. "Evansville." He checked a scrap of paper he had pulled from his pocket and added, "Eight-fifty-five Park Avenue."

The driver frowned. "That's almost three hours from here, you know."

Harold nodded. "Is that a problem?"

The driver's eyes widened; he quickly shook his head, "No sir," and pulled away.

As they left the terminal and pulled onto the highway, Harold tried to think how old Stewart's children would be. Andrew was eighteen when he had last seen him – at his high school graduation in the spring of '78 – which would put him at about twenty-two. Gloria had told him recently that Andrew was completing his first year of Medical School. *A respectable line of work,* he thought, as he tried to think how old Cynthia would be. Though Stewart and Jeannie had insisted on calling her Cindy, Harold had always preferred Cynthia. He sighed. She would be about 15 by now. Suddenly he grinned. *Ah…the irrepressible Cynthia Madison…*

"Grampa! We are so excited you've come to visit!"

Harold bent low, and she ran up and hugged him around the neck. He patted her on the back, surprised by the gesture. After all, they saw one another so rarely. "I wouldn't miss your fifth birthday for the world, Cynthia!"

She giggled. "Everyone calls me Cindy, Grampa, but Cynthia sounds so much prettier." She looked over her shoulder at her father, "...don't you agree, Daddy?"

Stewart grinned and nodded. "Yes, I do. We'll make a point of calling you Cynthia from now on."

But they hadn't. She had been Cindy up until the day Stewart died.

Harold closed his eyes and leaned back, the long flight from London having taken its toll. He must have nodded off, for soon he felt the cab slow, then turn onto a narrow street with houses on both sides. They stopped in front of the last house at the end.

"We're here, buddy."

Peter took care of the fare, and opened the door for Harold. He made an effort to help Harold out of the car. Harold batted his hand away. "I can still walk, Peter."

"Certainly, sir."

The cab pulled away and they stood there, staring at the house. It wasn't the home that Stewart had bought in McCordsville. That house had been sold soon after his death, when the family had moved to Evansville. No, this home was unremarkable in every way. Harold noted some chipped paint, and a gutter or two that had pulled away from the roof, but otherwise, it was in reasonable condition; the grass was mowed, the hedges trimmed. He stood at the foot of the walk, taking it all in, and, when he could put it off no longer, he started toward the house. Peter followed. They walked along a cement walk with dirt in the cracks where mud had caked after the last rain. As they climbed a few steps to the gray front door, Harold did his best to not think back on the home that his son had bought – and delighted in – 24 years ago...

"So, what do you think, Father?"

Revelation

Harold looked at the small house sitting on less than an acre of land, and had to fight not to roll his eyes. "Where will you plant the roses, son?"

Steward beamed, and waved Harold to the backyard. There before them was a four-foot-square patch with rosebushes blooming in brilliant fashion. In spite of himself, Harold grinned. "They're hardy, son...lovely, I have to say."

Stewart nodded. "It was what sold us on the place. The roses were already here...just waiting for a Madison to keep them growing..."

Harold cleared his throat and straightened his collar as he knocked on the faded door. He wondered if Jeannie had planted roses in this Evansville backyard. He shook his head. *Not likely.* He waited, then knocked again. He looked around. He was standing on a small porch which could use a coat of paint. Off to the side was a single lawn chair, with a small table sitting next to it. No other furniture; no pots, no planters, nothing to suggest that much more happened in that house beyond just getting by. He felt despair deep in his heart, and was glad when he heard the shuffling of feet on the other side of the door.

It was opened and he was greeted by a woman he barely recognized. Jeannie Madison had aged...and not just chronologically. She was wearing a baggy sweater and a faded pair of jeans, and, though her hair was combed, it had clearly not been colored or cut in quite a long while. There were deep lines on her forehead and around her eyes. She looked more like sixty instead of forty-three. It was clear that Stewart's passing, though a full ten years ago, still had her reeling. She smiled and her sallow skin looked as if it might crack. But the smile was genuine. Her eyes looked tired, but kind, and Harold fought a pang of regret.

"Thank you so much for coming, Har—Mr. Madison. Please come in."

Harold knew he should insist that she call him Harold...*I am her father-in-law, after all*...but he simply nodded as he stepped inside. His advisor followed.

"This is Peter," he said perfunctorily.

Jeannie reached out a thin, bony hand. "Nice to meet you, Peter."

Harold sensed that she was nervous, but he didn't smell alcohol. *A nice surprise.*

She walked them into the living room and offered them each a seat in two upholstered chairs that had seen better days. She sat on a couch across from them. She pushed a strand of hair behind one ear as she said nervously, "Can...can I get you something to drink?"

"No, thank you," Harold said quickly. Peter simply shook his head.

Again, she smiled, but this time it was with shame. "I'm sorry... the place...isn't—" She shook her head quickly. "I've—I've just been so upset, of late."

Harold had to bite his tongue as he glanced in the kitchen and saw an empty wine bottle on the counter and dishes in the sink. "Now, what is this problem that you need my help with, Jeannie?"

She looked like she was about to cry. She was shaking and he stood, walked over to her, and put his hand on her shoulder. She looked up at him and smiled weakly. Her blue eyes welled with tears as she said, "Cindy is in trouble."

PART I

DAY 1

"Three things cannot be long hidden:
The sun, the moon, and the truth."

~ Buddha ~

CHAPTER 1

Edinburgh, Scotland

The muscles in Maddi's thighs were burning, but still she kept running. Harder, faster...as if she couldn't run fast enough. The sun was only beginning its rise, and it cast long, looming shadows on the castle in the distance. It inspired her. She could imagine that castle in a similar light, those inside waiting for an attack from the British during the centuries-long battles that plagued Scotland and England, or perhaps an assault by the French during the Seven Years' War. Brave soldiers facing insurmountable odds as they fought for an ideal...their willingness to give their lives for freedom. She breathed in, heartened by the image, and by the morning air not yet tainted by the smell of diesel from the buses that would soon run up and down the primeval streets of Edinburgh.

This morning's run had taken her farther than the day before, and she felt it in every muscle of her body. She reached the end of the Royal Mile, looked over her shoulder for a final view of the castle, then sprinted toward Calton Hill. From there, the nursing facility was only three kilometers away.

She had made a similar run most days of the last few months, finding the tedium of sitting by Henderson's sick bed almost more than she could take. She had learned that the monotony was eased at least a bit when she took her own body to a limit she could barely stand. Then again, was it monotony she was running from? Or was it something else? What was it her mother used to say? *"Time to yourself is nice, Cindy, but too much time can make you dwell on things better left forgotten."* Maddi's life had been so crazy for so long, that she had had little time to think...to dwell. But now, as her lover lay in an unrelenting coma, all she had was time. Though she had tried to fill the hours with novels, senate intrigue, or chats with friends, she had had far too much time to think. And think she did…about her life, her loves, her past. And it was carving a hole deep inside her, as if the regret and shame had finally found a home. How she longed for the chaos of her DC life, or the wild journeys as she went in search of a man she thought had died.

Henderson hadn't died, but he had most certainly changed. And those changes were profound. She had yet to learn details; there hadn't been time before he fell into his coma to share all that he had been through over the last four years. So, it would have to wait. And, in the meantime, Maddi was left alone…with her thoughts…with her past.

Which is why she had decided to start running. It had come to her while she was watching the time trials for the summer Olympics in Greece, which had been held in the spring. The sheer pain and self-discipline it took for those distance runners to become the best had inspired her. *I'll bet they don't have time to think about the past.* But a simple jog wouldn't do it; Maddi needed to hurt…her muscles, her chest, every part of her needed to feel absorbed by the run. Only then would she be able to turn off her thoughts.

And it had worked. She had started slow. A kilometer or two just to stretch her legs had quickly become ten-kilometer mini-marathons in the heart of Edinburgh. Harder, faster, every day a challenge to run to the point of exhaustion…to the point when, at last, she could push it all away.

Push what away? she wondered as she started up Calton hill. It wasn't just her worry for Henderson, or her discovery that he was alive after four long years of silence. It wasn't even her recent captivity with six others in an abandoned schoolhouse, chained to chairs as the school burned to the ground. It wasn't the loss of her father when she was just a child, the loss of her mother to alcohol, or the murder of so many good men who had been assigned to keep her safe. It wasn't even the attempted murder of Maddi herself on far too many occasions. No, there was something more terrible, more threatening than all of those things…and that was what she was trying to get away from.

She grinded up the hill, her shallow breaths coming faster as her chest ached for air. She reached the top and, without slowing, ran past the National Monument toward the other side that would lead down the hill and back to the nursing facility.

She looked over her shoulder, glad to see Cravens at her heels in a black sedan that was being driven by a Scotland Yard police officer. Cravens had originally run with her, but once she passed the five-kilometer mark, he had recruited the car and driver, stating that '...*it's more responsible to have two of us on that road in those dark hours before dawn.*' Maddi didn't care how he justified it; she was just glad to have him.

Why? Who's after you, Maddi? What are you afraid of? The last question had become like a broken record, and, whenever it would enter her mind, Maddi would fall into an all-out sprint to try to push it away. *Everybody has secrets they're not proud of,* she thought as she braced herself for the steep run down the mound. "But not like this one," she muttered as she barreled down the back of Calton Hill.

She came to the bottom and looked over her shoulder for Cravens. She saw him and gave a quick wave. As she turned back around, she stopped. The sun had just come over the hill and was shining like a spotlight on the front of a police station. For whatever reason, it made her feel sick inside. Was it the architecture? Modern red brick, so different from the aged gray stones that were such an integral part of Edinburgh? Or was it its location...a single-story structure all alone with a park across the street?

Keep going, Maddi. She stared for a second longer, then forced herself to resume her run. *Only three kilometers to go,* she thought as she picked up her pace. She turned right onto Leith Street and began her final sprint to the nursing home. Her heart was pounding and, though it was a cool fifty degrees, she was sweating profusely.

Fifteen minutes later she had finished the run, and she waited for Cravens as he got out of the car and waved a quick goodbye to the officer. They walked inside and took the elevator to the third floor. They went to Henderson's room and, as Cravens had done every day for the past four months, he did a quick inspection. He nodded to Maddi that it was all clear, then took his seat just outside the door. Maddi walked in, gave Henderson a kiss on the forehead, then walked into the bathroom to shower.

She hadn't always bathed there. When they first arrived in Edinburgh, she and her agents had reserved rooms in a downtown hotel. But it soon became clear that it was of little use, as Maddi was spending every waking moment at Henderson's side, first at the hospital, then at the extended-stay facility. Once she realized she had access to a bathroom and a cot, the hotel was little more than a place to store her clothes. So, she had moved out of the suite, had secured rooms for her two agents, and had moved in with Henderson. His parents, Walter and Dora, had then thoughtfully arranged for a larger room with two beds, and Maddi had been there ever since. They had seemed to welcome her presence there; as if her steadfast devotion might be enough to bring him back.

She took a shower, then stepped out and dried her hair in front of the mirror. As she pulled away the towel, she caught a glimpse of herself. No matter how many times she saw it, she was still awed at how much she had changed. Over the last six months she had lost a good twenty pounds, leaving her thinner than she had ever been. Her cheeks were no longer full, her clothes barely fit. She had been relegated to buying new slacks in Edinburgh. It was a pair of those and a loose sweater that she pulled on now. She finished drying her hair, which had grown considerably longer, then pulled it behind her head.

I need to get it cut, she thought as she walked into Henderson's room. She looked down at him – eyes closed, hair pushed back, feeding tube in place – and was suddenly overcome. Every day it was the same…his eyes never opened; his expression never changed. As if he was a mannequin that she had been charged with overseeing.

She turned to the window with a sigh. Rain was threatening. *What's new?* she thought as she walked over and pulled back the curtain. She looked down at the street and frowned. Streaks of soot were present on stone houses that were lined up side by side on the narrow street. They could have been from anywhere; the tidy homes would have seemed just as natural in London, or even Boston or Philadelphia; it had all begun to look the same. As had the room itself. Other than her morning runs or her afternoon walks in the garden, her only reality was those four walls; her only company – most of the time, anyway – was the hum of the monitors by Henderson's bed.

Henderson had been moved to the private facility four months ago, after a month at an Edinburgh hospital. The move had been prompted by his parents, who had insisted that their only son, who was clearly not coming out of his coma any time soon, be cared for in luxury. *"He must have the best of everything,"* his mother Dora had said.

And Maddi couldn't blame her. After all, the son she had thought she had lost to a fire four years earlier was alive, but barely. He, along with the rest of them, had been held prisoner five months ago in an abandoned schoolhouse in Dalgety Bay. The bay was only twenty miles north of Edinburgh, but, as she thought of it now, it seemed a thousand miles away. All of them had come about as close to death as anyone could, and the memory of it often awakened her in those dark hours before dawn. She would shoot up from her bed, wait for her eyes to adjust, then rub her wrists where the shackles had left a mark. She would stare at Henderson to make sure he was still alive, then do her best to go back to sleep. When she failed, she would get up, put on her sweats, and go for a run.

But the solitude of the nursing home was preferable to how it had been at the hospital. Nearly every day in that hospital room she had been peppered with questions, most of them about Henderson. As she had sat stiffly in a Queen Anne chair, Britain's MI6, Interpol agents, and America's CIA had drilled her over and over with questions she couldn't answer. *"How do you know Matt Henderson? Where had you been prior to being taken from the square? Why had you gone there?"* And every time her answer was the same. *"I don't remember."*

And to some extent, it was true. A lot had happened, and Maddi had managed to forget at least some of it. But she knew what those interrogators were looking for; why they were so curious about her relationship with the man in the bed. Known as Matt to the authorities, his past was more than murky. Though Walter had vouched for him, his arrival in the Henderson world had been sudden and unexpected. Not only that; he had recently tangled with Cobra, offering himself in exchange for CIA agent Roger Clarkson. If nothing else, authorities were intrigued by what might have motivated the selfless act.

What they didn't know was that Matt was actually *Martin* Henderson, and the selfless act had, at least in part, been predicated on his hatred for his half-brother, Cobra. No one knew of that relationship, of course, and it was imperative they never learn of it.

But there was more to his need for secrecy. Martin was thought to have died four years ago in a hotel fire, but had been pulled from the rubble at the last minute. He had been transformed into a CIA assassin known as Phoenix, who had recently been accused of going rogue. Wanted in connection with the Lassa fever attacks that had taken place in January, he had changed his appearance in an effort to hide. Only Maddi, his parents, and Hank Clarkson knew the truth; not only that Matt was Martin, but that he was also the Phoenix. Maddi felt certain that he had played no role in the January attacks; there was no way the man she had met in Providence four years ago was capable of such a thing.

Which was why she had gone along with the charade, going so far as to dye his hair every week or so to keep his blond hair black. She would pick up the dye during a morning run, hiding the purchase by telling Cravens that she 'needed a moment alone' to buy personal items. She would apply the dye in the middle of the night, wash it out in an emesis basin, then empty the basin in the toilet. She kept the basin and the dye under the bed, and put the stained towels in a plastic bag to throw away when no one was looking.

She frowned as she looked over her shoulder at her handiwork; the black hair so different from the color it had been before. As a matter of fact, Henderson looked nothing like the man she had met four years ago; the tall, blonde, magnetic man who had swept her off her feet. Not only was his hair a different color, but his face had changed as well. He had undergone a surgery which had literally given him another man's face. But nothing had changed more than the man himself. Though Maddi had yet to learn just how much, she had sensed it instantly when the two had been reunited. The magnetism wasn't gone, but it had been altered. He carried himself differently; more careful...less kind.

She walked to the overstuffed chair where she spent most of her day, and leaned down to grab her phone from her purse. As she did, she spotted the black leather journal that Henderson had left for her in Latvia. He had known when he flew to Paris that his efforts to save Roger from the Cobra could likely lead to his death. He had given her the journal in an effort to be honest about who he was and what he had done those four years when everyone thought he was dead. But the journal had become like a thorn in her side, the few entrees she had read confirming her fears that even if he awoke from the coma, he most certainly wasn't well. There was heartache on those pages, and sin...

deep-rooted sin. She hadn't been able to read more than a few pages. His agony was palpable in every word. She had decided to wait until he could be with her to read the rest of it.

She brushed her fingers over the black leather, thankful to have the journal once again in her possession. She had locked it in a safe in Lyon just before she had left for that fateful journey to the square, where she had later been kidnapped by Cobra. After she was freed, she had wanted to go back for it, but had been unwilling to leave Henderson's side for the day-long journey to France. When it became clear that his condition wasn't likely to change any time soon, she had decided to go back. The trip had been a quick one. A flight from Edinburgh to Lyon, a cab ride to the hotel, the retrieval of the journal, along with the travel bag she had left in the suite, then a flight back, all in the span of about seven hours. Other than a bit of reluctance on the part of a front desk clerk, she had retrieved both the journal and the bag with little fanfare. She had been relieved that the hotel's cleaning staff, rather than prying open the locked safe, had taken it to a storage room behind the front desk. After showing the clerk two photo ID's, and verifying not only the dates of her stay, but who had checked in with her, she was permitted into the storage room, where she had opened the safe using the same code that she had created five months earlier. She had nearly wept when she saw the journal. Being reunited with his writings had made her feel a sense of wholeness…as if she had once again found the key to unlock the story of Henderson's transformation from respected magnate to hired gun. She still couldn't read it; that was asking too much, but at least she had it. She had shoved it in her purse, which is where it had been ever since.

She reached past the journal for the phone and set it on the table, then walked back to the window. The phone was new; her old one had been destroyed by Cobra soon after he kidnapped her. The new phone had a different number, which meant that very few were able to reach her. Which was fine with her; there were few she actually wanted to hear from, and even fewer she was willing to call.

It was nearly eight a.m. in the UK; three a.m. back home. She would likely get at least one phone call in the next hour or two. Her secretary Phil was an early riser, and called her nearly every day to fill her in on all that was going on in the Senate and in DC. She looked forward to the calls…Phil's colorful updates on Senate intrigue.

She had known soon after arriving at the nursing home that Henderson's recovery – if there was to be a recovery – would take a long time, and that she needed to find someone to fill her senate seat until she could return to DC. She had spoken with Indiana's governor, and he had agreed to appoint State Senator Jana Smith to fill Maddi's seat while she was away. The two had worked together in the State House, and Maddi was confident that Jana would hold true to her values. *"Now, this is just temporary, right Senator?"* the governor had asked. Maddi had assured him it was. *"You know how I love the Senate, Governor. I'll be back as soon as I get things taken care of over here."*

She leaned against the sill, a sudden pang of loneliness making her physically weak. She lifted the window, ignoring the squeak from hinges that had seen far too many storms, and breathed in. She could smell the rain and it made her smile. She had grown to welcome the omnipresent rain. The rare sightings of the sun only served to highlight all that had gone wrong; the good men and women who had died over the last eight months. Two Secret Service agents, the Secretary of State, a cop-turned-government-agent by the name of Victor Silva, and another trusted agent, Spencer Seacroft, who was fighting for his life in a Lyon hospital, a victim of the attack in the square. So much misery, so much death. And now, it was possible that the man she had mourned for four longs years would soon merit mourning again.

What does he think about as he lays there? she wondered as she turned to look at him. Was he negotiating? Trying to make amends for a past that had clearly been violent and cold, a set of choices that had been forced upon him by circumstances he couldn't control?

Because that was what Maddi was doing…all the time, it seemed. Trying to bargain with her Maker to somehow forgive her for choices she had made in a soulless moment, decisions that had been forced upon her by circumstances she couldn't control, verdicts which had been brought about by the actions of a truly treacherous man.

She stared at the black-haired man in the bed. Who was he? And who would he be when he finally awoke? *If he does, in fact, awaken.* She continued to stare, knowing that, whoever he was, they would both have confessions to share.

CHAPTER 2

Washington, DC

God, what is wrong with that woman? Edward Morningstar watched as his lovely Janet shot up from the bed and stormed into the bathroom without a word. The woman he had spent over half-a-year with had suddenly become flighty...unpredictable. Though he typically would've booted her out for her erratic behavior, he found it oddly provocative.

He sat up in the bed they shared at the Starlight Hotel, the out-of-the-way inn that had become their refuge. Nestled in the outskirts of Washington, DC, it offered them far more privacy than the downtown hotels. Which was a good thing. As he had told his sons time and time again, *"Keep your private life private...the wolves are always at the door."*

He lit a cigar as he looked out the window at the darkness. *So... where are the wolves tonight?* Who was out there trying to disrupt Morningstar's Master Plan? Was it the elite fools who were part of a secret organization, ironically known as the Morning Star, who had done their best to keep a magical warship hidden from the world? Or was it his once-favored son, Joseph – Martin Henderson – who had deceived him, first in deed, and now in actual appearance? Or was it Henderson's well-to-do father, Walter, who was using his army and his influence to try to stop Morningstar at every turn? Or maybe it was the fair-haired Cynthia Madison, who, as a member of the esteemed United States Senate, had done all that she could to bring down not only Morningstar, but the men with whom he did business? He sneered. It didn't matter who was trying to stop him. Every one of them were idiots.

He puffed his cigar, blew out a perfect smoke ring, then said aloud, "As the great Bard once said, 'I would challenge you to a battle of wits, but I see you are unarmed.'" He laughed and looked at a clock on the table. *Three a.m. Geez, Janet, can't you at least hold off your antics until sunrise?* He ran his fingers through his coal-black hair. *I need a haircut.* It was longer than it had ever been. Morningstar's father – the overbearing green beret captain who had made his life a living hell – had insisted early on that Morningstar wear his hair short. *"It shows discipline, Edward, something I can only dream that you will someday acquire."* Morningstar smirked as he felt the hair teasing the tops of his ears. *Maybe I'll let it go to my shoulders…that'll show him who is really in charge.*

He shoved off the covers and got out of bed. He walked to the window. The sky was completely black. No stars, no moonlight, just a thick patch of clouds that had eliminated all light but for a single lamp post about ten feet away. He could make out the shadows of a walkway that led to an uninspired garden, but that was it. The lights of DC had been dowsed for the night…the Work of the People done for another day. He smirked. *Work of the people, my ass…everyone in DC is after one thing…power.* He laughed. "Little do they know; it will be I who acquires it...all of it."

He turned from the window and stared at the bathroom door. *What is that girl doing in there?* He heard bath water being run. *Why in God's name does she need a bath at three in the morning?* He shook his head and walked out to the living room, grabbing a robe on his way. He pulled it on, tying it loosely around his waist as he sat at the desk and opened his laptop. "Might as well look in on the boys," he said as he set the cigar in an ashtray. "Now, what time is it in France?" He did the math. "Nine a.m. I'll start with Simeon."

His soldier son, Simeon, had been sent to France five months ago to join forces with another son, Naphtali, who had been sent there to find a warship known as the Morning Star. Named in honor of Morningstar's Nazi grandfather, it was a World War II German warship that, five months earlier, had been stolen from its secret location near Montbard, France, and taken to the mountains that spanned the eastern part of the country. There it had either been hidden or destroyed. Naphtali had killed the man who had stolen it, the German Vice-chancellor, Dolf Mueller, by dropping a bomb on his truck as he was trying to escape. Naphtali had been looking for the vessel ever since.

Simeon had joined the effort soon after the Dalgety Bay fiasco in mid-March.

Morningstar flinched as he recalled the incident at Scotland's Dalgety Bay. It hadn't gone as planned. Another son, Dan, whom the world knew as Cobra, had imprisoned seven prestigious people in an abandoned schoolhouse. Three of those prisoners were important to Morningstar, and he had done all that he could to convince Cobra to turn them over to him. Cobra had refused, so Morningstar had sent Simeon and another son, Gad, to Dalgety Bay to kidnap them. But the plan had gone awry. A fire had taken down the entire schoolhouse, but the seven prisoners had somehow survived. Cobra had run off, leaving the prisoners, including the three that Morningstar wanted, suddenly part of a Scotland Yard inquiry. Which meant they were now off-limits to Morningstar.

He bristled. Those same people had cheated death so many times he had concluded they must live under some sort of star. The only good thing to come of it was that Simeon, who had pretended to offer his help to save them, had cemented his identity as a member of an elite group known, ironically, as the Morning Star. That group had been tasked with watching over the very warship that Morningstar was trying to get his hands on. Simeon, posing as British engineer Johnny Canterbury, had been accepted as an heir to one of the original founders, giving Morningstar an inside track into the very secret, very elite group. What would it get him? He wasn't sure, but like so many of the ties he had established over the years, he felt confident that it would eventually pay off.

After playing the savior, Simeon had snuck away from the bay, avoiding the medics and Scotland Yard. Morningstar had learned later on that it was Simeon who had started the fire by throwing a grenade into the school to serve as a distraction. The authorities assumed it was Cobra, and as far as Morningstar could tell, five months later that assumption hadn't changed. They had yet to find any remnants of the grenade.

Once he had left the bay, Simeon had gone back to Edinburgh, where he had called Morningstar to fill him in on all that had happened. *"I didn't get your three prisoners, Father, but I managed to keep my identity. Senator Madison even wants to award me a medal."* They had both had a laugh at that. Morningstar had immediately sent Simeon to France to help Naphtali find the missing warship.

But they weren't the only ones looking for the warship. Walter Henderson had brought in a team of Latvian soldiers to search for it, as well. Morningstar's frustration that a Henderson was once again threatening to disrupt his plans had inspired him to send his soldier-son Zebulun to the Henderson compound, with instructions to kill the head of security and leave a message that implied that the attack was payback on behalf of Germany for the murder of their Vice-chancellor, Dolf Mueller. But it was a reach. Mueller's body hadn't been recovered and he was listed as a missing person. Morningstar was hoping that by implying that the Hendersons and Cynthia Madison had played a role in his disappearance, their lives would be upended...at least enough to keep them from meddling in Morningstar's affairs. The Hendersons needed to keep their Latvian soldiers out of France, and Madison needed to keep her nose out of Morningstar's business.

And, from the look of things, he may have succeeded...at least in part. Though Henderson's soldiers were still combing the French mountains in search of the warship, Walter himself, along with Madison, had spent nearly every minute of the last five months in Edinburgh, Scotland, at the bedside of Walter's nephew, Matt.

Why had Walter shown such devotion to his nephew? Morningstar had asked his technical aide and recently-anointed son Levi to look into it. From what Levi had been able to determine, Matt's appearance in the Henderson world had been somewhat of a surprise, as he was thought to have died in infancy. Clearly, he hadn't, and had recently returned to Latvia to gain favor from his uncle. And, seeing that Walter was willing to sit at the man's bedside day after day, it would appear that he had succeeded.

As for Madison's piety to the ailing Matt Henderson, the only thing Morningstar could come up with was that she had fallen for him. Which was ironic, considering that, at one time, she had been in love with his cousin, Martin. It had led Morningstar to conclude one of two things: either the girl was bound and determined to sink her claws into a Henderson, or Matt wasn't who he said he was. Could it be that he was actually the missing Martin Henderson? It was certainly possible. After all, Martin had undergone a revolutionary surgery – a face transplant –

just months before the cousin had seemingly materialized out of nowhere. What was to say that he hadn't transplanted himself into his cousin, Matt?

Regardless of Madison's motives for her devotion, it had kept her out of Morningstar's hair. *For now.* He knew that eventually he would need to have a more permanent solution for the senator. She chaired a sub-committee that was looking into improper government arms purchases, and she had actually had the nerve to call in Morningstar to testify. *The gall!* he thought, as he kicked the foot of the desk. Fortunately, he had covered his tracks well. She and her committee were no closer to catching Morningstar and his Bentley Group than they had been when they started. And now, with Madison stuck in Scotland, the hearings had been put on hold. But he knew, once Matt either awoke from his coma or died, she would return to DC and pick up where she left off. He had never seen a more tenacious woman. If he didn't hate her so much, he might even respect her. But hate her he did, which meant, sooner or later, he would need to kill her.

First things first, he thought as he dialed Simeon's number.

"Yes Father?"

"Status?"

He heard a deep sigh. "Nothing new…just like yesterday, and last week, and last month. There's no sign of the damn ship."

Morningstar stiffened at the man's tone, but urged him to go on.

Simeon cleared his throat. "Three days ago, Naphtali took me to the site where the truck exploded, and showed me the exact road the guy took out of the mountains. We have backtracked from there. There is no trace of that ship."

Morningstar cursed under his breath. "Did Naphtali get a good look at the warship when he was pursuing the truck?"

"No. Neither one of us have ever seen it. All we have is the very limited description that was given to me at the Morning Star meeting in France. It's about ten-feet around, holds a very powerful weapon, and runs without electricity."

Ah yes, the magical ship that makes its own energy. He tightened his jaw… *I must have it!* "Find the damn warship, Simeon!" he sputtered, then ended the call.

The next call would be to son Gad. He had also been at Dalgety Bay, and had escaped soon after the old schoolhouse went up in flames. But his story had been a bit different than Simeon's. First, he claimed to have witnessed an odd event while accompanying the psychiatrist, Samuels, and the ailing Nenita Villamor to the school. According to Gad, there had been another man present when they arrived, a man whom Samuels had referred to as Mark Justice. He was handsome, respectable, and quite pleasant. But then, without warning, he had changed on a dime, tossing off a wig and a pair of gloves, and ripping contact lenses from his eyes. Within seconds, he had become the Cobra, which hadn't only stunned Gad, but had impressed him. *"One of the best disguises I've ever seen, Father."* He had added, *"…and I really think, Father, that for the minute or two that he was Justice, he believed himself to be that man."*

Morningstar had scoffed at the suggestion, and had been tempted to dismiss it, concluding that Cobra had merely concocted a very effective disguise – which he was noted for – to carry out a portion of his plan. But, on a whim, he had asked Levi to look into it, and, lo and behold, there really was a Mark Justice from London. The man was actually quite reputable; he oversaw a Private Inquiry Agency and was highly regarded among local law enforcement. If Justice was a disguise, then Cobra had put his heart and soul into making the man real. Which had left Morningstar to conclude that it was, quite possibly, more than just a disguise. Was it so farfetched to think that the crazy Cobra might occasionally believe himself to be someone else? Stranger things had happened. Cobra was clearly insane; to think that he might have some sort of delusional personality disorder wasn't such a stretch, was it? Morningstar had left several messages for Justice at his London offices, but according to his secretary, he hadn't been there since March. Which had only lent further credence to the notion that the men might be one and the same. Cobra was on the lam, and Justice hadn't been seen since Cobra has disappeared.

But there was another part of Gad's version of the Dalgety Bay fiasco that differed from Simeon's. According to Gad, Simeon had knocked him out in an attempt to have him die in the fire. It wasn't the first time one of his sons had accused another son of trying to kill him. Back in February, Simeon was convinced that son Reuben, aka Pocks, had tried to have him blown up while they were tracking Madison in

Argentina. Morningstar had made it clear then that he didn't have time for such disputes. *"Keep your sibling rivalries to yourselves, boys."* He had challenged Gad, *"If Simeon knocked you out and left you to die, then how did you get out of there?"* Gad told him that he didn't know, only that he had awakened in a grove of trees not far from the burning school. He had run from the site and had hitchhiked across Scotland to Glasgow. His call to Morningstar had come from a youth hostel. He had lost everything in the fire and was in need of money and a new ID. Morningstar had wired cash to an overseas exchange, and had instructed Gad to use the money to buy clothes and a cellphone, and to secure a P.O. box. He had then had Levi and Janet work together to give him a new identity. Gad was to become Karl Koppel from Maardu, Estonia. They had sent a biography, along with the proper documents – a driver's license, a passport, and a credit card – to his new P.O. box.

Making Gad an Estonian had been a brilliant idea. If Gad played his cards right, Morningstar could soon have one of his own sons inside the Henderson estate. *"I want you to find a way into that Latvian castle as either a gardener, a driver, or a servant."* He had sent Gad the attachments from the same encrypted email he had sent to Zebulun five months earlier, which described in full detail the location and layout of the estate.

But getting a job at the Henderson compound didn't follow the same protocols as it did for a typical estate. One couldn't just schedule an interview and offer a resumé. For one thing, the castle was a well-kept secret, which meant that anyone who wanted to work there had to be recruited by someone already affiliated with the estate. So, after months of trying and failing to establish ties with someone who might offer him a valid pathway into the estate, Morningstar had told him, *"Just get in there, Gad. I don't care how you do it."* That had been two weeks ago. It was time to check on his progress.

He dialed Gad's number and waited through four rings. He was about to hang up, when he heard a whispered, "Yes, Father?"

"Where are you?"

"In a field across from the compound."

"What are you doing there?"

"Waiting." There was a pause. "I've come up with a way to get inside."

Morningstar chuckled. "Good. Let me know when you're in." He ended the call.

His next call would be to son Judah, a man whom America had gotten to know a whole lot better over the past five months. Judah was actually Jerome Knight, a senator from Florida who had recently been chosen to replace the sitting Vice-president, James Conner... *who I so cleverly forced from the role.* Morningstar had compelled Conner to leave the vice-presidency by using forged documents and a few well-placed lies. But not only had Conner been America's VP, he had also led the secretive Bentley Group, of which Morningstar was a member. That group had had a hand in nearly every war that had taken place in the last three years. Though Morningstar knew he should probably kill Conner to ensure his silence, he had decided to hold off. He could easily make the man's death seem like an accident – he had done the same thing many times before – but coming so soon after Conner's abrupt departure from the White House might raise questions. Besides, Morningstar felt confident that Conner wouldn't talk; he had way too much to lose. *To tell what he knows would be to sabotage his own cushy life, as well as whatever legacy he has left behind.*

Morningstar laughed. His manipulation of Conner had been one of his finest achievements. The man had folded quicker than a house of cards. Within hours, he had left his post as VP and had run back to his wife in Nantucket. *He's out of my hair forever.*

Morningstar checked the time. It was four-thirty. He dialed Judah's private cell, fully aware that he might wake the man. But those hours before dawn were the best time for them to talk. It was answered after only one ring. A sleepy voice said, "Yes, Father?"

"So, tell me, Mr. Vice-president, what's on tap for today?"

He heard a yawn. "We've started putting things in place for the campaign tour."

"Still heading to North Dakota?"

"Yes. It will be our final stop before coming back to DC."

"Are you joining the President on the trip?"

"We haven't decided."

Morningstar hesitated. "I think there would be wisdom in you staying in DC."

There was a pause. "Okay. Any particular reason?"

Morningstar grinned. "It's just good to have at least one of you in DC at all times, don't you think?" He paused. "It was a frequent complaint with the last administration; that they were always gallivanting around. You know…no one minding the store."

Another pause, this one longer. "I think you're right, Father. I'll suggest it."

"Good. Now go out there and be impressive, Vice-president Knight."

"Yes, Father, I will."

Morningstar ended the call. He leaned back, put his hands behind his head, and stared out the window at the darkness. All in all, things were going well. To have a Son of Jacob only a hundred yards from the Oval Office meant that Morningstar was one step closer to achieving his goal. And what was his goal? Absolute and unquestioned sovereignty…first, over America, then over the world.

And his other sons were on track, as well, each of them following the same well-designed blueprint. Simeon and Naphtali would soon find the warship, giving Morningstar the fire power that he would need to accomplish his goals, and Russian son, Zebulun, was preparing for what would be an undeniably historic event. Levi was working with Pocks to learn the identity of the man who was lying in a nursing home bed in Edinburgh, and, now that Gad had come up with a way to get inside the Henderson estate, Morningstar would soon have an inside track on one of the most formidable war machines in Eastern Europe.

He chuckled. He had positioned the right men in the right places, and because of it, things were moving along well. If things continued to go as smoothly as they had, he would be exactly where he needed to be by the end of the year. He nodded. *God knew what He was doing when He put me in charge.*

He laid his phone on the desk, then stood and walked to the bedroom. Janet was back in bed, her entire body – including her head – underneath the covers. He crept to the bed, then laid on top of the covers next to her. He pulled the blanket from her face and was about to whisper in her ear, when he saw that she had been crying. He bristled. "What the hell is wrong with you, woman?"

She buried her head in the pillow. He waited. Finally, she turned to look at him, strands of red hair falling across tear-stained cheeks. With a voice he hardly recognized, she said evenly, "Baby, I'm pregnant."

CHAPTER 3

Edinburgh, Scotland

Walter Henderson stood at the desk of his Edinburgh hotel suite, and held up the dirty, singed jacket that he had just received from a Latvian soldier. The soldier had picked it up from another soldier who had found it months ago at the site where a missile had taken out a truck being driven by Germany's Vice-chancellor, Dolf Mueller. Charred and covered in dirt, the jacket had somehow survived what Mueller had not. The Vice-chancellor had been in the process of stealing a warship, *Der Morgenstern*, which had been entrusted to the care of a select group of men who referred to themselves as the Morning Star. Walter was part of that group, and their mission was to keep the warship from falling into the wrong hands. Mueller had taken it by force in a misguided attempt to restore Germany to greatness as the leader of a Fourth Reich. But as he had been about to drive the warship to his native Germany, a fighter plane had begun pursuit. Mueller had hidden the vessel somewhere in the mountains that spanned eastern France, and had then driven his truck down to the highway that would take him to Germany. The plane's missile took out his truck, and Walter's soldier came upon the scene soon after. Though he hadn't actually seen Mueller's body, he had assured Walter the man was dead. *"No one could have survived it, sir."* The soldier had discovered the jacket not far away.

Walter carefully laid the jacket on a Victorian desk in the exclusive Edinburgh hotel suite. He and Dora had reserved the suite soon after Martin had been taken to a nearby nursing home after falling into a coma five months ago, a victim – like the rest of them – of the international assassin, Cobra.

Walter sighed as he thought of all that had happened since. Cobra had escaped, and the rest of the world had fallen into turmoil, brought about by regional wars, the assassinations of a few heads of state, and other plots that a conspiracy theorist might conclude had been purposely designed to disrupt the foundations of western civilization. Walter's Latvian compound had been targeted, as well, attacked by an intruder who had killed over thirty of Walter's soldiers, and Putin had begun flexing his muscles throughout the Baltic States in an attempt to restore the alliances of the former U.S.S.R. But all of it paled in comparison to the loss of the ship, *Der Morgenstern*. Not only was it the most destructive flying machine ever to have been created, but its technology was so far advanced that, in the wrong hands, it could quite easily lead to another world war.

Walter frowned as he brushed his fingers over the singed jacket, a symbol of all that had gone wrong. Though one of the sleeves was missing and the other was charred from shoulder to wrist, it was in surprisingly good condition. *"He must have tossed it out the window before his truck exploded,"* the soldier had said. Walter frowned as he stared at the coat. *Why would a man use his last seconds to save a simple piece of clothing?* There was nothing unique about it; a dark green military jacket, heavy material, deep pockets. He patted it, feeling for something to explain the man's behavior. He found nothing.

His plan was to send the coat to a private facility in Latvia for DNA verification to prove that it had, in fact, belonged to Germany's Vice-chancellor. The man had gone missing five months ago, and, though Walter was aware that Dolf Mueller was actually the neo-Nazi, Adolf Mueller, the German Government had no idea. They would most certainly balk at the notion that one of their leaders had been a neo-Nazi involved in the theft of a war machine for the purpose of establishing a Fourth Reich. The jacket would serve as proof that the Vice-chancellor had, in fact, been behind the theft of the warship.

Luckily, Walter already had Mueller's DNA. The Germans had led a worldwide search for their missing Vice-chancellor, and Walter had offered a regiment of Latvian soldiers to help. As a result, he had been given access to the man's DNA. Once he was able to test the jacket, he would have irrefutable proof that Vice-chancellor Dolf Mueller was the same man who had slain a private army and stolen a vital warship.

Not that he could use that information. He couldn't tell a single soul what had taken place five months ago. That warship was one of the best-kept secrets in the history of the last hundred years, and it needed to stay that way. *But at least I will know.*

The last man to see Mueller alive, the German Chancellor, had told authorities that he had said goodbye to Mueller early Sunday morning. Mueller had told him that he had a private matter to attend to north of Paris, and would be back by noon. He never came back. The only lead the German investigators found was Mueller's rental car, which had been abandoned hundreds of miles from Paris, at the side of a highway not far from where a pickup truck was said to have exploded. There was nothing inside the car to indicate where Mueller might have been going or why. But Walter knew. Mueller had driven that car to Montbard, France, so he could lead his secret army to steal a warship that could change the very fabric of the future.

Luckily, he had only partially achieved his goal. He had stolen the warship, but had been forced to abandon it somewhere in the mountains east of Montbard. A Latvian soldier, who had escaped the carnage in Montbard, had found the rental car nearby, and had attempted to follow the truck that was carrying the warship. He had tracked it into the mountains, but had lost it in the thick brush that covered the crags east of Montbard. Hours later, he had spotted the truck on a highway not far from the German border. He had followed it and, within minutes, had watched it go up in flames. He had ditched the rental car, wanting in no way to be tied to the vehicle or the man who had rented it, and had hitched a ride back to Paris. He had told Walter that there was no doubt in his mind that Mueller had been incinerated in the blast. *"I saw it, sir…there was nothing left of him."*

Walter sighed. *Except for this coat.*

He brushed a smudge from the shoulder of the jacket as he continued his inspection. An insignia on the collar suggested that it was standard issue from Germany's Nationale Volksarmee, which had been dissolved in 1990 after the fall of the Berlin Wall. Walter guessed the jacket was a holdover from Mueller's days as a commander in that army, and that he had kept it to keep himself anchored to the man he had been before he had become a part of the German government. Maybe that was why he had gone to such an effort to save it; it was a symbol of the only part of Mueller's life that he was proud of.

Walter had originally asked the soldier to bring the jacket to him after his lecture in Paris, which was to have taken place in March as a prelude to the NATO conferences. But when Walter had been lured to Lyon by Cobra, he had been forced to cancel the lecture, and had told the soldier to hold onto the jacket until he returned. The problem was, Walter didn't return. He was kidnapped in Lyon and taken first to a dungeon outside the basilica, then to an abandoned schoolhouse in Dalgety Bay, Scotland. When he was finally freed, he had tried to contact the soldier, but had been unable to reach him. He had thought about traveling to France to search for the man, but had no idea where he would even begin. He had let it go, his thoughts no longer on the jacket or the warship, but on his son, Martin, who had fallen into a coma. Then, just a week ago, he had received a message from his chief of security, Dimitri, telling him that the soldier who had originally found the jacket had been in an accident soon after Walter's kidnapping, and had nearly died. He was recovering in a Paris hospital. Walter had instructed Dimitri to send a Latvian soldier to Paris to offer Walter's unlimited support for the man's recovery, and to pick up the jacket and bring it to him in Edinburgh. Which was how it had landed on an antique Victorian desk in a posh Scottish hotel suite.

He looked again at the jacket. *Time to learn who you belonged to,* he thought as he searched the top drawer for the phone number of his private London courier. He had used the man before for sensitive transactions and knew he could be trusted. But the man's number had been in his cellphone, which had been destroyed by Cobra, so he had had to call his Latvian estate for the number. He had written it on a piece of scrap paper.

Now, where did I put that piece of paper? he mused as he rummaged through the drawer. He found it under a travel brochure. He closed the drawer and shoved the jacket to the side. He was about to lay the scrap of paper on the desk, when he noticed an odd bulge in the jacket. He patted it, surprised that his earlier inspection had missed it. He slid his hand into an oversized pocket, and, after a bit of probing, his fingers touched on a smooth leather casing. Whatever it was had lodged in a hole in the pocket, and was covered by thick pieces of material. He had to tease the item from under the material, and with a firm tug, was able to wrangle it from the pocket. He recognized the brown, leather-bound book, and his hands began to shake. He dropped the scrap of paper and held the three-by-five-inch booklet with both hands. *Dear god...it's Hitler's journal!* That journal had been given to the caretaker of their group by Eisenhower himself, just before he was sworn in as America's 34th President. Eisenhower, one of the original members of the Morning Star organization, had decided that there was too much risk to their secrecy for a man in such a notable role to continue as a member, so he had left the group, but had given the Caretaker the journal with a warning that whatever was contained in that booklet would someday be vital to the future of the vessel, and, quite possibly, the world.

The only problem; other than its cover, which contained a quote by Hitler, the book had been written in an ancient Germanic language that was no longer spoken or understood by modern-day linguists. Sean had spent decades trying to find someone to translate it, but had failed, and had finally given the journal to another member of the group, Arthur Kauffold, for safe-keeping. Kauffold, instructed to bring it with him whenever the group was to meet, had brought it to Paris five months ago. Sean had shared with them that he had finally found a translator, and Kauffold had given it back to him. Sean had taken it with him on his journey to Lyon to protect the vessel. He had died in that battle, and Walter had had his team of Latvian soldiers scour the warehouse for the booklet. They hadn't found it, and Walter had assumed that Sean had destroyed it when he knew he was about to die. As Walter thumbed carefully through the pages, he found himself overcome by the memory of the Caretaker, Sean MacPherson. He had known Sean for many years, and they had become close in much the same way that soldiers become close in the course of battle...a bond that is indescribable. The fact that the book that Sean had been trying to protect had somehow survived all the chaos of that terrible day was a stunning turn of events. *As if it was meant to find its way back to us.*

He read the cover. "Er allein, dem die Jugend gehört, gewinnt die Zukunft." *He alone, who owns the youth, gains the future.* He shook his head as he walked to the closet and took a cashmere scarf from a shelf. He wrapped the journal in the scarf, then slid it in his briefcase, which was sitting on top of a safe. The briefcase itself was new. The one he had used for the past thirty years – given to him by his father – had been left in the square in Lyon. He had asked the French police if they had found it during their crime scene investigation; they insisted they had not. Which worried him. Not only had the briefcase been a gift from Eisenhower to Walter's father, Jeremy, but it bore the symbol of the secret Morning Star organization: a church, a star, and a Russian saying. Would anyone grasp its meaning? Hopefully not. But of even greater concern was what was inside the briefcase. Drawings, twenty-two of them; constellations of one sort or another, that had been sketched by his father. Walter didn't know why they were important, only that they were. His father had spent forty years traveling the world in an effort to sketch the constellations accurately. What if they had fallen into the wrong hands? More importantly, what if they were lost forever? What if the years that his father had spent drawing those constellations had been wasted because of a madman in a town square? He shook his head; it wasn't likely. For one thing, Jeremy, a careful man by nature, had likely made copies, though Walter had yet to come across them. As for the briefcase itself, it was solid; a leather covering over reinforced steel. It wouldn't have burned, even with the C-4 that had been used in the square. And the only way to open it was with a numerical code and a Henderson fingerprint. Anyone who tried to force it open would be met with a burst of noxious gas. Which meant that it was likely still secure…just missing.

He looked again at the cashmere scarf which so carefully shrouded the brown booklet at the bottom of the case. *At least I have Hitler's journal,* he thought, as he secured the briefcase, then locked it in the safe. He walked to the desk and stared at the jacket. He did another pat-down, making sure that he had missed nothing more before he handed it off to his courier. Again, he was stunned that it was only mildly charred after what had clearly been a massive explosion. The soldier who found it had concluded that Mueller must have tossed it out the window before he died.

Suddenly, Walter frowned. What if that wasn't the case? What if the jacket had survived, not because it had been thrown from the truck, *but because Mueller had escaped the explosion?* It would explain why the jacket had been found so close to the wreckage, and why it was in reasonably good shape. Mueller could have jumped from the truck, then rolled away from the flames with the jacket on his back. But if that was the case, then where was he? And why would he have taken off the jacket? Walter looked again at the singed left sleeve. Maybe it had caught fire and, in an effort to escape, Mueller had shed the jacket rather than spend time dowsing the flames. Walter sighed. *There's no way. If Mueller had survived, one of us would have heard from him by now.*

But as he dialed the courier, he felt a familiar ache in the pit of his stomach. *What if Adolf Mueller is alive and well, just waiting to come back for that warship…so he can use it to change the world forever?*

CHAPTER 4

Edinburgh, Scotland

Agent Tom Cravens ran a thick hand through his thin, graying hair and sighed. He had been sitting outside Matt Henderson's nursing home room since getting back from the senator's sprint through town, and, even though he now followed her in a government sedan, he was exhausted just from watching her. It wasn't like she had spent her entire life running, or even the last year or two. No, Maddi had decided to "go jogging" only a few months ago, and those jaunts through downtown Edinburgh had now become mini-marathons. But that was Maddi. Whatever she did, she did well, with an energy that would leave most people – including Cravens – simply watching from the sidelines.

He didn't mind. Being responsible for looking after the vibrant Cynthia Madison felt like an honor. He had begun the task five months ago, soon after the Dalgety Bay attack, and had found the woman to be one of the most sincere, likeable people he had ever protected. And he actually welcomed her morning jogs; it got him – both of them – out of the lovely yet depressing long-term care facility for at least a few hours. Other than those morning runs or their walks through a nearby park in the afternoons, very little happened outside that room, or in the life of the senator. She spent most of the day just sitting by Henderson's bed.

The afternoon walks were Cravens' favorite, though most of the summer Maddi had been accompanied by either Walter and Dora, or by the lovely Tonna Kauffold. Cravens wasn't sure what it was exactly that tied Maddi and Tonna together, but it was clear that they were close as they talked and laughed and spent hours among the roses. As

Madison's bodyguard, he had had the privilege of walking the gardens with whomever was with her, and had been surprised to find that he enjoyed it...far more than he might have thought. Even now, when it was just him and Maddi, he looked forward to the walks. It was late summer and, unlike the steamy heat of Washington, DC, the Scottish air was cool and comfortable. The flowers were at their peak and, though he knew only a handful of their names, they were nice to look at. *If I'm gonna be stuck in Edinburgh for months at a time, at least I can walk in a garden full of pretty flowers.*

But he was struggling. Not only with the boredom that comes from being in one place for months on end, but with an ethical dilemma that he had allowed to go on for far too long. He sighed and shifted in his chair so he could see beyond the hallway outside Henderson's room as he listened for footsteps. When he felt certain that the hallway was empty, he reached under his chair and pulled out a briefcase. He set it on his lap, admiring for probably the fiftieth time the rich brown leather, the black leather trim, and the well-made construction. It had a numerical keypad, as well as a place for a fingerprint, suggesting that it would be almost impossible to open without the proper code and DNA. He stared at the engraved letters on the side, "JH," and frowned. The briefcase wasn't his, and he had no idea who it belonged to. All he knew was that by now he should have handed it over to the authorities.

He had found the briefcase five months ago while investigating the scene of an attack at a square in Lyon from where Cynthia Madison and Walter Henderson had been kidnapped. He had been searching the square for clues, and had stumbled upon the briefcase. Wedged between an overturned table and a tree, he had snuck it from the site, unsure what to do with it, but instinctively knowing it was important. He had shared the discovery with no one; not his partner, not his boss, not even the local police who were investigating the scene. Why? He wasn't sure. He had told himself it was because he didn't know who he could trust. After all, it was a French cop that had allegedly kidnapped Walter and Maddi.

But there was more to it than simply being unwilling to trust the police. The briefcase was unique. And once he had gotten a good look at it, he had known just how unique. On the side of the case, at the bottom right-hand corner, was a logo...an emblem that Cravens had instantly recognized. He had seen that same emblem on a medal in his Uncle Harry's bedroom when he was just a boy. Harry had been a decorated soldier in World War II, having had five beach landings with five silver arrow medals to show for it. Harry had gone on and on about the landings, and about the pride he felt toward every one of those silver arrows. But the medal with the emblem was different. For one thing, Harry had been unwilling to talk about it, other than to say that it had been given to him personally, *"...by the General himself."* Not for an act of wartime bravery, but for the simple task of keeping a group of men – very prominent men – safe and secure inside an old church. That was all he would say, other than the fact that the medal – and the meeting – had had little to do with the war. *"It was about the future, Tommy."*

The medal itself was unique. It was bronze, and instead of an eagle or a flag, it had an image of a church, a star, and a Russian saying. It was so unique that the minute Cravens saw that same image on the briefcase in the square, he had known right away that it was important. Not only important, but likely harboring a secret. And, as if Harry had been speaking to him from the grave, he had heard the old man say, *"Don't give it to the police, Tommy; it's not yours to give. Return it to its owner. His mission is far greater than any oath you may have taken or any code of ethics you may have vowed to follow."*

Cravens had listened to that voice, and that was what had resulted in his current dilemma. He had held onto the briefcase, and somehow a full five months had come and gone. Too much time for him to simply hand it over now.

The most surprising thing was that he hadn't told his partner, Larry Cross. He knew he could trust the man; he had trusted Cross with far more than a briefcase over the past six years. But he also knew that Cross would be forced to tell their boss; he would be *obligated* to tell the man. And if Cross, for whatever reason, chose to honor their friendship over that obligation, then he would be dishonoring his oath to the Service. So, against every protocol he had ever been taught and every vow he had ever taken, Cravens had told no one, and had simply held onto the briefcase. Waiting...for what?

He shifted in his seat. *Waiting for Shaw.*

Cravens had met Shaw – he wasn't sure if it was his first name or his last – about two months ago at an all-night diner in downtown

Edinburgh. Cravens went to the diner whenever he worked the night shift covering Madison. Cravens and Cross swapped days and nights every four weeks, so after Cravens would leave the nursing home in the middle of the night, he would stop at the diner for a bite to eat before going to his hotel room. Shaw was nearly always there, and Cravens had yet to learn if his night was ending or his day beginning. The man had intrigued Cravens. He was short and thick and solid as an ox, and his hair was long and gray. He typically had it pulled in a ponytail. He wore army fatigues, along with a pair of leather sandals, and his hands were misshapen; as if he had some sort of arthritis. He had stayed to himself, and Cravens had gotten the sense that the time alone was a sort of reprieve. But after weeks of being the only two in the diner at three a.m., the men had struck up a conversation. Shaw, in a thick Irish brogue, had eventually confided in Cravens that he had once been a criminal, *"...the best in the business when it comes to crackin' a safe."* Then, about two years ago, he had had a conversion of sorts, and was now on the British government's payroll. Officers from MI6 had arrested him during a bank robbery in Switzerland, and once they saw his talents and grasped his ties to the underworld, they had made an agreement with him. They would let him go if he would agree to infiltrate a Scottish mob that had terrorized downtown London for the past ten years. He had done so, and was able to help them shut down the mob. In return, he was granted his freedom, but it was made clear that he could be called upon at any time to use his unique skills to help them. *"So, you see, Tommy, now I commit crimes on behalf of the Crown."*

Cravens wasn't sure why the man had been willing to confide in him. He guessed it had to do with Cravens' role in the Secret Service... an element of respect for anyone who spent their days trying to outsmart bad guys. Or maybe it was a shared understanding about the similarities of good and evil. *"Tis a fine line between being crafty as a sinner and clever as a saint, Tommy. It all comes down to who you owe."*

Regardless, the relationship had proven to be providential, at least as far as Cravens was concerned. It offered him a solution. If Shaw could use his skills to get into that briefcase, then Cravens might be able to figure out who owned the damn thing. Then, once he was able to verify that the man had played no role in the attack in the square, he could return the briefcase and be done with it. *Just like Uncle Harry wanted me to do.*

But he was reluctant to give that briefcase to his new friend…even for just a day. After all, if Shaw was able to break into it, he would, of course, see what was inside. Cravens felt certain that whatever it was, it was top secret, and he worried that some vital piece of information would then be compromised…information that, by its very nature, should remain secret. Could Shaw be trusted with such information? Cravens had no way of knowing; he had only just met the man. But he had done all he could to learn about him, using his vast array of resources to dig into the life of the criminal-turned-spy. Other than an overnight stay in a British jail for IRA graffiti when he was seventeen, Shaw's history was exactly how he had presented it; a kid who had gotten good at being bad, but was now working for the good guys. So, after hours of deliberation, Cravens concluded that he had no other choice. He either learned who the case belonged to so he could return it, or give it to his boss and risk a reprimand, or maybe even a discharge from the Service. Whatever he chose, he needed to do it soon. He was getting an ulcer worrying about it.

He leaned back in his chair and sighed. *Tonight's the night.*

Though he was currently working the dayshift, he had decided that he would set an alarm for two a.m., so he could be at the diner by three. He would sit across from Shaw in the same booth they had sat in for the past several months, swear him to secrecy, then hand him the briefcase with the simple request that he find a way inside. *"The minute you're in, however, you need to forget you ever saw the damn case, or me, for that matter."* Would the man honor his request? Cravens rubbed the back of his neck. It was impossible to say. But it was his only option. He had let too much time go by.

He heard commotion near the elevator and shoved the briefcase under his chair. He checked his watch. *Nine-thirty…The Hendersons?* Not likely; they usually waited until after lunch to come to see their son. That was another secret that Cravens had been forced to keep. The man in the coma, Matt Henderson, who was believed to be a nephew to the esteemed Walter Henderson, was actually Martin Henderson, Walter's son. As far as Cravens knew, only he, Maddi, and the Hendersons were aware. And Maddi didn't realize that Cravens knew the truth. He had learned it by accident, about three months ago, while chatting with Walter's wife, Dora. She had let it slip, and had immediately regretted it. Cravens had reassured her, telling her that he had kept far bigger secrets during his time as an agent. But that actually wasn't true; he couldn't imagine a bigger secret than the fact that the Henderson heir had survived the fire that the world had thought had killed him four years ago. He didn't know the details; only that Henderson had spent the last four years taking part in some less-than-savory activities. Dora had implied that he was CIA, but Cravens' research could find no mention of the man in the CIA's records. Regardless, Henderson had clearly gone to a lot of trouble to alter his appearance, including a literal face transplant. Cravens didn't know the specifics; the whole thing seemed beyond belief. He had also dyed his hair black, and Cravens guessed that it was Maddi who made sure that it stayed that way while he was in the coma.

Cravens stood as he heard footsteps coming down the hall. Only one person, from what he could tell. The steps were heavy, likely those of a man. Cravens stepped in front of the door, made his revolver visible from inside his jacket as he crossed his arms on his chest.

The visitor rounded the corner. With a wide girth and a classy white suit, he could have been Santa Clause in the off-season. He had a white mustache and bushy white eyebrows. He carried himself well; obviously a man of means. His manner was reserved and cultured; he had likely been on the international stage. He walked up to Cravens and gave a subtle bow. "Good morning, sir. My name is Arthur Kauffold and I've come to call upon the senator."

Cravens' eyes widened. *Of course! Arthur Kauffold…the former ambassador to America.* He straightened. "Certainly, sir. I believe we met years ago, Ambassador."

The older man stared at him, his cheerful blue eyes seeming even more distinct under the thick white brows. He tilted his head and frowned. "So sorry sir, I don't recall."

Cravens nodded. "The Reagans…at the ranch, in '82. You had come 'across the pond' as they say, to discuss Argentina's invasion of the Falkland Islands." He paused. "I'm with the Secret Service, Mr. Ambassador. The name's Cravens, Tom Cravens."

The ambassador's eyes lit up. "Why, I do remember you, Cravens. A bit younger then, but weren't we all." He chuckled and his eyes gleamed. "I remember that visit well. Quite a lovely time we had, my Annabelle and I." He nodded sadly, then cleared his throat. "The Reagans were delightful hosts."

Cravens nodded. "Yes, they were good people." He sighed. "And I'm now responsible for the safety of Senator Madison. May I ask how it is that you know her?"

Kauffold stuck out his chest as he tugged at his lapels. "Why, I would like to think that I played a rather significant role in the woman's upbringing." He looked Cravens in the eye and said, "...but you are free to call MI6 to verify my good intentions." With that, he took off his hat and held out his briefcase for Cravens to inspect.

Cravens checked the hat and, as he lifted the briefcase to inspect it more closely, his heart began to race. The case was identical to the one he had just slid under his chair, only this one had the initials AK etched in the side. He stared at it, taking in every detail; the brown leather, the black trim, the fingerprint ID next to dials for a numerical code.

Kauffold must have picked up on his interest. "Is there a problem, Cravens?"

Cravens took a final look, then said to Kauffold, "That briefcase; it's...quite remarkable."

Kauffold returned his hat to his head, but continued to hold out the briefcase. "Yes, it is, my good man. There were only three of them made, as far as I know."

Cravens looked for the emblem. There it was, in the exact same location on the bottom right corner. He looked at Kauffold. "Only three were made? Why three?"

Kauffold's demeanor suddenly changed. He slid the briefcase under his arm. "That is really all I can say, Cravens. Now, may I please look in on the senator?"

"Uh, yes...certainly." Cravens did a quick pat down of the man, then stepped aside. As Kauffold walked into the room, Cravens stared at the briefcase that was now tucked protectively under Kauffold's arm. *Now I know for a fact that the briefcase is important...it's one of only three!*

As he pondered that fact, he gave a quick nod to another overweight man who had just rounded the corner. This man was far less sophisticated than the ambassador, dressed in overalls and carrying a toolbox. His face was pocked from what looked like acne scars, and he wore a pair of thick, black-framed glasses. He reached the door and stopped.

Cravens had seen him before…many times…and had already had him vetted; his name was Cameron Milligan and he was a maintenance man for the nursing home. He had been hired two months ago, and Cravens and Cross had had their boss in DC run him through the ringer. He had come up clean.

Cravens stopped him just as he was about to walk into Henderson's room. "Something broken?" he asked.

The man looked at him. His puffy eyes, barely visible through the thick glasses, were wide and uncertain. "Ye…yeah, yes sir. Sink appears to be leakin' again, it does, sir."

Cravens looked down at the man's toolkit. "May I check your kit?"

The man nodded, then nervously opened the toolkit. Cravens rummaged through the tools, then waved the man into the room. As Cravens returned to his chair, his thoughts were still on Kauffold's briefcase, and he failed to notice the man pull a small, three-inch camera from his pocket.

CHAPTER 5

Edinburgh, Scotland

Pocks – Herbert Cosgrove – hated these types of assignments, especially when he was under such direct scrutiny by a U.S. Secret Service agent. It was as if God Himself was looking down on him, ready to chastise him for his iniquity. But Pocks had been given no choice. Morningstar had made it clear that he wanted a full accounting, not only of Matt Henderson's medical progress, but of his appearance, as well. *"Get me a really good photo, Pocks."* The request seemed odd; why couldn't Morningstar just look the guy up through one of the government's surveillance sites? Could it be that Matt Henderson wasn't on any of those sites? Why wouldn't he be? *Everybody in the world is on the government's radar.* Regardless, Pocks had been the good soldier, and finally, today, was ready to do what Morningstar had asked, after spending the last two months establishing his credentials as a maintenance man at Edinburgh's elite extended-stay nursing facility. He had been spurred along by a call from Morningstar a few hours ago, insisting he get the photo today. *"Have it to me by seven a.m. my time…which is noon in Scotland."* Though Morningstar had requested only one really good picture of Matt, Pocks had decided that he would try to get several. Why? Pocks shifted uncomfortably as he walked into the sick man's room. *Because Matt Henderson is so damn handsome.*

Pocks looked away as his eyes fell on the man in the bed. Did Pocks hope to have a relationship with Matt Henderson? Hell no; Pocks had given up on ever finding a meaningful relationship with any man. It seemed like those he had had had only gotten him into trouble. But it was hard not to admire the man's remarkable face or his rugged build… even while lying comatose in a bed. *A man can dream, can't he?*

But Morningstar was getting antsy, which meant that Pocks had to get the photo today. He had put it off long enough. He would send a photo to Morningstar and keep the rest for himself. *And then I'll get out of this godforsaken place.*

It had taken time to cultivate his identity as a maintenance man for the nursing home. Though Morningstar had set him up with a flawless identity – he was Cameron Milligan, a mechanic with twenty years of experience – Pocks had needed to gain the confidence of the many people who protected both Matt Henderson and Cynthia Madison, including the nursing home security staff, as well as the two Secret Service agents who swapped shifts looking after the senator.

It had helped that Pocks was good at fixing things. He was a bomb-maker for the Pentagon, which meant that he knew how things worked. He had needed to repair a number of fixtures since his hiring two months ago. Dressed in a standard pair of overalls, he had worked late and covered shifts for co-workers, all of which had gone a long way to solidifying his ID. But he hated it, mostly because of where he was forced to work. The people at that facility were sick…very sick, and most of them weren't likely to ever get well. Which meant they would probably die. Pocks didn't do well with death. Thinking of it made him think of the afterlife, and – for him, anyway – he expected very little from the next world. He believed in heaven; he just doubted he would ever get there.

I'll be glad to get this over with, he thought as he looked again at Matt Henderson lying in the bed. Though he would miss seeing the handsome man, it would be good to never have to walk into that building…or that room again. He looked over at Cynthia Madison. She was sitting by Matt's bed like she always was, only this time she had a visitor. Pocks didn't recognize him. He was a big man, and respectable, from the looks of his fine white suit. Madison smiled at Pocks as he walked toward the bathroom. He gave her a quick nod, then turned away, knowing that his pocked cheeks had likely turned an embarrassing shade of red. The senator had a remarkably kind smile.

He hurried into the bathroom, disgusted by what he was being asked to do. *How did I get into this mess?* He had wondered that same thing probably fifty times over the past year. *Well, let's start with the fact that you're a gay man from a family that abhors homosexuality.* But there had been more to it than just his proclivity toward men. When he was twenty-two years old – and still living at home – he had fallen for a young man, a neighborhood boy who was only seventeen. They had been caught together. The boy was considered underage, so his parents, appalled to learn that *their* son was gay, had pressed charges. It was only because of Pocks' father's role as a prosecutor in their small town that Pocks had gotten out of it. But had he, really? Though his father was able to hide the statutory rape charge, Pocks knew that it was still out there... somewhere.

And his father had held it over his head, insisting that he join a catholic seminary to *"...wipe that sin from your soul, Herbert."* Pocks didn't mind the request; he loved his catholic faith and was excited at the prospect of becoming a priest. But when he was caught in a compromising position with one of the other students, he was immediately dismissed from the seminary, and summarily dismissed from his home.

Which was how he had wound up at boot camp in Fort Benning, Georgia. He was a six-foot-four, 250-pound man, who – in spite of his reticent nature – was deserving of respect. He was surprisingly quick on his feet and stunned them all when he was able to run the mile in less than six minutes. Not only was he fast, he had an extraordinary understanding of bombs; making them, disarming them, identifying the unique signature that was a part of every single bomb. Because of this, he was pulled in to work with Special Ops. Pocks had found his niche. But a back injury while on a mission in Iraq resulted in his exclusion from combat, and he had been delegated to behind-the-scenes bomb assessments for the Pentagon. The Chairman of the Joint Chiefs, General Alexander Daniels took an interest in him, and it had been left to the general's aide, Edward Morningstar, to complete Pocks' background check. That was when Morningstar learned of his history at the seminary. But the aide kept it to himself, at least initially. Pocks was brought aboard, and Morningstar then chose him to accompany him on a reconnaissance mission to South America. He had struck up a conversation with Pocks and had seemed nice enough; but it was what he had said on the way back that had ultimately defined their relationship. Though he had yet to learn the steamy details that had forced Pocks to attend the seminary in the first place, just with the information he had, Morningstar could ruin Pocks' life. It was 1996. To learn that a man was gay was one thing; to learn that he had defiled a soon-to-be-priest was another. It had been their bond ever since. *"You do what I tell you to do, Cosgrove, and I'll keep your secret."*

But Pocks knew it was only a matter of time until Morningstar learned about the statutory rape charge. That information could land Pocks in an entirely different kind of trouble. Though his 'rape' would be classified as a misdemeanor, Pocks had claimed on his admission form that he had never been arrested. The lie alone would force him out of the Pentagon, and would likely make him unhirable for any sort of meaningful work. He could only pray that if he continued to do what Morningstar asked, the man would be content to leave the rest of the story alone. He shook his head; he doubted it. He was counting on the decency of a man who had shown himself to be anything but. *What choice do I have*, he thought as he tugged at his overalls. *Morningstar holds all the cards.*

He knelt at the sink and frowned. His job was to mess with a few pipes, then loosen one of them just enough that in a few days it would leak, and the facility would call him again. It was intended to allow the Secret Service agent sitting outside the door to get used to him, as well as Madison and anyone else who might be visiting. He had pulled the ruse seven times already, and was astounded that they hadn't just replaced the entire sink by now.

Then again, money was tight. No one knew that better than Pocks. If it wasn't for Morningstar's paydays, he would have a hard time making ends meet. Housing in DC was expensive, utilities were expensive; hell, everything was expensive. The only thing that was cheap were the deals that were made in the fancy dining rooms or dark boardrooms of the Halls of Congress. Pocks had little to do with those...*thank God.*

He tinkered with a pipe, all the while peering into the bedroom to wait for his chance to snap a photo. Who was the man with her? And would his presence get in the way of what Pocks was trying to do? *I'll just have to wait for him to leave*, he thought as he continued to stare. Madison looked in his direction, and he quickly looked away. His hand was shaking as he held the camera, ready to snap, in the right-hand pocket of his overalls. He used a wrench to bang softly on a pipe. Several minutes passed and he heard the door open and close. Pocks stole a look into the room. *Thank god.* Madison's guest had left, and she had moved to the window. She lowered it to keep out a sudden burst of rain, and the hinges squeaked. *I should fix those hinges,* he thought absently. She was looking out, her wistful stare almost moving him to tears. *What is she thinking about?* he wondered, as he raised the camera and snapped her photo. He snapped another one, then zoomed in and took six quick photos of the man in the bed. He shoved the camera in his pocket. It was done. Assuming the photos were as good as he expected, this would be his last trip to the facility. He would call in tomorrow morning and claim that his mother in Aberdeen was dying of cancer, and that would be the end of it.

This time he tightened the pipe instead of loosening it. He put his tools in his kit, then stood to walk out of the bathroom. As he did so, he caught a glimpse of himself in the mirror. At Morningstar's urging, he had not only clipped his blond hair short, but had donned a pair of thick glasses with wide lenses, *"...to hide your ugly skin."* But he could still see it...the puffy eyes and even puffier pitted cheeks. He looked away, disgusted. He walked out of the bathroom, nodded timidly at the senator, then left the room.

He walked past the Secret Service agent without saying a word and went straight to the elevator. He took it to the first floor, then walked along a hallway to a metal door that led to the basement. He went down a set of cement stairs and slid out of his overalls; he was wearing street clothes underneath. He shoved the overalls and the toolkit into a box in the corner. It would be years before anyone looked in that box. If they did, all they would see was a uniform and some tools. Nothing to raise any suspicions. He adjusted his glasses. He would keep them; they were part of his disguise...a disguise that, according to Morningstar, he wasn't yet finished with.

He left by way of a back service entrance and walked six blocks through an alley until it dead ended. He turned right and walked to the corner of a busy street, where he waved down a cab. He gave the driver the name of his hotel on Edinburgh's west side. As the taxi pulled away, he stared out the window for a few minutes, then sat back and closed his eyes. He tried to think of something relaxing as the cabby embarked on the twenty-minute ride to his hotel. He thought of Matt Henderson and Senator Madison, and the undeniable love that the senator clearly felt for the man in the bed. Though Pocks was glad to be away from the depressing nursing home, he would miss seeing them…and that devotion.

Soon he felt the car slow. He was nearing the hotel. He checked the time. Ten-thirty a.m. He would have plenty of time to get Morningstar his photo. He reached in his pocket for the camera. It wasn't there. Panicked, he felt in every single one of his pockets, then checked the seat and the floor of the cab; the camera wasn't with him. Suddenly, his eyes widened. *It's in the pocket of my overalls!*

The driver pulled up to the hotel entrance and stopped. He mumbled, "Here you go, buddy."

Pocks leaned forward. "I need you to take me back to the where you picked me up."

The man looked over his shoulder at Pocks and frowned. "What? Why?"

Pocks sighed. "Because my whole purpose for being in this lousy country is back there."

The cabby looked like he was about to object, then simply shrugged his shoulders. "Whatever you say, buddy." He pulled out of the drive and got back on the road.

CHAPTER 6

Edinburgh, Scotland

Maddi stared out the window at the rain. Kauffold had left. He had been heading to a meeting at Holyrood Castle, and had stopped by on his way. *"I promise to drop by again when I can stay longer, Maddi."* He had given her a wool scarf, likely hand-loomed in Chesham. She draped it over her shoulders, glad for its warmth.

She walked over to a small record player that sat in the corner of the room. Dora had asked that it be brought in soon after Henderson's arrival, and the three of them had alternated the selection of music. Sometimes it was jazz, sometimes it was seventies rock...there was even the occasional military march, but for Maddi, it was almost always classical. She was in charge of the morning, and this morning she chose Mozart. Why? For one reason, the composer was a Henderson favorite. Maddi knew this from their time in Providence...that magical weekend from a lifetime ago...before the fire that had nearly killed him; before assassins and terror attacks that had nearly killed them both.

She closed her eyes as the first few stanzas of Mozart's *Requiem* filled the twenty-by-twenty suite. By now, she had practically memorized every movement, each rise and fall of the melancholy piece. She trembled as the haunting violin blended with the rain, creating a sad, soulful composition that seemed to echo Henderson's slow march toward death. For the first time in months, Maddi had begun to accept that he actually might die. She looked over her shoulder, trying to imagine what she would do if he did; if he died while she was sitting only inches away from him. She had already mourned him once...four years ago, but then, when the entire world thought he was dead, she had felt certain that he was alive…and she had been right. But this felt different. This time she could actually see him lying still, motionless, close to death. *He won't die…he can't.* The doctor had said *"He's as healthy as a horse."* Maddi had said *"Then why's he in a coma?"* The doctor had shrugged. *"I wish I knew."*

She looked again at the rain, sad to think that she might have to put off her walk through the gardens. Unlike the morning runs, which fought off demons in the darkness before dawn, the walks through the gardens could transport her to a better place, a better time. They made her think of Tonna, the young woman who had revealed just months ago that she was Maddi's biological daughter, the child that Maddi had given up at the tender age of fifteen. Tonna had been adopted by the Kauffolds and lived in Chesham, which was about six hours away by train. She had visited Maddi several times over the last few months, and nearly every visit would lead them to the gardens where they would stroll four hours. It had been remarkable how much they had to talk about; how much had been missed in their twenty-two years apart. Though, over the years, Maddi had caught glimpses of Tonna growing from a child to an adult, it had only been as a friend to Tonna's adopted father. But now she got to hear it as a mother; how it was to grow up the child of an ambassador, to travel the world, to see it through the eyes of a diplomat.

The irony was that Maddi had had no idea that the Kauffolds had adopted her child. She had traveled to England to stay with her grandparents until her baby was born. Soon after the birth, they had taken Maddi on a private tour of Buckingham Palace. It was there she met Arthur Kauffold, and they became fast friends. To learn years later that he had been the one to raise her child had been a welcome discovery. Maddi suspected that the adoption hadn't come about by accident. Though she had never had a chance to ask, she felt certain that her grandparents, who were close friends with the Kauffolds, had purposely placed Tonna with their dearest friends so they could watch her grow.

Maddi had been pleased to see that Tonna was as beautiful on the inside as she was on the outside. *Of course, she is,* Maddi had thought after their first day together. *She was raised by two remarkable people.* Tonna had laughed as she had shared what it was like to watch boyfriends shy away, intimidated by Kauffold's position in the British hierarchy. And she had shared the sorrow she felt when she lost the only woman she had known as her mother, the lovely Annabelle. But it had taken her weeks to get around to the topic that Maddi had been dreading: *"Tell me about my father…my biological father."* Maddi had looked at her and sighed. *"He wasn't a nice man, Tonna. Can we leave it at that?"* Thankfully, Tonna had honored her wishes, but Maddi knew there would soon come a time when she would insist on knowing more.

Maddi felt a sudden chill and reached for a quilt on the back of her chair.

Tonna had recently told her of her relationship with CIA agent Roger Clarkson. Maddi wasn't surprised. She had seen them at the Queen's Ball; it was clear they were attracted to one another. Because of the nature of his work, they had agreed to keep the relationship secret, but as Tonna had put it, *"If I don't tell someone, I think I'll bust."*

Maddi had then shared her rocky relationship with Roger's father, Hank. They had chuckled at the fact that they had fallen for a father and son. *"Good taste must be genetic,"* Maddi had said. She had made sure to tell Tonna that, though she and Hank were no longer together, she had never known a finer man.

Maddi sighed as she thought of Hank. *He really is such a good man.* Out of nowhere, she felt a longing for him, or at least for the relationship they had had. Simple, easy, comforting, sane. She missed his solidness, his lack of mystery. She looked over her shoulder at the man in the bed and sighed. Henderson was anything but.

Her phone rang; she jumped. Though she had had the phone for a full five months, the ring could still startle her. She walked to the record player, turned off the music, then hurried to the table and picked up the phone. She checked caller ID and smiled. It was Andrew. "Hey, big brother. How's that baby? Is he taller than you yet?"

There was a chuckle. "No, but he's about got Amanda beat."

"I don't doubt that. He'll be taller than her by Christmas."

He laughed. "How's Matt?"

Maddi sighed. "No change…still in a coma. The doctors can't explain it."

"I'm sure he'll wake up soon, Maddi. Just keep talking to him."

Maddi smiled. Even over the phone, Andrew was a comfort. "So, Doctor Madison, what do you think has made him like this?"

"Something that lunatic Cobra gave him."

Maddi nodded as she stared at Henderson. He looked like he was sleeping; as if at any moment he would sit up and say, *"Man, I'm hungry."* She smiled sadly. "Well, if he wakes up, I'll let him know that you asked about him."

"He'll wake up, don't worry." There was a pause. "Um…did you remember that Mom's birthday was in two days?"

Maddi flinched. "I did. Should we maybe call her?"

A longer pause. "You can…I don't think I will, Maddi."

Maddi nodded; she understood. Their history with their mother had been a difficult one, to say the least. She cleared her throat. "So, how's Amanda?"

"Doing well. She thoroughly enjoys motherhood."

"Well, tell her 'Hi' for me, and give Adam a hug from his Aunt Maddi."

"Will do. I'll talk to you soon."

Maddi ended the call and fell into her chair. She missed Andrew; she missed home. She hadn't been in the U.S. for nearly six months. How she longed for her house in DC, the familiarity of the senate chamber, the chance to see her brother any time she wanted. Her closeness with Andrew was like a lifeline, forged by the challenges they had faced after their father was killed in the line of duty. Their mother, Jeannie, had been unable to handle the loss and had turned to alcohol; it had destroyed their family. Neither Maddi nor Andrew had much contact with her, choosing to avoid anything that reminded them of those dark days after their father died and their mother fell apart.

Maddi sighed. If she tried really hard, she could recall her mother's laugh. It had been distinct; contagious. *"When Jeannie laughs, the whole world laughs,"* her father used to say. But it was getting harder to remember. She and Andrew had tried to get her help over the years, and for a while she would do better. She would sober up, fix her hair, straighten the house, even cook a meal or two. But then, the slightest stressor would push her to drink, and she would quickly spiral downward. Their hearts had been broken too many times. So, they had stayed away. But it had never gotten easier; it had never felt right to avoid the only mom you would ever have. Andrew and Maddi weren't like Tonna; they didn't get to have two mothers…they had only the one, and the poor woman was a mess. Maddi nodded. *I'll call her on her birthday.*

She rubbed her hands over the arms of the familiar chair. How long had she been either standing at the window or sitting in that chair with the embroidered silk and a missing brass button? *Too long.* She touched where the button had been with affection. Like Andrew's calls, it had been one of only a few distractions during the long, lonely days.

She switched on the TV, hoping to find something else to think about. A crisp British accent filled the room, making even the war-torn Middle East seem a bit lighter.

> *"Syria continues its onslaught into Oman. Neighboring Yemen has vowed to stay out of it. Though Yemen and Oman had been allies for a period of time, the assassination of Abdulkarim Al-Gharsi nine months ago ended all cooperation between the two countries, and Yemen is now vowing to withhold support…"*

Maddi suddenly began to shake. She was finding it hard to breathe. It was as if she had been transported from that Edinburgh nursing home to a New York City restaurant. It was a cold winter night, and her good friend, Abdulkarim Al-Gharsi was walking her into the restaurant. They were seated next to one another and, as they sat at an elegant white-clothed table, he said something funny. She laughed and turned to him. Suddenly, his head fell forward onto the tablecloth, and was quickly encircled by a pool of blood. Investigators had determined that he had been shot execution style by the leader of the Omani delegation, who had then turned the gun on himself. It had been a tragedy of epic proportions. Not only had her dear friend been murdered while sitting right next to her, but a Middle East peace process that had been years in the making had suddenly come to a halt. The regional war had escalated and had quickly encased the entire Middle East. Now, months later, it showed no sign of easing.

Maddi clicked off the TV. She stood and walked back to the window. Her legs were still shaking; she leaned against the sill. She looked out; the rain was coming harder. *How fitting*, she thought, as she stared at the sky, the street, the houses...all of it now just a blur of water-stained gray. The murder of Al-Gharsi had been a horrific event among many in her life; a final straw. There had been too much violence; too many men either gunned down or blown up. She had thought she would go crazy from it; she nearly did.

She walked to Henderson's bed and looked down at him. *Thank God, you're still alive. You've not been taken from me...yet.* She took his hand and leaned over and kissed his cheek as she smoothed his hair from his forehead. She stared at the black hair and the smooth skin of a face that had once belonged to someone else. She had wanted to ask him what it was like...to wear another man's face...to look in the mirror and see a stranger looking back. She had wanted to ask him so many things.

She sat down in the overstuffed chair and rested her feet on an ottoman that an orderly had brought in for her months ago. That room had become her home. The doctors and nurses now greeted her as if she was a part of the team. Meals were brought to her without a second thought. She knew the names of the night aide's children, the challenges of the charge nurse's ex-husband, the romance woes of the attending doctor, even the joys of the custodian as he delighted in his new grandson. Maddi knew it all; these people had become her world. And, though she had a world in DC – a world she missed – that world seemed a million miles away.

A monitor let out a beep. She looked up. Just a skipped heartbeat. She looked at Henderson's closed eyes and sighed. She wished she knew what he was thinking. *Maybe then I'd understand why you didn't reach out to me during the four years you were gone.*

They had talked only briefly since their reunion; first at the Henderson estate in Latvia, then in the dungeon outside Lyon where Cobra had held them hostage. They had had little time to really share, however. The only thing she had learned about those four years was that he wasn't proud of them. But it was more than that; whatever he had done as the Phoenix had left him so ashamed and disgusted with himself that to mention it would change him. His eyes would grow dark, his jaw would tighten; it was as if he would choke on the words if he dared to speak of the past.

Maddi flinched. She understood. She, too, had a past with dark secrets. She felt certain that she could reassure him just by letting him know. But she wondered if she would ever be able to share what had happened to her. Just like him; a past that seemed so awful that to breathe a word of it would destroy her, or, more importantly, would destroy anyone's ability to love her. Even talking about it with her therapist, Claire, had left her reeling. Yes, she had gotten pregnant at the age of fifteen and that had been hard. But it didn't compare to the horror of what she had done to the baby's father, Officer Evan Jackson of the Evansville Police Department...

"What if we go at this a different way, Maddi." Claire laid her hands on her lap.

"What do you mean?" Maddi's hands were clasped, her legs crossed; the armor firmly in place.

"Let's give him a different name. What might you call him if you didn't call him Officer Jackson?"

Maddi flinched. "I don't know, how about...Mr. Pain."

Claire nodded. "Okay. Now, let's start with the police station, after you bravely told...Mr. Pain...that you were pregnant."

Maddi shook her head. "I don't know if I can do this, Claire. You have no idea how bad it is."

Claire frowned. "No matter how bad it is, it isn't as bad as it's become in your mind. Trust me, Maddi."

Maddi looked at Claire's strawberry-blonde hair and warm green eyes; she did trust her. Maddi trusted Claire more than she had ever trusted anyone. But could she do this? Could she finally say the words? She took a deep breath. "I walked away, ready to handle the pregnancy alone. I was devastated, and my self-worth was all but gone, but I was ready." She paused. "I walked home, rehearsing in my mind what I'd say to Mom. Though she was drinking at the time, I still had to tell her. I reached the house, walked in the door, and called for her. She didn't respond. I walked back to her bedroom, thinking maybe she was napping. I opened the door, and then..." Maddi stopped.

Claire frowned. "What happened?"

Maddi swallowed. "She was passed out, an empty bottle on the floor beside her." She sighed. "So, I slammed the door and ran out of the house. I walked for hours to nowhere in particular. I had no place to go...no one to talk to."

"Where was your brother, Andrew?"

"He was away at medical school. I was so proud of him. Andrew was going to make something of himself in spite of all that had happened...unlike me." She paused. *"Anyway, I was wandering aimlessly when this car pulled up."* Maddi's legs had begun to shake; she put her hands on her lap to calm them. *"It was...Mr. Pain. I had somehow wandered into an alley and I was scared. But I wasn't going to let him know that. He slowed the car, rolled down the window and said, 'Need a ride?' I hate to admit it, Claire, but I almost got in; I was so hungry for someone to love me, so frightened of being alone...I almost let that slime bag lure me into that car one last time. Instead, I turned and walked away. He inched the car beside me and said, 'Listen, bitch, I know what you're trying to do, and two can play at that game.'"* Maddi cleared her throat. *"I...I stopped and looked at him. I saw the dark eyes that I had once thought were so appealing and smelled the Old Spice cologne; I wanted to vomit. I said, 'There's no game. I'm pregnant with your child, Evan.' He glared at me. I'll never forget the look in his eyes. He said, 'Well...one way or another, we're gonna resolve that...situation.'"*

Claire frowned. *"What do you think he meant by that?"*

Maddi sighed. *"Oh...I knew exactly what he meant."*

They sat silently. Claire said, *"So, what happened next?"*

Maddi shifted in her seat. *"I couldn't let him do it. Though I regretted how it had come about, I had somehow fallen in love with that child, or at least the thought of it."*

Claire nodded. *"I'm told that's how it happens."* She paused. *"So, what did you do?"*

Maddi hesitated. *"I stopped him."*

"How?"

Maddi stared at Claire, grateful for her kind eyes and patient demeanor, as she said evenly, *"I killed him."*

The monitor beeped, bringing Maddi back to the present. She looked at the rhythm. It was atrial fibrillation, and this time it lasted longer. *He's getting worse.* She squeezed his hand and laid her head on his chest. "Don't you die on me, Henderson."

All at once she felt his chest vibrate, as a raspy voice said, "I won't."

CHAPTER 7

Edinburgh, Scotland

Was it morning? Nighttime? Martin Henderson couldn't tell. Was he asleep? *Am I dead?* He had been trying desperately to get back to Maddi. For how long? He had no idea. It was as if he was imprisoned within his own body. He could hear her, and he could feel her take his hand. He felt the longing in her heart when she fell against his chest in despair, and he wanted to reach his arm around her to comfort her, but he couldn't. He had tried screaming, but nothing would come out. *What did that bastard do to me?"*

Then, he would fade, knowing – whatever it was – it was useless for him to try to fight it. He would give up. He would slow his heart and try to die. But he couldn't; his body wouldn't let him…as if some internal voice was telling his heart to keep beating.

I can't live and I can't die.

It had been that way for weeks, maybe months, as Henderson struggled…alone in the shell that was his body, taunted by the voices of Morningstar and Cobra as Maddi soothed his cold, clammy skin from a place he couldn't get to. *I'm in Hell.*

There were days when he was convinced it was true. But then it would occur to him that Maddi would never be anywhere near Hell. He would feel her tears touch his skin, and he would know…*it can't be Hell.* Then he would fight harder. He would take deep breaths and force his heart to beat harder, stronger; and each time he did, a monitor would go off and he would try to shout, "See, I'm here!" But he couldn't shout; he couldn't say a word.

58

Again, he heard Maddi's voice, her despair as she sat by his bed...
for how long now? How many days had it been? He had tried to keep
track, but it had been impossible. Days turned into nights turned into
days; nothing changed.

There, he heard it again. As if it was a thousand miles away, he
heard the sound of Maddi's voice. *"Don't you die on me, Henderson."*

Suddenly, he heard himself reply. *Did I just talk?* He felt her squeeze
his hand, and he was able to squeeze hers, as well. *I'm back!* A blurred
face – Maddi's? – was directly in front of his; he could *see* her. *Which
means my eyes are open!* She was crying, her hair was falling in her eyes, and
her smile filled him with so much joy that he thought his heart might
explode. *I can see you, Maddi!* The lights were so bright, impossibly
bright...it was painful, but still he forced his eyes to stay open. *I can see
you, Maddi.*

She crawled next to him and hugged him close. "Henderson, you're
back! Wake up! Wake up!"

He felt his arm move; he hugged her. Suddenly he coughed; he
was choking. Alarms began to sound and he could hear footsteps
running toward him. Maddi jumped from his side, but refused to let go
of his hand. A voice snapped, "Step away, Madam."

She replied, "I'm not leaving his side."

Stubborn Maddi. He tried to laugh, but only choked.

A voice said, "Take it easy, Mr. Henderson. In and out...slowly
now." He tried, acutely aware of each breath as it filled his lungs. Never
had breathing seemed so hard. *In and out...in and out.* Finally, he calmed
down, and the breaths came easier as he fell into what used to be so
natural. He clung to Maddi's hand as he tried to once again open his
eyes. It was blurry; he blinked several times. He felt something wet wipe
his eyes and he opened the lids wider. He was nearly blinded by
fluorescent lights. He turned away, first to his right, where nurses and
doctors were fumbling with monitors, then to his left, where Maddi was
still clinging to his hand. Tears covered the cheeks of a face that was
far too thin, but it was still the most wonderful face he had ever seen.
She squeezed his hand tighter; it almost hurt. He grinned. "Hey, Maddi."

She nodded; unable to speak. *That has to be a first,* he thought, then
he laughed. She laughed as well, both of them ignoring the doctors who

were screaming orders as the nurses checked and rechecked monitors. *Why aren't they stepping away? Don't they see I'm back?*

Suddenly, one of the nurses screamed, "We're losing him!"

He stared at Maddi; he could see it on her face. Something was wrong. He felt his lungs hungering for air. *Why can't I breathe?* Then he felt his heart stop. A heavy weight was on his chest, and Maddi had disappeared. As a doctor pounded on his weakened thorax, all he could think was, *Maddi, don't let go.*

CHAPTER 8

Edinburgh, Scotland

Pocks' taxi driver had driven him back to the same corner where he had picked him up, and Pocks had given him a twenty-euro bill to wait for him. He had then run back through the same alley to the nursing home, had snuck in through a side entrance, and had run down the stairs to the box where he had hidden his overalls. He had taken them from the box, had found his camera, then had stuffed them back in the box. He had then run up the stairs and out of the building. As he was leaving, he had overheard two nurses who had just arrived, saying that they had been called in because *"...the wealthy man in a coma just woke up."* One of them had mentioned that he had coded soon after, and Pocks had made a mental note to share the news with Morningstar when he talked to him.

He arrived back at the hotel at 11:20. He paid the fare and ran into his hotel, ignoring the front desk clerk who had said hello. He went straight to the elevator, then to his room. He hurried inside, quickly closing and locking the door.

He walked into the bathroom and relieved himself. He was about to walk out, when, once again, he caught his reflection in the mirror. He took off the glasses, frowning as he looked at his pocked cheeks. It was how he had gotten the nickname. A bad case of acne and an awkward personality, and *voilà*, he had gone from Herbert Cosgrove to Pocks. This time, he didn't turn away. *Look at yourself, Pocks. Look long and hard at the man you've become.*

He continued to stare, hoping that if he looked deep enough, he would see something – someone – different. But no matter how long he stared at himself, it was still him…still Pocks, the man who had sold his soul to Morningstar. He had always thought there would be a stopping point…some mythical line he wouldn't cross, not even to keep his secrets buried and to keep from getting fired. Was there such a line? He hoped so…he prayed that he had enough honor that when the time came – when Morningstar finally asked him to do the unthinkable, whatever that was – he would stand his ground. He searched his greenish-brown eyes for a sign…some hint that he had courage in his soul. He blinked, looked again, then turned away. *Who are you kidding, Pocks? You're a weak, pathetic man.*

He walked out of the bathroom, and sat at a small desk. He took out the camera and plugged it into his laptop. He smiled for a quick second as he looked at the pictures of Matt Henderson. He picked the one that was clearest, then sent it via an attachment to a secret Morningstar email address. It was eleven-thirty. *Plenty of time.*

He went to disconnect the camera from his laptop, when the photos of Cynthia Madison caught his eye. Just as he had snapped the second one, she had glanced over her shoulder at the man in the bed. He enlarged the photo, captivated by the love, the fondness he could see in the woman's eyes. As if she was actually speaking the words, 'I love you,' to Matt Henderson. Her unwavering faith in his recovery was astounding to see. Pocks felt a sudden rush of tears, and he quickly disconnected the camera. He shoved it in his pocket. He needed to call Morningstar.

I'll do it in a minute, he thought as he stood and wiped his eyes. He walked to the window and looked outside. It had started to rain…again. Pocks didn't mind the rain; he felt that it was cleansing in an odd sort of way. *Sort of like a baptism,* he thought, as he opened the window. The rain hit the sill and splashed onto the floor; he didn't care. He stuck out his head. He had learned that if he leaned far enough to his right, he could see a sliver of the River Thames. He leaned to his right, straining to see the river. It looked dirty; the entire city was dirty. He missed DC. He would be glad when he could go home.

He sighed. What he really wanted was to go back in time…to First Blood Seminary in upstate New York. Though he had been sent there by his father to 'cure' his homosexuality, the notion of becoming a priest had appealed to him. He had begun to see it as God's calling. Yes, it was a criminal act that had led him there, but he was content to think that it had been God's plan all along…that Herbert Cosgrove had been ordained to become the finest, kindest priest in all of New York. But it wasn't to be; his appetites in the bedroom had dictated a different path for the overweight man from Queens. There was no place for homosexuality in the priesthood. He had been let go with little fanfare, dismissed first by the bishop, then by his family…*and now – if I'm not careful – by the only place that will have me…the United States Government.*

He thought again of Morningstar's simple, yet unambiguous directive. *"You do what I tell you to do, Cosgrove, and I'll keep your secret."*

He stared at the dirt-stained building across from him, thinking about where his life had led him. Certainly not to a calling as a man of God. No, as he leaned even further to the right so he could catch that sliver of the River Thames, it occurred to him that he was about as far from God as any man could be. *Now I take my orders from a tyrant.*

CHAPTER 9

Washington, DC

How on earth can that stupid woman be pregnant! Morningstar had just returned to the suite after walking for the past hour or so through the dark streets of DC. Though it was early, he found that time of morning to be particularly soothing in a city where chaos reigned supreme. And soothing was exactly what he had needed. Janet's news had rattled him to the point that he had hardly been able to keep from beating the poor woman to death. After all, she had assured him that she had her reproductive obligations under control. *"How the hell did you get pregnant, Janet?"*

She had looked at him, first with fear, then defiance, and with her voice unwavering, had said, *"I wanted it, Edward. And once you accept it, you'll want it, too."*

He had grabbed the clock by the bed and had thrown it against the wall, and had then proceeded to tear the entire room apart. By the time he left, reproductions of Rembrandt and Van Gogh lay in pieces, while the lamp – with the light still glowing – lay broken on the floor.

But at least I didn't hit her, he thought as he tapped the keycard on the door. It clicked and he pushed it open. He waited for sounds of Janet fussing in the bedroom or taking a bath. There was nothing, and he was instantly struck with fear. *What if she left me?* he thought, but then quickly recovered, realizing that Janet would be nothing without him. He knew it, and – more importantly – she knew it, too. "Janet? Where are you, Janet dear?" He waited, his heart racing at the thought that he may have lost her.

"Hey Baby." Janet's sultry words preceded her as she walked out from the bedroom in nothing but a robe. He could see the outline of her breasts through the silk, and was speechless as he looked at his unrepentant lover. Should he chastise and berate her as he had done before he left? Or should he bed her and let it all go, ignoring the fact that the woman he was so fond of had deceived him? *Or...should I just kill her and get rid of two problems at once?*

He was stewing over the decision, when suddenly she put her hand to her belly and grinned. "It's a boy." She slid her tongue over her upper lip and added, "...I thought we could name him Benjamin."

Morningstar felt as if he had been struck by lightning. *Of course!* he thought as he quickly stumbled to a chair. He stared at his pregnant concubine with a mixture of anger and awe. *This was what God had intended all along.* For the past four years, God had told Morningstar to hold off finding the twelfth son...*and now I see why...this boy is him!*

He rubbed his eyes, fighting an urge to cry. He stood and walked over to her. He laid his hand on her stomach. It was hard and full. He rubbed it gently, then took his other hand and put it on her breast, squeezing so hard she groaned. "You deceived me, yet you bring me God's greatest prize." He squeezed harder; she bit her lip. "I can either kill you now, or I can keep you alive, then kill you once he's born."

She looked up at him, her bold green eyes showing no sign of fear. "There's a third option," she said with a coolness he couldn't help but admire.

"Oh yeah, what's that?"

"You could let me help you...let me be your Rachel...the Cleopatra to your Caesar." She smiled seductively, and he eased his pressure on her breast. She moved closer, so that their eyelashes were almost touching. "Besides, I know for a fact that you would be nothing without me."

His reaction was fierce. He reached back his hand and was about to smack her hard across her jaw, when she grabbed his wrist with a strength that surprised him. She stopped him just before he was about to make contact.

"Touch me, Edward, and I end not only this pregnancy, but all the work you've done."

He laughed bitterly. "You presumptuous bitch! Pray tell how you would end my work, dear Janet."

She continued to hold his wrist, her strong grip almost painful. "Surely you don't think I would have gone through all of this and not put in place a security clause."

He flinched. "A security clause?"

"A way to ruin you…even if I'm dead." She eased her grip, but only slightly. She moved closer and whispered, "Do you understand what I'm saying, baby?"

He was speechless. He had to admire her nerve. After another few seconds, he wrangled his wrist free, let go of her breast, and sneered. "Oh, I understand alright. But this isn't over."

She grinned, then turned and walked back to the bedroom.

That insufferable bitch, he thought as he started to follow her. *I'll beat her into submission.* He was nearly to the door of the bedroom when he heard a clock tower ring out a single chime. He checked his watch. Six-forty-five. He flinched. The weekly meeting of the Bentley Group was to start in just over an hour, and he had a lot of work to do before the meeting. *I'll deal with her later.*

He turned, walked to a corner desk, and took a seat. The altercation had unsettled him. What sort of insurance policy was Janet referring to? Tape recordings? Photos? Suddenly he sneered. It didn't matter. Janet would never do anything to undermine him; she was as addicted to power as he was…*and she needs me in order to have it.* But it was clear that his concubine had been paying attention. How many times had he said to his sons: *"Always have a backup plan…an insurance policy, even if you think you're dealing with a friend."* Janet had simply done what she had been taught to do…*by me.*

He adjusted his chair; it was time to get to work. Not only did he need to prepare for his meeting, but he was also expecting to receive a photo from Pocks at any moment. Pocks had been instructed to take a picture of the ailing Matt Henderson and send it to Morningstar, who would, in turn, send it to Levi, who would then run it through NSA's facial recognition software. The goal: to learn if Matt Henderson was, in fact, Martin. He had tried using what few photos he could find of Matt from his high school and college days, but they were old and grainy; not nearly clear enough to satisfy the requirements for a reliable facial

ID. It was possible that the ambiguous photos had been planted as part of Martin's elaborate masquerade. After all, if he was pretending to be Matt, he would need a solid backstory, including old photos in old school records as a way to verify his claim.

Why was it so important to prove that he was Martin? Because if the man in that bed was Martin Henderson, then not only did Morningstar need to punish him for his betrayals over the last nine months, but he needed to stop him from telling the world what he knew about Morningstar and his operation. Martin – Joseph – had been Morningstar's favorite son, and, as such, had had an inside track on much of what Morningstar had done over the last four years. He could ruin Morningstar if he was to ever share what he knew.

So, why hasn't he done it? Morningstar wondered as he sat back in his chair. He sneered. *Because it would destroy him...and his prestigious family.* Imagine the fallout should the world learn that a Henderson heir was also an international assassin. *Two Henderson heirs,* Morningstar thought with a chuckle. The notorious Cobra was a Henderson, as well. Morningstar laughed. *That's some hefty DNA.* Yes, Henderson had a lot on Morningstar, but there was no question that Morningstar had a lot on Henderson, as well.

But he couldn't count on the man's silence forever. What was to say that Henderson might not suddenly choose to sacrifice himself and his family to bring down Morningstar. *Which is why I must know if the man in that bed is Martin. If he is, then I must kill him.*

But it would be difficult. Morningstar was fond of Henderson. He had spent hours not only rehabilitating him, but training him to become one of the finest assassins in the world. And Henderson had been open to the training...at first. But when the time had come to actually kill a man, he had resisted. So, Morningstar had needed to use a bit of coercion, which had come in the form of a child named Lili. Morningstar had learned that the young girl was important to Henderson. He didn't know why; it didn't matter. He was able to use the threat of harming her to make Henderson do whatever he asked of him.

And things had gone along just fine until November of last year, when Henderson – for whatever reason – had decided to leave Morningstar. He had seemed to vanish into thin air until five months ago, when Cobra informed Morningstar that Martin was one of his Dalgety Bay captives. But when the dust had settled and the prisoners were all accounted for, Martin, aka Phoenix, aka Joseph, was not among them. Which left only three possibilities: he was never there, he was there but had somehow been taken away before others could learn of it, or he had *changed his appearance* and was actually one of the seven survivors. Three of the survivors had been women; he certainly couldn't have pretended to be one of them. One thing Martin could never get away with was masquerading as a woman. Simeon could do it; he had on many occasions. But Henderson was too solid; too *manly*. As a matter of fact, he was more of a man than anyone Morningstar had ever known. He flinched. *Except for me.*

Which left the four men who had survived the assault at the Bay. But every one of them had been accounted for. Scotland Yard's Chief Inspector, Lionel Pritchard, had been beaten to the point where he was nearly unrecognizable, but one would never mistake his slight frame for Martin's. And Walter Henderson was too well-known to be anyone but himself. There was a psychiatrist, James Samuels, but he was even smaller than the Inspector. Which left the nephew, Matt, as the only viable candidate. But in spite of the fact that Matt and Martin were the same height and build, Simeon swore that Matt couldn't be Martin. *"They look nothing alike, Father...there's no way they're the same man."* But Morningstar, never willing to bank on Simeon's word alone, had instructed his technical analyst, Levi, to dig into Matt's past with a fine-toothed comb. Levi had come to the same conclusion. *"Matt is Matt, Jacob...his historical footprint is solid."* Which had put Morningstar right back where he started. *Where in the hell is Martin?*

He stood from the desk and walked to a nearby coffee maker. He started a pot, then paced the room as he waited for it to brew. Could it be that the man he had hunted for the last nine months was lying comatose in a nursing home in Edinburgh, Scotland? If so, how had he pulled it off? Had he killed his cousin and then taken his face in an act of barbarity that would shame even the lowliest criminal? Wouldn't there be an aunt or uncle who could refute his identity? Levi had looked into that, as well. Apparently, Matt's mother was dead, and his father was in an institution suffering from the last stages of Alzheimer's Disease. Which meant that there was no one to challenge Matt's identity. *A brilliant choice, if it is, in fact, what Joseph has done.* The odd thing was that Martin's *own father* had bought into it, insisting repeatedly that the man lying in that bed was his nephew. Was Walter lying, as well? Or had he maybe been fooled by the ruse of a nephew whom he hadn't seen for years? Morningstar sneered. *I'll know soon enough.*

He checked his watch. Six-fifty; almost noon in Scotland. Pocks was to have the photo to him by noon, his time. *Hurry up, Pocks…I need to see him for myself,* he thought, as he poured a cup of coffee and carried it to his desk.

Getting the photo had presented a challenge. First, Morningstar had needed to come up with a way for Pocks to get inside Matt Henderson's nursing home room. He was closely guarded, not only by the Hendersons, who had instructed the facility that no one was to enter the room without their okay, but by Cynthia Madison's bodyguards. Morningstar had come up with the idea of Pocks posing as a maintenance man and, with help from Levi, had given him an identity as a top-rate handyman with a years-long history of working in and around Edinburgh. Pocks, with a feigned Scottish accent, had interviewed with the facility and had been hired on the spot. He had cemented the role by spending the last two months repairing broken lights, clogged toilets, and anything else that was malfunctioning, all the while just waiting for an opportunity to go into Henderson's room. That chance had come three weeks after Pocks had been hired; the bathroom sink had sprung a leak. He had entered the room, taken a quick inventory of the twenty-by-twenty suite, then fixed the leak. When he left, he had purposely loosened a bolt at the base of the sink, which would guarantee that he would be called to come back within the next few days. According to Pocks, it had worked like a charm. Every few days or so, he was called to the room to fix the sink. When they asked him why it kept breaking, he told them they needed a new sink, which he guessed – correctly – would take at least until the end of the summer to arrange. Which meant that he had been able to repeat the ruse two or three times a week for the last four weeks. Every time he went into that room and fixed the sink, he solidified his credentials a bit more. Now, almost a full month later, everyone was used to him…Madison, her bodyguards, even the Hendersons themselves. As long as he was careful, he should have no problem snapping a photo.

From what Pocks had told him, Madison was in the room nearly twenty-four hours a day. *"She eats there, sleeps there...she even bathes there, Jacob."* Morningstar wasn't surprised. Simeon had already told him that she and Matt were an item; her faithful vigil was just more proof of that fact. It was also further evidence that Martin and Matt were likely the same man. Prior to Martin's presumed death four years ago, he and Madison had struck up a relationship. It made far more sense that they had rekindled that relationship than that Madison had somehow fallen for Martin's cousin.

Morningstar stood and carried his coffee to the window. Though it was still dark outside, he could see a hint of sunrise in the distance. It was sure to be another hot one in the nation's capital. He had grown tired of the heat. *I need a vacation,* he thought, as he sipped his coffee and stared into the darkness. He chuckled and walked back to his desk. *Kings don't take vacations...not when they're about to expand the realm.*

He had just taken a seat at his computer, when his phone vibrated. "Yes."

"Hello, sir, it's me, Pocks."

"Have you got the photo?"

"Yes sir. It should be in your inbox by now."

Morningstar opened his laptop, typed in a password, then waited while he was taken to a login page. He typed another password, opened the email, and grinned. There it was; a perfect image of Matt Henderson. Clear, concise, the features as crisp as if the man had posed for it. His eyes were closed, which would make it harder for the facial recognition program to identity him, but Levi had assured him that the software would still be able to tell. "Good job, Pocks. Now what can you tell me about the man's status?"

"Well, I had needed to go back to the nursing home to pick up something, and, as I was walking out a side door, I overheard a nurse tell another nurse that she was being called in because the wealthy coma patient had come out of his coma."

Morningstar's eyes widened. "Was it Henderson?"

"I think so, sir. I'm pretty sure he's the only coma patient in the nursing home."

"I see. And you're telling me that he woke up from his coma?"

"Yes sir, just for a minute or two. Then he coded, I guess."

Morningstar stood and paced the room. Matt had come out of his coma. Which meant that he could do it again at any moment. Only the next time, he might stay awake. He frowned. *Near-death experiences do funny things to a man.* If that man was actually Martin, then it was vital that Morningstar get to him before he had a chance to tell anyone what he knew about Morningstar, his sons, or the Bentley Group. He frowned. "Here's what you need to do, Pocks."

He heard Pocks let out a deep sigh. "I'm listening, sir."

"You're going to make sure that you're nearby when that man wakes up."

"But I got rid of my uniform."

"You got rid of it?"

"Well, no, not exactly. But I left it in the basement at the facility." There was a pause. "You told me the assignment was over once I got you a photo."

Morningstar gritted his teeth. *What a whiny fat man.* "Yes, Pocks, but now I want you to go back there, put on the uniform, and place yourself in position to let me know the minute that man wakes up. Do you hear me?"

Another pause. "Um, yes sir. But how will I know? I can't really hang out there."

Morningstar had to fight to control his anger. But the man had a point. "I'll tell you what. Why don't you find a way to put a bug in the room."

"A bug, sir?"

"Yes…you know, a listening device. Wire it so that I receive the feed through my private cellphone."

There was a slow, deep sigh. "It will take me some time, sir."

"Why?"

Another sigh. "I'm not due back until this evening. Which should give me time to get everything together."

"Just hurry up and get it done, Pocks."

Morningstar ended the call. Bugging the room was brilliant. He would know the minute the man awakened. *Then I can do what needs to be done.*

He stared at the photo on his screen and frowned. *And what, exactly, is that?* He leaned back, his eyes still fixed on the screen. If Matt turned out to be Martin, which seemed likely, and if he awoke from his coma, which seemed like a reasonable probability, then that meant that Martin Henderson was alive and well in a nursing home in Scotland. *But only I and a few others would be aware of that fact.* Martin would be forced to maintain his identity as Matt, if for no other reason than he was a wanted man. Which would give Morningstar a brief window of time in which to kill him.

He continued staring at the photo, trying to see if Joseph was somehow present in the man's features. He wasn't. That face looked completely different from the man he had nursed to health after the hotel fire four years ago. He opened his phone, dialed, and, without waiting for a hello, said, "Levi, I'm sending you the photo I told you about. Run it through the software. You'll need to account for the fact that the face has been altered."

"Altered?"

"Yes…by way of a revolutionary surgery." Another pause. "But no one can know what you're doing, Levi. You must remove any evidence. Got it?"

"Yes, Father. I should have something in the next twenty minutes or so."

Morningstar ended the call and shoved the phone in his pocket. He checked the time. It was six-fifty-five. If Levi delivered as promised, Morningstar should know the truth about Matt or Martin before he left for his meeting with the Bentley Group.

He sent the photo to Levi's private email, then grabbed his empty coffee cup and carried it to the sink. He was surprised to see that his hand was shaking. Was he nervous? Frightened to finally learn the identity of the man in that bed? Or was it more? *What will I do if he's Joseph?* He flinched. *I'll kill him…that's what I'll do.* But it wouldn't be easy. Setting aside Morningstar's fondness for the man, Henderson would be tough to get to. He was well-protected, not only by the Henderson's, but by Madison's bodyguards. *So, I'll just tell the world who he really is.* But the minute he did, Henderson would no longer have a reason to not tell all that he knew about Morningstar. Morningstar shook his head. Though it was ironic, it was true: Matt's disguise was Morningstar's protection.

He was about to rinse his cup when he stopped. *Maybe I should just fly over there, flash my credentials, and walk into his room and kill him.* He could schedule his visit for the morning, so the Hendersons wouldn't be there, and order Madison to leave the room under the premise that it was a top-secret interrogation. Then he could suffocate him, claim he had had a heart attack or a stroke, and attribute it to a setback from the coma. A brilliant idea, except that Matt was a civilian, a foreign-born one, at that. What would justify a Pentagon aide flying all the way to Scotland to interrogate a non-military non-American who had just come out of a coma? He shook his head. *If only he was in the States, it would be so much easier. I wouldn't have to explain myself to anyone.*

Suddenly his eyes widened. *So...why not bring him here...to DC.* He rinsed his cup, plotting how to get Matt Henderson to America. He frowned. Even if he could come up with some clever justification, his biggest challenge would be Matt's 'Uncle Walter.' According to Pocks, Walter and his wife spent every afternoon in Matt's room. Whether the man in that bed was Matt or Martin, he was clearly important to them. Which meant, before Morningstar could get Matt to America, he would first need to get his powerful uncle out of the way. Which left Morningstar with two very distinct challenges. The first was to come up with a justifiable reason to bring Matt Henderson to America. The second was to get Walter out of the way long enough for him to do it.

He walked into the bedroom. Janet was asleep, but had picked up the broken lamp, had returned the clock to the table by the bed, and had rehung the damaged frames that had held the Rembrandt and Van Gogh reproductions. He chuckled as he stole to the closet and opened the door. *I can always count on that bitch to clean up my messes.*

He took out a dark gray Brioni suit and a pair of polished Berluti shoes. He was about to carry them into the bathroom, when suddenly he stopped. He laid the clothes over the back of a chair, set his shoes on the seat, and grinned. He had an idea.

He walked out to the living room and dialed his private phone. "Levi, I know you're working on that ID, but I need one more thing from you, and I need it quickly." He paused. "Actually, two more things...two documents that you'll need to fax to me in the next ten minutes." He proceeded to tell Levi what was needed on the documents, then gave him the number to a fax machine that he had installed in the suite a few weeks ago.

He ended the call and carried the phone into the bedroom. He grabbed his clothes and shoes from the chair, and walked into the bathroom. He hung his suit on the back of the door, set his shoes on the floor, and laid his phone by the sink. He turned on the shower and was about to step in, when he took a quick glance in the mirror. He smiled. He was a handsome man. In spite of the fact that he was fifty-five years old, there was no sign of gray in his black hair, and only a few wrinkles around his mouth and eyes. And though he was short – about five-seven – he was a large presence. *Bigger than any six-four man could ever dream of.* And today, once again…he would prove it.

CHAPTER 10

Edinburgh, Scotland

Maddi brushed her fingers over the soft wool of the scarf that Kauffold had brought her, as she sat in her chair and stared at the man in the bed. She had barely moved. She was afraid to even breathe. Henderson had come back for a moment, then he was gone. *A perfect metaphor,* she thought, as she watched his chest move up and down as if he was merely sleeping. It made her angry, far angrier than it should have. Wasn't it hopeful that he had come out of the coma? *No, it was only cruel...to give me...to give all of us...that glimmer of hope.*

Walter and Dora had arrived just minutes ago, likely called by the nursing staff the minute Henderson had awakened from the coma. Fortunately, they hadn't gotten there until after the code, which meant that they hadn't had to watch the doctors and nurses pounding on his chest. They were sitting quietly at Henderson's side, much like they had for the past five months...Dora with her hand on his arm, Walter with his arm around Dora.

It was obvious to anyone watching that the experience had taken a toll on both of them, but mostly on Dora. Her face was drawn, her normally-bright eyes left empty by grief. Her entire countenance was a testament to all she had been through. She had mourned her son's death four years ago, and, looking at him now, it was clear that she may soon be mourning him again.

She leaned forward and put her hand on his bruised arm. There were tubes and wires hanging from every part of his body. His skin was mottled from the chest compressions, and his eyes were fluttering. Was he aware? Did he realize that he had almost come back? Was he now forced to face the fact that he may *never* come back? Was it time for all of them to face that truth?

She stood and walked to the window. The rain was showing no signs of stopping. She had always liked the rain, ever since she was a child; especially when she was a child. She and Andrew would spend hours jumping in puddles as the summer rain drenched them in warm wonderfulness. Tears filled her eyes and she quickly wiped them away.

She looked over her shoulder. All she could see from where she was standing was Henderson's dyed black hair. She flinched. No matter how many times she saw it, it made her uneasy. Was it because she had fallen in love with him when his hair was much lighter? Or was there another reason that the coal-black hair made her uneasy? She reached for the blanket on the back of her chair, threw it over her shoulders, and stared out at the rain. She didn't want to admit it, but there *was* another reason…a person she couldn't help but think of whenever she saw that coal-black hair…

"Describe him for me, Maddi."

"I thought I already did."

"Yes, but I'd like you to do it again."

Maddi looked at Claire and frowned. "Why? Why would I want to describe the awful man who nearly ruined my life?"

"It's important. Not just his appearance, but why you were first drawn to him. I want to hear it."

Maddi said nothing for nearly a minute. Finally, she looked at Claire and said evenly, "He was tall, with brown eyes…light brown, almost copper. He had a mustache, and his hair was cut short, but not too short."

"What color was it?"

"Black. Very black."

"Did he remind you of someone?"

Maddi flinched. "The hair…it was the same color as my father's." She added quickly, "…but he was nothing like my father."

Claire nodded. "I'm sure he wasn't." She narrowed her eyes. "How old was he?"

Maddi frowned. "I don't think he was as old as my dad, but he had been his partner, so he had to have at least been in his mid-thirties."

Claire shook her head. "Old enough to know better." She shifted in her chair and sighed. "So, tell me more about that day in the alley."

Maddi shook her head. "What I told you last week is all I'm going to say, Claire. I probably shouldn't have told you that much."

"Why?"

"Because that was part of the arrangement."

"What arrangement?"

Maddi sat back in her chair and sighed. "I can't tell you."

"You can't...or you won't."

Maddi looked at Claire. "I am not at liberty to say."

They sat in silence. After a minute, Claire nodded and said, "Maybe next week."

Maddi stood and was about to walk out the door, when she stopped. She turned and looked at Claire. "I doubt it. Like so many other things that that man ruined for me, he ruined my ability to trust anyone...even you."

Claire smiled sadly. "It's okay, Maddi. You'll get there. We'll get there..."

Maddi looked again at Henderson's black hair; the hair that reminded her so much of Evan Jackson. She shivered and wrapped the blanket tighter. What she wouldn't give to wash out that black dye, so he would at least resemble the man she had met in Providence four years ago...*instead of the man who ruined my life twenty-two years ago.*

As the rain fell harder against the glass, she thought about the cop from her youth, and all that had happened in Evansville, Indiana. A terrible man had coerced her to have sex with him at a very young age. From that horrid experience had come a child...who was now a beautiful, loving young lady. Maddi shook her head and sighed. She had been lucky. *Thank God that man had had no other children.*

CHAPTER 11

Philadelphia, Pennsylvania

"Johnny Malone. An ugly case. It'll piss you off. Look into it."

Police officer Todd Jackson combed his fingers through his short black hair as he looked over at the oversized cop who had come out of nowhere. The man had taken a seat beside him on the park bench and was staring straight ahead, his thick eyebrows making it hard to tell where he was looking as he delivered the cryptic message.

Todd frowned and said, "Okay...and then what?"

The officer crossed his legs, upsetting two pigeons that were fighting over a piece of bread. The birds moved a few inches away. "You'll know what to do." He stood, causing the bench to shift. He walked away, his massive legs working like steam engines as he plodded down the sidewalk with his hand on the grip of his gun.

Jackson narrowed his eyes. He was new; he had joined the force just a few months ago. And, at only twenty-five years old, he was thankful to get the job with the esteemed Philadelphia police force. After all, he wasn't from Philadelphia...he wasn't even from Pennsylvania. Todd had been born in Evansville, Indiana. *Midwest boy through and through,* he thought with a chuckle.

He pondered the cop's words. *"Look into it...you'll know what to do."*

He shook his head. *What does he mean by that?* But he knew exactly what the man meant. That police officer had just given him a ticket in... his rite of passage into an organization that few even knew existed.

He kicked at one of the pigeons, causing them both to fly away. He leaned back and stretched his thick, muscled legs, crossing them at the ankles. He grabbed his hat from the bench, smoothed back his hair, and put it on. *Johnny Malone.*

After another few minutes, he stood and strolled in the direction of the police station, shielding his eyes from the rising sun as he glanced at his watch. *Seven a.m.* His shift didn't start until eight, but he liked to be early. He was working the day shift on Philly's south side, and things were busy; he rarely got home before nine or ten p.m. But that was okay; there was no one to go home to. He didn't even own a dog. It was just him alone in a small apartment on Avon Street in North Philly. His mother was his only living relative, and she lived back in Evansville. Though he called her once a week, he had vowed to never go back there; to never go back to that dead-end town. That town was where his father was killed and, though he didn't remember him, he knew the stories; Evan Jackson was a brave officer who had died in the line of duty.

Todd walked into the station and poured a cup of coffee. *Johnny Malone.* He went to a computer in the back of the room and typed in the address of a website listing felons, past and present. He scrolled the names. He found Malone under "dismissed cases," and saw that the "incident" that had put him on that list had taken place three months ago...

> *"Johnny Malone: aggravated assault, manslaughter, and possession of a firearm. Robbed a grocery store and shot and killed the owner. No evidence at the scene, but he was viewed clearly on a video camera as he was running out of the store. His attorney successfully faulted the officers for obtaining the video without a properly executed warrant, and Malone was eventually let go."*

Following the summary was a photo of Malone. He had a thin face with dark eyes, and a deep scar running from his forehead down his left cheek. He wore a scraggly beard, and a corner of his lip turned upward, pulled by the scar. Todd imprinted the image in his mind and left the site. He clicked to another site which listed the addresses of all suspects for the last three years. He found Malone's name and most recent address. *Westfield Heights, South 9th Street, Apartment C6.* He scribbled the address on a scrap of paper and stuffed it in his pocket. He left the site, cleared his searches, and logged off. He looked around to be sure no one had been watching. Though most of the cops knew of the Blue Brotherhood, the true purpose of the organization was a well-kept secret. It needed to stay that way. Todd only knew of it because of his friendship with an instructor at the police academy. The man had told him on his last day there, *"There's a way for you to make it work, you know."* The comment had surprised him. *"What do you mean, make it work?"* The man had leaned closer. *"There's an…organization…that will allow you to clean up the streets…right society's wrongs, if you get what I mean. Pay attention, Jackson; someone will ask you; I'd bet money on it."* He had added, *"And when they do, you do what they tell you…ya hear?"*

Todd grinned. *I hear, alright.*

His partner had just arrived and was sitting at a desk on the other side of the room. Todd grabbed his coffee, walked over and took a seat. "Hey Jimmy."

"Hey Todd." Jimmy was average height, average build…average in about every way. But he was a halfway decent cop, and he had a good sense of humor.

Todd took a sip of the coffee and set it on the desk. "Any news yet on last month's double homicide?"

"Nah…tied up in court. Nothing but bullshit."

"I hear that." Todd leaned back and sipped his coffee. *Johnny Malone.* He knew exactly what he was being asked to do. Could he do it? Of course, he could; there was a part of him that had been waiting for the chance his entire life.

He leaned forward and thumbed through a stack of paperwork. As he rifled through the pile, his eyes drifted to a picture in a gold frame placed prominently on a corner of his desk; it was a picture of his father. The man was standing proud in his dress blues, his hat angled just right, his copper-brown eyes unmistakable. Jet black hair hung an inch or two lower than the cap, and his face bore the expression of an officer who was proud of who he was and what he stood for. It was the photo from when he had been promoted to captain of the Evansville Police Department. As Todd stared at the picture, he wondered what might have happened if his father had lived. What might it have been like to have had a dad around who could show him how to fish, how to hunt, how to bang women? He would never know; his father's life had been cut short by three morons trying to rob a convenience store. He shook his head. One of them had never been caught. The other two were doing time in a prison in upstate Indiana. As far as he knew, all three were still alive. *They live, but my daddy's dead.* He leaned back and crossed his hands behind his head. It wasn't fair, and he promised himself – someday – he would do something about it.

CHAPTER 12

Edinburgh, Scotland

Walter frowned as he watched Maddi go from the chair to the window, then back to the chair. Her grief was palpable, and he decided that – though it was painful to see the aftermath of the compressions on Martin's chest – it had probably been far worse to actually watch it all take place.

He and Dora had been notified immediately after their son had come out of the coma. They had left the hotel, and were informed on the way that he had coded. They had arrived to see him with his mottled skin and the added tubes and wires. And now, as they sat at his side, Walter was struck by his own lack of power, his inability to fix his son. He couldn't call in a favor from a well-heeled diplomat, or maneuver his highly-skilled troops…he couldn't pay for more help, more specialists, more answers. He had already tried all that and this was the result. All he could do now was wait. He wasn't good at waiting. Nor was he used to having no solutions. His entire life had been spent solving problems, nationally and internationally. Fixing things was what people like Walter did, but his dying son wasn't to be one of them. He couldn't fix him.

He looked at his wife and his heart broke. Though she would normally be reading aloud from either Lawrence or Shaw – two of Martin's favorite authors – today she hadn't even tried. Too much had happened; too much had changed. Martin had come out of the coma, only to return to its dark depths, the prognosis worsened by the severity of how close to death he had come. Poor Dora had buried her son already; wasn't once enough? Wasn't the grief that she had endured after the hotel fire four years ago enough? Again, he grimaced at his total lack of power. Not only could he do nothing for his dying son, but he could do nothing for his heartbroken wife, either.

I need to get out of here. He checked his watch. It was noon. He was to meet the courier who was picking up Mueller's jacket at 1:00. He leaned closer to Dora and whispered, "I need to go to the hotel to handle a bit of business, but I'll come right back."

Dora nodded, but said nothing. Her despair was obvious. He gave her hand a squeeze, nodded at Maddi, then stood and looked down at his son. He shook his head, his grief almost disabling. He turned and walked out the door, nodding at Tom Cravens, one of two Secret Service agents who had sat dutifully outside his son's door for the past five months. He went to the elevator, took it to the first floor, then walked out and hailed a cab. "Edinburgh Hotel," he said, as he slid in back. The driver nodded and pulled away.

They reached the hotel within minutes, and Walter took the elevator to his suite. He walked in and went straight to the jacket sitting on the desk. He stared at it, and was suddenly furious. His anger over his son's misery – over *all* their misery – had somehow morphed into that scorched jacket...as if it had become a symbol for all that had gone wrong...as if it held not only the DNA of the neo-Nazi Adolf Mueller, but a trace of the world's darkness – and his own.

He cringed, suddenly mindful of his own cruelty through the years; infidelity to his wife, shielding a killer who had then been able to kill again. Were he and Mueller really so different? *Yes,* he thought with a sigh. He could only pray that when he faced his Maker, there would be a sliver of mercy granted for intent. Walter had carried out his sins unwittingly and unwillingly; Mueller had pursued his goals with hatred and spite.

Walter was about to pick up the jacket, when he noticed a newspaper sitting next to it on the desk. He had been about to read the paper when he had gotten the call about Martin. A headline, which he had failed to notice before, now got his attention. *"Local psychiatrist using shock therapy to try to cure schizophrenia."* He read the first couple of lines. He had never heard of the psychiatrist, and he wasn't particularly interested in schizophrenia, but he was suddenly reminded of the last words of his mistress Nenita as she lay dying in his arms. *"Find Dr. Samuels, Walter…let him help you save our son."*

Samuels was the psychiatrist who had accompanied Nenita to Scotland. Walter had never learned why Samuels had made that journey with Nenita. All he knew was that the man had somehow given Nenita hope that within Cobra there lived another soul, a man named Mark Justice, who was kind and honorable. And she had clung to that hope. Even in the end, when she and everyone she loved had nearly been killed by her very own son, she had found a way to believe in the boy's goodness. Where had that faith come from? He frowned. *From a psychiatrist by the name of Samuels.*

Though Walter had felt her faith to be misplaced, he had known that, sooner or later, he would need to find Samuels, if for no other reason than to honor the woman's dying wish.

But how could he even dare? Hadn't he spent the last five months doing all that he could to put the affair with Nenita behind him? His amazing wife, Dora, had somehow forgiven him; she had even given her blessing for him to fly to the Philippines to spread Nenita's ashes. Shouldn't that have been the end of it? He shook his head. As long as the son that he and his Filipino mistress had created was alive and wreaking havoc around the globe, Nenita would be a presence in his life. They had brought the world a killer, and even something as simple as reading the morning newspaper would remind Walter that their killer son was still out there.

And now she has left it to me and a doctor I barely know to somehow try to save him.

He frowned. *Save him from what?* It wasn't like he could somehow find Justice, pull him from inside his warped son's psyche, and let him live free among them. Regardless of how good and kind Justice might be, the body he inhabited had killed many. Which meant that, even if Walter and Samuels did somehow 'save Justice,' it would be a wasted gesture. The best they could hope for would be to appeal to the courts to spare the man's life. Justice would still go to prison, likely forever. *But at least he would be alive…and Cobra would be dead.*

Walter narrowed his eyes, suddenly realizing that that was the crux of it. If he could somehow find a way to save Justice, he would inevitably kill Cobra…forever.

Walter had dug up all he could about Dr. James Samuels. With the help of a friend in UK's medical society, he had learned quite a bit about Samuels. He was a Vienna-trained psychiatrist, and had been in practice for over forty years. He was respected within the London psychiatric community, but was considered an outsider, not only because of his ties to Vienna, but for his dogged belief in the teachings of Sigmund Freud. Though Freud was known as the Father of Psychiatry, nearly all of his teachings had been deemed archaic and out of touch. Samuels had maintained his trust in those teachings, however, which had left his fellow psychiatrists to view him with disdain. But they had forgiven him to some extent, mostly because of his willingness to tackle the most difficult cases…those patients whom no one else dared touch, those clients whom other psychiatrists had all but given up on. They would call Samuels and ask for his help, acting as if they hadn't ostracized him for decades. And, from what Walter had been able to determine, Samuels would always oblige. The sort of man who held no grudges, simply taking on the plight of whatever poor soul he was asked to care for with the confidence that, in the end, he could help them.

Which was, Walter guessed, how he had ended up seeing Mark Justice. Cobra's alter ego had likely come to Samuels's office in an effort to ease his mental anguish after having tried other, more conventional approaches. Whatever the reason, Samuels had clearly tried to help him, going so far as to travel to the Philippines to gain insight from the troubled man's mother, Nenita. Together, she and Samuels had made the journey to Dalgety Bay, and somehow, during that journey, Nenita had learned of the kindness of Cobra's alter ego. How had she put it? *"Our son is not just a wicked killer, there's another man inside him who is good and decent; his name is Mark Justice."*

Walter shook his head. He wouldn't have been so willing to believe Nenita if he hadn't seen hints of Justice with his own eyes. In the dungeon outside Lyon, Cobra had spent nearly a full hour ranting and raving at two unseen individuals. The first was a child – whom Walter guessed was Mark as a boy – and the second was a man named Justice. Did that confirm what Nenita had told him…that there was a good man somehow living inside the bad? An honorable man battling to escape? An alter ego by the name of Justice, who was imprisoned inside the body and mind of a madman?

Walter checked his watch. He had about twenty minutes before he was to meet the courier. He pulled out his phone and scrolled through his contacts until he found the number that he had plugged in five months ago. He thought again about Nenita's final words. *"Find Dr. Samuels, Walter...let him help you save our son."*

It had been five months since Nenita had asked it of him; five months that he had been struggling to follow through on her request. But now, for whatever reason, the need to act was overwhelming.

Why?

Again, he thought of Martin, fighting to live...struggling for every breath, every heartbeat. He stiffened as images of his beleaguered son filled his mind. Mottled flesh, the lifeless expression of a man who had little life left in him...*all because of my other son...the son who has tortured so many with his crimes.*

He stared at his phone. He had put it off long enough. It was time to call the one man who actually saw a way to save his son, while at the same time, rid the world of a killer...forever.

CHAPTER 13

London, England

"Betty, this afternoon looks to be every bit as busy as the morning. Would you please make sure we have plenty of tea?"

Samuels' receptionist smiled, her knowing grin a comfort to an old man like him. "Certainly, Doctor. Would you like me to have a sandwich delivered since you worked through lunch?"

The psychiatrist clapped his hands. "That would be splendid, Betty."

The woman nodded and left his office. Samuels, who was standing at a small table, poured the last of a pot of tea into his cup. As he carried it to his desk, he looked around at the room where so much good work took place. At least that was how he saw it. As a Freudian psychiatrist, much of his therapy involved deep, hours-long conversations with his patients. He did his best to avoid medications, or at least use very few, convinced that the answers to nearly all of a patient's problems lay within them, imprisoned in their psyches…just waiting to be set free.

He sat at his desk and sipped his tea as he checked his ledger. Like most of his days, the ledger was full, and he smiled with joy for the challenge of what lay before him. Mable Stone was scheduled for 1:10 p.m. He checked his watch. *Twenty minutes from now.* Mable had been coming to him for many years now, and, though most would likely note little progress with the poor woman's obsessive-compulsive behavior, Samuels had seen considerable improvement. For one thing, she no longer felt the need to circle her chair five times before sitting down. Yes, she still had to arrange her purse by her chair three times, but she was definitely making strides.

The man who had just left, Ramsey Sprite, had only been coming for a short time, and had been reluctant to say much at all. But he was slowly developing trust, and Samuels had been delighted just to see the man continue to come back. He hadn't stayed for the fully allotted time, however, skittish at the direction their conversation had gone. Which was why Samuels now had an extra twenty minutes to be alone with his thoughts.

He stretched his legs and crossed them at the ankles. He was glad for the extra time, if for no other reason than to embrace the fact that he was alive.

Dr. James Samuels had been part of what had been dubbed the Dalgety Bay Attack. He and six others had been chained to chairs in an abandoned schoolhouse, and put through physical and verbal torture by the infamous Cobra. The seven of them had been carefully chosen, each one playing some role in the development of the killer. Samuels' role had been small. He had simply been the doctor that the man's alter ego had chosen in an effort to gain relief from debilitating headaches. As it turned out, those headaches served as the mechanism by which Cobra and the alter ego, Mark Justice, relinquished their hold over the body. Samuels hadn't realized this at first; neither had Justice. The discovery had been overwhelming for both of them. But before Samuels could alert the authorities that he had, in fact found Cobra, or could place Justice in a long-term psychiatric facility, the man had escaped and had quickly resumed his role as Cobra. He had then murdered a young mother in a dark alley in Calais, France, and Samuels had owned that murder as if he himself had killed the poor woman. He had vowed to try to find the man and stop him before he could kill again. His search had taken him all the way to the Philippines, Cobra's boyhood home, where Cobra's mother, Nenita, had still been living. Cobra had ended up inviting both Nenita and Samuels to the Dalgety Bay schoolhouse, where they had joined the other five prisoners: Inspector Pritchard of Scotland Yard; Senator Cynthia Madison from America; philanthropists Dora and Walter Henderson from Boston, and their nephew Matt. Nenita had divulged to Samuels that Walter Henderson was Cobra's father; Samuels had been dumbfounded. How had a killer like Cobra come from a man like Walter Henderson? What on earth could have caused a highly-regarded man like Walter, who had a stunningly beautiful wife, to stray to the arms of an exotic lover halfway around the world? Though Nenita was also lovely and deeply kind, as Samuels had had the pleasure to learn, she was about as far removed from the life of the erudite and cultured Walter as any woman could be.

Samuels had yet to fully understand how it had come about, but one thing was clear: Cobra's existence was a challenge for the Hendersons. Though up to now the secret had been kept, were it to ever be revealed that a Henderson heir was an infamous killer, it would be disastrous, not only for them, but for the many who relied on their good name.

Samuels sipped his tea, shaking as he thought back to the schoolhouse at the bay. He often wondered what Cobra might have done to them had there not been a fire. Its timing had been fortuitous. Cobra had been forced to flee, which had given them all a chance to escape. Cobra's mother, Nenita, who was already ill, had died outside the school, and Matt Henderson had fallen into a coma…a coma from which he had yet to awaken. The other five had been beaten and bruised, but had otherwise come out unscathed. Well, that wasn't completely true. No one knew better than Samuels how Cobra's verbal attacks had likely affected them all as he had made a point of telling each of them not only how they had failed him, but how they, too, possessed evil in their hearts. *"Don't lie to yourselves…there's a Cobra inside every one of you."*

Ironically, Samuels had barely been touched. He wasn't sure why. He had concluded that, though it had been Justice who had initially approached him, it was Cobra who, in some way, must have felt Samuels' compassion, not only for Justice, but for how and why Cobra had come to be. *As if I was his only friend in his lonely journey from troubled child to psychopathic killer.* It was the only explanation.

And Cobra wasn't wrong. After the killer escaped, Samuels had found himself secretly cheering the fact that he might still have a chance to save the man's alter ego, Mark Justice. Was it a longshot? Yes, but longshots were Samuels' specialty.

He finished his tea, then stood and was about the go for another cup, when there was a knock on the door. "Yes?"

"Doctor, there is a man on the phone who insists on speaking with you."

"Who is it, Betty?"

"He says his name is Henderson…Walter Henderson."

Samuels' eyes widened. "Put him through."

"Yes sir."

Betty left the room, and, within seconds, the phone on the desk beeped. Samuels lifted the receiver. "Hello?"

"Is this Dr. Samuels…Dr. James Samuels?"

"Yes, it is, Mr. Henderson. How may I help you?"

He heard the man clear his throat. "As I'm sure you recall, we were together at…the bay." There was a pause. "And I'm guessing that you picked up on my unique…relationship…to Cobra?"

Samuels sighed. "Yes sir, I did. A difficult situation, I'm sure."

"Yes. It has been very difficult for both me and his mother."

"Nenita."

"Yes. I think you were aware that the poor woman…passed at the site."

"Yes, she was clearly ill to start with, and I'm certain the stress of the events that afternoon took their toll."

"Yes, they did. But she had one final request. It is that request that has prompted me to make this call."

Samuels raised an eyebrow. "What was her request?"

He heard a deep sigh. "She…she said that you told her that there was…another man living inside Cobra." A pause. "It sounds so odd to say it out loud."

"Let me help you, sir. I did discover – quite by accident – that your…son possesses an alternate personality…an alter ego, if you will. It was that man, Mark Justice, who came to see me not long before the events at Dalgety Bay." He paused. "Poor Justice had no idea that he was sharing his psyche with a killer, and when he uncovered that fact during one of our sessions, it took him to a terrible place." Another pause. "He tricked me and ran away before I could get him somewhere safe. I felt certain I would never see him again, and was so very pleased when it was Justice who greeted Nenita and I at the school." He sighed. "His presence was short-lived, however."

"Fascinating," the man said, more to himself than to Samuels. He cleared his throat. "Uh…according to Nenita, it's that…alter ego… Mark Justice, that she wants me to find. She was convinced that he embodies the uh…good side of our son, if you will, and she made me promise to enlist your help to find him." The man laughed awkwardly. "Again, it seems absurd, Doctor, to even say the words."

"It is not absurd, Mr. Henderson. Nenita is exactly right. I believe with all my heart that Mark Justice is a good man, and that if he is given the chance to triumph, he will show himself to be worth saving from the death that I am certain awaits him."

Walter coughed and again cleared his throat. "Such a thing would be a miracle, Doctor. I am at your service. What must we do to find – and save – Justice?"

Samuels felt a pang of joy. He had accepted that his quest to save Justice was his and his alone, but now he had an ally...a man who had actually known Mark before he had become a killer. His heart was racing and he took a few deep breaths to calm down. "We...we must try to think like him if we hope to find him," he said as he tugged at his beard. "And we must do it soon. For I'm certain they're looking for him." He hesitated. "And if they find him, Walter, I'm almost certain they will kill him."

There was a pause. "So, how do you propose we do that, Doctor?"

Samuels hesitated. "We use the events at Dalgety Bay to guide us." He frowned. "What do you feel was his primary goal that afternoon in the schoolhouse?"

Another pause. "To make my nephew suffer."

Samuels shook his head. "Though I think that is true, I actually think it was you whom he wanted to hurt the most." He paused. "So, I think, sir, that you should ask him to come to you."

The answer came quickly, and with a sternness that surprised the doctor. "With all due respect, Samuels, you saw what happened the last time we were together."

"Yes sir, I know. But this time will be different." He paused, unsure if he should go on. *I may never have another chance to say what needs to be said.* "Walter, this time you must reach out to Mark as a member of your family," he held his breath as he added, "...it is time to become a father to your son."

CHAPTER 14

Washington, DC

Morningstar's taxi pulled up to the Morgan building just as a nearby bank clock rang out eight chimes. He had come up with a plan – as he always did – and was ready to put it into action. But he would need help from the men he was about to meet with, the six men who, along with him, now made up The Bentley Group.

His challenges were three-fold. First, he needed to create a justification for bringing Matt Henderson to DC. Second, he had to time it so that Madison and her agents couldn't interfere. Third, he had to figure out how to distract Walter so that he wouldn't get in the way of the transfer. But before he could do any of it, he would need to know for certain that Matt and Martin were the same man. He checked his watch. Levi had told him twenty minutes…*over an hour ago.* He flinched. *Get your ass in gear, Levi."*

Fortunately, Levi had gotten him the two documents, and he patted his briefcase as he stepped out of the cab in front of the tall, nondescript building in downtown DC. He was paying the cab fare, when his phone vibrated. It was Levi. "It's about time."

"Um…yes sir." There was a pause. "It took me a bit longer because of not having the eyes open, but I'm 98 percent certain that it's him. I don't know how he did it, sir…um Father, but I'd bet money on the fact that that man is Martin Henderson."

Morningstar clung to the stair railing. How long had he been looking for his errant son, and now, finally, he had him. He had Henderson…the Phoenix…his once-beloved Joseph, right where he wanted him. *And now, I must find a way to get him home.*

92

He managed to say, "Good job, Levi," then shoved the phone in his pocket. He climbed the steps, doing his best to ignore his shaking legs. *This morning is no different than any other,* he told himself as he walked into the building. *Except that now, I have Henderson.* He took a deep breath; he would need to be composed if he was to carry out the next part of his plan. After all, he wasn't dealing with a bunch of idiots. The Bentley Group was made up of some of the most powerful men in government and business.

He smoothed down his suitcoat as he walked to the elevator. He pushed a button and waited. He reviewed in his mind what he was about to do. Fortunately, a couple of the members of the Bentley Group would be in a position to help him. But he would need to act quickly; the wolves were circling. Not the least of which was the senator from Indiana, Cynthia Madison. She had begun her own personal crusade against gun maker Silverton Arms, Inc., the same company that was secretly supplying arms for the Bentley Group's various war ventures. She claimed that the arms manufacturer was skirting the law. The fact that she was right was immaterial. She had become an obstacle in Morningstar's path, and, like Henderson, she needed to go.

But how many times had he tried to kill that woman? He had set in motion her demise more times than he cared to think about. She was obviously well-protected. Not only by her bodyguards, but by Henderson himself. He had saved her far too many times, which was why Morningstar was so eager to destroy them both. *It's where you come in, boys.* The Bentley Group would help him take out a prominent U.S. senator and the heir of a prestigious family, all at the same time...*and they won't even know they're doing it.*

He grinned as he waited at the elevator. It was only because of him that the men in that group had any power at all. He had shown them the way...educated them on how to rule from behind the curtain. Morningstar had single handedly transformed a weekly gathering of shoddy old men into a force that could bring countries to their knees. As a result, every one of them was a millionaire. *They owe me,* he thought, as he ran a hand through his dark hair. There had originally been eight of them, but five months ago, Morningstar had urged the U.S. Vice-President, Jim Conner, to resign, not only from the Bentley Group, but from his party's ticket. *"It's an election year...a good time to make a change,*

Conner." The VP had initially resisted, but with the help of a rumor, a lie, and two documents, Morningstar had made him see the wisdom of the move. Conner had left, and, though the others suspected that Morningstar had set it all in motion, none of them knew the extent to which he had orchestrated the downfall of the great James Conner.

The elevator opened and he stepped in, along with an attractive woman in a sundress, an elderly man with a cane, and a young man wearing a three-piece suit. He waited while they punched the numbers for their floors, grinning at the woman with his distinctive charm. Like most women, she fell for it, and gave him a quick, alluring smile. He chuckled as he smiled back. *It'll have to wait, Sweetie...I have a world to destroy.*

When the last one had gotten off the elevator, he pulled a key from his pocket, inserted it into an opening at the side of the panel, and turned. He was quickly taken to the top of the building. The door opened and he walked into a large, oval room with expensive artwork on the walls and a crystal chandelier over the center table. He absently looked for the two bodyguards who had stood there for so long; the secret service agents who had accompanied the Vice-President to every meeting. They were, of course, no longer there. He chuckled. With Conner gone, Morningstar had become the presumptive leader of the group. There had been no vote, no coronation; the others had simply recognized that it was he, Edward Morningstar, who bore the qualifications to lead them.

He walked to his chair, set his briefcase on the table, and went over to the bar. He poured a cup of coffee and carried it to his seat. He sat in a rich leather chair and pulled a cigar from his coat pocket. He lit it slowly. None of the men had the guts to tell him to hurry. Conner had always rushed him...*and look what happened to him.*

He leaned back, blew a perfect smoke ring in the air, then cleared his throat. "Good morning, gentlemen."

There were a few nods and grunts.

Morningstar laughed. "I see it's up to me to get things started." He took a sip of coffee. "We have a lot to go over." He looked around the room. Six pairs of eyes were on him as he reached for his briefcase, opened it, and pulled out two documents. "I was originally going to use this meeting to update you on our recent successes overseas." He paused. "But I have uncovered some interesting information."

The six pairs of eyes widened in chorus. Though the men at that table had no idea what he was about to tell them, they could be sure it would disrupt or destroy something …or someone. He hid a sneer as he laid the first document on the table. "We now have more proof that the CIA's rogue assassin, Phoenix, was behind January's terror attacks."

No reaction. It wasn't news to them. Morningstar had been telling them that from the beginning. Though they didn't know the details, they were well aware that the Phoenix actually worked for Morningstar, not the CIA. They had no idea, however, that he had once been the respected entrepreneur, Martin Henderson. They, like the rest of the world, thought Henderson had died in a DC hotel fire four years ago. How would they react if they were to learn that Morningstar had turned such a highly-regarded man into a killer? He chuckled. *They would be impressed, but not surprised…it's what I do.*

He went on. "This document corroborates what I've been saying since February. Phoenix – once a devoted American patriot – has gone rogue." He looked around the room and sighed. "Which means that he must be eliminated."

He waited. This was normally when VP Conner would ridicule Morningstar for not having already killed the missing assassin. No one said a word. He added, "And I think I may have found a way to do it that won't put any of us in jeopardy." Still nothing. *Where's your spunk, fellows? I'm starting to miss Conner.*

He picked up the second document. "And this piece of paper is our way to do just that." He paused. "This memo, discovered among the belongings of a former Pentagon employee, suggests that Phoenix may not have acted alone." He watched the men. Their eyes had narrowed. He had their attention. "And the man who's been implicated in helping him is currently lying in a coma in an Edinburgh nursing home."

Again, no one spoke.

Finally, Senator Sam Lawford from Texas said, "So what?" Morningstar hated him. His Texas drawl was annoying, but even more annoying was his belief that he held some clout among the men at the table. *I need to take him down a peg.*

Morningstar feigned indignation. "So what? Are you crazy, Lawford? You don't get it, do you? The man I'm referring to is Matt Henderson. He's a member of the prestigious Henderson clan and, in a matter of days, he'll be charged not only with playing a role in the poisoning of scores of Americans, but will also be implicated..." he paused for effect, "... in the assassination of the Phoenix." He waited; they merely looked at him. "The man has motive and – with a little bit of help – he will soon have means and opportunity." He paused. "The only problem is that I can't get to him."

"Why not?" Lawford again. "Just wave your Pentagon ID, and go get him."

Morningstar rolled his eyes. "I can't do that, *Senator Lawford*...one, because Matt Henderson is not an American citizen, and two, because the man's uncle, the esteemed Walter Henderson of Boston, would never permit it."

Lawford smirked. "Surely you have more power than he does?"

Morningstar bristled. "No...actually, I don't...not in this instance. Not only is Walter worth millions, but he also happens to be one of the President's closest friends." He paused. "Which is why we need to come up with a way to distract him, so I can get his nephew back to the States, where I can 'interrogate' him and then put him to work."

Lawford shook his head incredulously. "Put him to work? Doing what?"

Morningstar had to fight not to yell at the man. "Assassinating the Phoenix," "*...you dumbass,*" he wanted to add, but held back.

"But Matt Henderson is in a coma." Lawford wasn't letting up. "How can he assassinate someone...especially a man as skilled as the Phoenix?"

Morningstar wanted to punch him. "His condition has changed, Lawford. My understanding is that in the next day or so, he'll either die or come out of that coma." He paused. "And I have been told that he is every bit as skilled as the Phoenix."

Lawford frowned. "Okay, but you're saying that we have to somehow distract Walter Henderson, one of the most well-connected and influential men in America." He shook his head. "How on God's green earth are we gonna do that?"

Morningstar flinched. *You overestimate the Hendersons, Lawford…and you underestimate me.* "Glad you asked, Senator." He paused. "We need to start a fracas."

"A fracas?" This time it was their newest member, a fifth circuit court of appeals judge, Bill Carson. The man was old and slow, but he was shrewd.

"Yes, Judge…a fracas."

"What sort of fracas?"

Morningstar narrowed his eyes. "We need to threaten his precious Latvia."

"Latvia?"

Morningstar nodded. "The man has a home there; actually, a castle, replete with an army of highly motivated soldiers. If Latvia is threatened…by Russia, for example, Walter will feel compelled to return to his beloved Latvia to lead his army as they try to stave off the threat." He paused. "And, while he's busy putting out fires in a Baltic country that nobody cares about, I'll be bringing his nephew to the United States for questioning." Morningstar waited; no one said a word. He grabbed the documents and shoved them in his briefcase.

"So, how do we create a 'fracas' in Latvia?" It was the fifth circuit judge again.

Morningstar closed and locked his briefcase and set it by his chair. He leaned back and locked his hands behind his head. "We get Putin to attack Latvia…and soon."

CHAPTER 15

Edinburgh, Scotland

The blare of a police siren outside the window made Maddi jump. She had fallen asleep in the chair by Henderson's bed. She sat up and quickly checked his monitors. She was relieved when she realized it was merely a crisis outside the window, not inside the room, or, even worse, inside his overworked body. She looked across at Dora, who gave her a quick smile and a nod. Maddi smiled in reply, then leaned back in her chair.

For years, sirens had made her think of her dad; the man whose life had been lost while he was protecting the citizens of their small town in Indiana. Every time she would hear them, she would feel the loss of the man who had been her hero…the man who had been killed by thieves during a robbery gone bad. But now, sirens made her think of something far different. They made her think of another police officer; a man who had changed forever not only her image of the police, but of her fifteenth year of life. She shook her head and frowned. *Why am I so obsessed with that man all of a sudden?*

She stood and walked to the window, listening as the sirens faded, watching the taillights of a police car as it disappeared down an alley. She felt a wave of nausea. She had never seen that alley in downtown Edinburgh…she had never walked its narrow darkness, but, nonetheless, it felt familiar. She frowned. *Maybe all alleys feel the same…*

Claire smiled. "Let's try again. What happened in the alley, Maddi?"

The minutes ticked by and Maddi said nothing. Finally, she sighed. "I already told you…I killed him. What else do you need to know?"

Claire nodded. "The details...the how, the why...all of it."

Maddi was about to refuse to answer, as she had done for the past four weeks, when, all at once, she felt an overwhelming need to talk about it. How good it would feel to finally let someone else know what took place on that awful day in 1982. She tucked a strand of hair behind one ear as she leaned forward, looked at Claire, and said, "I didn't mean to do it." She hesitated. "Well, maybe I did. After all, I had the gun with me."

"Where did you get a gun?"

"It had been my father's; a spare he'd kept hidden in the kitchen at the house in McCordsville. He didn't think I knew about it, but I had secretly watched him clean it many times. I had overheard him tell mom, 'This gun isn't registered. We have it for protection...in case I'm ever gone and there's trouble.' Mom had brought it with us to Evansville and had hidden it in a drawer in the den. I decided my entire life had become 'trouble,' and I grabbed the gun from the drawer before I ran out of the house. I'm sure Evan was shocked when I pulled it out. But he wouldn't quit talking about putting an end to the pregnancy." Maddi's eyes narrowed. "I was beginning to see that he would do whatever it took to get rid of my child...to get rid of any evidence of his own indiscretion."

Claire nodded. "So, when did you pull out the gun?"

Maddi flinched. "I remember him saying, 'You're powerless, girl. All I gotta do is force you into this car and take you to the clinic. I'm an officer of the law, sweetie...and don't you forget it.'" Maddi trembled as she gripped her hands into fists. "He pulled the car sideways in front of me, angling it so I couldn't get past. He grinned, and I felt like I was going to be sick. He said, 'Unless maybe you wanna reconsider,' he pushed open the passenger-side door and added, '...maybe one more roll in the hay before we go?'"

Claire waited. Finally, she said, "So what did you say...to Evan?"

Maddi cleared her throat. "I reached in my pocket and pulled out the gun. He was shocked. I aimed it at him, and said 'I'd rather fry in Hell than have sex with you again, Evan. You weren't even that good.'"

Claire chuckled. "I'm guessing that made him angry."

"Yes, it did. He turned beet red and leaned across the front seat. 'Get in here now, bitch! Put the damned gun down and get in this car. We both know you don't have the guts to shoot me...now get in!' His eyes had grown dark; they looked black as he stuck out his hand, waiting for me. I came closer, and I spat at him. He jumped out of the car and ran around the back. He was standing only a few feet away, and he came at me, ready to...I...I don't know. My hand began to shake. I backed up,

and found myself pressed against a brick wall. 'St—stay away!' I said. He grinned and kept coming. Never had I seen an uglier man. 'Stay away!' I said again. He laughed. 'Listen, bitch, you either go to the clinic willingly, or I'll get you there with force. Now what's it gonna' be?' I thought about it; I thought, Just go with him. End the pregnancy, and end any tie to him. Get him out of your life and start over.'"

"What stopped you?"

"What he said next." Maddi closed her eyes. "He said, 'your mom's a drunk, your dad's dead, your brother's nowhere to be found. You got no one but me, bitch.'"

Claire waited. "And?"

Maddi had begun to shake. But her voice was even as she said, "I hated him more in that instant than I have ever hated anyone before or since. It was like I was someone else. He was still coming for me, and I was scared to death, but somehow I managed to look him in the eye and say calmly, "Evan, you're a fool. My dad's dead, but he died a hero. My brother's away at medical school and will someday be a great physician. My mom's a drunk, but only because she suffered an impossible loss… and I have so much more than you'll ever have, Evan. I have…a child.' And then I pulled the trigger."

The sound of an alarm pulled Maddi from her trance. She rushed to Henderson's bedside and checked the monitors. This time, the EKG showed V-tach, and she and Dora stepped back from the bed as nurses and doctors stormed into the room. They worked on him for several minutes, and were able to stabilize him, but Maddi could tell; he was getting worse.

She was shaking and she leaned against the wall, crossing her arms on her chest to keep anyone in the room from noticing. But they weren't watching her. They were focused on the man in the bed, the man who seemed determined to die in spite of how much Maddi begged him not to. As she watched them reattach monitors and insert IV's, she thought, *I can't do this much longer, Henderson. You've got to come back to me.*

Then it occurred to her. *This is my punishment…my penance.* She frowned. *I killed a man…and now I must watch a man I love die before my eyes.*

CHAPTER 16

Washington, DC

There were quandaries in life, and then there were dilemmas. Quandaries involved such things as 'What do I cook for dinner?' or 'Can I get to the store before it closes?' Simple challenges met with simple solutions. Therapist Claire Porter had certainly had plenty of those, especially since she lived alone in Washington, DC.

But now she was faced with a dilemma; a true problem that lacked an easy answer or a suitable outcome. And, though she'd also had her fair share of those in her fifty-odd years, the challenge she faced now seemed far greater than anything she had ever known.

She rose from her desk and went to a corner table where she had steeped a pot of tea. *Earl Grey…the only tea worth drinking,* she thought as she poured another cup. Though it was lunchtime, she wasn't hungry…which was odd for her. *Maybe I'll lose a few pounds,* she thought as she grabbed two cubes of sugar and dropped them in her cup. *Not like this, you won't.* She knew she should go with artificial sweetener. But there was nothing artificial about Claire Porter, not even the sugar.

She chuckled as she went back to her desk, taking a quick look down at her loose blouse, which was intended to hide the twenty-or-so extra pounds she had carried most of her life. *It's my blanket,* she thought. *My cozy retreat from my problems and my fears.*

Claire hadn't had a bad life; she had simply had to overcome a reticent father and an overbearing mother. They had battled silently for as long as she could remember, with her often winding up in the middle. That was when she had acquired the blanket. It had taken a Harvard education and years of psychoanalysis for her to stop mediating the struggles of her parents. *Life's too short for battles that aren't mine.*

Fortunately, she was more like her father; reticent without being withdrawn. She liked to think of herself as 'thoughtfully quiet.' It was helpful to her work; better to be a good listener than a forceful advisor, she had decided. She would leave the 'forceful advising' to her mother.

But being a good listener had now landed her in quite a predicament. Because of her openness and her gentle persuasion, she had managed to learn a secret. And not just any secret…one far bigger than any she could imagine. It would have been better if someone had told her the codes for the nuclear arsenal, or confided in her the name of the second shooter in the Kennedy assassination; she could have handled that. But this secret was far more troubling. Not because of the content, but because of the consequences. Its revelation would change things for many in Washington, DC…maybe even the world.

Eight months earlier, Cynthia Madison, a prominent member of the United States Senate had come to her in terrible pain. Not physical pain, but emotional agony. The poor woman had just watched her dear friend, the president of Yemen, get shot in the head as he was sitting right next to her. The incident itself was bad enough, but the fact that it had come on the heels of the violent deaths of so many other men in her life had unnerved her…to the point that she was having a hard time not only focusing on her work in the senate, but getting through her day without breaking down in tears. It was at the advice of a friend that Maddi had called Claire, and they had hit it off immediately. Which was part of the problem. It had taken only a few weeks for Maddi, a nickname that only her closest friends were privy to, to tell Claire quietly and in no uncertain terms, that she had shot a man to death twenty-two years ago in an alley in Evansville, Indiana. And not just any man…an Evansville police captain. The case had presumably been solved, but to no one's satisfaction, and Claire was certain the Vanderburgh County Prosecutor would be eager for information regarding the murder of one of Evansville's finest.

Claire shook her head. "Evansville's finest? Hardly." The man that Maddi shot sounded like a true scumbag. Did that make it okay? As far as Claire was concerned, it did…especially when one considered the circumstances surrounding the shooting.

She set her tea on her desk, and glared at a stack of paperwork. She shoved it aside and turned to the window, where a soft rain had begun to fall. She closed her eyes, letting the patter of rain against the glass soothe her. It was late August, the end of summer, and roses and amaryllis were in full bloom. She could see them from her chair. She had planted them when she bought the place, knowing they would be visible outside that window throughout the long summer months...*a comfort to my patients,* she had thought at the time. But they were a comfort to her, as well.

Which was exactly how it worked. Give and take. As her clients found solace from their psychological pain, so did she. She would listen, cajole and comfort, helping her clients to reclaim their lives, and their victory would quickly become her own. It was like nothing she had ever known. To see the light go on in dark, empty eyes...it was magical for both of them. But the current dilemma had disrupted that give and take; it had challenged Claire to her very core. Contrary to what most people believed, all revelations in a psychologist's office were not protected by privilege. Most were, but not all. What were the exceptions? There were only two. The first involved the threat of harm to another person. If Claire felt that a client was dangerous, it was her obligation to report it as such. The second exception involved what was referred to as a capital crime. *"An act by an individual that is so serious that it may be punishable by death."* The best example was murder. In most states, Claire was required to report any capitol crime divulged to her by a client, regardless of the circumstances. Which meant that she was expected to inform the Indiana authorities of Cynthia Madison's killing of the cop. But Claire was certain that the senator – who had been nothing even close to a senator at the time of the shooting – had confided in her the ugly details of that event, believing it would stay between them. After all, the poor woman was convinced that she had, in fact, committed murder. Claire felt it was more a case of self-defense. Maddi, who had been Cindy at the time, had had words with the man earlier, and had grabbed a gun to carry with her...just in case. In case of what? That was the question. Had Maddi feared for her life? Or had she hoped – on some internal level that she could never have been aware of – that Jackson would, in fact, come for her and she would *need* to shoot him? Unfortunately – or maybe fortunately – he had come for her. But from what Claire had been able to put together, he hadn't pulled his weapon. *"He didn't need to,"* Maddi had told her. *"He would've been quite capable of killing me with his bare hands."* Regardless, she had felt threatened, and had responded by putting a bullet in the man's chest, possibly followed by several more. *"Make my day,"* Claire had thought at the time, an image of Clint Eastwood's 'Dirty Harry' squinting over the barrel of his .44 magnum clear in her mind. Self-defense or not, Cindy Madison had unequivocally killed the cop.

Claire hadn't been prepared for Maddi to reveal that fact. If she had, she would have warned her. She would have said, *"Maddi, wait. If you tell me of any sort of capital crime, regardless of whether or not it was justified, I will be compelled to inform the authorities."* As it was, Maddi blurted it out, and, once the words had been said, Claire didn't have the heart, or the courage, to tell Maddi that she was obligated to report it. So, she had spent the last six months trying to figure out a way to avoid doing what she knew she had to do. *I'll address it tomorrow* she had said to herself too many times to count.

She had talked it over with another therapist; her best friend, Marge. *"You don't understand, Marge. If I tell the authorities what my client did, it will bring down a remarkable woman who is truly making a difference."* Her friend had shaken her head. *"Claire, regardless of who she is or how remarkable she is, it's your duty. You don't have a choice."* That had not been what Claire had wanted to hear, so she had sat on it for a few more weeks, and then had decided to call a friend of hers in the Justice Department. *"What do you think, Bill? A hypothetical client shoots a terrible man twenty years ago, and reveals it to me in psychotherapy. Would I have to tell the authorities?"* Bill had paused. *"It depends on where the murder took place...which state."* Claire had said, *"Indiana."* She had heard Bill typing away, and then, with a deep sigh, he had said, *"I don't see any way around it, Claire. If the murder took place in Indiana, then you have to turn in your 'hypothetical' client."* That conversation had taken place a month ago.

So now, here she sat, knowing exactly what she needed to do, but wanting very much not to do it. And worst of all, she couldn't even tell Maddi what she was about to do. The woman had taken a leave of absence from the Senate, and Claire had no idea where she was. Claire had tried calling her cellphone several times over the past few months, but it had never connected. Had Maddi lost her phone? Maybe gotten a new one? Either way, it appeared that Claire wouldn't even be able to warn Maddi that the trust she had placed in Claire would soon result in public humiliation, a possible arrest, and a likely dismissal from the Senate. *You don't know they'll dismiss her, Claire.* She shook her head and said aloud, "Yes, they will. If not, she'll be voted out at the next election. Either way, Maddi loses, simply by trusting me with her deepest darkest secret."

The thing was, Maddi hadn't wanted to share it. Claire had coerced her into revealing that secret, knowing it was eating her alive. Maddi had *needed* to share it. And, though Claire was still working on Maddi's take on the events in that alley, Claire had seen instantly the relief in her face once she had said the words aloud, *"I killed him."*

A sudden wind swell forced a limb against the window, and Claire jumped. Clearly, the branch was trying to get her attention. She put down her tea, walked to the window, and cracked it just a bit. She breathed in the cool damp air, suddenly noticing a bold red cardinal sitting on a branch just inches away. Claire had a fondness for cardinals. They seemed somehow elevated over other birds; some might even call them self-aware; as if they were actually engaged in the world around them...*as if they were...exigent.* She chuckled and said aloud, "My dear Exigent Cardinal, I have an awful decision to make."

And, as if the bird had answered, a voice in her head said, *"I gather that."*

Claire frowned. "I wish she had never told me."

The bird flitted to a nearby branch. Again, as if she was hearing it, a voice in her head said, *"I understand, but your client isn't stupid. What did she think would happen?"*

Claire tilted her head to the side. "What do you mean?"

The bird tilted its head, as well; Claire would have sworn it was considering what to say. *"She had to know there was a risk that you might be obligated to report it."*

The thought had never occurred to her. Was it possible? Could it be that Maddi had *expected* it? Maybe even *welcomed* it...a chance to do penance for her crime? Claire pondered the thought as she shut the window and walked to her desk. She sat and sipped her tea. *Maybe this is exactly what Maddi needs...what she had been looking for all along.*

She pulled her rolodex close to her and thumbed through the cards. Months ago, Maddi had given her a direct number to her secretary, in case – as Maddi had put it – *"You ever need to find me in an emergency."* Claire had never dreamed she would need the number, but, after many attempts to dial her directly, it had become apparent that if she was to ever speak to Maddi, she would need to go through her secretary. She picked up her pencil, tapping it on the desk as she dialed. After a minute, she heard a kind male voice say, "Good afternoon. Senator Madison's office. May I help you?"

Claire hesitated. It was as if she had suddenly been cast mute. *Maybe those who can't speak, don't want to,* came a thought from nowhere. "Um, yes," Claire managed to say. She cleared her throat. "Go—good afternoon. My name is Claire Porter and I am acquainted with the senator on a personal level. Though I don't want to cause concern, it is urgent that I speak with her as soon as possible."

There was a pause. "I'm sorry, Ms. Porter, but the senator is currently out of the country. I will tell her you called the next time I speak with her. Would you like to give me a number where she can reach you?"

"Do I have to?"

"Of course, you have to, silly girl."

"Fine, mother…" "Um, yes." Claire rattled off her number. *So, how long should I wait? This nice man might not talk to her for days.* "Excuse me, sir, but do you have any idea when you will speak with the senator?"

"Please, call me Phil. And yes, I hope to speak to her later today." A pause. "You say it's urgent?"

So urgent I've sat on it for over six months. "Yes Phil, it is."

"I'll see what I can do."

"That would be greatly appreciated. I'll await your call."

She hung up and laid her pencil on the desk. She stared at the pencil and sighed. Now, she would wait. *But for how long?* Half an hour? Half a day? Half a year?

She leaned back and stared out the window. *You've waited months, Claire, what's one more day or two?* What was it the cardinal had said? *"She had to know that there was at least a risk that you might be obligated to report it."*

Revelation Part I

Claire watched the rain, thinking about the cardinal's insight. She chuckled at the thought that not only had she sought guidance from a bird, but she had received it.

'Tis better to talk to a cardinal or an elf,
then to deliberate alone, with only myself.

She laughed at her cleverness as she set the tea aside, grabbed the stack of papers on her desk, and pulled them close. She let out a deep sigh and nodded. *You'll call me, Maddi...and I will tell you what I'm about to do. Then...just maybe, you can heal.*

CHAPTER 17

Edinburgh, Scotland

Maddi stared at Henderson's mottled skin, her heart sickened by the number of times a nurse or doctor had pounded on the poor man's flesh. *Maybe they should just let him die*, she thought, but then quickly shook her head. No, no matter what, those doctors and nurses had to do whatever they could to keep Henderson – and hope – alive.

She sighed as she looked around the room. She was alone. Walter had come back, but only for an hour or so, and had done his best to read headlines from the Financial Times to his lifeless son. Normally, he would spend at least an hour reading articles aloud and discussing the topics of the day, pausing now and then as if waiting for Henderson to reply. He would then move on as if Martin had, in fact, responded. But today there had been no such give and take, and soon he was standing at the door with his wife at his side, offering a solemn goodbye as he and Dora left for an early dinner. *"Would you like to join us, Maddi?"* he had asked. They had invited her many times over the past five months, but always her answer was the same. *"No, thank you, maybe next time."*

The physical therapist had also come and gone. Maddi knew him well. His name was Harper and they had become good friends over the past several months. Every day around five o'clock, he would come into the room, and he and Maddi would chat back and forth as he put each of Henderson's limbs through a series of exercises that would keep his muscles at least somewhat functional should he ever wake up again.

Maddi sighed. *Should he ever wake up again.* The therapist had left about an hour ago, and Maddi had done nothing since but sit by

Henderson's side…waiting for him to wake up again. She had put on no more music; she had read him no more books. She had simply sat there…waiting.

A few minutes ago, an aide had brought her a tray with tea, scones, and a bit of butter and jam, but she had simply stared at it, unable to take even a bite. *At this rate, I might die right along with you, Henderson.* And that would suit her just fine. What wouldn't suit her was to sit there and watch him die.

But it was exactly what was happening…just like before. After four long years, he had finally come back to her, but had been taken by Cobra. And now, after five agonizing months, he had come back again, only to be carried off to the underworld of the coma.

Finally, she pulled out a book by Sir Walter Scott and began reading aloud a poem she had read many times in that dark, lonely room, "Flora MacIvor's Song…"

> *"There is a mist on the mountain, and night on the vale,*
> *But more dark is the sleep of the sons of the Gael.*
> *A stranger commanded –, it sunk on the land,*
> *It has frozen each heart, and benumb'd every hand!"*

She stopped. The poem spoke of a Scotland that had lost at war, and the challenge of its countrymen to imagine their future. Would they find triumph in loss? Or would they simply give up, and never again fight for freedom as fearless Highlanders. Night after night, she had read the bold stanzas that spoke both of triumph and defeat…

> *"Tis the summons of heroes for conquest or death,*
> *When the banners are blazing on mountain and heath:*
> *They call to the dirk, the claymore, and the targe,*
> *To the muster, the line and the charge…*
>
> *"Be the brand of each chieftain like Fin's in his ire!*
> *May the blood through his veins flow like currents of fire!*
> *Burst the base foreign yoke as your sires did of yore,*
> *Or die like your sires, and endure it no more!*

Maddi trembled, the words finding their mark. *"Or die like your sires, and endure it no more!"* There was no victory in death…at least not as far as Maddi was concerned. She certainly didn't feel victorious. After the events of the day, all she really felt was exhausted.

She stared at Henderson, wondering if he could even hear her… *or am I just reading this poem for myself?* She frowned, suddenly curious about what he could, in fact, hear, or even see in his mind while he lay comatose on that bed. *What do you think about when you're in there, Henderson?* She had asked herself the question so many times, watching for signs of what might be going on inside his head. She imagined that she knew…a hint of a smile meant he was thinking of her…a frown suggested a memory from the past. *Or maybe none of it means anything; just the biologic responses of a man on the brink of death.*

Maddi closed the book and laid it on the table beside her. She pulled her quilt over her lap and leaned back in her chair. It was well after seven; the nursing home was slowing down for the night. Visiting hours had ended, but fortunately, Maddi had been deemed a co-resident in the room, and the restrictions didn't apply. Thank god for that. She couldn't have stood it knowing he was alone as he was fighting not to die.

She shook her head, trying to get her mind on something else. She looked down at her purse and frowned. *Should I?* She took a deep breath and sighed. She reached down, took her phone from her purse, and laid it on the table. She stared at it. *Don't do it, Maddi…you're only torturing yourself.* Suddenly, she grabbed the phone, opened it, and pushed a single button that dialed a number she had memorized from months before. She closed her eyes as she held the phone to her ear.

"It's me. If you're her, leave a message."

Tears filled her eyes. Henderson's voice…the raspy voice that she had barely heard since Dalgety Bay could move her to tears in an instant. And it had done so off and on for the last two months. But it didn't help her; it only made her miss him more. Though she was tempted to call it again, she held back and simply closed the phone.

She had learned of the message by accident. She and Henderson had only texted back and forth; she had never called him. But then, two months ago, overwhelmed by a desperation unlike anything she had ever felt, she had dialed the number, never imagining it would still be in use. After all, Henderson hadn't had a phone since sometime before Dalgety Bay. She had been stunned when she had heard those words, left on a message machine in the hoarse whisper she had grown to love. *"If you're her…"*

She had never left a message. He wouldn't be able to retrieve it. He was in a coma, and his phone was gone. She wondered what had happened to it. It didn't matter. That singular connection to the man's voice had kept him alive for her. *How can he die when I hear him speak to me so clearly?*

She rubbed her eyes and leaned back in the chair. She looked again at the food on the tray. She should eat. She reached over and grabbed one of the scones. She bit off a piece and chewed it slowly, trying to imagine how Henderson would feel when – if – he took his first bite of food. He had been fed through a tube for such a long time. Chewing, tasting, swallowing…all of it would need to be completely relearned.

Her phone rang and she jumped. She checked caller ID and smiled. "Finally. I thought maybe you moved to Canada, Phil."

He laughed. "Don't think I haven't thought about it." He paused. "So sorry I didn't call earlier. There was a big vote in the Senate today. They interrupted their August recess specifically for that vote, and now everyone's hurrying to get out of here. Jana needed my help to finish some research." Another pause. "How is Mr. Henderson?"

"Holding his own," Maddi lied. "So, what is Jana working on?"

"That's the reason I called, actually. It's the same War-on-Terror committee that you were looking into before you left town."

Maddi's eyes widened. She had forgotten about the committee, which had literally been called the WOT Commission. She had learned of it back in March, just before she was getting ready to leave for London. She had been exploring Edward Morningstar's involvement in what she felt certain were illegal arms sales, and one of his subpoenaed documents had revealed the existence of the committee. From what she could tell, it had been founded on the premise that uniting various government agencies under one umbrella would be more beneficial than working cases in isolation. But Homeland Security had been created for that same purpose, so Maddi had been curious why someone had felt a need for the commission, and why it had been such a secret. Shouldn't a committee designed to share and shed light be totally transparent? She had tried to learn more, but had been unable to dig up anything other than that it had been created sometime after 9-11, and that it was Top Secret. "What have you found, Phil?"

He cleared his throat. "Well, miraculously, I came across an agenda and the minutes from one of their meetings. It looks like the documents were supposed to have been shredded, but had been filed instead in a folder labeled 'War on Terror.' I was lucky to find them." A pause. "From what I can tell, there were eight members."

"And Morningstar was one of them?"

"Yes, I actually think he might have been the one who called for the committee in the first place." A pause. "But here's what's interesting. As I tried to nail down the members, I began to discover that...most of them have died."

Maddi frowned. "How many?"

"Five."

"Out of eight?"

"Yes, and their deaths have all occurred within the last year or so."

Maddi felt a sudden chill pass over her. She took the blanket from her lap and wrapped it over her shoulders. "Go on."

"Each member represented one of seven major branches of government. CIA, FBI, TSA, Secret Service, Homeland Security, the State Department, and the Pentagon."

"The Pentagon is Morningstar. He's obviously still alive. So, who died?"

"There was another Pentagon agent...he died of a heart attack while jogging. He was the first to go." There was a pause. "The second one was an FBI agent who was killed in a single-car crash back in late December. The third one was a CIA agent who...uh...died in Jacksonville in January."

Maddi swallowed, her chest heavy as she recalled the events of the sarin gas attack at the Jacksonville hotel. Two CIA agents had died during that attack. "Sarin gas?"

"Yes."

"Keep going, Phil."

"The fourth death involved, um...the Secretary of State, Jane Harper."

Maddi's hands began to shake. She wanted to tell him to stop. She had been at the Queen's Ball when Harper was killed. "Jane herself was a member of the committee?"

"Yes. I reached out to the State Department. Her private aide told me that because she had been in New York City on 9-11, she took the attack personally and felt it would send a stronger message if she attended the meetings herself."

Maddi coughed; she was finding it hard to breathe. Her proximity to the last two victims' deaths had begun to unnerve her. "And...the fifth one?"

"A TSA human resources director. She was found hanging from a storeroom ceiling fan, a suicide note pinned to her chest. That happened about three months ago."

"Did the investigators verify that it was her handwriting on the suicide note?"

"Yes, and they had her husband attest to it. He also told them that she had been fighting depression."

Maddi frowned. Five deaths. A heart attack, an accident, two murders, and a suicide. "Could it be a coincidence, Phil?" She had asked the question mostly to herself.

"I don't think so, Senator." Another pause. "But here's the part that I think you'll find interesting...actually alarming."

Maddi tensed. Again, she heard Phil clear his throat. "Um...it looks like Hank Clarkson was on that committee."

Maddi grabbed her stomach, feeling as if she had been punched. She stood and began to pace the room. "Representing Homeland Security, no doubt."

"Yes, and like I said, he's one of only three who are still alive."

"There's Morningstar and Hank...who's the third one?"

"A Secret Service agent named Kennedy...Hal Kennedy. No relation to...you know, the Kennedy's, but well-respected within the Service. He's the lead agent assigned to protect the President." A pause. "I'm sure the Service decided that he'd be their best representative due to his direct knowledge of the President's whereabouts."

Maddi shook her head. She didn't like it; not one bit. Why had the committee been such a secret? *And why have five of its members died just in the past year?*

She cleared her throat. "Did either the agenda or the minutes reveal anything else?"

"No, they were apparently from the very first meeting, and simply addressed the purpose and formation of the committee."

Maddi frowned. "So, why was Jana looking into it?"

"The vote today was to sanction more money for the Iraq war. Jana had seen a reference to the WOT Commission in a Pentagon document, and asked me to look into it. I recalled that you had asked about the same commission, so I went back to my notes, and then I did some digging. That's when I found the documents." He paused. "They were dated for November of last year...about eight months after we dropped the first bomb on Iraq. None of this was helpful to Jana, but I thought you might be interested."

Maddi narrowed her eyes. "See if you can find any more notes that might tell us what went on at the meetings." She paused. "And thank you for letting me know, Phil."

"I'll call you if I come up with anything more, Senator. Take care."

"You too, Phil." She ended the call, shaking her head as she tried to put it all together. Hank was on a committee that he hadn't bothered to tell her about. Had he been instructed to keep it a secret? If so, why? Transparency across all agencies had been stressed, especially after 9-11. And what about the other members? Five out of eight were dead. Phil was right; it seemed like more than a coincidence. Not only that; they had all died within the last eight months. Maddi shook her head. *But Hank is still alive.* Had his life intentionally been spared? If so, why? More importantly...*is he in danger now?*

She stopped at the window and stared out at the fading daylight, trying to imagine why Hank had never mentioned his involvement in the committee. She needed to talk to him. But she hadn't spoken with him since Dalgety Bay, when she had finally told him that Matt Henderson was actually Martin. She had thought it best that they not talk...to avoid piling onto the secret that he was already being forced to keep. *The secret he's keeping for me.*

But this was different. It was quite possible that Hank was in trouble. She opened her phone and scrolled down until she came to his name. Though she hadn't called him since getting the new phone, she had plugged in his number, knowing at some point she would want to talk to him...that she would *need* to talk to him. *And that time is now.*

She had to know more, and Hank was the only one who could give her answers. Why had the group been formed? Had there been an ulterior motive? Had they disbanded? What had they accomplished? She trembled as she dialed Hank's number. *And why are five out of eight of them now dead?*

CHAPTER 18

Edinburgh, Scotland

Walter walked the same path around the sofa, the chair, and the Victorian desk that he had for the last hour, stopping only to reread the notes he had taken during his call with Dr. Samuels. He had paced the Edinburgh hotel suite since he and Dora had returned from dinner, trying to figure out two things: First, how he could even consider reaching out to his killer son, and second, how to do so without inviting Cobra back into his life.

He passed by the desk and stared down at his notes, his eyes fixating on one item in particular: an address in downtown London. The address belonged to Mark Justice, Private Inquiry Agent. Walter's conversation with the psychiatrist had been revealing, mostly because it had confirmed what Nenita had already told him: Cobra possessed an alter ego who was kind, well-mannered, and highly-regarded by the British hierarchy. The revelation, though hard to believe, had given him hope that if he managed to somehow make Justice the dominant personality, it would, in turn, force Cobra to vanish forever. And what he wouldn't give to make it so. Watching Martin's slow march toward death wasn't only unbearable, but it had seemed to underscore the fact that Walter's only living heir might soon be a serial killer known as Cobra. *If I could banish forever the very notion of Cobra...then no one would ever have to know about the madman I gave life to.*

But there was one person who would balk at the idea of Walter trying to 'save' his other son; his wife, Dora. She had forgiven his affair with Nenita; she had even blessed his journey to the Philippines to spread Nenita's ashes over the garden outside her home. But to ask Dora to support his efforts to essentially save the life of the man who had put her son in a coma – who had potentially *killed* him – was asking too much. To ask her to back Walter's efforts as he tried to protect the serial killer who, just months ago, had kidnapped and tortured her, along with Walter and five others, wasn't only unfair, but was criminal of its own accord. Worst of all, perhaps, was that her trusted aide, Kate, had been found not far from the school, all evidence suggesting that she, too, had been killed by Cobra. Dora would hold no forgiveness in her heart for such a man, nor should she. Which meant that if Walter chose to reach out to his son Mark, he would have to do it behind Dora's back. He cringed. *Which means that I will have to lie to her…again.*

He stopped at the bedroom door and listened. Nothing…no radio, no TV, no subtle sound of pages turning in a book. Dora had gone into the bedroom the minute they had gotten home from dinner, and, though it was barely eight p.m., she was clearly asleep. She had been sleeping a lot lately, but Walter didn't blame her; he understood. To lose a son, then get him back, then watch him die slowly before your eyes… well, sleep was her only reprieve from the agony of feeling it all again.

He resumed his pacing, replaying in his mind the phone call with Samuels. The psychiatrist's suggestion that Walter should reach out to Mark as a father to a son had resulted in a heartfelt protest. *"Don't you think I've tried to do that, Doctor?"* Samuels had then suggested that, instead of trying to appeal to the boy, Mark, Walter should appeal to Justice in a way that would leave Cobra completely unaware. Again, Walter had protested. *"How on earth do I talk to one without talking to the other?"*

The psychiatrist had sighed; a slow, audible sigh that had spoken volumes. *"I have tried more than once to coerce Justice into overpowering Cobra, but to no avail. The Cobra personality is definitely the dominant one, and will not give up without a fight. My guess is that he has gotten stronger since Dalgety Bay."* He had added. *"Which is why I think it will be up to you, Walter, to find a way to lure Justice to the fore."*

Fortunately, Samuels was willing to help. *"Your first step will be to get a message to Justice. He's most proud of his work as a Private Inquiry Agent. To reach him without alerting Cobra, your best bet would be to leave a message at his Belgrave office address."* He had read off the address and phone number, then had added, *"But just so you're aware, Walter, I've left several messages, and I've yet to receive a call."*

Walter stopped at the desk and stared down at the address: "Justice Enterprises, fourth floor, Apprentice Office Building, Belgrave Square." It was followed by a phone number.

He shook his head as he looked at the other notes he had jotted down. There were several lines about how Cobra had come to be, and what could cause a personality like Mark Villamor to dissociate. *"If an already-troubled boy feels trapped and alone, he might very well create his very own savior. In this case, I believe that savior was Cobra."* Walter had balked at the notion of Cobra being a savior, but Samuels had gone on to say it was likely that the headmaster's abuse toward the boy had abated soon after Cobra arrived on the scene. Walter couldn't argue the point. As a matter of fact, it was likely that Cobra had killed the headmaster just before Mark was expelled from the school.

Walter flinched. Though he hadn't known of the abuse, he felt an overwhelming sense of guilt that it had gone on as long as it had. Maybe if he'd made more of an effort to visit Mark at the school, he would have sensed what was going on. *Then I could've been the one to stop it, so Mark wouldn't have needed to create a killer to protect him.*

Samuels had gone on to give him a detailed description of Justice: *"He's blond, blue-eyed, fair-skinned, and well-dressed, and he faithfully wears a pair of quality kid gloves."* He suggested that the gloves were a way to hide his olive skin, and that he likely used makeup on his face and neck. The hair was obviously a wig, and the blue eyes had been achieved by wearing contact lenses.

Walter read through the description and sighed. *How do I make you the dominant personality, Justice?* According to Samuels, the answer was simple. *"We just need to give him the proper tools."* Walter had asked how they would go about giving an alter ego anything, especially tools. *"Wouldn't we be giving those same tools to Cobra?"*

The doctor had replied, *"You may be right, Walter. It has been my goal from the start to give Justice a way to escape his wicked moorings, but I've clearly failed."* He had paused. *"Perhaps it is as you say…to educate Justice is to educate Cobra."*

Walter was startled by the vibration of his phone. "Hello?"

"Walter, it's Maddi. I just wanted to update you on Matt before you and Dora went to bed for the night. He's stable, and the good news is that there haven't been any more codes. His heart has returned to its normal rhythm. I think he's resting peacefully."

Walter thanked her and ended the call. They had agreed to refer to Martin as Matt whenever they were on the phone, just in case their calls were intercepted. As for 'Matt' resting peacefully, Walter didn't buy it. How could anyone rest peacefully while lying comatose in a nursing home bed? What did the poor man think about? Was he aware of what was going on? As much as Walter wanted him to be cognizant if and when he awoke, it would be agony for him to be fully aware as he lay there so helpless. *Probably even worse than the helplessness I feel every single day as I watch my son – who looks nothing like my son – fight for every breath.*

It was even harder on Dora, which was why they had limited their visits to the afternoons. Even those few hours would take their toll, and Walter would see his poor wife fading along with the late day sun. So, he would rise and say it was time to go to dinner. Dora wouldn't argue. He would make a point of asking Maddi to join them; she would politely decline. They would stop at a favorite café, Dora would barely eat a bite, and they would come back to the suite, where she would retreat to the bedroom until the following morning. Walter felt certain if things didn't change soon, she would fall into an even deeper depression than she had the last time they dealt with the loss of their son.

So, how can I even consider resurrecting my mistress's child?

He sighed as he walked to the large bay window. He stared out at the evening sky. The sun was barely a glimmer over a distant knoll, leaving a black veil covering much of the surrounding landscape. He could see shadows in the garden below, but little else. He waited for his eyes to adjust, or for the sunlight to somehow emit a last gasp and light up the evening sky. It wasn't to be.

He continued to stare at the enveloping darkness, trying to conjure a way to reach Justice and not Cobra. Samuels had suggested that Walter should try to find a point of commonality between him and Justice; something that only the two of them might share. Walter had been skeptical. *"Don't he and Cobra occupy the same mind? Wouldn't a secret shared with one, be shared with the other?"* The doctor had answered quickly. *"Not necessarily. Justice learned only five months ago that he shared a psyche with a killer. Think of all that had happened to each of them prior to that knowledge. I think it's likely they know very little about one another."* He had paused. *"Take Justice's fondness for coins. I learned of it at our first meeting. He admired a rare and ancient coin that was sitting on my desk, identifying it instantly as a silver shekel from Israel's First Revolt in 66 A.D. It was a remarkable observation, something only a true numismatist would recognize."* Another pause. *"As for Cobra, I doubt he knows a thing about coins. Or if he does, he has dismissed it as a foolish hobby that is shared by only you and the boy."*

Walter had then asked Samuels how he knew that Walter and Mark had shared a fondness for coins. Samuels had told him that Nenita had been kind enough to let him see Mark's old bedroom, *"...where an array of coins were displayed proudly in his book case."*

It had disturbed Walter to think of anyone being in that bedroom and seeing Mark's darkness on full display. *It was bad enough for me to have to face it again,* he thought as he continued to stare out the window. His journey to the house to spread Nenita's ashes had about done him in. Just looking at that old house had brought back all they had been through...Nenita's illness, the unrelenting anguish of raising a killer for a son. While there, he had boxed up the coins and had had them sent to his home in Boston. He had left the scrapbooks on the bookshelf in Mark's bedroom. Once the house had been emptied of the few items that mattered, Walter had had it burned to the ground.

So, why on earth would I invite any of it back into my life? he wondered as he watched a taxi drop a guest in front of the hotel. He had said pretty much the same thing to Samuels. *"With all due respect Doctor, why should I reach out to a man who only months ago tried to kill everyone that I hold dear?"*

Samuels had said calmly, *"Don't you understand, Walter? It's not Cobra who you'll be reaching out to; it's your son. It is imperative that you see it that way."*

"But that boy no longer exists, Samuels. He died long ago."

"But he hasn't died...not really." Samuels had added, *"Mark is the common thread between Cobra and Justice; he's the source of them both. He created Cobra to save him from abuse. He created Justice to battle the evil that had arisen from Cobra."*

Walter had scoffed. *"I'd say Justice failed to do his part; wouldn't you agree?"*

"Not necessarily. I believe it's too soon to say. If you're able to pull Justice from Cobra, and can find a way to make him stay, the boy's goal for Justice will have been met. Justice's very existence is the repudiation of Cobra."

Walter shook his head and sighed. *Whatever.*

He walked away from the window and went to a sideboard along one wall. He poured a glass of red wine and carried it to the sofa. A newspaper was lying open on the coffee table, and he looked at a headline on page ten, probably for the twentieth time that night. "2004 Coin of the Year." He quickly skimmed the article.

> "In 2003, the British Royal Mint announced that starting this year, 2004, there would be a new series of designs for the One Pound coin. Featuring the Forth Railway Bridge that crosses over the Firth of Forth in southern Scotland, the coin will honor the work of Sir John Fowler and Sir Benjamin Baker. The bridge, built to carry the two tracks of the North British Railway, shows three cantilever towers that were constructed by Sir William Arrol. The bridge was begun in 1883, and was opened on 4th March 1890 by the Prince of Wales (later Edward VII). To celebrate this new coin, there will be a jubilee in Aberdeen, Scotland, on Saturday, October 30th. This one-day event will feature coins from around the world, and will showcase this memorable 2004 'Coin of the Year,' which highlights the historic bridge that unified a country."

Walter sipped his wine and sighed. He had found the article two days ago and had saved it, thinking he might try to attend. That was assuming that his son was even still alive in October. But now he wondered; could the jubilee serve as a way to appeal to Justice without alerting Cobra? Was what Samuels had said correct? That only the boy and Justice shared Walter's love of old coins? If so, then wasn't it likely that, even if Cobra did somehow learn of the event, he would feel no need to attend? If Walter was able to appeal to only Justice, then was it possible that only Justice would come?

With the newspaper in one hand and the glass of wine in the other, Walter stood and walked to the desk. He looked again at the address he had written down; the address in Belgrave Square. Could it work? He thought of the ramifications should he succeed. *An end to Cobra…forever.*

Then he thought of the risk…the fact that he might be inviting a killer back into his life. Finally. he thought of Nenita, the dear, kind woman who had asked so little of him. *"Find Dr. Samuels, Walter…let him help you save our son."* He shook his head and sighed. *For her…and for the legacy that is my family…I have to try.*

CHAPTER 19

Edinburgh, Scotland

Maddi was pacing the suite. She had tried to call Hank twice now. He hadn't answered either time. She had chosen to not leave a message. *I'll try again in a few minutes.* Though her concerns for his safety were unnerving, she had to admit that it felt good to focus on something besides Henderson's painful journey to death.

She had made her nightly call to Walter to let him know that Henderson was resting peacefully. She wasn't sure why she did it; it certainly didn't change anything. *It lets Walter and Dora sleep a bit easier,* she had concluded. She hoped it was true.

She checked the time. Nine p.m. ...four p.m. in DC. It had been thirty minutes since her last attempt to call Hank. She opened her phone and was about to dial, when the phone vibrated in her hand. "Hello?"

"So sorry to bother you again, Senator, but it's me, Phil. I forgot to tell you earlier that a Claire Porter called. She's trying to find you. She said it was important."

Maddi frowned. *Why would Claire be calling me?* "What did you tell her?"

"Just that I would give you the message. I didn't know who she was or if you would want to talk to her."

Maddi sighed. "Her number was in my old phone. Did she give you a number?"

"Yes, Senator."

He rattled it off. Maddi wrote it on a scrap of paper, thanked him, and ended the call. She looked around the room. It was just her and Henderson...which meant that she was, essentially, alone. A perfect time to talk to her therapist…right? No one to hear, no need to whisper. She was about to dial, when she heard a knock on the door. She walked over and opened it. The maintenance man who had worked on the sink earlier that day was standing at the door, his pocked face a distinct shade of red.

She smiled. "Is everything okay, Cameron?"

The man nodded. "Yes Ma'am." His cheeks had turned brighter red, and he lowered his eyes. "I…I was asked to take a look at the window…I was told that it squeaks."

Maddi frowned, wondering why he would choose that hour to fix the window. Then again, it would be nice for it not to screech every time she went to open it. She stepped back and motioned him into the room. He went to the window and got to work. A few minutes later, after a bit of WD-40 and an adjustment to one of the latches, he was done. He shuffled out without a word, offering a quick nod as he left the room.

Maddi walked to the window and lifted it, nodding as it opened without a sound. It was no longer raining, but the air was thick with the smell of rain. She breathed it in as she tried to decide who to call first. Hank, to warn him and learn more about a committee whose members were dying…or Claire, who had taken the unprecedented step of calling Maddi's secretary with a cryptic message that Maddi needed to call her. She stared at her phone, still trying to decide, when suddenly she heard it…the violin. The same violin she had listened to every evening for the last four months.

Each night it was the same…around nine p.m., the somber music would break through the twilight, giving voice to her sorrow. She would listen, her heart breaking at the sound of it, then an aide would walk in and insist that she close the window, per the nursing facility's rules. Maddi would beg him, *"Please, let me listen."* He would shake his head, but, always, in the end, he would let her keep the window open.

Tonight, was no different. The aide walked in, she asked him to let her leave open the window, and again, after some hesitation, he gave in. She listened to the melancholy melody of Bach's "Come, Sweet Death" and her heart broke. She had to fight not to cry. *It's just a song, Maddi.* But it was more…it was a requiem…a funeral dirge for the many in her life who had died. And, ironically, it had been one of her mother's favorites...

"So, what happened after you shot Officer Jackson?"

Maddi frowned. "Isn't that enough?" She shook her head. "Isn't it enough that I told you I murdered a man – in cold blood? What more do you want, Claire?"

Claire said nothing, her eyes a comfort in the cold silence of confession. "It sounds more like self-defense to me. After all, he was coming for you, wasn't he?"

Maddi frowned. "Yes, I guess he was. But the thing is, I wanted him gone... I wanted him dead. So, aren't I a murderer either way?"

Claire shook her head, her short hair bobbing on full cheeks. "No, Maddi, not if you were protecting yourself from a terrible man."

Maddi whispered, "That's the problem, Claire...I don't know if I was."

Claire simply looked at her. "What do you mean?"

Maddi hesitated. "I was protecting myself...but I'm not sure that he would have hurt me...any more than he already had."

"You don't think he was a threat?"

Maddi shook her head. "Not to me. I think he was a threat to my unborn child."

"Dear god, Maddi...that is a threat to you."

Maddi sighed. "Maybe, but I don't think he would've gone through with it."

"Why?"

Maddi sighed. "In retrospect, that man was just a bully...all bark, no bite."

"Yes, Maddi, but he had bullied you. You couldn't know what he was capable of."

"Yes...but did that give me the right to shoot him?"

Claire leaned back, her eyes narrowed as she stroked her rounded chin. She sighed. "I think it did. You were afraid, Maddi. That man had raped you—"

"I had gone along all too willingly, Claire."

"But you were too young to know, Maddi. It's called statutory rape. And I feel certain from what you've told me that he was capable of violence, as well." She sat up straighter. "Maddi, I think it is a clear case of self-defense."

Maddi looked at Claire long and hard. Though everything Claire had said was true, for whatever reason, Maddi couldn't let it go. She sighed. "It doesn't matter, Claire, I shot him. I'm guilty...I did it...I killed that man...in cold blood."

Claire said, "How many shots did you fire?"

Maddi frowned. "I...I don't remember."

"Think about it."

Maddi tried to recall. Was it one? More than one? She shook her head. "I don't know. Why does it matter?"

Claire frowned. "Maybe it does, maybe it doesn't." She shifted in her seat. "Okay, so tell me what you did next."

Maddi closed her eyes. She didn't want to talk about it, but knew she had to; it was why she was there. That death – that murder – was the key to so many things. She looked at Claire and sighed. "It's the damnedest thing, Claire…my mom saved me."

Claire's eyes widened. "That's interesting. Tell me more."

Maddi frowned. "There I was, standing over a dead man…a cop…and I didn't know what to do. Operating on some sort of instinct, I guess, I shoved Evan's body behind some trash cans. I covered him with a piece of old cardboard, then grabbed a blanket I found in the garbage and threw it over top of him. I ran the two blocks to my house. Even though Mom wasn't doing too well herself, she was all I had. I burst into the house and there she was, sitting at the counter, just getting ready to pour herself a drink." Maddi's jaw tightened. "I said, 'Don't, Mom…I need you.'"

"Did she listen?"

Maddi nodded. "She did. She shoved the bottle out of the way, and put her shaking hands in her lap. Then I told her what happened."

"What, exactly, did you tell her?"

The words came in a rush. "That I had fallen for a cop and had gotten pregnant. That the cop turned out to be an awful man. That I went to tell him about the pregnancy, and he mocked me in front of an entire police station. That he threatened to end the pregnancy, and I hated him with all my heart. That I had taken a gun with me just in case he…got violent. That he came at me…and I shot him." Maddi bowed her head.

Claire said, "So, what did your mother do?"

Maddi sighed. "She nodded and said, 'It'll be okay, honey.'"

"What happened next?"

Maddi sighed. "Here's where things got interesting. Dad was dead, Andrew was away at college, and it was just the two of us. I hadn't felt close to her in so long, but – for those few hours – Mom and I were a team." Maddi paused. "She shoved the bottle even further out of the way. She pulled the phone close, took an address book from the drawer, and skimmed through it. She found the number she wanted and dialed. I asked who she was calling. She put a finger to her lips, waited,

126

then spoke into the phone. 'Harold, it's Jeannie Madison, your son's...wife.' Silent tears flowed, but her voice never wavered. 'We...have a bit of a problem here. I was hoping...you could...help.'"

Claire said, "Who's Harold?"

"My grandfather. He and my grandmother Gloria lived in Darlington, north of London. They were quite wealthy. Their son, who was my dad, had come to America against their wishes. They were disappointed when he became a cop. And I'm pretty sure they never approved of mom." Maddi looked at Claire. "Can you imagine what it must have taken for Jeannie to call him like that?"

Claire nodded. "A considerable amount of love for her only daughter."

Maddi said nothing.

"So, what did Harold do?"

Maddi hesitated. "He did what most wealthy people do..." She looked at Claire with a mixture of pride and regret. "He bought off the Evansville Police Department..."

Maddi looked outside. The music had stopped. There was nothing but the hum of the machines that seemed to be marking Henderson's inevitable march to death. She thought back to all that had happened so many years ago...her terrible choices...her grandfather's intervention.

She was still holding her phone trying to decide who to call first, Hank or Claire, when, suddenly, she found herself dialing the number for her brother Andrew.

He picked up after the first ring. "Everything okay?"

Maddi sighed. "No, not really."

"What's up?"

Maddi hesitated. "A lot, actually. Washington intrigue...Middle East unrest." She sighed. "But for some reason, I find myself thinking way too much about what happened back in Evansville."

There was a pause. "Why even go there, Maddi?"

Maddi sighed. "I don't know. I just keep thinking about the cop... what I did...and grampa...and what he did."

Another pause. "You have too much time on your hands, Maddi." She heard him sigh. "But I know that that isn't likely to change any time soon, so I'm going to say something that I probably should've said long ago. You did nothing wrong, Maddi. That cop was evil. And Grampa did what any decent grandfather would do. He saved you."

"Only by buying off and extorting people."

"It was necessary, Maddi. Yes, maybe it didn't completely follow the constructs of the law, but neither had Jackson. And we both know that he would've gotten away with it." He paused. "And God knows what he would've done to you, to your life."

Maddi nodded. It was true. If she hadn't shot Evan Jackson, and if her grandfather hadn't covered it up, then Maddi would be leading a far different life...*and Tonna would probably not even be here.* "But why do you think I'm thinking about it so much now?"

She heard a sigh. "Like I said...you have too much time on your hands. For the first time in your adult life, you have time to think about it, Maddi."

She nodded again. He was right. "Well, enough about me. How are things with you?"

She heard a chuckle, and found herself fighting a barrage of tears. "You mean since this morning?"

She laughed. "Yes. We both know that a lot can happen in the course of a day."

"You're right about that." He paused. "Things are perfect here, Maddi." Another pause. "Now, hurry home so you can meet your nephew."

She sighed. "Will do, Andrew. Thank you. I'll talk to you soon."

She ended the call and fell into her chair. The tears came, but she wiped them away quickly, knowing that the last thing Henderson needed was a sobbing girlfriend sitting at his side.

She thought again about her grampa. He had cleaned up her mess well. But, in spite of it...in spite of the fact that twenty-one years later the events of that day had somehow managed to stay buried, Maddi was always left to wonder...*what will I do if...when...someone finally learns the truth?*

CHAPTER 20

Washington, DC

Morningstar was giddy. Though he was irate that it had taken Pocks almost nine hours to get the listening device into Henderson's room, it had gotten results within minutes. *Of course, it did…God is guiding my every move.* Morningstar's goal had simply been to know the minute that Henderson awoke from his coma, but he had been blessed with so much more. He had endured a violin; he had even put up with the incessant hum of sickbed monitors, but it had been worth it. Madison had just told of her involvement in something dicey. But he was unsure what to do with it; the information was far too incomplete. All he knew was that the revered Cynthia Madison had a secret…a big, ugly secret from the sound of it. It involved her younger years in Indiana – Evansville, to be exact – as well as a cop and a payoff by her grandfather. How had she put it? *"Only by buying off and extorting people."* Could Morningstar somehow use the information to his advantage? *Not until I know more.* He pulled out his cellphone and dialed.

"Yes, Father?"

"Levi, I need you to look into something for me. It has to do with an event that happened years ago in Indiana, when Cynthia Madison was a young woman. Something to do with a cop, a coverup, and her grandfather using money to somehow save her ass."

There was a pause. "Wow. Um…okay…so, where do I start?"

Morningstar bristled. "I don't know, Levi…figure it out. That's what I pay you for." He paused. "And be quick about it. I'd like to use it soon, if I can."

"Yes sir…right away, Father."

The call ended. He shoved his phone in his pocket. He paced his office, trying to imagine what could have happened in Evansville in the 1980's. Whatever it was, it had been illegal, why else would Madison's grandfather have needed to pay someone off? *And why would she be stewing over it all these years later?* Most intriguing of all, a cop was involved. *Which means someone, somewhere still remembers what went on.*

He grabbed his phone and again dialed Levi. "Start with one of Evansville's older cops; maybe a retiree, or a veteran in the force. But don't tell him who you work for."

"Who should I say I represent?"

Morningstar sneered. *Must I spoon feed every one of them?* "Just say that you're investigating questionable incidents involving Evansville police officers over the course of the last thirty years." He paused. "You can tell them you're with the Department of Justice…and that this is a routine audit of all major police departments in America."

"Um…okay. I'll see what I can find."

Morningstar shook his head as he ended the call. *You do that, Levi.*

He walked to the window and stared out at the late-day sun, which had just crested over the Capital. Suddenly, he laughed. He had no idea what he had stumbled onto, but he felt certain it was big…very big. Something that – just maybe – might bring down the untouchable Cynthia Madison. *Maybe I won't need to kill the bitch, after all…maybe I'll be able to bury her with her own secrets.*

CHAPTER 21

Philadelphia, Pennsylvania

It was late afternoon in South Philly and the police station was hot and steamy, the rays of sunlight like lasers on the metal chairs and desks. Though the building had air conditioning, it never seemed to be enough during the hottest part of the day. Todd Jackson leaned back in his chair, wiped the sweat from his forehead, and looked at his watch for the fifth time in the last ten minutes. *Four-thirty-five.* He had done his best to stay busy, eager to take care of the assignment he had been given that morning by the oversized officer with the cryptic message. *"Johnny Malone...look into it."* He would look into it, alright. By the time he was finished with Johnny Malone, the poor bastard wouldn't know what hit him.

The day had been a busy one, and call after call had kept him and his partner occupied for most of their shift. But he had had trouble focusing; all he could think about was Johnny Malone and the night ahead. He had been given a challenge, a chance to prove himself...and he was ready. But a part of him was unsure; would he would be able to do it? Was he capable of murder? *Hell yeah,* he kept telling himself...*if it's justified.*

He and his partner had just finished a routine drug bust at a downtown pawn shop and had returned to the station. Todd was busying himself with paperwork, when his radio squawked. *"Attempted robbery, convenience store, 1816 Christian."* Todd stood, grabbed his hat, and looked at his partner. "Let's go."

The two men left the station, jumped in their cruiser, and drove to the store, which was just a few blocks away. They burst through the door with their guns drawn, and saw a man lying on the floor. Another man, who Todd guessed was the shopkeeper, was standing over him with his foot on the man's back. He was holding a ball bat over the man's head, ready to strike.

Todd raised his hand to the man with the bat. "Hold it right there." The man froze, his arms shaking as he held the bat over the other man's head. Todd said, "Are you the shopkeeper?"

The man gave a quick nod.

Todd looked at the would-be crook squirming under the shopkeeper's foot and chuckled. Jimmy walked over and knelt down to check on him. Jimmy looked at Todd and nodded. "He's okay. There's a welt swelling up on his arm – probably from the bat – but he doesn't need a medic." Jimmy looked at the shopkeeper. "What happened?"

"The prick tried to rob me."

Todd laughed. "Looks like he picked the wrong guy."

The store owner nodded. "You got that right. This asshole...he can't even speak English." He kicked at the man, who groaned as he looked up and muttered something in Spanish. The shop owner raised the bat higher.

Todd ran up and grabbed him by the wrist. "Stop. Though I'd have no problem with you beating the shit out of this asshole, you'll only hurt yourself if you hit him again." The shop owner scowled but finally lowered the bat to his side. Todd patted him on the back. "Don't worry; we'll take care of him." He bent down and put his mouth close to the ear of the man on the ground. "Get up, Comprendè?" He yanked him up by his collar and forced him face-forward against a wall. He pulled his hands behind his back, slapped cuffs on his wrists, and motioned for Jimmy to take him to the car. Jimmy pulled a translator card from his back pocket, and read him his Miranda rights in Spanish as he dragged him out the door. Todd took down the store owner's statement, assuring him the man would be punished. But even as he said it, he knew better. *The asshole will probably sue the owner for assault...and win.*

He walked out to the car and he and Jimmy drove the criminal back to the station. Most of the trip was spent listening to the man rant in his native tongue. Both men shook their heads as they did their best to ignore him. Just before they reached the station, Todd decided he had had enough. He reached back, pulled away the protective screen, and smacked the suspect's face as hard as he could with the back of his hand. "Shut up!"

The man's face fell to the side. He raised it slowly, licked blood from his lip, and glared at Todd, but said nothing more as they pulled into the back lot of the South Philly police station. They processed the man, then went to their desks to write up the report.

Jimmy typed a last sentence, leaned back in his chair and sighed. He looked at Todd. "I'm thirsty. Ya' wanna' get a beer with some of the guys at O'Malley's?"

"No, I've got something to take care of. You go ahead. I'll read through the report and make sure nothin's missing. I'll see ya' tomorrow."

Jimmy stood and put on his hat. "See ya' tomorrow."

Todd nodded and looked at his watch. *Five-twenty-five.* He grabbed the report, read through it quickly, and took a pen from his drawer. After the last sentence he wrote, *"The perp was taken to holding after trying to assault Officer Jackson, who was compelled to use force to restrain the unruly prisoner."* He chuckled. *Just in case.*

He stood and grabbed his hat and keys, his eyes falling on the small picture that sat on the corner of his desk. The familiar face stared back at him; the proud police officer dressed in full uniform, the stiff captain's hat resting on jet black hair. Todd grinned as he put on his own hat. *This is for you, Dad.*

He left the station and walked to his refurbished 1986 Monte Carlo. He slid behind the wheel and pulled out of the lot. *South Ninth Street.* It was only twenty minutes away. Hopefully, Johnny Malone would be home. He drove in silence; no music, no news, only the quiet hum of the engine amid the horns and screeches of late day traffic. He had to get his head just right...*it's not every day I intentionally kill a perp.*

Minutes later, he turned into an alley and pulled up behind a rundown apartment complex just off South Ninth Street. He edged behind a produce truck parked off to the side, shielding his car as he looked for building C. It was the smallest of the three buildings and sat back from the others with a parking lot separating it from a vacant lot next door. "Perfect," Todd said, under his breath.

He pulled out of the alley and drove two blocks further south, turning into a parking garage off Sixth Street. He rounded the corner of the first level, noting a video cam angled on one of the walls. He couldn't let his car be seen anywhere near Malone's apartment. He knew what to do. *Go fast through the garage, don't stop, and park as far from the camera as possible, preferably behind a truck or SUV.* He drove two more levels until he found a Ford pick-up near the end of the row with an empty space on the other side. Without slowing down, Todd jerked the Monte Carlo into the space beside it, then pulled up far enough that he was out of sight of the camera. He turned off the engine and just sat there. What he was about to do would change him forever. *Good.*

He adjusted his hat in the rearview mirror. It covered his hair, though strands of black could be seen below the rim. His mustache, the same color as his hair, looked just like his father's, and he smoothed it down as he stared at the face looking back at him. He barely recognized the brown eyes. He turned away. *Some would call what I'm about to do a crime,* he thought, *but I know better…it's justice.* The world had gone crazy and the crooks had all the rights. He rubbed his forehead. He had never done anything like this. He had believed in his oath and had intended to honor it. *How better to protect and serve than by getting rid of this piece of shit who slipped through the system on a technicality.* He took one more look at the face in the mirror, still bothered by the eyes. His mother had always told him they were the color of sweet caramel, *"…just like your daddy's."* He flinched. *Well, Daddy's dead…killed by scumbags like this one.*

He reached into the back seat and grabbed a wrinkled white button-down. He took off his hat, his shirt, and his badge and shoved them on the floor of the passenger seat. He removed his police-issue Glock and hid it beneath the hat. He grabbed an unregistered pistol from under his seat and secured it around his ankle. He took a pair of tactical gloves from the glove compartment and stuffed them in his back pocket. He pulled on the shirt, buttoned it, and tucked in the tails as he stepped out of the car, making sure to stay low and behind the truck, out of the way of the camera. He slipped into the stairwell, ran down three flights of stairs, and out a back door. He jogged the two blocks to the rundown apartment complex. He reached building C and scanned the area, looking for bystanders or mothers with children. The place was deserted. He walked to the door and snuck inside. He looked at the names on the mailboxes along one wall and saw 'Malone' hand-written on a piece of tape over a box with a number six etched in the metal. He went upstairs and crept down a poorly-lit hallway, finding apartment six at the very end. He pulled on the tactical gloves and listened at the door. A radio was playing some sort of rap music. He knocked three times. He heard footsteps. The door was opened by a thin man in a white muscle shirt. The whiskers and the scar on the face were exactly the same as the photo, though heightened by an ugly scowl. "What do you want?"

Todd grinned as he glared at empty eyes. "Are you Johnny Malone?"

"What's it to ya'?"

In a split second, Todd had stepped around the man and was inside the apartment. "You here alone?"

"Yeah…what's it to you, asshole?" Malone had one hand on the open door, and was using the other to gesture with his middle finger. "Now get out!"

Todd raised his hand and karate-chopped the arm holding the door. The man pulled back in pain. Todd slammed the door shut and locked it. Before Malone could recover, Todd punched him in the jaw, then shoved him to the floor. Malone landed on his back. Todd pushed his boot into Malone's neck. He listened for sounds of anyone else in the apartment; he heard nothing. He stared down at Malone, who was squirming under his boot. "Quit movin', ya dick-weed." He pushed the boot harder. "Ya know that man you killed when you robbed the grocery store last year?" The man continued to struggle under Todd's boot. Todd pushed even harder. "Remember? Well, he had two children. *Little children*, you asshole!"

Malone tried to say something, but he choked instead. He reached his hands around Todd's thick calf and tried to pull him to the floor. Todd held his position and pushed harder against the neck. Malone was gasping for breath, his legs jumping in an effort to get free. Todd reached down and took the unregistered gun from around his ankle. He pulled a silencer from his pocket, screwed it onto the barrel, and aimed the gun at Malone's forehead. He said coolly, "In the name of justice," then pulled the trigger. The bullet hit Malone directly between the eyes. He gave a last gasp as his head rolled onto the floor, his eyes wide open. Todd stared at him, his gun aimed and ready, waiting for him to move. Though Todd's hand was trembling, it was steady enough to shoot the man thirty more times, if necessary. But Malone didn't move; his chest was still, his breathing silenced. Todd knelt down, took off one of his gloves, and felt for a pulse. Nothing; the guy was dead. He took a camera from his pocket, snapped a photo, then slid it back in his pocket. He removed the silencer and stuffed it in the pocket with the camera. He strapped the pistol in his ankle holster, found the spent casing, and shoved it in his pocket, as well. He stood and walked out of the apartment as quietly as he had come, locking the door behind him. He took off the gloves and shoved them in his pants. He would get rid of them later. He left the building, looking around for witnesses; he saw no one. He could barely breathe; his entire body was shaking. But the hit had been easy, far easier than he had thought it would be. And, in spite of his shaking hands, it had felt natural…like he was fulfilling his God-given role.

He did his best to walk calmly back to the parking garage. He climbed the three flights of stairs and clambered over a railing to his car, careful to stay out of the camera's eye. He sat on the cement, his back against his Monte Carlo, and took slow, deep breaths. He checked his watch. *Six-twenty-four.* It had taken only fourteen minutes to eliminate a piece of filth from the streets of Philadelphia. And, though he struggled with the line he had just crossed, he knew in his heart he had done the right thing.

He opened the car door and slid behind the wheel. His hands were sweating; he wiped them on his pants. He tried to slide the key into the ignition, but his fingers were shaking. He leaned back against the seat and closed his eyes. *Scum…that's all he was.*

After a minute the shaking eased, and he was able to put the key into the ignition. He started the engine but left the gearshift in park as he stared out between the thick cement columns of the Sixth Street parking garage. Thin rays of fading sunlight were glimmering on the pavement, and Todd couldn't help but grin. He had done it. He had just sealed his place in the band of brothers; he would soon become an official member of the Blue Brotherhood.

After another minute, he threw the car into gear, backed out of his spot, and sped down three levels to the exit. He paid the attendant in cash, making sure to avoid making eye contact. The man seemed uninterested, and opened the gate. Todd accelerated and turned onto a side street, checking his rearview mirror to be sure no one was following him. There they were again; those copper-brown eyes. He flinched. They had changed; they now belonged to a stranger. Yes, he had crossed a line, but it had needed to be done. Not only in the name of justice for the grocery store owner and his family, but in the name of justice for his father. *I'll avenge your death, Daddy.* And he would...one killing at a time.

DAY 2

TUESDAY, AUGUST 24TH, 2004

"Beware the fury of a patient man."

~ John Dryden ~

CHAPTER 22

Washington, DC

Edward Morningstar checked the time. *Two a.m. Why am I still awake?* He sighed as he stared up at the ceiling in his Starlight Hotel suite bedroom. He knew why. He was troubled…by several things, not the least of which was that his betrayer son, who had been lying in a coma for the past five months, might soon awaken. The confirmation that the man in that bed was Martin and not Matt had left him reeling…and concerned. If Henderson awoke, which seemed far more likely now that he had done so once, then he might tell the world what he knew about Morningstar and his operation. Morningstar was surprised he hadn't done so already. Once Morningstar had sent him the photo of Lili lying lifeless in the snow, he had had no reason to hold back; there was no longer anyone to protect. So why hadn't he shared the insider knowledge he possessed regarding Morningstar's operation? He sneered. *Because he has his own crimes to worry about.*

It seemed clear now that Henderson had spent at least the first month or two after his departure from Morningstar building a new face, a new life, a new identity in an effort to hide from the authorities. Then, luckily for Morningstar, it wasn't long after that that he had been kidnapped by Cobra, who had somehow put him in a coma that had kept him incapacitated for the past five months. Which had worked perfectly for Morningstar. Henderson had been unable to tell anyone anything about him or his operation. *But now, he could awaken at any moment.* And if he did, he would have a chance to tell the world, or at least Cynthia Madison, what he knew.

And God knows she'll be right there to hear it. Madison had sat at Henderson's side almost nonstop for the past five months. And that devotion concerned him. After all, Madison had made it her goal to take down Morningstar for his role in illegal arms purchases from Silverton Arms. If she were to team up with Henderson, who knew what they might do to Morningstar and his operation.

Which was why the information he had gotten from Pocks' listening device was so vital. Could a simple secret be his answer to finally ruining the woman who had become such a thorn in his side? The woman he had tried to kill on countless occasions? If he was to learn that Madison had done something immoral, or maybe even illegal a couple of decades ago, perhaps he could short-circuit not only her efforts to take down his arms-for-profit scheme, but any collusion she might eventually have with Henderson.

He had immediately put Levi to work to learn more about what had taken place in Evansville, Indiana so long ago. *"It has to do with some sort of coverup involving Madison, a cop, and her grandparents."* That had been nearly twelve hours ago. The man had yet to call him back.

He looked over at the woman next to him…Janet…his lovely, pregnant concubine. She was sleeping peacefully, and, even with her full belly and messy hair, the woman was a work of art. He was about to reach for her, when he heard his phone vibrate on the table by the bed. He grabbed it and opened it before it could vibrate again, then stood and walked naked into the front room. He closed the door behind him as he whispered into the phone, "Finally. What have you got for me, Levi?"

"Not much. Either it's been too long, or no one's willing to talk." There was a pause. "But I did find one thing you might be interested in."

Morningstar could feel his heart pounding. He grabbed a blanket from the back of the couch, wrapped it around him, then walked to the desk and sat down. "Tell me."

"Like I said, it was almost impossible to find anyone who seemed to know anything from back then. So, I decided to put in a call to the McCordsville police station; McCordsville is where Madison grew up. One of the old-timers there recognized the name; apparently her father was a cop, but he was murdered when she was a child. It was soon after that that the family moved to Evansville." There was a pause. "When I spoke to police officers in Evansville, they denied knowing anything about Cynthia Madison." Another pause. "So, I decided to look into her grandparents. They're all dead now, but I decided that if they were in a position to bribe and extort, it was likely they were rich. That definitely didn't apply to her grandparents on her mother's side, but, as it turns out, the Madisons of England were incredibly wealthy landowners."

Morningstar narrowed his eyes. *How did the son of a wealthy British landowner wind up as an American cop?*

Levi went on. "It would appear that the ultra-rich Madisons rarely visited the United States, especially after their son died."

"And when was that again?"

He heard Levi flipping through notes. "In 1972. A jewelry heist that went bad. Stewart Madison was given a hero's funeral."

Morningstar did the math. *Madison would've been only five years old.* "Go on."

"Here's the part I think you'll find interesting. In January of '82, after years of staying away, the grandfather flew to Indianapolis. I have a record of his plane flight, but that's about it. He didn't rent a car or a hotel room, and he flew back that same night."

Morningstar frowned. *That's a long way to go for just a day.* "Did his wife come with him?"

"No. He brought someone else."

Morningstar's eyes widened. "And who might that be?"

"His financial assistant."

Morningstar grinned. *Bingo.* "Go on."

"About a month later, the Evansville police department received a sizeable endowment for the establishment of what soon came to be known as the Madison Foundation." There was a pause. "It's still active today, and has financed the education of a number of police officers."

Morningstar chuckled. *Grampa bought off an entire police department? Ballsy fellow, I'll give 'im that.* "Any idea why he might've wanted to bribe Evansville's police department?"

"No sir. Like I said, the Evansville cops are pretty tight-lipped."

"Okay, not bad, Levi. But I'll need more than that if I'm to use it for anything worthwhile. Keep digging."

"Yes sir…yes, Father."

Morningstar closed his phone. It was good…but it wasn't enough. No specifics; no real dirt that could effectively tarnish the Teflon senator from Indiana.

Suddenly, his eyes lit up. *I can always pretend that I know more than I do. I'll bet it would get her attention if I let slip a comment about a cop and a payoff from her past.*

He stood and, with the blanket still around him, began to pace the room. His mind was racing. *Maybe I can do even more than that. Maybe her dirty little secret will allow me to address all of my problems at once…her efforts to take me down for arms trading; her devotion to my greatest enemy, Martin Henderson; Henderson's devotion to her…and any willingness they might share to take me down.*

He nodded and glanced at a wall clock. It was two a.m. …seven a.m. in the UK. If he played his cards right, he might be able to put a stop not only to Madison, but to her alliance with Henderson…by the time the sun set over the magnificent Edinburgh castle.

He frowned. But how would he communicate what he had learned about her? It wasn't like he could simply call her on the phone and tell her that he knew a secret about her past. And he certainly couldn't fly over there, waltz into Henderson's nursing home room, and drop that bombshell in her lap. He would need distance from the dirt. Otherwise, it would seem self-serving, especially since Madison had been probing his arms trading not that long ago. *If I want to bury her with this, it can't appear to be politically motivated.*

He let the blanket fall to the floor as he walked to the window and looked outside. The curtains were open, and, yes, he was naked. But it was two a.m. The only ones who would see him were the bums on Montana Avenue. *Let 'em look,* he thought, as he stared out at the darkness. Other than a streetlamp just outside the window, there was nothing. No moonlight, no stars. He stared at the black sky, trying to think how he could use what he had just learned to its maximum effectiveness. *I'll need to be creative,* he thought, as he sauntered back to the desk. He took a half-smoked cigar from a tray, and rolled it between his fingers as he searched for a lighter. He found one in the top drawer and lit the cigar. He puffed several times, then walked back to the window, trying to come up with a clever way to tell the lovebirds in

Scotland that someone with power had become aware of a Cynthia Madison dirty secret.

He had already started the ball rolling on a plan to bring Henderson back to DC if and when he awoke from his coma. If the plan was effective, then it was likely that Madison would come with him. Assuming she did, was there a way to maybe leak the gossip to one of the DC papers?

He frowned. No paper on the planet would publish innuendos without at least a fact or two; especially regarding a popular female senator. Besides, he was in a bit of a time crunch. According to what Pocks had told him, Henderson could awaken at any minute. Morningstar had to have Madison away from him before they had a chance to compare notes and join forces against him. The only way he could use the limited info he had obtained would be to make Madison think that he knew more than he did…soon. Which meant that someone would have to tell her as much…soon.

I'm sure one of my boys could help me out. But all of his 'sons' were tied up with tasks. Simeon and Naphtali were in France looking for his warship, Gad was in Latvia trying to work his way onto the Henderson estate, Levi was in in DC digging up dirt on Morningstar's enemies, Zebulun was on a mission in New Jersey, and Judah was tied up with a reelection campaign for his Commander-and-Chief. There was always Pocks, who was actually there at the nursing home, but he was a terrible choice to deliver a threat.

He began to chuckle. *There's one left,* he thought as he stared out at the dark night. *Dan…the ever-elusive Cobra.* But no one had heard from Cobra since the debacle at Dalgety Bay. The last that anyone had seen of him, he had been running up a hill and away from a burning schoolhouse. *Should I try to call him? Will he answer?*

Morningstar walked back to the desk and stared down at his phone. He went to grab it, and was surprised to see that his hand was shaking. Of all the sons, Cobra was the only one who had the power to actually frighten Morningstar. Though every one of the sons had the capability to be callous and cold, only Cobra displayed those traits twenty-four-hours a day. He was intimidated by no one; not even Morningstar. It had been a tightrope from the beginning…enlist the killer's help without incurring his wrath.

"To hell with him," he said as he grabbed his phone from the desk. "He's my son…and he'll do what I say."

CHAPTER 23

Edinburgh, Scotland

Secret Service agent Tom Cravens stretched his arms as he tried to suppress a yawn. He had had a late night and, though he was paying for it now, he felt a sense of relief that he had at long last given the "JH" briefcase to someone else to worry about.

The enigmatic criminal-turned-government-agent Shaw had come to the diner as expected, and Cravens had told him the details of the briefcase…the conditions under which he had found it, the significance of the insignia in the corner, his reluctance to turn it in, and his whole-hearted belief that whatever was inside that case was vital…and likely top secret. *"Which means that I'm gonna need you to forget you ever saw it: the briefcase, the contents…even me."*

Shaw had merely nodded. *"Shouldn't take me long, Tommy. I'll call ya."*

Cravens had been touched – and a bit unsettled – by Shaw's repeated reference to him as Tommy. Only three people in his entire life had called him Tommy. His mother, his wife, and his Uncle Harry. He felt it to be a good sign…an omen that his trust in Shaw was well-placed.

God, let's hope so, he thought as he tried to suppress another yawn. Why had he been willing to trust the man with so much? He sighed. *Necessity.* Cravens had gotten himself into quite a predicament with that briefcase, and he needed a way out. Who better to help him than a former criminal-turned-legitimate agent with an obvious propensity for keeping secrets? Not only that; over thirty years with the Secret Service had given Cravens a keen sensibility about people; he knew who to trust, and he was rarely wrong. *Let's hope I've gotten this one right,* he thought as he stifled yet another yawn.

He had been sitting outside Matt Henderson's nursing home room since four a.m., having foregone most of a night's sleep in order to get the briefcase to Shaw. Fortunately, his watch so far had been quiet. Rain had kept Maddi from going on her jog, there had been no visitors, and Walter and Dora didn't usually come until the afternoon. There hadn't even been a sink to fix, which meant that the handyman, Milligan, hadn't come by to interrupt Cravens' time alone outside the room. He was glad…he was tired.

But in spite of his fatigue, his mind was spinning. Thoughts of Shaw, the briefcase, and what might be inside twirled in his head like a top. He had promised himself that if the owner of the briefcase had no criminal ties, he would return the case to him without a word. He would never tell anyone of its discovery…not his partner, not his boss…and the world would go on as it had, no one the wiser that trusted Agent Thomas Cravens had sat on evidence from a crime scene…for months.

He winced and shifted in his seat. As much as he hated to admit it, that was exactly what he had done. He had knowingly and intentionally removed evidence from the scene of a crime, kept it hidden for five full months, and – after paying a former criminal to break into it – was still unwilling to turn it in.

Why? Was it simply because the insignia was the same as the image on his uncle's medal? Or did it have something to do with the fact that he had practically *heard* his dear uncle telling him from the grave not to turn it in. He shook his head and sighed. Whatever had motivated him to hide the evidence, he had done it, and the sooner he got rid of the damn thing, the sooner he could get past what he had done.

But what if Shaw finds something that implies that the owner of that briefcase is a criminal? What will you do then, Tommy-boy? That was the question he had been unwilling to answer; the challenge he had yet to resolve. Because if there was something unlawful about the contents of that briefcase, or about the man who owned it, then Cravens would not only be forced to turn it over to the authorities, but would also have to admit that he had impeded an investigation. Not knowingly, but he had done it, nonetheless. Who knew how many crimes might have been averted had he come forward five months ago?

He cleared his throat, and once again shifted in his seat. He didn't want to think about it. But as he stretched his arms for probably the twentieth time and stifled yet another yawn, suddenly it was all he could think about.

CHAPTER 24

Edinburgh, Scotland

Walter awakened to the sound of a vendor outside the hotel. "Bagels, get your toasted bagels!" He had heard the man before. Every morning at 8:00 a.m., a robust voice would shout out the arrival of "*... fresh-baked, honey-flavored bagels,*" and Walter would instantly sit up, his sleep irreparably harmed by the intrusion. *He's like a damn rooster.*

He pulled himself out of bed and walked to the bathroom. Dora was somehow able to sleep through the vendor's decrees, which was good…especially today. It would give him a chance to review the plan he had come up with the night before.

As he finished up in the bathroom, he stared at his face in the mirror. He had aged considerably. His salt-and-pepper hair, once a sleek black with only hints of silver, was now mostly gray, and there were far more wrinkles around his pale blue eyes. He rinsed his face and sighed. *My roadmap of the last four years.*

He left the bathroom, grabbed his robe from a chair, and walked to the front room. He went to a counter and started a pot of coffee. Though Dora favored traditional British tea, Walter had learned early on that he wasn't worth a damn without his morning coffee.

As he waited for it to brew, he walked over to the Victorian desk. He stared down at his notes from the night before and frowned. Would it work? He shook his head and sighed. *There's no way.*

The newspaper article about the coin jubilee was lying next to his notes, and he read it through, trying to imagine Justice meeting him at the event. He wished it was sooner. October 30th was over nine weeks away. Then again, it might take that long for Justice to break free of his alter ego.

That is assuming I can get a message to Justice without alerting Cobra. Could he do it? Assuming he could, if Justice did show up at the jubilee, how could Walter be sure he wasn't Cobra in disguise? *That wouldn't happen,* he thought, ...*not according to Samuels, anyway.* The psychiatrist had insisted that Cobra's dislike of Justice was so great that he would be loath to voluntarily adopt the man's dress or mannerisms...even to deceive his father.

Which meant that if Justice showed up at the jubilee, the odds were high that he would, in fact, be himself. *So, the challenge is to get a message to Justice without Cobra being aware.* Walter thought back to those few hours in the dungeon outside Lyon, when Cobra was clearly being taunted by his alter ego. It had been frightening, yet fascinating to watch as Cobra went back and forth with the imaginary Justice. *And who won that battle, Walter?* He shook his head and sighed. *Cobra...Cobra definitely came out on top.*

He recalled the interplay between the psyches. *How does it work? Are they both living inside one man?* From what he had witnessed, it looked like they were. But how much did they know about each other? Cobra was aware of Justice, that much had been clear; and Justice most certainly was aware of Cobra; he had taunted him endlessly in the cave. But what about the boy, Mark? According to Samuels, it was the child who had created the two men. So, he obviously knew of them...but did they know of him? And, if so, to what extent? Cobra had been created to save the boy...which meant that Cobra was aware of the boy. But what about Justice? Walter thought again of what Samuels had told him about how Justice had come about. *"My guess is he was created to battle Cobra...to tame the urges of the killer."* Did Justice know that his very existence had been predicated on the wishes of a young boy?

Walter rubbed his chin. *If he does, then that means that each psyche is aware of the other.* The question was, to what extent? A faint passing knowledge? Or an intimate awareness of all that goes on with the other two? Again, he thought of the dungeon. Cobra had been goaded by them; he had felt them to be *external* to him. Which meant they were not part of his inner psyche...their existence was outside of his thoughts and fears. Was that the case with all of them? If so, then how did one explain Justice's uncanny appreciation for the origins of an ancient coin? Samuels had suggested that Justice had been created only recently, evidenced by his short time as a PI. *"I'd stake my career on the fact that he didn't exist before that, Walter."* Which meant that he hadn't had time to learn all he seemed to know about coins. But he had to get that knowledge somewhere. The only psyches he had access to were Cobra's and young Mark Villamor.

Maybe he acquired it in his role as a PI. It was possible...but not likely. Even if he had been pulled into a case involving ancient coins, to have the knowledge required to identify Samuels' relic would involve years of study; years that Justice hadn't likely had.

Walter walked to the counter and poured a cup of coffee. He threw in milk and sugar, then carried it back to the desk. Though the sun was starting to rise, it was battling rain that had been present since last night, as well as distant rolls of thunder. He turned his chair to face the battle, sipping his coffee as he silently cheered on the sun.

He looked over his shoulder at the article on his desk, noting the date of the jubilee. October 30, 2004. Over two months away. It would give Justice plenty of time to plan for the event. How much time would he need? Would more time give him a better shot at being the dominant personality? If so, then Walter's best chance at success was to get the invitation to him as soon as possible. *But how?* Though Samuels had given him the address for Justice's offices, there was no way Walter could travel to London, especially not now, so soon after his son had come out of his coma. Yes, he had once again fallen into its grip, but the odds of him waking for good had increased significantly, at least according to his doctor. *"I think, Mr. Henderson, he'll either awaken soon...or he'll die."* Walter rubbed his eyes. He was so tired...tired of waiting for his son to die.

And how would he explain such a trip to Dora? *"I need to leave you and our son who is clinging to life, so I can invite the killer son whom I conceived with my mistress to a coin show."* He shook his head. No, he couldn't go to London. *I'll have to call, instead.*

He stood and carried his coffee to the window. The sun was winning its clash with the rain, and it now shone brilliantly on a row of hydrangeas outside the window. Though the grass and trees were still a rich green, he could already see hints of yellow. As if a thin sheet of buttery silk had been draped over summer as a prelude to fall. It was breathtaking. The cool air of Scotland had allowed for an array of colorful flowers that rivaled some of the best London gardens. *I should take a walk,* he thought as he stared at an old stone entrance to a park less than a block from the hotel. He sighed. *Maybe after I make the call to Justice.*

He walked to the desk and looked down at his notes, rereading the message he had written the night before.

> *"This message is for Mark Justice, Private Inquiry Agent. My name is Walter Henderson. You and I share an acquaintance with Dr. James Samuels, whom I recently spent time with at Dalgety Bay. He has told me of your interest in rare coins, and I would like to request your presence at the dedication of the 2004 Coin of the Year, to be held Saturday, October 30th, 2004 at Hazlehead Park in Aberdeen, Scotland. I'm attending the event with Dr. Samuels, and would be honored to have you join us. I feel that your appreciation for old coins, as well as your high regard among the London elite would be a welcome presence at our table. I will wait for you outside the front gate at noon."*

Walter frowned as he parsed the message in his mind. He hadn't yet clued in Samuels to his plan. He wanted to hear from Justice first. But he had purposely included references to the psychiatrist, as well as to Dalgety Bay, thinking they might inspire Justice to take control of the psyche and keep Cobra away. Was that how it worked? Could one psyche will the others away? That was how it had seemed in the dungeon. Cobra had pushed back against the specters battling for control, and from what Walter could tell, he had won. How? How did one of them gain control, only to lose it down the line? He shook his head. He didn't understand any of it. One thing was clear, whatever he decided to do, it was going to be a longshot.

And at what cost, he wondered as he continued to stare at the message. Not only did his carefully crafted words have to reach Justice and only Justice, but Walter had to make sure that a meeting with the man didn't put other lives at risk...including his own. It would do Dora no good to regain her son, only to lose her husband to a foolish notion of restoring the sanctity of a killer.

What am I doing? What on earth makes me think that I can will evil out of a man? And why am I willing to risk another encounter with Cobra? He shook his head. *For Nenita. I made a promise to a woman I cared for deeply, and now I must keep it.*

But it wasn't just the pledge that he had given to his dying mistress that was compelling him to follow through with the plan. He understood that now. His motives had far more to do with his own preservation… or at least the preservation of his family and their name. To permanently bring Justice to the fore would relegate Cobra to the past…forever. Though it would never remove the heartache of what the killer had done over the years, or the lives he had ruined, it might at least keep the world from ever learning of his ties to the Henderson clan.

Walter gathered up his notes, both on the desk and in the top drawer, double-checking to make sure he had every last scrap of paper. Holding back the message for Justice, he carried the scraps to the closet, opened the safe, and locked them inside. He went to his desk and picked up his phone. He dialed the number that Samuels had given him the night before. As he waited for either a secretary or an answering machine, he read through the message one more time. Would it work? He could only pray that it did. *Then, if things go well, I'll meet Justice in October, entice him to stay, and bid Cobra farewell…forever.*

CHAPTER 25

Edinburgh, Scotland

What day is it? Mark Justice opened his eyes, squinting at a ray of sunlight as it glared through a small, square window. *Where am I?* He was lying across an unmade bed, and he sat up, the effort taking far more out of him than it should have. He felt a sudden pain in his temple, and put his hand to his forehead. *Abominable headaches!* He had spent the last several years trying to get rid of them, but clearly, he had failed.

He stood and stumbled to the window, doing his best to make sense of his surroundings. He spotted a castle and immediately recognized its formidable bulwark. *How on earth did I get to Edinburgh?* The last thing he remembered was being at Dalgety Bay, which was about twenty minutes north by train. When had that been? He tried to recall. "It was in March...the blooms had just come out on the rhododendrons."

He continued to stare, trying to piece it all together. He looked from the castle to a row of flowers just outside his window, and felt an ache in his stomach. The fading blooms he was looking at now belonged to late August; they were not the spring blossoms he recalled from the Bay. *Dear lord, have I lost an entire summer?*

It wasn't the first time he had lost time. It had happened frequently over the past several years. But never for so long. *A lot can happen in a summer,* he thought, as a sudden chill ran through him. He tried to imagine all the horrible things that his alter ego might have done while Justice was 'away.' *What sort of hell hath Cobra wrought for the people of the UK? Or for the world, for that matter?*

Justice had only recently begun to grasp his tie to the infamous killer Cobra, and the realization – that he literally lived *inside* the man's psyche – had left him completely unnerved. Justice's brief appearance outside the Dalgety Bay schoolhouse had been an attempt to wrest control from Cobra…to win the battle over who would be dominant. But he had failed…miserably.

Suddenly, he cringed. "Nenita…what happened to Nenita?" He thought back to that brief moment when he had caught sight of the beautiful, yet tragic lady…the gentle woman who had somehow borne a killer. What had happened to her? He couldn't recall. Her sad eyes were his last recollection, and yet a full summer season had come and gone.

"I need a newspaper," he said as he looked around the room. It was clear that he was in a hotel…*and a not-too-elegant one, at that.* The wallpaper was stained and peeling from the corners, the carpet was faded, the baseboard was chipped. The bed was barely big enough to hold a man, and at its end was a crumpled brown bag sitting on top of a wrinkled coverlet. He walked to the bag and poured the contents onto the bed. There was a box of blue-tinted contact lenses, a blonde wig, white gloves, makeup, a wallet, and two cellphones. He recognized one of the phones. He opened it, sad to see that the screen had been cracked to the point where he couldn't read the day or date, but relieved to at least make out the edges of his screensaver – a photo of a Van Gogh – which meant that it was, in fact, the same phone he had had for the last two years. He clicked to the list of contacts to see if they had been saved, but was unable to read any of the names due to the cracks.

He picked up the second phone. It wouldn't turn on; the battery was dead. He set both phones on the bed, then opened the wallet. There was his Private Inquiry card, as well as a credit card in his name and four hundred pounds cash. He slid the wallet in his pocket, surprised to see that he was wearing his customary off-white suit. But it was filthy; he would need to go shopping, that much was clear.

There was no mirror in the room; he would have to get ready without it. He unpacked the contact lenses and slid them in his eyes. He ran his fingers through his hair. It was long enough for him to see stringy, black ends. He pulled on the wig, taking care to hide every strand of the ugly black hair. He looked at the skin on his hands and his stomach turned. It was the deep olive of his counterpart, Cobra. He opened the makeup, covered his face and neck as best he could, then put on the gloves. They weren't the high-quality kid he was used to. He frowned. *I must have been desperate when I bought these.*

But had *he* bought them? He must have; Cobra would never have allowed for such purchases. *Then why can't I remember?* He frowned as he threw the empty bag in a rubbish bin next to a dresser. He grabbed the phones from the bed and was about to leave the room, when the charged phone began to vibrate. He fumbled to open it. "Y—yes?"

There was a pause. "Is this...Dan?"

Justice frowned. "Dan? Why no...I believe you must have the wrong number."

There was a pause, followed by a chuckle. "Such a distinguished British accent. Could this be Mark Justice, the eminent Private Investigator from Belgrave Square?"

Justice's eyes widened. "Why, yes, I'm Mark Justice. And who might this be?"

Another pause. "My name isn't important. Just know that I work for the United States Government, and I have an important task for you."

CHAPTER 26

Edinburgh, Scotland

Maddi sat up in bed and rubbed her eyes. She stared at the clock. *Eight-forty.* It was the latest she had slept in weeks, maybe months. *I missed my morning jog.*

But she hadn't slept well. She had decided to wait until today to try to reach Hank. Her two attempts the night before had failed, and she hadn't wanted to interrupt his evening at home with something as mundane as a disbanded government committee. But was it mundane? She frowned. *That's what I'll ask when I call him later today.*

She had spent a good part of the night standing at the window… thinking. And though much of that thinking had involved Henderson, a good bit of it had also involved her life…her accomplishments…her failures…her past.

She flinched as she stood and stretched her arms. She walked over to Henderson, did a quick assessment to make sure he was still alive, then kissed him on the forehead. "Good morning, Love." She walked to the window and pulled back the curtains. Though rays of sunlight were trying to cut through the ever-present clouds, she could tell that it had been raining, and she heard thunder fading in the distance. She probably wouldn't have been able to go for her jog anyway. She stared down at the houses with their stone chimneys and brick bulwarks and sighed. Nothing had changed; nothing ever changed.

She turned away from the window and walked to the bathroom, grabbing a change of clothes on the way. As she walked into the bathroom, she made a point of not looking in the mirror. She was tired of looking at her empty eyes and sunken cheeks. She freshened up, put on the clothes, then left the bathroom. She walked past Henderson and fell into her overstuffed chair. She sighed. *My past.* Not since her actual conflict with the cop from Evansville had Maddi been so caught up in it…so entangled by the emotions of all that had taken place back then. But for some reason, it was all she could think about. *Why?* For years she had been able to bury Evan Jackson's memory. But now, for whatever reason, it was as if he was there in the room with her, as if he had never died…*as if I had never killed him.*

She frowned as she thought back to that moment when she finally told Claire the truth of that day. Though Maddi had felt a sense of relief, she had sensed a change in Claire…a disruption to their easy give-and-take. Maddi thought at first that she had offended the counselor, but gradually began to see that it had nothing to do with Claire's opinion of her; it had more to do with Claire, herself…

"So, was that the end of it?"

"What do you mean?"

"Once your grandfather got involved…was that the end of it?"

Maddi frowned. "More or less. It certainly put a stop to any further investigation." She paused. "But it wasn't the end of it with me…it lives on inside me."

Claire nodded. "In what way?"

"I killed a man, Claire. It is everything I don't believe in."

"Then make it right."

Maddi frowned. "Make it right?"

"Yes, tell someone. Explain that you were only defending yourself."

Maddi frowned. "I can't do that, Claire…I have too much to lose." She sat back and crossed her arms. "And was I defending myself?"

Claire narrowed her eyes. "I think so…but only you can really answer that."

"What does it matter? Either way, I pulled the trigger and I killed a man."

"How many times?"

Maddi frowned. "How many times what?"

"Did you pull the trigger."

There it was again; Claire's obsession with how many bullets Maddi had fired into the chest of the cop. "I already told you…I don't recall. Can we move on, Claire?"

"How many times?"

Again, Maddi tried to remember. Was it once? Three times? Did she empty the chamber into the awful man's chest? She shook her head. "I... I can't remember."
Claire nodded. "Well... once you do, then you'll have your answer."
"What answer?"
Claire sighed. "Did you kill him? Or did you save yourself?"

Maddi leaned forward and looked at Henderson. She reached for his hand and held it tightly with both of hers. He looked calm... maybe even peaceful. When was the last time she was at peace? *Not for a very long time.*

She hadn't answered Claire's question, in that session or in any of those that followed. They had moved on, but the question had hung in the back of her mind. Did she murder Evan Jackson? Or was she protecting herself... or her baby. *Maybe both?*

A tower in the distance rang out nine chimes. She scooted her chair closer to the bed and clung to Henderson's hand, trying to think how many chimes she had heard in that room. How many days had she watched morning fade to night, then ease back into morning? She leaned her head on his chest and sighed, wondering if he, too, counted the days and nights. Could he feel time pass? *What does he think about as he's locked inside himself? Does he know I'm here? Has he felt my tears on his cheek?*

As if in answer, she suddenly felt his hand squeeze hers. She raised her head and looked at him. He was staring at her and she gasped. "Henderson, you're back."

He gave a weak smile. Then, in the gravelly voice she had become so fond of, he said, "Yes, and I plan on staying this time."

* * *

Before he squeezed her hand, he watched her... her hair falling onto his chest as she waited for him to come back. The tired eyes he had imagined a thousand times as she fought sleep out of fear that he might be dead when she awakened. He knew those feelings, every one of them, for he had felt them himself... time and time again. He knew what it was to feel incomplete... as if you had taken only half a breath as you waited for your other half to finish it. As he watched her, he wondered how he could feel so much love for another human being. It was beyond anything he had ever known. As she raised her head and looked at him, he knew in that instant that, no matter what happened, he would stay with that woman forever. *If she'll have me.*

"Have…you slept…much, Maddi?" It hurt to talk.

"Yes."

"You're lying. Not…a good…foundation…for a relationship, you know."

She grinned and his heart stopped. A monitor rang out and a nurse rushed into the room. He looked at her and smiled. "Don't…worry, Patty, it's just my…lovelorn heart."

Patty giggled as she looked at him warily. "Yer back then, Mr. 'enderson? I 'ope ye stick around longer than last time." She frowned. "How do ye know my name?"

"I've heard it said enough times over the last three months." He swallowed. His throat hurt. "Or has it been four?" He turned to Maddi. "How long have I been lying here?"

Maddi practically crawled on top of him, oblivious to Patty who was looking on with a stunned grin. Maddi turned to Patty. "What's it been, Patty? Four months, one week, and two days?" She paused. "Or something like that."

Patty chuckled and turned away. "Somethin' like that." As she walked out of the room, she said over her shoulder, "I'll let the doctor know yer back." She grinned. "Now don't ye go getting all excited, Mr. 'enderson. Yer not out of the woods yet, ye know."

Henderson pulled Maddi close. He could smell her; her hair, her skin, smells that had stayed with him for four long, lonely years. She seemed unreal; like he was watching someone else trace the skin on his cheeks, his lips. He leaned up and kissed her forehead. "God, how I missed you."

Maddi said nothing, silent tears a testament to all they had been through. She grabbed a damp washcloth from a nearby table, and wiped it gently over his eyes, his forehead, his cheeks. She brushed back his hair, and traced the barely visible scars beneath his left eye and along his jaw. "Do they hurt?"

He closed his eyes. *Yes, they hurt…everyday they sting like the fire that caused them.* He gave a weak smile. "Not so much."

She kissed his cheek. "Who's lying now?" She put her lips on each of the scars, kissing them gently, slowly as she moved from one to the next. He closed his eyes, trembling, certain his heart was about to explode. Again, a monitor rang out and she stopped. She looked at him and grinned. "I guess maybe I should hold off."

He shook his head. "Don't. It would be a remarkable way to go out, you know."

She chuckled and shook her head. "No, I just got you back. I will not permit you to go away again, Henderson. My heart can't take it."

He pulled her closer, surprised he had the strength for it after so much time lying in the bed. "I won't. Not unless I can take you with me."

She leaned up on one elbow. "I'd go, you know."

He frowned, wishing he hadn't said it. "No, it won't be necessary. I'm not going anywhere."

She closed her eyes and laid her head against his chest. He put his arm around her. He coughed, but she didn't move. He coughed again, then fell back against the pillow. "I don't know what that bastard gave me, but it doesn't seem to want to let go."

"Like me," she said with a grin. She sat up and kissed his cheek, then again laid her head on his chest. He tucked his arm around her, and they lay there, silent and still.

After another minute or so, she looked at him and sighed. "They'll be in here soon, you know…the doctors and nurses fussing over you. They'll make me get up."

"I'll fight them," he said with a laugh, which was followed by another coughing spell. He quickly recovered, then pulled her closer. After several minutes, he looked at her and said, "What are you thinking?"

She looked up at him. "I want time to stop. I know this horrid sickness will take you away again; that's what it does. It gives you to me, then it takes you back." She frowned. "It's rather cruel, as sicknesses go."

"Yeah, it's as if he knew."

"Who?"

"Cobra. It's like he knew what his drugs would do to me."

"But he hasn't given you anything in months."

Henderson nodded. "Exactly."

She shook her head. "Well, I won't let him have you."

He closed his eyes and sighed. "Have they found him...Cobra?"

Maddi shook her head. "No. Roger's still looking for him."

Henderson's eyes widened. "So, Roger made it? He's okay?"

Maddi nodded. "Yes...thanks to you." She smiled. "And he returned the favor by saving you from the burning schoolhouse."

He shook his head. "Of all the monsters Roger had to be assigned to." He paused. "How about the Chief Inspector? Pritchard's his name, right? Is he okay?"

"He's had quite a battle, but he's finally on the mend."

"Good." He paused. "And the psychiatrist?"

"Barely hurt. He went back to his home in London that same night."

"I wonder why Cobra didn't do more to him."

Maddi shook her head. "It's hard to say."

"What about Mom and Dad?"

Maddi's eyes lit up. "They're wonderful. I've never seen two people together for so long who still seem to be so much in love."

His eyes widened. "Are we talking about my mom and dad? Walter and Dora Henderson?"

Maddi grinned. "Yes, they're fun to watch...like teenagers."

He laughed. "Teenagers, huh?" He paused. "I knew they were here...but I could hear only bits and pieces of what they said."

"Well, they'll be here soon, I'm sure. The nurse likely called them the minute she saw that you were awake. They've been staying at the hotel down the street."

Henderson closed his eyes. "What about the really thin woman... Nenita."

Maddi laid her head on his shoulder. "She died at the scene. But it was peaceful. Both Dora and Walter were at her side."

"You've got to be kidding me. *Dora* sat with *Nenita* while she died? I've awakened in an alternate universe." He paused. "You know who she was, don't you?"

Maddi nodded. "I know enough." She pulled herself up on her elbow and looked at him. "It's strange to see what happens when people are facing the end. It's beyond strange…it's magical. Like a lifetime of anger and hurt just disappears."

He frowned. "You could see all that just by watching my parents with Nenita?"

Maddi nodded as she lay next to him and stared at the ceiling. "Yes."

He grinned, trying to imagine his parents happy together again. Though they had put on a good show for most of his life, he had always thought that theirs was not a relationship to envy. But hearing Maddi speak of it now, it sounded as if things had changed…as if they had managed to somehow start over after all the pain.

He sighed. If only it was that simple. If only the pain he had caused had come from something as simple as a love affair. *My sins are so much worse.* They laid quietly for several minutes, then he said, "You sat here for five long months with nothing to do."

She laughed. "I had plenty to do. You've always been a fulltime job."

He chuckled in spite of himself. Though he didn't want to ask the next question, he knew he had to…he had to know. "So…have you read the journal?"

She looked up at him. "Just the first few entries. Like I told you in the dungeon, I won't read it until you can read it with me."

Henderson frowned. He had hoped that she had changed her mind and had read it…every last word. That she now knew everything there was to know about who he was and what he had done over the course of the last four years…that the fact that she was still at his side meant that she had forgiven him…for all of it.

But she hadn't read it. Which meant that she didn't know what he had done; who he had killed, the pain he had caused. And though the thought of holding her in his arms had been the only thing that had kept him breathing for the last five months…there was a part of him, a very small part, that had wanted her to read it so she would see him for who he was…and she would leave him. She would see that the man she had fallen in love with existed no more and she would leave him behind, finally realizing that she would be better off without him.

He pulled her closer, his eyes stinging at the thought of not having her next to him. But he knew, once she realized what he had done, she would be horrified. Even then, she would find a way to forgive him, because that was who she was, but she would be wrong to do so. The things he had done – the men he had killed – it was unforgivable. Though many of those men were evil, not all of them were. Martin Henderson had killed at least one good man…a peacemaker. Only a broken man could do such a thing, and there was no undoing it…no apology could ever make right the harm he had done and the pain he had caused. Maddi needed to know it…all of it…*so she will know the madman, the killer, that she is holding in her arms.*

He cleared his throat. "You should have read it, Maddi."

She turned onto her side so she was looking directly at him. "It won't change how I feel, Henderson."

He sighed. "Maybe it won't…but it should."

She moved even closer. His entire body tingled as he felt the warmth of her skin. She whispered. "You can't decide that for me. Only I can decide if your past matters to me." She sighed, "…just like only you can decide if my past matters to you."

He chuckled. "Your past? Maddi, I doubt you've done anything to be ashamed of in your entire life."

She said nothing. The silence felt odd…awkward. He was about to ask, "Have you?" when he thought better of it. After all, who was he to question anyone's past.

She sighed. "Maybe we both have things to share…or to hide." He was about to reply, when she kissed him long and hard, and he forgot all of it…his sins, her forgiveness. He pulled her closer, his heart pounding as he felt her in his arms. Again, the alarms went off, and again, Maddi pulled back and laughed. It was like music to his ears.

She laid next to him. "Henderson, whatever you've done, I'll find a way to forgive you…I promise. And it won't be hard." She leaned up and kissed him again, this time more cautiously. She sat back and smiled. "Why? Because I love you…so very much." She looked at him, her blue eyes glistening with years of unshed tears. "As a matter of fact, I already forgive you." She laughed. "There. It's done."

Henderson nodded, but he had to fight his own tears, for he knew, though she meant it, she wouldn't likely feel that way for long. *Once I remind her of what I've done.*

CHAPTER 27

Edinburgh, Scotland

Justice stared at a bit of the torn wallpaper where the wall met the ceiling. He had just returned to the sleazy hotel room and was sitting on the bed, unable to look away from the tragedy of the cheap wallpaper. He was looking forward to getting back to his London apartment with his Fratelli Basile four-poster bed and his sophisticated artwork.

But not until I straighten out this mess. The call from the American had thrown him. Not only because of the curious way the man had described himself, but because of his request. *"I need you to deliver a message."*

"What sort of message?"

"A warning."

"To whom?"

There had been a pause. When the man spoke again, he had changed his tone; he had become more confident, almost cocky… maybe even a bit angry. *"An American senator, Cynthia Madison."*

Justice had been taken aback when he had heard the woman's name. He knew Madison; not well, but better than many, mostly because he had done research on her not that long ago. The research had been done in March at her request. She was trying to learn the identity of a mystery stalker. Her Secret Service agents had determined that the stalker was in London, but had been unable to learn much more. Madison and her agents had flown to London hoping to find the man, but had been unsuccessful. Madison had consulted Justice and, true to form, he had uncovered the identity of her stalker. It was none other

165

than her biological daughter, Tonna, whom she had given up when she was only fifteen years old. Justice hadn't had a chance to tell her that, however, because soon after, he had once again lost time. He understood now that the loss of time represented the takeover of his psyche by Cobra, but he hadn't known it then. By the time he had managed to come back around as Justice, Madison had left town. He had tried to find her, but had been unable to do so before he changed once again into Cobra.

He wondered if she had ever learned that it was her own daughter stalking her. How lovely it would be to have an excuse to speak to her again. He had said as much to the mystery caller. *"I would be glad to deliver a message to that fine woman, sir, but how do I know that you are legitimate?"*

There had been a pause. *"I am closely tied to the upper echelons of America's government. I can direct you to a website that lists some of those for whom I work. On the site, they speak to my credibility. Would that satisfy your curiosity?"*

Justice didn't have a laptop; he barely had clothes. But he needed something to go on before he took on this man's request. *"Yes. I'm sure Princess Street has a library or a computer café. I'll call you back as soon as I review the information."*

"No, I'll call you in thirty minutes." The mysterious agent had given Justice an address and a password for the website, then he had ended the call.

Justice had found a key card on a table by the bed, had shoved it in his pocket, and had run out of the room, placing a "Do not disturb" sign on the door. He had taken the stairs to the lobby, which was in worse shape than the room, and had gone in search of a computer. He had found one ten minutes later at a library on Princess Street, and had instantly typed in the address. A page appeared with a logo for the United States Army. In the middle of the page was a blank line. Justice typed in the password, and was taken to another page with the same logo at the top, followed by a statement: "The names listed here serve as verification that the agent who reached out to you – a man who must remain anonymous – is working on behalf of the United States Government. He should be shown every courtesy." The statement had been followed by three names with corresponding signatures: Chairman of the Joint Chiefs, General Alexander Daniels; Director of Homeland Security, Jason Hanover; and the last name, which had definitely gotten

Justice's attention, Jerome Knight, Vice-President of the United States of America. Justice had gone so far as to look up the men's signatures on public documents, and was able to confirm that the signatures on the website were, at the least, a very close match.

But reading a statement followed by a list of prominent men in no way guaranteed that the caller was actually affiliated with them. *I must speak to at least one of them,* he had decided, and had quickly run back to the hotel.

He was sitting on the bed and staring at the wallpaper when his cellphone rang.

"Satisfied?"

Justice flinched. His fondness for the agent was decreasing by the minute. "I would like to speak to one of those men. My choosing."

There was a pause. "Time is short, Justice...but I guess I can make that happen. Who would you like to speak to?"

Justice considered it. *When in doubt, aim for the top.* "The VP...Mr. Knight."

Another pause. "Do you have a pen?"

"I don't need a pen. My memory is impeccable."

The agent rattled off a number. "Call him. I'll call you back in five minutes."

The call ended. Justice checked the time. It was ten a.m. in London, which meant it was only five a.m. in DC. *Hopefully, the chap is an early riser.* He dialed the number.

"The White House." came the reply. "How may I direct your call?"

The White House? Why not the Vice-President's office? "I...I apologize for the early hour, Ma'am, and I'm sure this is a bit irregular, but I would like to speak to...to your Vice-president. Is he available?"

"Your name, please?"

"Uh...Mark...Mark Justice, Private Inquiry Agent, London."

Justice could hear a shuffling of papers. "Yes, Mr. Justice. Your name is on our list of authorized individuals. Please hold."

Justice's eyes widened. *Authorized individuals?* He cleared his throat as he sat up straight and smoothed down his jacket.

"Mr. Justice?"

"Um...yes...yes sir. Is this Jerome Knight?"

"It is. I'm pleased you called."

Justice frowned. *You are?*

The man went on. "I only recently became aware of you...of your work for the Crown." He paused. "I would normally be at my office in the Eisenhower Building, but the President is leaving today to campaign out west, and I'm staying here so I can handle any emergencies that might come along."

"I...I see. It is awfully early in America, sir."

"Yes, I'm an early riser. It's good to get a jump on the day, wouldn't you agree?"

"Oh yes, most definitely, sir." Justice swallowed. "I'm calling in regard to an agent who reached out to me just moments ago. He was unwilling to give me his name."

"Yes, Mr. Justice. I am aware of the man. He's working on behalf of our government. I can't say much more, except that the message he is asking you to deliver is vital to U.S. security interests overseas. Does that help?"

Justice was stunned. "Yes...yes it does. Can I ask why the message is so vital?"

He heard a sigh. "Let's just say that it concerns the safety of several of our agents. I'm sure you can appreciate why we're eager for your help."

"Certainly, sir...Mr. Vice-President. I will do what I can."

"Thank you, Justice. Your assistance will not go unnoticed by our government."

The call ended. Justice stared at the phone. His hands were shaking. He had just spoken with America's Vice-President...or had he? It could still be a setup. Though by this point, it would have been quite an elaborate one. His phone rang and he answered.

"Now are you satisfied?"

"How do I know that the man I just spoke with was who he said he was?"

There was a pause. "Do you still have access to a computer?"

"No."

"Well, when you do, look up the number I had you call. You'll see that it does, in fact, connect directly to a private line of the White House." There was a pause. "Now, time is of the essence, Mr. Justice.

Ms. Madison is at Sacred Hearts Nursing Home, just off Trust Street in Edinburgh." He paused. "So, are you in Edinburgh or Manchester?"

Justice frowned. "How do you know that I am in either, sir?"

The man laughed; Justice liked him even less. "You forget that you told me in our first call that you thought you could find a computer on Princess Street. I can think of only two Princess Streets of significance. One is in Manchester, the other is in Edinburgh. Either way, you're within a few hours of the nursing facility by train. Am I right?"

Justice shook his head. *Lucky guess,* he thought, but was forced to admit to the man that he was in Edinburgh.

"Perfect." The agent paused. "Now, will you deliver my message?"

Justice cleared his throat. He had had about enough of the arrogant agent. "Are you aware, sir, that you are speaking to one of the most highly-regarded Private Inquiry Agents in the UK?"

There was a pause followed by a laugh. "I don't care who you are, Justice. But I'm glad you're well-credentialed. I'm sure it will be helpful as you carry out this task."

Justice bristled. The man's impudence was infuriating. "Tell me, sir, is it wise to trouble the dear senator with an obscure message as she recovers from whatever has put her in need of a nursing facility?"

A pause. "You refer to her as the 'dear senator.' Do you know her?"

Justice sighed. "As a matter of fact, I do."

"Intimately?"

Justice shifted uncomfortably. Though he would like to say yes, it would be a lie. "No, but I do know the woman...rather well."

"Good. That will be helpful." He paused. "Actually, that could be quite helpful down the line." Another pause. "But Madison isn't the one who's residing at the nursing home. There's a man there by the name of Matt Henderson. She's in love with him and refuses to leave his side, but her vigil is putting both of them in danger. And though I doubt you have any regard for Henderson, it is clear that you think highly of the senator."

Justice frowned. "Is that the message? That her devotion to Matt Henderson is putting them at risk?"

"No...not exactly. It's a bit more nuanced. I represent a group of men who know quite a bit about Henderson...his actions over the last four years...what he did in January, for example." He paused. "Your

task will be to convey to her that if she doesn't leave him…for good…
then all of it will be brought to light." He added. "And tell her that these
men also know about his family; his father, his mother…even his half-
brother."

Justice narrowed his eyes, his curiosity suddenly burning a hole in
his gut. "I see."

"I doubt you do. But I'm counting on you to do as I say,
regardless."

Justice was losing his patience with the man. "Though I'm not
above doing work for the good of those involved, or even for a friendly
government, can you tell me why I should do this? What is in it for me?"

There was a long pause, followed by another sigh. "Let's just say,
Justice, that those who don't do what I ask often end up floating in a
river."

Justice trembled in spite of himself. *The nerve,* he thought, though
something told him that the man had meant every word. "May I ask
why it is so important that Madison leave that man…for good, as you
say?"

Another sigh. "The safety of several of America's overseas
operatives requires it." Another pause. "So, are we agreed?"

"I have agreed to nothing."

"You're impertinent, Justice. I don't like impertinence." A pause.
"Regardless, I'm confident that you'll deliver the message, if for no other
reason than your fondness for Madison. Please know that the men I
represent could ruin not only Henderson, but your dear senator with a
few phone calls." Another pause. "One more thing. The message must
be delivered by noon today – your time – if you want to guarantee her
safety."

Justice frowned. "Why on earth must this message be delivered so
quickly?"

Another long pause. When the man spoke, his voice was even
colder than before. "Justice, if I say that it's urgent, then it is. So just
shut up and do as you're told."

Justice had to fight not to end the call right there. But he needed
to see if through, if for no other reason than to protect Cynthia
Madison. The man on the phone was clearly capable of hurting her. He
cleared his throat. "Where again will I find the senator?"

"Sacred Hearts Nursing Facility…just off Trust Street." He added, "Keep in mind, Justice, if you fail to do as I've asked, then you and the senator will be dead by nightfall."

The call ended. Justice stared at the phone. *What an obnoxious man.* Nonetheless, if what he had said was true, then Justice needed to get moving. It was after ten, which meant that he had less than two hours to write and deliver the message.

He leaned back and thought about the man who had made the call. He was clearly used to getting what he wanted. And Justice felt certain that, not only was he more than willing to follow through on his threat, but on some level, he would enjoy it.

He combed his fingers through his blond wig, irritated at the mystery agent, but pleased at the prospect of once again seeing the lovely Cynthia Madison. And now, because of the overbearing agent, he had two reasons to reach out to her. Not only to tell her the identity of her stalker, but to inform her of the American agent's threat.

But there was one thing he couldn't wrap his head around: the motive for the request. The agent had said that it was to keep foreign operatives safe. It had been confirmed by the Vice-president. But how did Madison sitting dutifully at the side of the ailing Matt Henderson jeopardize foreign agents? *Why does the U.S. Government care if the lovely senator is spending time at this man's side?* That was the real question, and, once Justice delivered the message, he would make a point of finding the answer.

CHAPTER 28

Washington, DC

Dr. Hank Clarkson sat in his second-floor office at Homeland Security with his computer in front of him. It was still dark outside, but it was no longer unusual for Hank to be at the office before the sun came up. He had been a Deputy Director with Homeland Security for just under a year, and on his watch, there had been a bioterror attack which had killed scores of Americans. He had been tasked with finding the culprit and bringing him to justice. He shook his head and frowned. *No big deal…just find the monster who unleashed a poison into four separate cities in America.*

He checked his watch; it was 4:30 in the morning. *I need coffee.* He stood and combed his fingers through his hair, noting for probably the fiftieth time that it was too long. The longer it got, the curlier it got, and he hated it. But he had had no time to get it cut. He had had little time to do anything other than look for a mass murderer.

As he walked out of his office, he checked his cellphone. He had received two calls the day before – from a number he didn't recognize – while he was in a briefing regarding new protocols to address the rising threat at the southern border. Whoever it was hadn't left a message, and he had decided to not call them back, thinking that if it was truly important, they would call again. There had been no further calls from the number, leaving him to conclude that it was likely either a wrong number or a telemarketer of some sort.

He walked into a nearby kitchenette and was glad to see that a pot of coffee had been brewed. There was only one other staffer there at that hour, a surveillance analyst who had been in his office since ten the night before. Hank poured two cups of coffee and took one to the analyst.

"Thanks, Dr. Clarkson."

"Don't mention it, Hal."

Hank walked back to his office and sat at his desk. Early yesterday, he had been notified that the Pentagon had uncovered a memo that more or less confirmed that the bioterror attacks in January had been carried out by the rogue agent, Phoenix. As the only physician in an administrative role, Hank had become the point man on the attacks. He had recently learned Phoenix's true identity from of all people, Maddi. As the police had been trying to secure the Dalgety Bay schoolhouse scene, Maddi had shared with Hank that Phoenix was actually Martin Henderson, who was currently pretending to be Matt Henderson, who at that time had been in the back of an ambulance on his way to the hospital. She had sworn Hank to secrecy, and, as far as he knew, he and Maddi were the only ones who knew Matt's true identity. Matt had fallen into a coma soon after that, and had yet to awaken. Hank knew he should inform his director of Phoenix's true identity; his obligation to the U.S. government should outweigh his promise to Maddi. But he had yet to do so. Was it blind devotion to Maddi? Or did it have something to do with the fact that Phoenix was being blamed for the bioterror attacks? Though Hank and Henderson hadn't always been on the best of terms, Hank felt certain, just as Maddi did, that Henderson couldn't have done it.

Most of those who were in charge saw it differently, however. Vials had been left at the scene of three of the attacks, and fingerprints on those vials belonged to Phoenix. And, unfortunately, the memo that had just come through seemed to bolster the case. Credited to a deceased Pentagon analyst, who, by coincidence, had been a member of a committee that Hank was also a part of, it had been found just days ago in a locked drawer of the man's desk. It had been handed over to Homeland Security sometime yesterday morning. It recapped the attacks, then described in detail the vials with Phoenix fingerprints. It also contained a link to video footage that placed Phoenix in each of the cities affected by the attack at the time they had taken place. Hank's boss, Jason Hanover, had called him with the news. *This reinforces that Phoenix was responsible for the attacks, Hank.* Hank felt certain that if

Hanover knew that Phoenix was Martin Henderson, he would agree that there was no way that Martin could be behind the attacks. But as much as Hank wanted to tell him Phoenix's true identity, he couldn't. Why? *Because Maddi asked me not to.*

He ran his hands through his thinning hair and sighed. He was tired. His office had been nothing but chaos for the past eight months, and not just because of the terror attacks. So much had happened since January; the annihilation of an entire village in Argentina, the murder of America's Secretary of State in London, multiple attempts on Maddi's life, and – last but not least – the detention of seven notable people in an isolated schoolhouse in Dalgety Bay, Scotland. It was like the world had gone mad. And with all that chaos came an increasing number of threats against America, many of them up to him to assess. And the stress of it was showing. His large frame, already primed for arthritis by years of abuse on a college football field, had begun to ache, especially the leg that had been shot by Maddi's would-be kidnapper at the Queen's Ball five months ago. He rubbed it as he stared at his screen, which displayed a copy of the memo. It was damning, of that there was no doubt. Giving dates and video evidence, it put Phoenix at every one of the sites directly before and after each attack. It mentioned the fingerprints, then went on to describe the terrorist as six-four with blond hair and scars on his hands and face. Hank sighed. *A perfect description of Martin Henderson.*

He turned off the computer. He needed a walk. He was about to get up, when he glanced at a photo on his desk. He grinned. It was a new one, added a few months ago, shortly after returning from France....

'Will she be waiting?' Four simple words that suddenly meant everything as Hank did his best to push the Eurostar to Paris. He had been forced to stay an extra two days in Dalgety Bay – Hanover's instructions – to tie up loose ends about all that had happened both there and in Lyon. He hadn't wanted to stay; he had wanted to get back to Jenny, who had promised to wait for him in Paris, beneath the Eiffel Tower, every day at noon. But she had also said that she wouldn't wait forever.

It had been a remarkable turn of events. After all, he and Jenny had been divorced for sixteen years. But their time at the bedside of their son, Roger, as he was recovering from a near-fatal bout with Cobra, had brought them together, and, in the course of watching and waiting, they had fallen in love all over again. But Hank had felt compelled to follow Roger when he left the hospital, to have his back should he once again come up against Cobra. He and Jenny had said their goodbyes in the middle of a Paris hotel lobby. That was when she had told him she would wait for him...but not forever.

'Like something out of a damned movie,' he thought, as he checked the time. It was 11:10. The train was on time, but he would be pushing it to get to the Eiffel Tower by noon. His cellphone had died and he didn't have a charger. He didn't know Jenny's number to call from a land line...which meant that there had been no way to get word to her that he was coming. Would she wait? Or had she already waited too long?

He saw the outskirts of Paris and his heart pounded. He tapped the armrest as he saw the Arc de Triomphe looming in the distance. 'I'm close.'

The Eurostar pulled into the station and came to a stop. He waited impatiently for the passengers to leave the train, then jumped from the top stair, running past them to the terminal. He had rehearsed the route from a map he had grabbed in London, and, as he reached the front of the station, he burst through the doors, turned left, and sprinted to the La Chapelle train station. He boarded a train to Charles De Gaulle Etoiles, then took a bus to Trocadero, getting off on the other side of the river. This put him directly across from the Eiffel Tower. He ran through the Trocadero Gardens, reaching the base of the Tower just as a tower rang out the first of twelve chimes. He looked everywhere for the familiar brown hair but couldn't find Jenny. There were tourists covering every square inch, and he had a hard time scanning the faces. He walked around the tower, then underneath it, shoving his way through the crowd. He yelled, "Jenny! Jenny Clarkson!" but other than a few stares from passersby, there was nothing. After fifteen minutes of pacing and looking and pacing some more, he sat on a bench under the tower. He was exhausted. He hadn't had any real sleep in days. He leaned forward with his elbows on his knees and rested his head in his hands. Jenny was gone; she hadn't waited. He couldn't blame her. After all, she had waited sixteen years.

He shook his head. It was time to go home...time to get back to his life. But that life had changed...dramatically. Maddi was gone, and he had blown it with Jenny. And Roger was hunting a killer. What life was he going back to?

"Why bother?" he said aloud, ignoring the glare of a woman standing next to him.

A soft voice said lightly, "Well, it depends."

He didn't look up; he was sure he had imagined it. 'I'm just tired,' he thought. He waited; he heard it again. "I mean, if 'why bother?' means why did you run halfway across Europe? The answer is 'for the love of our son.'" There was a pause. "On the other hand, if 'why bother?' means, why did I come back to Paris?' Well, I hope the answer is…for me."

Hank looked up, the sunlight blocking his view. He shielded his eyes and grinned. It was Jenny. "You waited."

She nodded. "Of course, I waited."

He took her hand and pulled her beside him. "Actually, the 'why bother' was in reference to the table I reserved at L'Arpege Restaurant for tonight at 7:30." He smiled. "Because I've just remembered – you don't even like French food."

She laughed and his heart skipped a beat. "Well, it's the strangest thing. I've recently acquired a taste for foie gras."

"Good. There's only one problem. I've got nothing to wear."

"Then let's go shopping…"

Hank grinned. They had shopped and then they had rested before dinner. Well, they hadn't actually rested. He chuckled as he stood and walked to the window. Yes, the world was going to hell, but he hadn't been this happy for quite some time. He was glad to be back in DC and had no plans of leaving, other than to visit Jenny in Ohio.

His phone rang. "Clarkson here."

"Hank, it's Hanover. You need to go to Edinburgh."

"As in Scotland?"

"Yes."

Why?"

"I just got a call from an Edinburgh long-term-care facility. Matt Henderson woke up from his coma about thirty minutes ago." There was a pause. "You need to go over there and question him about the bioterrorist attacks."

Why would I question Matt? Does Hanover know that he's actually Martin? "What're you talking about, Hanover? Matt had nothing to do with those attacks."

Hanover paused. "Yeah, well…maybe he did." Another pause. "You know that memo I sent you last night?"

"Yeah."

"Well, there was a second memo. It said that Matt Henderson was involved."

"Why didn't you tell me about a second memo?"

"Because to put it bluntly, I don't believe it."

"I don't either...not for a second." He paused. "Involved how?"

"You remember Morningstar, don't you?"

"Edward Morningstar...from the Pentagon?"

"Yes."

"I remember him, but I don't really trust the guy, Hanover."

"Me either, but he's our liaison on the terror attacks. The second memo he sent over implies that Matt was instrumental in helping Phoenix pull off the attacks."

That makes no sense...they're the same man! "There's no way, Hanover. Matt Henderson risked his life to save Roger. He's one of the good guys."

"I know. And I thought it wouldn't matter, since Matt had been in a coma for so long." Hanover cleared his throat. "But now that he's awake, Morningstar insists that we bring him to the States for questioning." There was a pause. "Just fly over and talk to the guy. If you get the vibe that he's innocent, then leave him alone." Another pause. "But if he knows anything...anything at all...you'll need to bring him back."

Hank wanted to kick something. "Hanover, Morningstar's an ass."

"I know. But being an ass doesn't disqualify him from issuing orders...or at least requests."

"I don't think this is necessary."

"Me either. But I have a plane waiting for you at Andrews Airforce Base."

CHAPTER 29

Edinburgh, Scotland

Justice sighed as he paced the ten-by-ten hotel room. Though the agent had said that time was of the essence, Justice had yet to leave his room. Why? Because just as he had been about to walk out, it had occurred to him that not only was he the respectable Mark Justice, but he was also a serial killer by the name of Cobra. Were the authorities aware? Had Samuels told them of the dual identities? If so, they could be waiting for him. It was quite possible that the American agent was simply luring him into a trap.

I'll need a disguise. He looked down at his crumpled suit and sighed. He didn't have time to pull together an elaborate disguise. It was already 10:30. *This will have to do,* he thought as he smoothed down the wrinkles on the sleeves and lapels, then did the same with the pants. He would pick up a hat and a pair of dark glasses at the station. Hopefully, that would be good enough to at least get him to Trust Street.

The nursing home was on the other side of town. Though the train would take a few minutes longer than a taxi, he felt it was his best bet to avoid being identified. Cab drivers were often alerted of criminals on the run.

Luckily, the train station wasn't far. If he hurried, he might be able to catch the 11:15 train, which would have him outside the nursing home by 11:50 at the latest. *Then what?* Would he simply walk in and give Madison the message? *Of course not.* If Samuels had told police that Justice was also the Cobra, then, even with a hat and dark glasses, he was likely to be caught. It was a sure bet that after the Dalgety Bay attack,

178

Madison's bodyguards had been warned to be on the lookout for a man fitting Justice's description.

He frowned. *So, I'll buy a windbreaker, as well…and try to get the message to Madison when her agents aren't nearby.* He shook his head. Her agents were always nearby. Maybe he could greet her as she was coming out of someplace private; a bathroom, for example. Again, he shook his head. *Not if Spencer Seacroft is still her bodyguard.* Seacroft had come with Madison to Justice's office in March; he would surely recognize Justice, no matter what disguise he wore or where he met the senator. Assuming the agent was aware of his and Cobra's shared identity, he would detain Justice on the spot. *So, the first thing I need to do is find out if Seacroft is still Madison's bodyguard.* He nodded. *My secretary Sally can find out for me.*

But he needed to go if he hoped to catch the 11:15 train. *I'll call her on the way.* He was about to leave the hotel room when, at the last minute, he grabbed the paper bag from the rubbish can. It held the empty contact lens casings, as well as tags from the wig and gloves. Not only would those items have fingerprints, but they might also imply a disguise…a disguise he was counting on to get him at least as far as the nursing home.

He walked to the door, took a final look back to make sure he had left nothing behind, then left the hotel room and took the stairs to the lobby. He walked out the front door and turned right, dropping the paper bag in a large garbage bin several blocks away. He was glad that the train station was only a mile-and-a-half from the hotel.

On the way, he stopped at a stationary shop in downtown Edinburgh. He bought a quill, black ink, and gold-embossed note cards on high-quality paper. *If I'm going to write a letter to a proper woman, I must do so properly.*

He left the shop and resumed his walk to the station. He pulled out his cellphone and dialed the number he knew so well; the number for Justice Enterprises. As it began to ring, it occurred to him that after such a long absence, it was quite possible that his secretary had given up on him and had quit. Fortunately, because such absences were becoming more common, he had arranged to have all his personal and professional bills – including Sally's salary – on automatic payments with the bank. His account was well-funded as a result of the success of

Justice Enterprises, and the bank would use that account to make the payments. *So, at least Sally will have been paid while I was away.*

It continued to ring, and he began to get nervous. Just as he was about to hang up, the cockney voice he remembered so fondly said, "Justice Enterprises, may I 'elp ye?"

Justice smiled. "Sally, it's me…it's Justice."

There was a pause, then a tear-filled voice said, "Oh my God, Mr. Justice. I thought for sure ye were dead. Are ye doin' okay? Where 'ave ye been?"

Justice laughed in spite of himself. "I'm fine, Sally. I just had some things to take care of. It took longer than I thought. Have I received any messages?"

"Blimey, Mr. Justice, ye have quite a few, I'm afraid."

"I see. Can you give me just the most urgent for now? I'll try to get to the office later this week to address the rest of them."

"Certainly, sir." There was a pause as she rifled through papers. "Scotland Yard called a couple of times. An Inspector Perkins would like to speak to you."

Justice frowned. *Where is Pritchard?* He was about to ask, when she added, "…and a psychiatrist has left at least five messages. He would like for you to call him."

"Samuels?"

"Why, yes sir. Do you need the number?"

"Yes. My cellphone screen is cracked and I can't read any of my contacts."

Sally rattled off the number; Justice memorized it with little trouble. She went on. "And ye got a message from the States, sir…from a Pentagon aide."

Justice's eyes narrowed. *Another American. A coincidence?* He picked up his pace as he turned onto Princess Street. "Did he leave his name? Or why he was calling?"

"No, sir, 'e just asked for you to call whene'er ye got in."

"Can you give me his number?"

Sally rattled it off; again, Justice memorized it. "Anything else, Sally?"

"Ye got an interestin' message about an hour ago…an invitation, actually."

"An invitation?"

"Yes sir. From a Walter 'enderson. 'e asked that ye join him at a coin jubilee on the 30th of October."

Justice's eyes widened. *Henderson…is he related to the man lying in Sacred Hearts Nursing Home?* Suddenly he felt a sharp pain in his temple and put a hand to his head. *No…I can't have a headache now!* He managed to say, "Did he leave a number?"

"No, sir. 'e simply asked that ye meet 'im in Aberdeen, outside the gate at Hazlehead Park on Saturday, October 30th at noon"

Justice quickened his pace even more, still rubbing his temple as he memorized the information, tucking it away with the phone numbers she had given him. "One more thing, Sally. Can you maybe tell me… what day it is?"

There was a pause. "What day it is, sir? Why, it's Tuesday, 24, August, 2004." Another pause. "Are ye sure yer alright, sir?"

The end of August…dear God! I have, indeed, lost the summer! "Uh…yes, I'm fine, Sally. I couldn't read the date on my phone, and my watch says it's the 25th. I wanted to double check." He forced a laugh. "Glad I did." He cleared his throat. "Any other urgent messages?"

"I wouldn't say they're urgent, sir." She went on to list several more, all from people seeking help to find a lost loved one, or to address their suspicions regarding a philandering spouse. But Justice barely heard her; he was still processing the fact that Walter Henderson had invited him to an event; a coin show of all things. He recognized the name, though he wasn't sure how. He felt like it was important…like it mattered. And what a coincidence that in the last hour he had been asked – ordered – to address a matter regarding another Henderson.

"Is there anything else, sir?"

"Yes, Sally, it's actually the reason I called. I need to know if Senator Cynthia Madison from America still has Secret Service Agent Spencer Seacroft protecting her."

"Okay, sir, but 'ow do I find that information?"

He hesitated. Though he was leery of giving Sally access to his computer, it was the only way he would learn what he needed to know. "Sally, what I'm about to have you do is confidential." He had reached Waverly Station, but stopped short of the door, moving to an alcove so no one could hear him. "The minute you complete this task, I'll need you to forget whatever you find, as well as the passwords I gave you. Understand?"

There was a pause. "Why, yes sir. I'll do exactly as ye say."

"Excellent. I want you to go to my computer and type the following." He waited for her to walk into his office and turn on his computer.

"I'm ready, sir."

He walked her through his three-step login, giving her the proper password as she reached each page. When she had completed the login, he said, "Now, at the top of the page, I want you to type in the website for the U.S. Secret Service." He gave her the agency's address, along with the password, praying silently that it hadn't changed since he had hacked the site back in March. He waited as she frantically typed on the keyboard.

"Okay, sir, I'm…I'm in."

"Good. Now, do you see a tab that says 'Protectees?'"

"Yes sir."

"Click it and type in the name Cynthia Madison." He waited.

"Okay sir."

"There should be two agents listed beside her name." Again, he waited.

"Yes…yes sir. There is a Thomas Cravens and a Lawrence Cross."

Justice sighed, relieved. No Seacroft. But he was curious as to what had happened to the affable agent who had sat across from him not so long ago. *You can look into all of it, Justice, once you get this damn message delivered.*

"Is that all, sir?"

"Yes, Sally, thank you."

He ended the call and leaned against the wall outside the station, reviewing the messages. The psychiatrist was no surprise; Justice had confided in the man not so long ago, and had found the doctor to be remarkably kind. As for Scotland Yard, he could only imagine what they might want. Inspector Perkins had either learned the truth about Justice's alter ego and wanted to bring in Justice as a way to get to Cobra, or the Yard needed his help as they had in the past to find the elusive killer.

Justice closed his eyes, trying to get a sense for where Cobra might be or what he might have done for the past five months. He had always had a sixth sense about Cobra, and of course, now he knew why. But for some reason, he saw nothing; he felt nothing. It was as if Cobra had disappeared. Was it too much to hope that maybe the killer was gone for good? Justice shook his head and sighed. *Cobra won't die until someone kills him.*

But it was the invitation by Walter Henderson that puzzled him the most. An unexpected and curious request. Should he go? Walter hadn't left a callback number. Had that been purposeful? Justice sighed. The jubilee wasn't to take place until the 30th of October, which meant that he had plenty of time to look into it. *And look into it, I will.*

Suddenly he shivered. *But...what if I'm not...me...in October?* It was quite possible that Justice may have reverted back to his Cobra persona by then. If so, he might miss the chance to meet the curious Walter Henderson...at a coin show, no less. The invitation implied that Walter was aware of Justice's interest in coins. Had Samuels told him? *If so, what else did Samuels share with him?* He frowned. Was Walter's invitation simply a way to lure Justice to the jubilee, so the authorities could, in turn, nab Cobra?

He heard a tower clock begin to chime. *Eleven...I need to hurry.* He again smoothed down his suitcoat and walked into the station, pondering the urgency of delivering his message to Madison by noon. What was the significance of noon? Was it possible that at that hour something bad would happen to Matt? *Or to the lovely senator?*

He stopped at a sundry shop, and purchased a hat, dark glasses, and a charcoal-colored windbreaker. He put on the hat and glasses, then pulled on the windbreaker as he ran to the ticket counter. He waited in line, catching his breath as he adjusted the glasses on the bridge of his long, narrow nose. He looked down at the windbreaker and scoffed. His flimsy disguise might keep him from inviting scrutiny in the station or on the train, but it wouldn't get him past Madison's bodyguards, regardless of who they were. Not if they had been instructed to look for a tall man with shoulder-length blond hair and blue eyes. He shook his head. It was time to face the truth. To confront Madison directly would be a risk he simply couldn't take.

He reached the counter, bought his ticket and ran for the train. As he climbed aboard, he sighed sadly. *Which means, unfortunately, I will have to find someone else to deliver the message to Ms. Madison.*

CHAPTER 30

Washington, DC

Morningstar sat at his desk in his corner office of the Pentagon and checked the Homeland website for the fifth time that morning. *Finally!* he thought, as he read through a memo that had been posted ten minutes ago. It stated that the Department had received a lead regarding the January bioterror attacks, and was assigning an agent to investigate.

It was the first step in Morningstar's clever but convoluted plan. Assigning an agent to investigate meant they had signed on to the premise of the documents he had given them yesterday. He had dropped off the papers after his meeting with the Bentley Group. They were the same documents he had presented to the group, and he had asked the Homeland secretary to give them directly to Hanover. The first document reinforced Phoenix's involvement in the Lassa fever attacks, the second one implied that Matt Henderson had aided and abetted his efforts. Morningstar knew that Hanover would have no choice but to assign an agent to look into it. How could he not? Matt had just become a possible accessory to the worst bioterror attack in U.S. history. *Now, if Henderson will just wake up so they can send that agent over there to bring him back to the States.*

But how would Morningstar know when he awoke? He had had Pocks put a bug in the room the day before and, though it had given him a treasure trove of information regarding Cynthia Madison, it had quit working sometime during the night, leaving him blind and deaf as to what was happening in that room. Which meant that he would have no way of knowing if or when his prodigal son awoke. Then again, if

185

he was to learn that the Homeland agent had boarded a plane to Scotland, he would have a pretty good idea.

Though the website hadn't indicated which agent was being assigned, he had every reason to think it would be Dr. Hank Clarkson. The Deputy Director had served as the liaison between Homeland and the Pentagon during January's Lassa fever attacks; his knowledge of the case was extensive. Morningstar was counting on it being Clarkson. Why? He chuckled. *Because he's the one man that both Henderson and Madison trust.*

He leaned back in his chair and kicked his feet on his desk. He had always known that Clarkson would come in handy. He laughed. *It's why I haven't killed him...yet.* But he would need to kill the man soon...he would have no choice.

About a year ago, Morningstar had formed a committee which he claimed would aid in the War on Terror. No one had questioned it; the country's fear of another attack far outweighed anyone's cynicism over yet another secret committee. The premise was that they could share sensitive information without alarming the public. But it's true purpose was to give Morningstar access to those within the government who could reveal secrets that would allow him to expand his reach around the world. It had worked. He had learned more from that committee than he could ever have learned on his own.

But there had been one problem. The more he used the information, the more the members began to question if they had a mole within the committee. A CIA agent had shared that his agency had secretly infiltrated a cartel in Argentina and, within days, there was an attack on the nearby village of Mariupol. The Secretary of State had mentioned an effort by Scottish Nationalists to seek independence, and days later, the brutal murder of a Scottish Nationalist aroused the passions and ire of the Scottish people.

It had been effective, but it was dangerous. Which was why, once he had gotten what he needed from the members, he had decided to slowly, carefully kill them off.

And it had been easy. The first to go had been a man from his own Pentagon; an underling who had been asked to do an audit of Morningstar's department. The man was a bit overweight; a perfect candidate for a 'heart attack' as he was out jogging one cold morning in

November. It was his death that Morningstar had used – nine months later – to plant evidence that implicated Matt Henderson in the January bioterror attacks. *Never let a murder go to waste.* The second committee member to go was an FBI agent with a poorly hidden history of drinking. Morningstar had had Simeon remove the brake fluid from his car while the man was inside a bar, then wait for him to crash on his way home on a snowy Christmas Eve. No one even questioned it. As for the killing of the third member, it was, ironically, Cynthia Madison who had unwittingly set the stage. In January she had put together a retreat for high-ranking officials. Because of its prominent nature, the CIA had decided to have a presence there. Simeon's sarin gas – though it didn't kill Madison – did kill two agents, and was the perfect cover for the murder of the committee's CIA agent. The fourth member, Secretary of State Jane Harper, had also had a well-timed death. Cobra, who had been working for Morningstar at the time, had been running roughshod through the UK. His killing of Harper was simply in keeping with his tirade across the British Isles. The fifth murder, this time involving the director of the international sector of America's TSA, had been made to look like a suicide. The woman, who had a history of depression, chose a rainy May afternoon to hang herself. Though her family had insisted her death be investigated, there was little to dispute. Simeon had forced her to write a suicide note by holding a gun to her head, and had then proceeded to hang her. But Morningstar couldn't allow her contribution to go to waste. So, before Simeon had put her head in the noose, he had made her sign off on the release of an internationally-sanctioned airline mechanic's uniform and badge, that would allow the wearer and bearer onto any airport tarmac in the Western world...a useful tool for sure.

Five of the eight had now effectively been taken out.

Which left only himself and two others...a Secret Service agent whose value would soon become apparent, and Homeland's Deputy Director, Dr. Hank Clarkson. Why had Morningstar spared Clarkson? *For times like this...when what's needed is a man both Henderson and Madison can trust.* And from the look of things, Morningstar's restraint had borne fruit. Did Clarkson know that Matt was really Martin? It didn't matter. Assuming he was, in fact, the agent assigned to investigate Henderson, the second memo had basically ordered him to bring Matt to the States for questioning the minute he awoke from his coma. The fact that Clarkson was Henderson's onetime friend and his lover's former lover would inspire Henderson and Madison to trust him…at least long enough to get Henderson to America. They would assume that Hank could protect him from any overbearing interrogators. Morningstar chuckled. *And, of course, they will be wrong.*

As for the next part of his plan; it had fallen into place completely by accident. It had involved Gad's revelation regarding the shared psyche between Cobra and Justice. Though Morningstar had been skeptical, the minute he had dialed Cobra's number and the man had called himself Justice, he had known that Gad's suspicions were correct. The man on the other end of that line truly did believe he was Mark Justice. Morningstar had instantly seen an opportunity. Why not utilize Justice to deliver his message to Madison? Not only would Morningstar not have to deal with Cobra's insubordination, but Justice had said that he had met the woman, and that he *"…knew her better than most."* If that was true – and Morningstar had no reason to think that it wasn't – then a warning from Justice would be far more convincing than a threat from someone she feared.

Morningstar was eager to learn how well the PI did, in fact, know Madison. Could he possibly shed some light on her mysterious encounter with an Indiana cop over two decades ago? He would explore it more once his current plans were in play.

Justice was clearly no slouch. He had insisted on having some form of verification before proceeding with Morningstar's request. Morningstar hadn't been unraveled by it; as a matter of fact, he had quickly pulled together a rather ingenious plan. Within minutes of his initial call with Justice, while the Private Investigator was off finding a computer, Morningstar had had Levi construct the website with the names of the three men who could vouch for the 'mysterious agent.' He had then called Knight, telling him that a Mark Justice might call for confirmation. As for the other two – Homeland's Director Hanover and Morningstar's boss, General Daniels – Morningstar had enough clout to pull their strings if the need arose. He was the spokesperson for Daniels; he could vouch for absolutely anything on that man's behalf. As for Hanover, Morningstar could easily tell the director that he was overseeing a top-secret mission and needed his support on a verification call. But that would have been pushing things. Morningstar didn't like to ask for favors…especially from an agency administrator whom he despised. Luckily, Justice had chosen the highest-ranking of the men – Jerome Knight – to verify the American agent's legitimacy, and the Vice-President had played his role perfectly.

So now, I simply wait…for Levi to learn more about Madison's secret, and for Justice to deliver the letter that will compel the bitch to leave Henderson.

He sat back and grinned. Why was it so important that Madison leave Henderson? Because Henderson alone could never convince anyone of Morningstar's misdeeds. To be believable, he would have to admit his own crimes and risk shaming his family and losing his freedom, if not his life. But if he were to share what he knew with Madison – a respected U.S. senator who already had it in for Morningstar – it was possible that she would be able to convey Morningstar's transgressions in a way that would be believable. Not only that; it was clear by her unwavering devotion to a man who had lain in a coma for nearly half a year, that leaving him would devastate her, and render her useless…at least for the foreseeable future. As for Henderson, he would awaken from his coma not to the face of the woman he loved, but to the knowledge that she had left him. He laughed. *It will destroy him…it will destroy both of them.*

He stood and walked to the window, staring out at the darkness as he considered the only potential flaw to his plan. What if Henderson never awoke from his coma. Or, worse yet, what if he died? Morningstar shivered and hiked his collar. He had been forced to consider the possibility ever since he had learned that Matt was, in fact, Martin. Though it would eliminate any chance of Henderson betraying Morningstar's secrets, it would also eliminate any chance of Morningstar being the one to kill him. If Martin Henderson died from whatever Cobra had done to him, then that would mean that Cobra had basically been the one to kill him. *And – per God – that is supposed to be my job.*

Morningstar had also been forced to consider the fact that, if Henderson did come out of the coma, Madison might be too weak to leave him. She was, after all, a woman, and she was clearly in love with him. What if she decided that it was better to stay with him and have his life ruined, than leave him and have her life ruined? To counter that possibility, Morningstar had come up with an insurance policy to practically guarantee that the lovers would split. While Madison was weighing whether or not to leave Henderson, Morningstar would find a way to convince Henderson that it was in Madison's best interest that *he* leave *her*.

He laughed. *My version of "The Gift of the Magi."*

But it wouldn't be easy to convince a man like Henderson to leave the woman he loved. He had learned long ago that the only thing that could motivate Henderson was a threat to someone he cared about. And that was where Madison's curious 'secret' had come into play. Immediately after the second call to Justice, Morningstar had put in a call to Pocks. He had faxed him a letter written in his own hand that basically told Henderson that he knew secrets about Madison that would destroy her. He mentioned a cop – to give it validity should Henderson share it with Madison – then finished with, *"...leave her forever, or I'll ruin her."* Though he had been hesitant to handwrite it, he knew it was the only way to convince Henderson that he did, in fact, have the information he claimed. *One thing I never do is bluff.* Henderson would know that; Morningstar had drilled it into him repeatedly. Morningstar had sent the letter to Pocks by way of a fax machine, and had told Pocks to hand Matt the letter the minute he awoke from his coma.

"What if he doesn't wake up?"

Morningstar had bristled. *"Then you won't deliver the damn letter, Pocks!"*

"But how will I know he's awake?"

That was when Morningstar remembered the broken listening device. Could he risk sending Pocks into the room one more time to fix it? He had decided not to. It would be a mistake to create suspicion around Pocks before he was able to deliver the letter. He had chosen, instead, to put Janet on full alert. *"Monitor Homeland's website, and let me know if you see any activity regarding an agent's sudden trip to Scotland."* He had told Pocks to wait for his word. Once he could verify that Matt was awake, Pocks was to find an excuse to go into his room and wait for that second when he was alone. *"Give him the letter, let him read it, then grab it and get the hell out of there."* He had added, *"...and grab the bugging device, too. I don't want anyone finding it and suspecting foul play."*

Pocks had agreed in his typical timid fashion. *"Okay...I'll do it."*

Morningstar chuckled. Everything was in place. Assuming Matt woke up, Madison would leave him to keep him from being punished for his crimes, and he would leave Madison to keep her secret from being revealed. But there was still one final challenge: Walter Henderson. Morningstar knew, if Matt awoke and an agent came to take him to America, Walter would move heaven and earth to try to stop him. Which meant that Morningstar would need to distract Walter. He felt there was only one thing that could compel Walter to leave his son's side long enough for Morningstar's plan to be put into place. And that was an attack on his beloved Latvia. *So, bring on the bombs!*

But he couldn't wait until Matt was awake. He needed the attack to take place as soon as possible if he was to ensure that Walter was out of the way if and when the agent came for his son.

The assault would be carried out by a private team of mercenaries, a ragtag group of disaffected former soldiers whom Morningstar had groomed to be one of the most capable tactical teams ever assembled. "Jacob's Ladder," he called them, and they had trained nearly all of his 'sons' over the years. More importantly, they had been pivotal in spurring uprisings in foreign lands. And now they would do it again by attacking Riga, the capital city of Latvia. A member of the Bentley Group would supply them with Russian ammunition, and they would take advantage of the insurgents who lived in Latvia. The attack would convince Walter – and the world – that Putin had finally pulled the trigger on his longstanding desire to restore the former USSR. Morningstar laughed. *And then...Walter will rush home to save a country that no one gives a damn about.*

He checked the time. Six a.m. The assault was to begin in a matter of hours. General Daniels would be notified the minute the attack was underway, which meant that Morningstar, as his aide, would be notified, as well...possibly even before the general.

He walked back to his desk and pulled a cigar from his briefcase. Ignoring a 'no smoking' sign posted outside the door, he clipped the end and lit it. He breathed in, embracing the rich aroma as it filled the room. *The smell of victory,* he thought as he walked back to the window. He stared out at a small courtyard, appreciating the sun's first rays on bold azaleas which were in full bloom around the patio. He grinned as he puffed his cigar. Things were going well. Assuming Matt awoke from his coma, Morningstar would destroy both him and Madison, not by killing them, but by taking the one thing from them they couldn't live without: their love for one another.

He laughed. *Then I'll kill them.*

His private cellphone vibrated. He pulled it from his pocket and checked caller ID. He grinned. *Janet.* "Yes?"

"I've got some news."

Morningstar's heart began to pound. "What is it?"

"He's awake."

Morningstar closed his eyes; his entire body had begun to shake. "When?"

"About forty minutes ago. An alert from the State Department."

"Excellent!" he said, his heart beating out of his chest. Suddenly, he frowned. "But why was the State Department made aware?"

"Because of an alert that was sent to Homeland, which I'm guessing had something to do with the documents you left for the Director yesterday. Apparently, Homeland reached out to State requesting a transport plane," she laughed again, "…believe it or not, the agencies really do communicate."

He chuckled. "Yes, I guess they do."

She cleared her throat. "But here's the part I think you'll like even more." She paused "Deputy Director Hank Clarkson has just been slated to travel on that transport plane – equipped with a full medical team – to Edinburgh, Scotland. It's on its way as we speak."

Morningstar's eyes widened. *Shit…I did it! I got an entire government agency to do my bidding.* He started to laugh, then fell into a coughing fit from the cigar smoke.

"Are you okay, baby?"

He recovered and cleared his throat. "Oh yes, girl, I'm perfect." He shook his head and smiled. "Good work, Janet." Seductively, he added, "I'll reward you later."

He ended the call. It was done. Not only were Henderson and Madison about to be undone by their secrets and decimated by the ending of their love affair, but Matt Henderson, aka Martin, aka Phoenix, aka Joseph was on his way home.

CHAPTER 31

Edinburgh, Scotland

Maddi could barely contain her joy. Any exhaustion she had felt over the past several hours had been replaced by the exuberance of Henderson's return. But with his return had come doctors and nurses who were now hovering over their beleaguered patient, and she found herself resenting the fact that she couldn't be alone with this man who she had yearned to be with for so long. *"Everybody, just get out of here!"* she wanted to scream. But of course, she couldn't. The man had nearly died several times on their watch. She knew that they would do whatever it took to keep him alive.

She checked the time. Nearly noon. He had been awake for about two hours. It was a good sign. He seemed far more alert this time compared to the last time he had come out of the coma. His smile had overwhelmed her; she had felt like her heart was going to burst. She had climbed in next to him and had never wanted to leave. But after a few quick hugs and hurried kisses, the nurses had relegated her to a corner of the room.

Which was where she had been now for well over an hour, pasted against the wall, watching as others attended to the man she longed to be holding in her arms.

"Maddi, let's go for a walk." It was Cravens. He was standing at the door with his jacket over his arm. "You could use some fresh air, don't you think?"

Maddi was about to decline, when she looked again at the swarm of medical staff hovering over Henderson. Two more doctors had joined the group, and they gave no indication they were leaving any time soon. She was only going to grow more frustrated as she stood there doing nothing. She sighed. "Okay, but we can't be gone long."

He nodded. "Fair enough."

She grabbed her jacket, along with the scarf Kauffold had given her, and walked to the foot of Henderson's bed. "I'll be right back," she mouthed over the shoulder of a doctor who was leaning over Henderson with a stethoscope glued to his chest. Henderson nodded and smiled; again, her heart felt like it might burst.

She and Cravens left the room and walked to the elevator. They took it to the first floor and walked outside. Maddi was surprised to feel rays of sunlight on her face for the first time in days. It felt like an omen. As they crossed a wide, four-lane highway, she breathed in the cool, crisp air and smiled. *Henderson is back...he'll be waiting for me – arms ready – when I return from this walk.* It seemed fleeting and unreal...like a hummingbird that flies off before one has a chance to acknowledge that it's there. Would Henderson 'fly off?' She shook her head determinedly...*no, not this time.*

They walked a block-and-a-half to Pittencrieff Park, the same park where she and Tonna had taken their many walks over the past four months. As they passed through the gate, she smiled. After years of solitude, her life was finally falling into place. Her child had come back to her, and now so had the man she had loved for what felt like a lifetime.

Her feet seemed to glide over the gravel as she and Cravens walked without a word, their silence a testament to the vigil they had been a part of for so long...as if they were honoring the magnitude of what had happened. For five full months not only Maddi, but Cravens, too, had waited for Henderson to wake up; every day starting with a faint glimmer of hope, every night ending with the realization that he might never come back.

But now, finally, he had.

Maddi looked up. The sun was working hard to hold its place in the clouds. And it looked to her like it was winning. Could it be that Edinburgh might actually have a sunny afternoon? She laughed at the thought as more and more sunlight broke through, warming the air. Scotland rarely saw temperatures above sixty-five degrees, even in

August, but the sun's rays made it feel like summer in DC. She closed her eyes, soaking it in.

"Ouch!" she said, wincing as she felt the sudden poke of a rake handle in her side.

"Oh…excuse me, Madam…I am so sorry." The man, short and unassuming in a pair of khakis and a wool coat, was carrying a bucket, along with the rake that had poked her. He bowed, then bowed again. "I…I am so clumsy…so very sorry, Madam."

Cravens had run up and had instantly inserted himself between her and the man. Without taking his eyes off of him, he said to Maddi, "Are you okay?"

Maddi rubbed her side. "I'm fine, Cravens." She turned to the gardener and, in spite of the ache in her side, she forced a smile. "It's… it's quite alright."

The man reached out his hand. "No, Madam, I must make it up to you."

Cravens moved even closer, and practically shoved the man out of the way. But not before the gardener had managed to slide something into Maddi's outstretched hand.

She instinctively folded her fingers over the item; it felt like a rolled-up piece of cardboard. "Cravens, I'm fine," she said, then nodded at the gardener. "Really, sir, don't worry about it. It was an accident."

The man stepped back and bowed. "You are very gracious, Madam." He turned and hurried away.

Cravens watched him go, then turned to Maddi. "Are you sure you're okay?"

Maddi smiled. "Of course, I am, Cravens. Now let's go."

They resumed their walk, but this time Cravens pasted himself to Maddi's side. She was shaking, but did her best to hide it as she clutched the item in her hand. It felt like a rolled piece of cardboard, or maybe an envelope. Though she knew she should tell Cravens about it, the very nature of its delivery told her that it was meant for her and her alone. Which meant that, whatever message had just been given to her, it was important…and private.

* * *

Justice had watched the exchange from behind a row of thick blue spruces. His timing had been fortuitous. He had arrived outside the nursing facility just as Madison and her bodyguard were crossing the street to the park. Just seeing her again had made his heart skip a beat, though she had clearly been through quite a lot in the five months since they had last spoken. She had lost at least ten pounds, and her hair, which had lost a bit of its luster, had grown several inches. But she was still remarkably beautiful, and he hissed at the fact that he wouldn't be able to speak to her personally. Then again, if she did as his letter instructed, he might soon have his chance with the remarkable woman.

The letter had been easy to write. He was able to imagine the lovely Cynthia as he wrote each word, and his hope for an outcome that might eventually allow him to become a part of her world had made the words practically flow from his hand.

He had left the train and walked to the nursing home, taking care to use trees and bushes for cover whenever he could. He had stopped just shy of the entrance, and had spotted Madison and her bodyguard only a minute later heading for the park. He had followed them, staying a safe distance back, and had stopped just outside the gate. He had seen a gardener pruning rose bushes not far from where he was standing, and had waved the man over. The gardener had approached him cautiously, and Justice had made a quick offer of 100 pounds if the gardener would find a way to get a letter to the woman wearing the scarf. *"You will be doing the Queen's work, my good man."* He had added, *"But here's the thing; she mustn't know about me…or from where this message has come."*

The man had frowned. *"Ye say I get a 'undred quid for this?"*

Justice had nodded. *"As long as she gets the letter…and you keep me out of it."*

From what Justice could tell, the man had completed the task as instructed.

As Justice watched Madison grip the envelope in her hand, he smiled. He had done it. He had carried out the agent's request, and had hopefully advanced his own cause, as well. What he wouldn't give to watch her read his carefully-crafted words, but there was no way. She had pocketed the envelope and would read it only when she could be certain of her privacy. Which had, after all, been his intent…to have her read the letter in secret. But he had taken the bold step of including his cellphone number, hoping that once she had done what he asked, she might consider giving him a ring.

* * *

Maddi continued to clutch the cardboard as they started another lap around the garden. Suddenly, she stopped, looked at Cravens, and sighed. "We need to get back."

"Are you sure, Senator. It's been only fifteen minutes."

Maddi nodded. "Yes, we need to go."

Cravens sighed, and walked her to the gate. They left the park, walked the block-and-a-half, then crossed the wide road to the nursing facility. They went into the lobby, and Maddi excused herself to use the bathroom.

She walked in and locked herself in one of the stalls. She opened her hand and unrolled the cardboard; it was a notecard-sized envelope. She smoothed it on her lap, stunned by the gold trim and the elegant handwriting. *"Senator Cynthia Madison"* was scrolled in ink across the front. She held it away from her as she pried open the edges, in case it held a toxic powder. *The fear left to us by the madmen who attacked a tower on a beautiful Tuesday morning…much like this one,* she thought with a sigh. There was no powder, simply a blank note card, also embossed with gold trim. Inside was a folded sheet of high-quality paper, elegantly penned with quill and ink.

My dear Cynthia Madison,

I hope you remember me. My name is Mark Justice, and we had the occasion to meet when you came to my offices in the spring. I don't know if you ever learned the identity of your stalker, but I'm eager to share the news whenever we have an opportunity to meet again. However, that is not the purpose of this letter.

I'm sorry to say that secrets have come to light regarding Matt Henderson, a man who is apparently lying ill in the nursing facility close to where this letter will be given to you. I have learned that you are quite fond of him, and that you have been sitting faithfully at his side for the past several months. Though I'm not privy to the secrets involving Mr. Henderson, I've been told that he has done terrible things. I don't know if it's true, but I do know that very powerful men are willing to expose those secrets in an effort to destroy not only that man, but his entire family. I've also been told that if you would be willing to tell Henderson goodbye – by the end of today – those same powerful men will destroy any evidence of the secrets and will never reveal them to a single soul.

If you refuse to relinquish your hold over the man in that bed, then the powerful men I speak of will move forward with their efforts to destroy Matt Henderson and his family. They will share secrets of what he has done over the past four years, including whatever he did in January. They will also share the secret of his half-brother. The man who contacted me insists that the revelation of these secrets won't just ruin Henderson, but his entire family and all they represent.

Ms. Madison, I am quite fond of you, so I regret being the bearer of such bad news, as I know it will hurt you. That is the last thing I want to do. But the man who reached out to me doesn't just represent a group of powerful, unsavory individuals; he is quite ruthless of his own accord. I believe him, and I feel certain that he will carry out the very threats he has outlined. If you can find it in your heart to say goodbye to Mr. Henderson, then I feel confident that you will be saving not only him, but his entire family. You must do whatever you feel is best, but I do believe that if you choose to ignore this warning, Matt Henderson will find his reputation – and perhaps his life – forever ruined.

Fondly yours,
Mark Justice
+44-20-8985-458

Maddi stared at the letter, too stunned to move. Who was the man Justice had referenced? The agent who represented a '...*group of very powerful men?*'

And what a coincidence to hear from the investigator she had sought out months ago to help her find her stalker. Her cheeks flushed as she recalled her meeting with Justice. Remarkably handsome and self-possessed, he had reminded her of someone, though she had been hard-pressed to place who it was. She had felt an instant bond with him however, and had quickly grown to trust him.

The question was, could she trust him now?

She recalled an instance in the dungeon outside Lyon when Cobra had mentioned the name Justice. Was it the same man? She had never had a chance to ask anyone about it, certain she didn't want to know how the two were connected, if, indeed, they were.

She continued to stare at the elegant writing with the ominous message. She heard a toilet flush next to her, and quickly folded the letter and stuffed it in her pocket. *What should I do?* She didn't know, but if the author of that letter was telling the truth, then she had to decide soon.

She waited until she heard footsteps leave the bathroom, then walked out of the stall. She stood at the sink and stared in the mirror. It didn't matter who had given the information to Justice. It didn't even matter who those powerful men were who had prompted the message in the first place. All that mattered was that they clearly knew the truth about Henderson, and about his family's ties to Cobra. There would be no way to stop them, unless she left him behind. Which meant that, within the next few hours, Maddi had a choice to make. *Either I leave him now and hopefully preserve his secrets, or I stay by his side, and risk destroying him — and his family — forever.*

CHAPTER 32

Washington, DC, Strongsville, Ohio

"You know I don't want to go, right Jenny?"

"I know. But it's part of your job, Deputy Director."

Jenny's voice, even on the phone, was reassuring. Hank grinned. "Yes, it is."

There was a pause. "I guess Maddi is still keeping watch over Matt Henderson?"

Hank closed his eyes and sighed. *Yes, she is.* He had ignored it as much as he could as he prepared for the trip overseas. "She means nothing to me, Jenny."

Much quieter, Jenny said, "We both know that's not true." Then, as though throwing him a life raft, she said, "But, perhaps things have changed."

"They have. I swear it, Jenny; you have nothing to worry about. I have never loved anyone – not even you – as much as I love you now." He chuckled. "You know what I mean."

Silence. Then, "I believe you, Hank. I really do. I just wish you weren't forced to test the theory so soon."

"I'm ready, Jenny. Trust me."

He heard a sigh. "I do, Hank, I really do."

"I love you, Jenny." She echoed him and he ended the call.

Just hearing her say that she believed him had felt good. It had reinforced not only that she trusted him, but that he trusted himself... that he was solid in his relationship with his ex-wife, and was, in fact, ready to see Maddi. But, as he hurriedly packed his files into his briefcase, he couldn't help but wonder, *Am I ready? Am I ready to see Maddi?*

* * *

Jenny hung up the phone. The sun was just starting to rise, and a ray of light shone on a photo propped on the corner of her desk. It was a new addition to the cluttered bureau, and it made her smile. The photo had been taken in France the night she and Hank had gone to dinner at *L'Arpege*. The maître d' had come by to check on *'the happy couple from America,'* and had offered to snap a photo. Hank had nodded and had moved closer, placing his arm around Jenny's shoulders. Never had something felt so natural, so right. She had leaned into him as if she had done it a thousand times…and she had, but it had been so long ago. As the photo was snapped, Hank whispered in her ear, *"I wonder if he can tell how much I love you?"* The picture caught him with his face turned, his lips half-open, and Jenny's eyes wide as she grinned like a school girl.

It had caught her off-guard; the expression of love after years of nothing more than casual greetings between them. And those casual greetings had killed her. Each "Hi Jenny" said as a friend, not a lover, felt like a knife to the heart. But maybe that was what they had needed all along; an alliance that had nothing to do with high school romance or the bonds of an unexpected baby. Now, instead of habit or obligation, they had only their desire to be together. Jenny lifted the picture and held it to her, as if protecting it from the challenges of life… or time apart…or Maddi.

It was foolish to think that Hank cared nothing for Maddi; he had loved her for nearly fifteen years. *That doesn't just vanish.* And Jenny herself was living proof of that fact. She and Hank had been together since middle school. They had married when they were nineteen and had stayed together for eleven years…*until Hank met Maddi.* Though she felt certain that Hank hadn't cheated on her during their time together, it had become clear that he had fallen in love with another woman. And Jenny had been powerless to stop him. *Like now,* she thought.

She returned the photo to the desk and walked to the kitchen of the house on Milford Street, where she had lived for the past fourteen years. She and Roger had moved there after the divorce, and she had been there ever since. *You have to trust him,* she thought, as she busied herself with the dishes. But could she? It wasn't that she thought he was being deceptive; she knew better. The man didn't have a deceptive bone in his body. No, he had simply loved the senator from Indiana for much of his adult life. And that same senator had, for a while, loved him back. Jenny frowned as she wiped her hands on a dishtowel. *Don't think about it.*

She had recently put the house up for sale and boxes were everywhere, waiting to be filled with her life; their life…hers and Rogers. They had lived a lot of years in that house – a decade-and-a-half of love, skinned knees, and broken hearts – but now it was time to move on. There was nothing holding her to Strongsville any longer. Hank was in DC, and Roger was…who knew where?

She wasn't sure where she would go. She and Hank had discussed her moving into his townhouse in DC, but it seemed too sudden; too soon after such a long time apart. Then again, life was short and there was no rule that said they couldn't pick up where they had left off. *But he is on his way to see Maddi.* What if what he and Jenny had reignited couldn't compete with the love the man seemed to forever harbor for the senator from Indiana? What if he got to Edinburgh, walked into that nursing home room, laid eyes on her, and suddenly realized – though he loved Jenny – he loved Maddi more? What would Jenny do? Could she survive it…again? *Of course, I could.* But even as she thought it, she knew that she definitely couldn't.

CHAPTER 33

Philadelphia, Pennsylvania

The pudgy receptionist from the South Philly station, Becky, had been better in bed than Todd had thought she would be. Or maybe it had just seemed that way because of his satisfaction with what he had done to Malone. Either way, the sex had been good; he had liked having so much of a woman to hold on to. He had sent her away quickly, however, wanting to be alone to think about the hit on Malone. He didn't even remember telling her goodnight. The slamming of the door might have been an indication that she was pissed about it. No matter, Becky was easy; she would forgive him in the morning. More importantly, just hours earlier, he had ridded the Philadelphia streets of another worthless thug. Though he had ended up with a sleepless night, by the time the sunlight peered through his bedroom window, he had come to terms with what he had done. It felt good to know he had made a difference. *One less scumbag to poison this town.*

He had gotten up and had driven to the station early, planning to work on a few outstanding cases before everyone else arrived. His first task had been to check on the status of the Malone hit. He hoped that the Philly police wouldn't expend too much effort to find the man's killer; the guy wasn't worth it…not at all. *The bastard got what was coming to him.*

Becky called in soon after 7:00 saying she didn't feel well, and that she would be in later that morning. Todd chuckled. *The poor girl probably can't walk.*

At 8:00 a.m. he decided to go for a stroll. He left the station, glad that the morning air was still cool. He bought a bagel with cream cheese from a street vendor, then went to the same bench he had sat on nearly every morning since he had been hired four months ago. As he looked around at the busy street traffic with high-end brokers and low-end bums, he smiled. They were all part of his world now…his domain. This was Todd's town. *Or it soon will be.* He breathed in the summer air of his South Philly province and sighed. Yes, Todd had found his niche. He hoped the members of the Blue Brotherhood were aware of what he had done to Malone; he knew the hit was a test.

As he stretched his legs and leaned against the bench, the same policeman from the day before walked over and stood by the bench. He gave Todd a nod; Todd nodded back, then felt the bench give as the man sat next to him. They both looked out over a small garden with a few brightly-colored flowers.

The policeman said, nonchalantly, "Nice day, eh?"

Todd nodded.

The man continued. "Should be a nice evening, too."

Todd cocked an eyebrow and looked at the man.

The cop shifted and the bench shifted with him. "I think a few of the boys are getting together at Steinke's house on North Street." He paused. "In his basement."

Todd narrowed his eyes, then nodded.

The cop added, "You probably shouldn't mention it to anybody. We like small groups, if you know what I mean."

Todd nodded and stared at the flowers. "Of course. Where on North Street?"

"Twenty-one thirty-six. Seven o'clock."

"Got it. I'll be there."

The cop stood and again the bench shifted. As he walked away, Todd crossed his ankles, pulled his cap low over his face, and stifled a grin. *I'm in.* He was now a member of the Blue Brotherhood.

It was only 8:15, but the sun was getting hot. He leaned back and let it bathe his cheeks; it felt good. He finished the bagel, then stood and walked the few yards to the station. He was starting to sweat. He didn't mind; it felt good. He looked up at the sun, embracing its warmth…its intensity. He had done it. He was now part of the most exclusive group in the police underworld. He didn't know what to expect, but if he got to handle business the way he had with Malone, it was going to be a great fit.

He walked inside and smiled at the receptionist who had just arrived and was sitting at her desk near the door. "I see you made it, Becky."

Becky looked up from a stack of papers and glared at him. "Whatever."

He chuckled. "I guess there's some 'buyer's remorse' eh?"

She sneered. "You're a pig, Jackson."

Todd laughed. "Is that what they call it now?"

He walked to his desk and laid down his hat as he took a seat across from his partner, who was reading through a stack of papers. "What's up, Jimmy?"

Jimmy shook his balding head. "Not much. A robbery over on twelfth, but the boys from Central are handling it. Nothin' else going on."

Todd nodded and turned on the computer. As he waited for it to load, he took a pencil and tapped it on the desk, fidgeting with some papers. "Hey Jimmy, you ever been with Becky over there?"

Jimmy looked at Becky and grinned self-consciously. "No, but I hear a lot of the guys have. Have you?"

Todd nodded proudly. "Oh yeah. A nice piece of ass that is."

His computer had loaded. As he opened the Philadelphia Police website, he saw Johnny Malone's name pop up on the screen. He felt his shoulders tighten. "Hey Jimmy, did you see this one? Johnny Malone."

Jimmy nodded. "Yeah. Looks like a low-life got what was comin' to him."

"Yep, that's what I think, too. Who do they think did it?"

"Does it matter?"

"I wonder if they're workin' it hard."

Jimmy looked up from his monitor. "Why do you care?"

"Oh, I don't know. Just curious, I guess." He paused. "The store owner that he killed...he had two little children. It just pisses me off."

Jimmy nodded. "I hear that."

Their radios chirped, "Alleged rape on the 2400 block of Christian and Vine."

Todd stood and grabbed his hat. "Let's go."

They ran to the squad car. Jimmy climbed behind the wheel. Todd rode shotgun and turned on the siren. "Nothing like a rape to get the day started," he said with a laugh.

Christian and Vine was a well-known corner for prostitutes; it was unusual to hear of a rape in the area. Todd looked over at Jimmy. "I wonder how they know."

"Know what?"

"That it's a rape, when it's a damned hooker who gets poked? Seems to me that's her job, isn't it?" He winked. "How can you rape the willing?" He laughed heartily but Jimmy didn't join in.

They arrived at the scene and jumped out of the car. A busty, scantily-clad woman was standing between two others dressed about the same. They were trying to comfort her. Though it was hot outside, all three women were shaking, likely chilled by the coldness of the world around them.

Todd walked up to them. "So, which one of you is saying you got raped?"

The woman in the middle glared at Todd. Her makeup was smudged and her blouse torn. "It was me."

Todd nodded. "I see. Your name?"

The woman bit her lip, still shivering, slow to reply.

"You got a name, ma'am?"

"Porsche."

Todd laughed. "Porsche...like the car?"

She nodded; he grinned. "Okay, *Porsche*...so who did this so-called rape?"

"I don't know his name."

"Should we maybe call him 'John'?"

The woman scowled. "I don't know his name."

Jimmy jumped in. "Just tell us what happened, ma'am."

Porsche shifted her weight to her other foot, and the other two women stepped back, giving her room to speak. "I...I was with this guy and we had made...plans." She paused. "I asked for the money up front – I learned that the hard way. He refused to pay, so I told him to get lost. He said, 'Hell no, bitch; I'm gonna' get what I came for.' Then he grabbed me and practically carried me over behind that dumpster." She

pointed to the trash bin. "Then he ripped off my clothes and…well…
you know."

Todd smirked. "I see. Now, let me get this straight. If he had paid
up, that same thing would have happened anyway, right?"

Porsche's eyes were glaring. "No, not like that."

"Okay, not like that. Can you describe the guy?"

"Yeah, he was skinny, about six-foot, with long, stringy brown hair,
and tight jeans."

Todd motioned to Jimmy to write it down. "Anything else?"

"Yeah." Porsche trembled. "He had…a tattoo…left side of his
face." She paused and said almost in a whisper, "It was of…the devil.
Orangish-yellow…ugly as hell."

Todd raised his eyebrows. "Now there's something you don't see
every day. A devil tattoo…on a man's *face*." He put his hand on her
shoulder. "Porsche, we'll do all we can to find the man who did this to
you." He stifled a grin, though he found himself feeling a small bit of
pity for the woman. "Now go clean yourself up."

He turned and walked back to the car. Jimmy ran after him.
"Shouldn't we arrange for a rape kit?"

Todd stopped and stared at Jimmy. "Now what the hell are they
going to find, Jimmy? Bruises? Semen? Tears? All those things would
be present on every one of the girls on this corner. There's no way to
do the kit, and there would be no evidence that would convict 'devil
face' in a court of law." He paused. "Don't misunderstand, Jimmy. I'm
not so hard core that I don't feel Porsche's pain, but – let's face it. She's
in the wrong line of work if she's gonna get upset every time a john
doesn't pay for the meal but still expects to eat."

"I think we have to do one, Todd."

He sighed. "Fine. Call the boys and have 'em take her to Philly
General." Over his shoulder, he yelled, "Don't take a shower, Porsche."

Jimmy made the call, hanging up just as they reached the car. He
stopped. "Look at 'em, Todd."

Todd turned. The girls were huddled arm in arm like a church
choir. He looked at Porsche's eyes. Though they were hard as steel, Todd
saw a sadness that over time had become despair. She had lost so much
of herself, and now, what little bit of dignity she had left had been taken
from her by an ass with a devil tattoo on his face. At that instant, Todd

truly did feel sorry for her. But there was nothing to do about it; it was a hazard of her job. Besides, what he had told Jimmy was true. They would never be able to get a conviction for the rape of a whore. Though Todd was certain everything she had told him had happened just the way she had said, he knew the lawyers would eat her alive in court.

His radio squawked and he frowned. "Let's go, Jimmy. They need help with a robbery on South Street."

The two men jumped in the car and Jimmy drove away. As they turned the corner, Todd looked back at the women huddled together; their faces blank, their eyes empty. *Maybe there is something I can do for them...with the help of the Blue Brotherhood.* He made a mental note to tell the group about 'Devil Face.' He adjusted his cap and readied himself for the next battle. *Probably another lost cause, where the perps have all the rights.* God, he couldn't wait to get to his meeting.

CHAPTER 34

Somewhere over the Atlantic

The plane was waiting when Hank arrived at Andrews. Hanover had called him on the way. *"Go to Edinburgh, ask Matt a few questions, then, unless you're convinced that there is literally no way in hell that he could've conspired with Phoenix to pull off the terror attacks, bring him back with you."* Hank already knew the answer; there was no way in hell that Matt could have conspired with Phoenix; Matt and Phoenix were the same man. The question he had to answer was whether he thought that Martin Henderson had it in him to carry out those attacks. *Impossible.* Nonetheless, he would go to Edinburgh, interrogate the man, get a full-throated denial, then turn around and come back home...alone. *Hopefully, I'll be back by tomorrow morning.*

He had promised to call Jenny the minute he was on his way home. But he had heard it in her voice; she wasn't going to be okay until he was back in the States and she could see in his eyes that he hadn't fallen in love with Maddi...again. He would be glad to reach that point, as well.

He hesitated as the car stopped in front of the private 747. He sighed. *Just get it over with, Hank.* He and two military aides got out of the car, walked the few steps to the plane, and climbed aboard. There was a medical team already on board, with what looked like a fully-stocked hospital room. Monitors, IV's, everything that would be needed to bring a man who had just come out of a coma safely back to the States.

The jet, supplied by the State Department, looked to be far more accommodating than the military transports Hank was used to. The

State Department had insisted that they not only play a role in the mission, but oversee it, citing potential international implications. Hank didn't care who oversaw it; he just wanted to get it over with.

He found a seat and strapped in. As the plane sped down the tarmac, he leaned back, confounded by a problem he had yet to resolve. *What will I say to Maddi?* He had promised her months ago that he wouldn't tell anyone who Matt Henderson really was, and that he would do his best to protect him. Very few were aware that Matt was really Martin; only Hank and Maddi, as far as he knew. But the fact that Hank was being sent to interrogate the cousin had complicated things. *Either way, a Henderson is being accused of a horrible crime.* In spite of the fact that they had found Phoenix's fingerprints on the Lassa fever vials, there was one thing both Maddi and Hank agreed on: Henderson couldn't have carried out those attacks. So…had he been framed? If so…by who? *By the bastard who killed innocent Americans…that's who!*

Hank had wanted to tell Hanover the truth about Martin Henderson ever since Maddi had told him at Dalgety Bay. But he had held off, hoping that the actual culprit behind the attacks would be found, and Matt could come forward and reveal his true identity. Then Martin – Phoenix – would be off the hook, as would Matt. But now, Hank was being sent to Scotland to bring Matt in for questioning. It felt like the net was getting tighter. And Hank knew, if it was ever discovered that Matt was Martin, or that Martin was Phoenix, it would complicate things for the entire Henderson clan. But what would be even worse was if either one of them – Matt or Martin – was indicted for the January attacks. It would destroy not only Martin Henderson and his family, but Maddi, as well.

And she's been through enough.

The plane was climbing fast. After another few minutes, it leveled off and Hank loosened his seat belt and stretched his legs. The plush seats and large windows made it feel more like he was on a vacation than on a mission to retrieve a potential terrorist.

The highspeed jet was expected to arrive in Edinburgh in about seven hours, which would put him at the nursing home just after 9:00 p.m., UK time. He tried to think what he would say to Henderson. The man had just come out of a coma; it didn't seem right to put him through a full interrogation. But Hank's instructions had been clear. He was to question Matt to determine if he had played a role in the Lassa fever attacks. Though Hank already knew that he hadn't, he needed the man to tell him something that would convince Hanover and anyone else who might have doubts that he was unequivocally innocent of any collusion in the attack.

After another few minutes, he grabbed his briefcase and pulled out a stack of files. He rifled through them until he found the one that he was looking for. He made himself comfortable as he read for probably the tenth time the summary of the U.S. Government's secret weapon, the Phoenix....

Prepared by Edward Morningstar, aide to General Alexander Daniels, for the Department of Homeland Security as part of the joint effort to hunt down the man or men responsible for the bioterrorist attack that took place in January, 2004.

"*The Phoenix was born from the ashes... rehabilitated for the sole purpose of serving the United States of America. Intended as a secret weapon, he was helped through his recovery by the oversight of the brilliant soldiers of the U.S. Army. He was then given the challenge of covert international negotiations.*"

Hank frowned. *International negotiations, my ass. The guy was an assassin.* He read on.

"*Though asked to carry out hostile actions during his four years with the Pentagon, the tasks requested were essential to the preservation of those ideals that define our nation. America owes him a debt of gratitude.*

"*With one exception. It appears the man went AWOL in late fall, 2003, and has not been seen since. Though he has likely changed his appearance, there is one thing he could not change: his fingerprints. They were discovered at the three sites of the bioterror*" *attacks which took place across America in January of 2004. Though no one has come forward identifying Phoenix as the perpetrator of those attacks, fingerprints don't lie. There is also video surveillance that places Phoenix in the vicinity of each of the attacks at or around the time they occurred. It is felt that the man, in a state of PTSD, lost his mind and turned to terror to alleviate his pain.*

"He is considered armed and dangerous. The Pentagon requests that he be taken alive, in honor of the service he had provided this country prior to his transformation. We are hopeful he can shed light on several other murders that have taken place since his departure from the Service. Like many nameless soldiers who have been asked to fight surreptitious wars, the Phoenix will be both honored and despised when the time comes to eventually lay him to rest."

Hank closed the folder. *"…eventually lay him to rest."* He shook his head. The Phoenix had already been 'laid to rest.' He existed no more, having somehow morphed into Cousin Matt. *So, who are you, Henderson? Are you the Phoenix? Or are you the man I'm about to interrogate…Matt Henderson?*

Hank yawned as he stared at the closed file. He knew Henderson; fairly well, as a matter of fact. Years ago, Hank had actually worked for Henderson's company, Marker Insurance. Not long after that, it was Henderson who had saved Hank from a hotel fire that had subsequently trapped Henderson and nearly killed him. Then, about five months ago, the two men had traveled from Latvia to Paris to save Hank's son from the Cobra. While there, Henderson had persuaded Cobra to take him instead, and Henderson had nearly been killed again. He had risked his life, first for Hank, then for Hank's son.

Hank shook his head and sighed. *A man like that could never kill innocent Americans with vials of poison.*

Which could mean only one thing.

Hank sighed as he leaned back and closed his eyes. *Someone sure went to a hell of a lot of trouble to frame him.*

CHAPTER 35

Edinburgh, Scotland

Henderson rubbed his eyes, then stared again at a two-page letter he had just been handed by a man who was clearly some sort of maintenance worker at the nursing facility. Remarkably, Henderson was alone. His parents had gone to dinner, and Maddi was in the bathroom taking a shower. The doctors and nurses were in the middle of a shift change, and he guessed the new crew was being updated on his progress.

The frumpy handyman had clearly been waiting for such a moment, and had burst into the room, had shuffled to Henderson's bedside with his head down, and had handed him the note. He had walked to the window, had run his hand over the blinds, then had run out of the room without a word.

Henderson had wanted to stop him; to ask who he was and why he was delivering a letter to a man who had just come out of a coma, but he had been too stunned to say a word. Especially once he had gotten a good look at the handwriting…

> *Hello, Henderson. If you're reading this, then what I heard is true and you've awakened from your coma. Congratulations. I've come across a bit of info you might find interesting. It involves your sweet little love interest, Cynthia Madison. Apparently, the girl got into some trouble with a cop when she was young. I have it on good authority that she asked for help from her wealthy English grandparents, and they came through with flying colors. Suffice it to say, there is now a Madison Foundation in Evansville,*

Indiana that is dedicated to the support and betterment of police officers in and around the city.

Extortion, I believe we call it here in the States.

The Foundation still exists, which means that whatever provisions were agreed upon at that time are still in place. The revelation of Madison's role in such a scheme would result not only in her dismissal from the Senate, but in an indictment and a likely conviction for whatever part she played in such an unseemly affair. It would destroy the reputation of your lovely senator, and might even put her freedom in jeopardy.

So, I'm giving you a chance to save the poor lass. All you have to do is let her go. Tonight. Forever. That's it; just say goodbye and forget you ever knew her. Don't tell her why, just go.

I hope you're doing well. I look forward to seeing you soon.

Yours, fondly,
Edward Morningstar

Henderson's heart was pounding, he clenched his fists as he read the note, then read it again. It had likely been printed from an email or a fax; there was no way that Morningstar would have crossed the ocean to write it personally. And there hadn't been time to mail it overseas. Which meant that the man in the overalls had played a role. Who was he? Had Morningstar gotten himself a new son? Henderson shook his head and frowned. Whoever he was, Henderson guessed that he was long gone.

He closed his eyes, reviewing the note word by word, especially the part that said *"All you have to do is let her go."* In a fit of rage, he tore up the note and dropped the pieces into a trashcan by his bed. He tightened his jaw. *No, I can't…I won't do it.*

What could Maddi have done – as a child or a teenager – that would have resulted in a need for her grandparents to save her? *And why hasn't she told me about it?*

He scoffed. It was like asking why *he* hadn't told *her* about all the horrible things he had done. *Because she was afraid that I would leave her.*

Morningstar had said that it involved a cop. Maddi was one of the most law-and-order members of the Senate; there was no way she had

had a run-in with a cop.

So, I'll just ask her about it, he thought. He nodded. That's what he would do; he would ask her about it, and then, if it was true, the two of them could face it together.

He frowned. He couldn't ask Maddi about it. For one thing, if she had wanted him to know about it, she would have told him. For another, the minute he did ask her about it, the revelation would force her to confide in him. He would become the man she relied on...*and I am hardly that man.* Morningstar would carry out his threat, and the only person Maddi would have to cling to would be a man who had at one time done the bidding of the man pulling the strings. Henderson was powerless against Morningstar; he had always been powerless against him. Why? *Because he knows what I've done.* And from the wording of the note, he had also learned that Matt was actually Martin.

So, what was Morningstar's plan? What did he hope to gain by forcing Henderson to leave Madison. *My downfall,* he thought, as he tried to imagine his life without Maddi. But how would Morningstar know that losing Maddi would destroy him? He frowned. *He knows...I don't know how, but he knows.* So, his options were simple. Either he let Maddi go and save her from Morningstar's dangerously long reach, or he stay with her, defy Morningstar, and let the man take them both down.

He shook his head, the realization devastating. Maddi needed an ally; a man she could rely on...not a former assassin with blood on his hands. *I am the last thing she needs,* he thought, and he began to cough, nearly choking on the truth of it.

Maybe he's bluffing, he thought as he shifted in the bed. He frowned. *Morningstar doesn't bluff.* In all the time he had known him, the man had never bluffed. If he said Maddi had a secret, then she did. If he said that he would destroy her with that secret, then he would. Henderson felt desperation taking hold. It was a feeling he knew far too well. *But maybe now that I'm awake, I can stop him...I can learn the where and the why of whatever happened to Maddi years ago, and put a stop to Morningstar's efforts.* Again, he shook his head. There wasn't time. The letter had said that if he didn't leave her by tonight, Morningstar would come forward with Maddi's secret.

He's got me, he thought with a sigh. Morningstar, having figured out that Matt was Martin, was using Maddi's devotion against him...against them both. But there was an even bigger threat at play. Henderson knew, now that Morningstar had become aware of the depth of their love for one another, it wasn't just her secrets that were at risk...it was her very life. *She is in danger...if I don't let her go.*

He was struggling to breathe. His hatred for Morningstar was smothering him. He took a deep breath. *Mark my words, Morningstar... I'll make you pay...for all of it...even if it means I must spend an eternity in Hell.* He scoffed. Who was he kidding? He was already slated for Hell; he had set that table years ago. He had no soul left with which to bargain.

He leaned against the pillow and sighed. He felt overwhelmingly tired. But in a strange sort of way, he also felt relieved. He had always known that he could never really come back to Maddi...that he could never be the man she needed him to be. She had fallen in love with him when he was a good man, a hopeful man, a man whose purpose in life was to do good. But that man was dead...he died in a hotel fire four years ago.

He heard Maddi fussing around in the bathroom and, again, his heart broke. What had he been thinking? Maddi hadn't signed on for this...for a broken man lying in a bed, his past metastasizing like a cancer that was killing not only him, but everyone around him. Henderson had done terrible things as the Phoenix...things that were unforgivable. And, even if Maddi could find a way to forgive him, he couldn't let her...because he didn't deserve her forgiveness.

Maddi was sunlight; he was darkness...it was that simple.

And now, he had put her very life in danger. Which meant that within the next hour or two, Henderson had to come up with a way to make Maddi leave him...for good.

CHAPTER 36

Edinburgh, Scotland

Maddi, fully clothed, stood outside the running shower with the bathroom door locked. She took another look at the letter in her pocket; the mysterious note that had been written by Mark Justice and delivered to her secretly by a gardener. She had spent the entire afternoon trying to figure out what to do. Though she knew she should share the letter with Cravens, she couldn't; she could never let anyone know what was in that note. To give it to Cravens would be to basically give it to his boss, who would then ask questions and learn far too much about Martin, the Phoenix, Matt, and Cobra.

She guessed that the man who had reached out to Justice had understood this. His role in such an underhanded task would never come to light, because the secrets themselves could never come to light…not by Maddi, anyway. But who were the 'powerful men' he was supposedly representing? How did they know so much about Henderson? *And why do they care if I leave him?*

She looked again at the signature. It included Justice's phone number. *Should I call him?* She continued to stand outside the shower, unable to move. She felt sick inside. The letter was a warning, but it was so much more. It was clear now that Henderson's secrets were known by more than just him and Maddi; they were known by a group of despicable men who wouldn't hesitate to tell the world what they knew. Maddi frowned. *So, let them.* Let those men tell anyone who would listen, not only the things that Henderson had done as the Phoenix, but his tie to one of the most notorious killers of all time. Why not? Maybe they would all be better off if the world finally learned the truth.

No, Maddi thought, *too many would be hurt.* To disgrace the Henderson name would bring shame and destruction to more than just the Hendersons. The highly regarded Boston family oversaw an empire that had aided Presidents and kings for over half a century, if not longer. To reveal to the world that Martin Henderson was the Phoenix would tarnish that legacy; to reveal Walter's ties to the Cobra would destroy it.

Maddi grimaced as she folded the letter, then shoved it deep in her pocket. *I need to fight this...I need to find a way to prove to the world that whatever Henderson did as the Phoenix, he was ordered to do by his government. And that Walter's indiscretion was simply that; a misguided man made a terrible mistake.*

But would it really matter? Maddi shook her head. People wouldn't care *why* Henderson had done what he had as the Phoenix, and they certainly wouldn't care why Walter had strayed from his loving wife. No, all they would see was the fall from grace of a glorious family. *And some – the weak-minded among us – would celebrate that fall.*

Suddenly, out of nowhere, she heard a voice. A voice she had heard before...the soft whisper of a child...a little girl. *"You mustn't leave him... no matter what."*

Maddi looked around the bathroom, unsure what she was expecting to see. There was no child in that room; that much was for sure. She made a perfunctory check behind the shower curtain and sighed. No little girl. So, where had the voice come from? *My mind,* she thought with a sigh. *You're just hearing what you want to hear.*

She waited. She heard it again. *"You mustn't leave him...no matter what."*

Maddi stared into the mirror. *Why do I keep hearing the voice of that girl...of Lili?* Maddi might have been able to write it off as a fantasy of her own making, except that Henderson had heard it, too...back in Dalgety Bay. They had both heard her, and it had confounded Maddi. She thought back on what Lili had told her over the past several months. In Maddi's living room, the girl had said *"I told him we would wait for him,"* and had added, *"He's coming...then we'll dance."* In Roger's hospital room, the girl had asked if Ricardo, the young boy who had survived a terrible atrocity in Argentina, had given Maddi her message: *"He hopes you forgive him."* Maddi had assumed that Lili was referring to Henderson, and, yes, she had forgiven him. For what? She had no idea, but it didn't matter; she would forgive him for anything. Then, in Dalgety Bay, Lili had urged

Maddi to let Henderson know – as he was passed out beside her – that Maddi did, in fact, forgive him. Maddi had written it off to some delusion she was experiencing as she was facing death. But then, in that very same instance, Henderson had heard the girl, as well. Which meant that the child was real…or was at least a mirage that they both shared.

Which is simply ridiculous, she thought as she threw her hands in the air.

But it was more than that; it was more than the child's words. There was an *essence* about Lili. She exuded love and hope and joy…in a way that Maddi couldn't explain. She was beyond exceptional; she was kindness and truth wrapped up in a tiny little voice…*and I don't even know if she's real.*

Maddi moved closer to the mirror, as if it would allow her greater insight into the source of the magical voice. Where had Lili come from? And why did she continue to reach out to Maddi? "Will I ever have a chance to know you, Lili?" Maddi whispered.

She waited for a reply…words that might tell her something more about the child.

There was only silence.

After a minute, she stepped back and wiped her eyes. She still didn't know what to do about the note in her pocket that was threatening Henderson's very existence. Lili had said, *"Don't leave him."* Maddi felt certain that Lili didn't know the risks should she decide to stay. She had to leave him. It was the only way to have at least some hope that he and his family would stay safe, and that their legacy would remain intact.

Suddenly, her legs buckled and she gripped the sink. The very thought of it was crushing her. Had all her years of waiting and hoping and crying for Henderson culminated in this? Had she finally gotten him back, only to lose him to a choice that no one should ever have to make. *Must I leave him to save him?*

"No," said the sweet little voice out of nowhere. *"You mustn't leave him…ever."*

Maddi choked back a new round of tears. *Kind, gentle Lili.* If only she knew what she was asking. Yes, Maddi could stay and let the threats that Justice had outlined play out. She could sit back and watch as a great man and a great family were brought to their knees in shame. Or, she could leave him now…tonight…and trust that what Justice had said in the letter was true; that those who knew the truth would bury that truth forever.

She narrowed her eyes. But would they? What guarantee did she have that even if she did tell Henderson goodbye, those 'powerful men' wouldn't simply reveal his secrets anyway? *But at least I'll have done all I could to keep it from happening.* If there was one thing she had learned from the murder of her dear friend, Al-Gharsi, the destruction of a single man – or in this case, a single family – could result in years, even decades of death and despair. And there was no way that Maddi could be responsible for such a thing.

She rinsed her face and dried it, then smoothed down her sweater and combed her fingers through her hair. She looked again at the face in the mirror. She knew what she had to do. She reached in and shut off the water to the shower, waited a minute to suggest that she was getting dressed, then took a final look in the mirror. *Go, Maddi.*

As she reached for the handle of the door, she heard the voice again.

"I'm telling you…you mustn't leave him, Special Lady."

Maddi closed her eyes and gripped the handle, shoring up her resolve. She opened the door and stood there, looking at Henderson lying in the bed. His eyes were closed, his chest moving with the ease of a man whose life was no longer in danger. Her love for him, that had seemed unsurpassable just moments ago, had grown even more, and she felt that her heart might break from the power of it. How on earth could she leave him?

The truth was, she couldn't. She loved him more than life itself, and knew that he felt the same. Lili was right; she mustn't leave him. But it was more than that; she *couldn't* leave him…ever. She would never survive it. Which meant that, within the next hour or two, she would have no choice but to throw Henderson – and his family – to the wolves.

Suddenly her eyes widened. *Unless I can come up with a plan.*

She stepped back into the bathroom, closed the door, and pulled out her phone. She looked up the number of the most powerful man she knew, and dialed. Her voice was unsteady as she whispered, "Mr. President, it's Cynthia Madison. I…I need your help."

CHAPTER 37

Washington, DC

Claire checked the clock for about the fiftieth time. It was three-forty-five; her last client of the day had left her office fifteen minutes ago and she was alone. It had been over twenty-four hours since she had called Maddi's secretary, and about an hour since she had called him again; still no word from Maddi. Claire was about to pull out her hair… *every last red-streaked strand.*

She had gotten the red hair from her father, and – though she loved him – she didn't love her hair. It was coarse and unmanageable. She had tried wearing it long, then short, finally settling on the chin-length bob that she had worn now for the past fifteen years. It suited her; not too flashy, not too tame.

She stood and walked to the window. Though the day had started with sunshine, it had rained about an hour ago, and the sky was now a dusky gray. The roses were in full bloom, their bold red a contrast to the ashen sky that seemed unending as it merged seamlessly with the wet, steel-colored pavement. Claire needed to make a decision and she needed to make it soon. Why? *Because today – now – I have the courage to do it.*

Claire sighed. What if Maddi's duties had put her in a position where she couldn't get back to Claire for days, or even weeks. How long could Claire wait? How long could she sit on the news she had so painstakingly dragged from her client…her friend? She had known that Maddi needed to tell her story, she just had no idea how dreadful – *and illegal* – that story would be. Though Claire had waited six months to do what she should have done the minute Maddi told her what happened, she suddenly felt an urgent need to report it. She once had a client tell her, after years of considering whether to divorce his wife, when he finally decided to do it, it couldn't happen quick enough. This felt the same. Now that she had decided to do it, she had to do it soon...*before I lose my nerve.*

She walked to her desk and sat down. She stared at the stack of papers on her desk. Maybe if she threw her energy into her paperwork, it would keep her mind off of Maddi. She picked up a pen and was about to get started, when, all at once, she whipped the pen across the room with such fury she found herself shaking. *Good god, Claire, pull yourself together.* But she couldn't. She was angry that she had to do this; that "the Law" was *making* her do it. She shook her head. *The sooner I get it over with, the better.*

She checked the time; three-fifty-five. The DA's office would close soon; if she was going to do it today, she needed to do it now. She picked up the receiver, then slammed it down and sat back in her chair. *Do it, Claire...you have to do it!*

She rubbed her neck, sighing as she finally leaned forward and again picked up the receiver. She pulled a small day planner in front of her and opened it. Her finger was shaking as she dialed a number that she had etched in the planner four months ago. She waited as she heard first one, two, then three rings. *Maybe they won't answer.*

"Evansville Prosecutor's office. May I help you?"

Darn! "Um, yes, my name is Claire Porter; I'm a therapist in Washington, DC. May I have a word with the Prosecutor, please?"

CHAPTER 38

Edinburgh, Scotland

The flight had gone by surprisingly quickly, and Hank and his two agents stepped off the plane at the Edinburgh Airport at 9:00 p.m. sharp. They had no bags to retrieve, and passed easily through customs, their credentials and a call from the State Department serving as green lights to the officials at the checkpoint. They were followed by a team of medics who also passed through easily. Once through, Hank led the way to the front of the terminal, eager to get the entire matter over with. He didn't want to do what he was about to do, and, the sooner it was done, the better. He walked outside and looked for a black sedan, along with the van he had been promised before he left, that would hold the EKG machine, canisters of O2, and the necessary monitors.

The evening air was cool and damp. *England never disappoints,* he thought with a grin. But the cool mist was refreshing after the long plane ride. He loosened his tie as he looked around for the vehicles. He spotted a sedan and a van sitting half-a-block away; he motioned to the others. They hurried to the vehicles. He showed his badge, then he and his agents slid in the back of the town car, while the medics carried their equipment onto the van. "Sacred Hearts," he said as he checked his watch. *Nine-twenty…Henderson's probably trying to sleep.* He had, after all, just come out of a coma. Though Hank didn't like the thought of waking a man who had just come out of a coma, he had been given clear instructions: *"Go over there, question him, and if there's even a chance that he knows something, bring him back to the States."* So, question him, he would.

As they pulled away, Hank thought again about how much he hated what he was about to do. Though it was likely that Henderson had indeed carried out some of the assassinations attributed to him in his "Phoenix" file, Hank knew that the man he had known, the esteemed Martin Henderson, couldn't have done them all. And he most definitely couldn't have carried out the Lassa fever attacks. Which meant that someone was doing all he could to tie Henderson to at least one very terrible crime. *And Henderson is powerless to defend himself.*

Hank looked outside at the last gasps of a fading sun, marveling as it shone on the majestic Edinburgh castle. He had seen a similar fortress not that long ago – the Henderson castle in Latvia. And he had been treated well there. Could that man – the man who had risked his life to save first Hank, then Hank's son, Roger – have done what he was being accused of? For the hundredth time, Hank felt certain that the answer was no.

He sighed. *But what if he did?* What if Henderson, from whom everything had been taken, had experienced some horrible break from reality, and in an act of crazy desperation, had unleashed a deadly virus on America. Hank couldn't even imagine it. But, he knew, in spite of his appreciation for all that the man had been through, if it *was* true, then Hank would never be able to overlook such a thing…*not even for Maddi.* He leaned back, watching as the castle faded along with the sunlight. He shook his head and sighed. *Which is why I will carry out my orders as instructed.*

CHAPTER 39

Washington, DC

Morningstar was in the middle of a call to his general, when his private cellphone vibrated. He checked caller ID. *Shit...it's Janet.* He was tempted to ignore it, but found himself unable to do so. Janet rarely called when he was at work. *Something's up,* he thought as he felt the vibration stop, then vibrate again.

"Excuse me, General, but I'm getting a call from our contact in Estonia. I'll call you right back, sir." Without waiting for a reply, he answered Janet's call with a stern "What!"

"She didn't leave him."

Morningstar frowned. "What are you talking about?"

"Madison...she didn't leave."

"How the hell do you know that?"

"She put in a call to the State Department."

"She did what?"

"She put in a call to the State Department. Well, *she* didn't...the President did."

"The President? As in Wilcox?"

"Yes. On her behalf, he requested transport for four."

Morningstar bristled. "Transport to where?"

"An undisclosed location."

"Who is she bringing with her?"

"He didn't say."

Morningstar was beside himself. "Madison has the power to have America's President request a transport plane *on her behalf*...without offering a destination or a list of who is going with her?"

"Apparently so."

"It's picking her up in Scotland?"

"I believe so…though that, too, was listed as undisclosed. All I know is that the plane is coming out of France."

Morningstar bristled. "France? My god…that's right next door." He flinched. "That plane could get there before Clarkson does. When do we expect it to arrive?"

"The memo just said 'ASAP.'"

Morningstar stood and paced his office. What was Madison up to? Where was she going? *And who is she taking with her?* Was she running away? Taking her two agents and Henderson and flying off into the sunset? There was no way. Her agents would never go along with it. Which left only one possibility; she was taking the entire Henderson clan…all three of them…*so she can hide Henderson and his family from the ugly truth of who they are and what they've done.* He bristled. Why would the State Department agree to transfer Henderson, if they had already facilitated a transfer for the same man through the Department of Homeland Security? *Because Madison didn't tell the President that one of her passengers is Matt Henderson, the man they are about to retrieve.*

He squeezed his hands into fists. He had clearly underestimated her. Though he had expected she might weaken and choose her love for the man over her devotion to his wellbeing, he had never expected her to come up with an exit strategy for all four of them.

Suddenly, he stopped. He had already taken this into account. His backup plan was that Henderson would leave *her.* And though Madison was weak, Henderson was not. Henderson knew what was at stake if he didn't leave her. He knew what Morningstar was capable of. *But he's just come out of a coma…what if he weakens, as well?* He smacked his hand on the desk.

"Edward, are you still there?"

"Get me Pocks…now!"

He ended the call. Though he would have typically dialed the awkward man himself, Pocks had been instructed to leave Edinburgh the minute he delivered the note to Henderson. It was possible he was in a place where he couldn't speak freely…like on a train or a bus. If so, Janet's text to him would simply instruct him to get to a location where a phone call couldn't be overheard, then have him call Morningstar at once. Janet would know to do this. He sneered. *Why? Because I taught her to know such things.*

Morningstar resumed his pacing, trying to think of a way to ensure that the lovebirds went their separate ways. Especially now. Madison had defied his threat. If Henderson was to confide in her that Morningstar had written him a letter with a similar theme, they would put two-and-two together, and could make his life a living hell. *Thank God I had Pocks take that letter from Henderson.* At least there would be no proof that Morningstar had reached out to Henderson…just his word against Morningstar's.

His cellphone rang. It was Janet.

"He'll call you in five minutes." She paused. "Baby, can I ask why this is so important to you…that Henderson and Madison leave one another?"

He was about to scream at her for daring to challenge him, but had learned his lesson. *Yelling at Janet never goes well.* "Janet dear, the only way I know to put it is this: Though I'm strong without you, you have aided me. At the risk of giving you more credit than you deserve, I do believe that we've achieved more together than we could ever have achieved apart."

He heard her laugh, and he sneered. "What's so funny?"

"Oh, nothing, Babe…I'm just glad to hear that after all this time you're finally willing to admit it."

Morningstar stiffened. "I admit that you would be nothing without me; that's all I have admitted." He took a deep breath. "I hope your stupid brain is able to grasp what I'm saying. Madison on her own can do little to hurt me. She can run her committee until she's blue in the face, but she won't uncover any more than what she already has." He paused. "And Henderson can tell anyone who will listen that I'm the reason he killed all those men, but it would be the word of a known assassin against a respected Pentagon aide." Another pause. "By themselves, they can do nothing to me. But if they were to team up; a popular, powerful Senator joining forces with the son of an international icon…well, it's quite possible that people might start to listen." He felt his phone vibrate. "Gotta go. It's Pocks." He transferred the call. Without waiting for a hello, he said, "Did you deliver the letter, Pocks?"

"I did."

"Good job." He paused. "Your next task is to get me a private phone number."

"Landline or cellphone?"

"Cellphone."

"Whose?"

"Madison's."

There was a pause, followed by a deep sigh. "Give me about an hour, sir."

Morningstar checked the time. It was four-twenty in America, which meant that it was nine-twenty p.m. in the UK. Clarkson was expected to arrive at the nursing home in Edinburgh by nine-thirty. But Madison's transport plane was coming from France. It was possible that it would get there before Clarkson had a chance to take Henderson into custody and bring him back to the States. He frowned. "I don't have an hour. I'll give you ten minutes."

He ended the call, then walked over to his desk phone. He dialed the private number to the General, bristling when he heard the gruff voice say, "Took you long enough, Morningstar. Why are you talking to Estonia?"

Morningstar cleared his throat. "I reached out to them, sir, based on intelligence I received about thirty minutes ago relating to Putin and a possible move on Latvia."

He heard a laugh. "That's ridiculous, Morningstar. Putin would be a fool to attack a NATO country."

Morningstar tightened his jaw. *Idiot.* "I agree, sir. But I felt it best to make sure we had a battalion in place, just in case." He waited. Would Daniels buy it?

A pause. "Never hurts to be prepared. Good work, Morningstar. Keep me posted."

Morningstar sighed. "Yes sir." He hung up the receiver with a slam. *I'll keep you posted, dumbass. Once I take over this world…with your assistance, you patsy.*

He walked to the window, trying to distract himself while he waited for Pocks to get him Madison's number. What would he do with it? What could he say that would compel the selfish wench to leave the man she was so desperately in love with…*instead of flying him off to who knows where?* He tried to think how he had effectively persuaded people in the past. Secrets or money; usually both. But he had already threatened her with secrets. If she didn't care about exposing the Henderson family secrets, it was doubtful that she would be persuaded by an offer of cash.

He continued to pace, trying to think what he could say that would compel a do-gooder like Madison to walk away from the love of her life. It had to be bigger than her, bigger than Henderson, bigger than money. Suddenly, his eyes widened. "I've got it!" he said, and once again smacked his desk.

His cellphone vibrated. It was Pocks. Morningstar barked, "Well?"

"Um…it took some doing, sir. Thank god for my contact at the NSA," he hesitated, "…but I have Madison's cellphone number."

CHAPTER 40

Edinburgh, Scotland

Maddi forced a smile at Dora, who had just gotten up to get Henderson a glass of water. Though he hadn't swallowed anything for months, he was able to sip water as long as he was careful. Dora handed him the glass and sat next to him, ready to help, if needed.

Just tell them, Maddi…tell them what you're about to do. She frowned. She had yet to share her plan to fly them all to an unnamed location before the Henderson secrets were exposed. Would they accept it? Or would they despise her for letting it happen in the first place? Would they resent her once she told them that if she had just been willing to say goodbye to Henderson, their secrets would be safe? That she was choosing her love for Henderson over preserving the integrity of the Henderson name? Assuming they did forgive her, how would she convince them to board a transport plane on nothing more than her word? She had concluded that her best move would be to not tell them anything until the driver who was taking them to the plane had arrived.

But it was more than just their name that was at stake. That was what she had concluded while standing in the doorway of Henderson's bedroom. The men who were willing to ruin him and expose his family's secrets were capable of far more than just character assassination. She trembled. Maddi knew better than most what men like that were capable of. *But what then? What will we do once we've escaped?* She sighed. She had yet to solve that one. *I'll deal with it once I know that Henderson and his parents are at least out of harm's way.*

She checked the time. It was 9:30. The President had arranged for a car to come for them once the plane was ready. Maddi had no idea when that would be, but guessed it would be soon. What if Walter and Dora chose to go back to their hotel before the car arrived? Maddi sighed. *Then I'll just have the driver pick them up there.*

It had been out of sheer desperation that Maddi had reached out to President Wilcox. Though they were friends, she had made sure to never use that friendship to secure a favor. But this was different; lives were at stake. And it wasn't an overstatement to suggest that the fates of several countries were at stake, as well.

Wilcox was beginning a campaign tour, and had taken her call as he had been about to board Airforce One. He had been supportive, but had balked when she had been unwilling to offer him details. *"Can't you at least tell me who you're transporting?"*

"I would prefer not to, sir, out of consideration for their safety."

"And you won't tell me where you want to go?"

"No sir...for the same reason."

With a deep sigh, he had finally given in. *"Because it's you, Maddi, I'll do it. I'll go through the State Department. They'll find a plane from a country close to your current location. I'll send a car once it's ready...the driver will text you at the number you're calling me from. The jet will have no formal flight plan, no tracking capability, and a capacity for...how many did you say again?"*

"Four"

"Do you need a military escort? Or at least a team of soldiers to keep you safe?"

"No sir, the fewer who know about this, the better."

"Will you at least take one of your Secret Service agents?"

Maddi had considered it, but had then dismissed the idea. *"With all due respect, sir, it would be intolerably unfair to him. We may be gone for quite a while."*

A pause had been followed by another deep sigh. *"Consider it done, Maddi."*

Consider it done, Maddi thought as she watched the Hendersons dote over their son.

Walter and Dora had come back to the room just moments ago, and it was clear that Dora's strength had been renewed by Henderson waking from the coma. The conversations had covered everything from Dora asking *"How do you feel?"* to Henderson asking *"How are Charles and Nelly?"* Maddi knew of Nelly from the quilt that Dora had given her soon after the hotel fire four years ago, and was amused to hear how she, the maid had had a secret romance with Charles, the chauffeur at the Henderson home in Boston. Periodically, Dora would fight tears, and it was then that she would take Henderson by the hand and say softly, over and over, *"You're here...you're really here."*

Maddi sat back and watched it all...the love that floated between them like shared smoke from a late-night fire...the warmth that filled the room as father and son reunited, not in a cold dungeon outside a Lyon Basilica, but in a comfortable room in the outskirts of Edinburgh. And the mother and her boy; they had clearly been close, brought closer she guessed by the strain of the affair.

As Maddi watched them, the magnitude of their misdeeds seemed to fade with the twilight. So what if Henderson had become an assassin; he had done it all on behalf of the U.S. Government...right? And so what if Walter had strayed and had somehow become the father to a mass murderer? He had played no role beyond contributing his DNA. All of it felt like ancient history. Henderson was no longer the Phoenix, and Walter was no longer the straying husband. Dora had gotten past it; couldn't the world do the same?

Maddi shook her head; she knew better. Those transgressions were huge. The best she could hope for was that by the time their secrets became public, they would all be thousands of miles away.

She had tried to talk to Henderson prior to Walter and Dora's return from dinner to let him know what she was about to do, but had been unable to come up with the right words. She felt certain that he would ask why, then try to talk her out of it. He would tell her that his sins couldn't be eradicated simply by forcing his parents and his lover to go into hiding in some remote location.

And he wouldn't be wrong...not entirely, anyway. After all, how long did Maddi expect the four of them to stay hidden? Forever? Though she could live with it, she knew it would be a terrible burden on Walter and Dora. They had obligations; others in their lives who relied on them. But what else could she do? Either she stayed with Henderson and the secrets were exposed, or she left him and her world fell completely apart.

The irony was that she didn't even know Henderson's secrets. Not a single one of them. What would she do when she learned what he had done while they were apart? How would she feel? Claire had challenged her with a similar question…

"So, tell me, Maddi, if he is alive, what do you suppose he's been doing for the past four years?"

Maddi looked at Claire and sighed. "I don't know."

"If I were you, I'd need to know. After all, he didn't even tell you he was alive."

"That's true," Maddi said, and looked away. "But maybe I don't want to know."

Claire nodded. "I get it…what if he's not the man you fell in love with, right?"

Maddi leaned back. "You know, Claire, there's so much I've told you about him; so much I've let you see about that weekend and the circumstances that brought us together…and then ripped us apart. But there's one thing I've been unable to recreate."

"What's that?"

"Whatever it was that we had…or have…it kept us separate from the rest of the world. As if the worries of the day didn't matter…as if nothing could touch us."

Claire nodded. "We've said before…love isn't tied to the hands of a clock. Well, it isn't tied to its surroundings, either. Love is love; it has a life of its own." *She paused. "So…is there anything he could say about the past four years that would change that?"*

Maddi sifted through the possibilities: Theft, murder, even another woman. She shook her head. "No, I can't think of a single thing…"

The Hendersons continued to talk. Maddi kept waiting for one of them to ask him what he had done for the past four years…*so I don't have to.* Finally, as the sun faded and the room grew dark, Dora said, "These things you've done, Martin; in the past. Are there any repercussions for your future?" She frowned. "You know…is anyone *after you?"*

Walter frowned. "Maybe now isn't the time, Dora."

Dora nodded. "You're right. I just thought that perhaps you could intercede, Walter. You know…make a few phone calls; that sort of thing."

Henderson laughed, but it wasn't the light, joyful laughter Maddi expected. It was bitter; it hurt to hear it. He said, "Mom, there are just some things in this world that you or Dad can't fix." He looked away, and Maddi's heart broke…again.

* * *

Henderson was tired. In spite of how good it felt to be awake, reunited with his mom, his dad, with Maddi, Morningstar's letter was crushing him; weighing on him like some incurable flu. He felt physically ill, and was relieved when Walter finally said it was time for him and Dora to go back to the hotel. *Two less people to hold witness to the awful things I've done.* They hugged him and agreed to return first thing in the morning.

After they left, Henderson looked at Maddi and frowned. "You know, Maddi, I…I love you more than you could ever know." She smiled and crawled in bed next to him. He trembled from the feel of her skin against his and he had to fight not to cry. *Don't weaken now, Henderson.* He cleared his throat. "Which is why I wish you had read the journal."

She shook her head. "No, I'm not reading it until you're ready to read it with me."

He frowned. "There isn't time."

"Isn't time…what do you mean?"

"Never mind," he said.

Maddi hesitated. "Henderson, I don't care what you've done…it doesn't matter."

He closed his eyes. "It will…once you remember."

Maddi frowned. "Remember? Why would I remember? You never told me."

He sighed. "Yes, I did." He hesitated. "Not only that; you were there."

She looked at him, clearly perplexed, and his heart ached for her… for him…for both of them. The thought of leaving her scared him more than beatings or bullets or fire. He had suffered all of those things, but he knew that what he was about to do would hurt far worse and leave far deeper scars than any of it. But before he did what Morningstar was making him do, he had to come clean; tell her face-to-face what he had done, not just to strangers she had never met, but to a friend of hers…a good friend, as it turned out…

The Yemen leader, Abdulkarim Al-Gharsi, appeared at the door of the restaurant, flanked by body guards and guests. Henderson watched as they were led to their table next to the Omani delegation. He pulled on thin black gloves, and was about to take his pistol from his back pocket, when he stopped. He had spotted a guest walking next to Al-Gharsi, laughing, holding his arm. It was Maddi… his Maddi. He felt like he might smother. He loosened his tie and opened his collar. He tried to look away but he couldn't. 'Maddi and Al-Gharsi are friends!' He took a drink of Chianti to calm himself. 'How can that be? How does she know Al-Gharsi? Why do they seem so… close?'

He thought of Lili – the little girl Morningstar vowed to kill if Henderson didn't do what he asked – and he knew he had to carry on. 'Nothing's changed,' he told himself.

A hostess led Al-Gharsi and his guests directly past Henderson to a table only a few feet away. Maddi didn't seem to notice him. But he could feel his temperature rise as she passed so close he could smell her. He turned away and tried to focus, but had to turn back and look at her. His chest hurt as he watched her smile at the Omanis as her group was seated next to them. The two leaders exchanged nods. A waiter handed out menus, another poured water, a third brought in a bottle of wine and was preparing to open it.

Henderson felt for his .45 caliber USP in his back pocket, silencer attached. He grabbed it and put it in his lap, using his napkin to hide it. He turned so he had a clear view of both tables. His hands were shaking. 'Just another hit,' he thought as he lifted the napkin, raised the gun, and fired a shot directly into Al-Gharsi's forehead. Al-Gharsi fell forward onto the table. Henderson got up and instantly became a part of the crowd, running and pushing in every direction. The Omani leader had been shoved under his table for protection. Henderson edged close to that table, then dropped down and slid underneath. He shot the leader in his right temple, put his gun in the man's right hand, and crawled from under the table. He walked calmly to the kitchen. He stopped at the door and looked back. He saw Maddi sitting at the table, a look of horror on her face. He closed his eyes. 'What have I done?' He forced himself to turn around and keep moving, but he knew he'd never forget that look as her eyes registered the murder of her friend. As if he'd changed their very color, he knew they – and she – would never be the same….

"Maddi, I don't think you understand why I—why *the Phoenix*—was created."

Maddi frowned. "What do you mean? Who 'created' you?"

Henderson tightened his jaw. Could he do this? *Should* he do this? He thought of Morningstar's warning, suddenly grateful for a reason to follow through with what would be the hardest thing he would ever do. He recalled something his mother had told him long ago. *"Whatever you do, son, be sure to be honest in your dealings with those you care about."* Though she had likely said it from the pain of her own betrayal, Henderson had done his best to abide by it. *At least I'll have been honest before I make her go.*

He held his breath and took her hand in his. "Maddi, I killed someone."

* * *

"So, what if he tells you that he murdered someone…someone powerful, or – even worse – someone good."

Maddi shook her head. "That would never happen; he would never kill a good man." She frowned. "Why are you doing this, Claire? If he's alive, that will be enough."

Claire sighed. "I'm trying to prepare you, Maddi."

"For what?"

"For whatever has kept this man who loves you away from you for so long…"

Maddi was holding her breath. *Here it comes. Finally, I'll know why he stayed away.* The timing was right; it would be good to know before it was leaked to the world.

She took his hand in hers. "It's okay, Henderson; anything is okay."

He looked at her and the tears came. His pain was palpable; she could feel it, every bit as much as she felt the scars on his arms or the dyed black hair that fell against the nape of his neck. She pushed a strand of it from his forehead. "I promise…it's okay."

His raspy voice whispered, "Maddi, I killed more than one man… I killed many."

Maddi swallowed; she was prepared. The first pages of his journal had implied as much. And though she didn't understand why or how he could do such a thing; she had prepared herself. She stroked his cheek. "It's okay. I'm…I'm sure there were reasons."

He shook his head. "You don't understand, Maddi. I killed people...at the behest of a...terrible man. And, though most of the men I killed were bad—" he lowered his eyes, "—sometimes, they were good men."

Maddi shifted in the bed; she was becoming uneasy. He had said that he had already told her what he had done. She tried to recall their conversations since their reunion. There had only been a few, and those had been short. Certainly not substantive enough to include a confession. "You said that you already told me...when?"

He sighed. "Before you knew I was alive."

Maddi closed her eyes. *The emails!* He had reached out to her in emails. And those emails – which she had somehow pushed out of her mind – had gotten her attention for one reason and one reason only. *Because the author had admitted to committing a horrible crime.* She began to shake. *No...I won't believe it.* She stared at him, unsure if she wanted to hear more. She cleared her throat. "It's okay, really, it is." But the words weren't as convincing; even she didn't believe them.

In a hushed whisper, Henderson said, "Maddi, I killed a friend of yours."

* * *

The minute he said it, he wanted to take it back. On some level, he was holding out hope there would still be a thread of love between them, some tie that – should things change – they could reunite. He shook his head. *There's no way she'll be able to love you after this, Henderson... and, why should she? You're nothing but a killer.* Again, he thought of Morningstar's letter. He shook his head and sighed. He had no choice; he had to send her away. *To think; that asshole has given me the resolve that I'll need to let her go.*

She sat silent, staring at him. He reached for her; she pulled away. "Maddi, I—"

"Give me a minute." Her entire countenance had changed. Though she was sitting right next to him, she was miles away. She had begun to shake, but her words were measured as she said, "Tell me who you killed that you think was my friend."

It's over. You had her for what — a whole ten hours? You're an idiot, Henderson.

"Please, Henderson…I need you to tell me who you killed."

He couldn't do it…but he had to. She had to know who he was and what he had done before he made her go. That's when it hit him: if he told her the truth – the ugly, unforgivable truth – she wouldn't need to be forced to leave, she would do it on her own…*on her terms.* "Maddi, I—"

"Just tell me, Henderson."

He reached for her hand, and, though this time she let him take it, she didn't squeeze his in return. She was closed off…arming herself for the truth. *Just get it over with…just tell her.* "Al-Gharsi. I was the one who shot Al-Gharsi…while you were sitting right next to him. It was me who did that, Maddi." He looked away. "It was me."

* * *

The evening was cool. Al-Gharsi offered Maddi his coat. "No thanks. I'm fine."

"But you are not fine, Senator. You shake. Please, take my coat."

Maddi took his jacket and wrapped it over her shoulders. It had been a long time since she had seen the Yemen leader, and when they had visited last, he was simply the Minister of Foreign Affairs. His selection as President was one of the things they were celebrating as they went to dinner at the famed Almanti's in New York City. The other was the peace negotiation he had managed to pull together with the leader of Oman. Though the two countries had fought for years, Al-Gharsi's gesture had been well-received and it was one more step toward peace in the Middle East.

They were led to their table. Al-Gharsi waited as Maddi was seated next to him. Though the two had been friends for nearly a decade, they hadn't seen each other for over two years. She was eager to hear about the challenges he faced as President of Yemen, and to know more about his two little girls, Sasha and Jade. She tried to think how old they were. She was about to ask when the waiter popped the cork on a bottle of wine and offered her a drink. Al-Gharsi said something funny. When she turned to laugh, she saw him slump forward, his head falling onto the table with a horrifying thud. A red stain covered the white linen and Maddi gasped as she realized what had happened. The President of Yemen – her dear friend, Al-Gharsi – had just been assassinated…

Maddi felt sick. She remembered the night well; it had lived in her dreams, night after night for weeks. It was what had led her to Claire… the final straw in a life filled with the violent loss of so many. Al-Gharsi's murder had brought to the fore the many others in her life who had been brutally killed – either by her or by others – and she had been unable to sleep without seeing his forehead slumped on the table, the bright red blood pooling around it like some misguided halo. She thought back to the emails. Suddenly, she could see that very first email as if it was sitting right in front of her…

"I'm not sure how to say this. I am sorry about your friend, Al-Gharsi. I wish I hadn't done it, and would give anything to take it back. I will do all I can to make it up to you."

Her hands began to shake and again, she pulled away. *"I wish I hadn't done it."* It had been there all along…an admission by the very man she was sitting next to. How had she missed it? *Perhaps I chose to,* she thought, as waves of nausea forced her to grab her stomach. She was suddenly cold. Her entire body was shaking and it wouldn't stop. She stared at Henderson, but was no longer sure who or what she saw. There was the man she loved, who had endured impossible challenges; the fire, the painful recovery, the loss of everything. But she also saw a killer; the eyes, the face, the demeanor of a man who had killed far too many times…*and she was afraid.* She was finding it hard to breathe. She had never been so close to an assassin…*a man who kills for a living.* Though she had guessed that he had done terrible things, she had never imagined that he would be capable of killing a man like Al-Gharsi. Her eyes hurt; they stung like they had when she was forced to watch her mother fall apart after her father's murder…or when she finally saw Evan Jackson for who he really was. As she looked at the man who had defined her existence for the past four years, she had no idea what she felt. Her heart was pounding, breaking in two as she loved, despised, even feared the man lying next to her. She tried to stand up from the bed, but her legs wouldn't hold her and she fell into her chair.

He shook his head. "I shouldn't have told you."

Nothing has changed, she told herself. But that wasn't true. A lot had changed. She now knew why he had been so hesitant to tell her what he had done. Not only had he killed a good man, but he had destroyed a vital peace process that would have saved the lives of many. *How could he do that?* she wondered. She closed her eyes. With a voice she barely recognized, she said, "I assume your government asked this of you?"

Henderson seemed to hesitate. Then he whispered, "No."

Maddi's shaking had gotten worse. She leaned forward and grabbed the bed railing with both hands. "You…you killed a good man and no one asked you to do it?"

"Maddi, you don't understand. I had to do it."

"Why? Why did you *have* to do it?"

Henderson looked at her. His eyes were bloodshot and empty… she looked away. His voice cracked as he said, "I just had to."

* * *

Why can't I tell her? Even as he watched her pull away, he couldn't seem to bring himself to say the words. *Just tell her, dammit! Let her know that you did it all to stop Morningstar from killing a little girl!* He sighed. He wasn't going to tell her; he knew it now. This was how he would force her to go. He would let her see who he truly was; what he had done to a *good friend of hers,* and she would be so repulsed that she would walk away…forever. And he would let her. Morningstar's letter had given him the will to do what he should have done months ago.

He raised his eyes to look at her. Her head was turned, as if the very sight of him made her sick. "Maddi, I did what I did from pain… despair. I'm ruined. Please…just go."

It was clear she was struggling as she sat on the chair. Never had he seen her so… broken. Her shoulders were sagging, he could feel her shaking. She looked at him and he wanted to disappear as he looked in her wounded eyes. She said, "Just tell me one thing."

He nodded, afraid of what she was going to ask. "Anything."

"Did it hurt you to kill Al-Gharsi? Did your soul tremble at least a little when you took the life of a good man?" She continued to look at him, her eyes impossible to read, hopeful perhaps, as if they were begging him to give her a reason to forgive him.

Yes, dammit, it hurt me so badly I have never recovered. But Henderson wasn't going to let her forgive him; he couldn't. Not now. Morningstar's note had been clear; he had to leave Maddi in order to protect her. And he could see now that it was the best gift that he could give her. He looked her in the eye and whispered, "No, not really."

* * *

The color drained from Maddi's face but she didn't look away. She simply nodded. "I see." Henderson's words had stunned her; they had hurt her deep in her soul. But still, she wouldn't leave him...she couldn't. In spite of what he had done to one of the finest men she had ever known, she would stay at his side and weather the storm with him. She would find a way to forgive him...to get past what he had done.

She was about to tell him as much, when her phone vibrated on the table next to her. Though she wanted to ignore it, she couldn't. It was likely a text from the driver who was taking them to their plane. She opened it. It was a text, but it wasn't from a driver...

"You underestimate me. Ask Henderson about Lili; don't tell him why. Then leave him...now...or that little girl dies."

Maddi stared at the text. She began to shake. She didn't need to ask Henderson about Lili; she knew of her...the girl who had magically spoken to her so many times, and to her and Henderson in Dalgety Bay. She read it again. "*...leave him...now...or that little girl dies.*" She choked. *These monsters are going to kill a child?* But whoever had texted hadn't used the plural 'us;' he had said 'me.' *Who is he? And why does he care so much that I leave this man?*

She was struggling to breathe. *I need some air.* What should she do? She had made up her mind to run off with Henderson. She had been willing to expose his entire clan not only to shame, but to danger, and in Henderson's case, to a life on the run. But now, a child's life was at stake. Though Maddi had yet to actually meet Lili, she felt as if she knew her; the girl had spoken to her when Maddi was most vulnerable, when her faith in God and love and life were at their lowest, when she and Henderson were facing death from the Cobra. Lili had managed to show up when there was nothing left...*and somehow, she made it okay.* And that same child had shown up less than an hour ago, telling Maddi that she mustn't leave Henderson. *But that was before someone threatened the poor girl's life.*

Maddi swallowed; her throat felt like it was closing. Though she had no idea how she would survive it, there was no question now; she had to leave...by herself, just like the letter had told her to do. It was up to her to save Lili from the reach of a clearly diabolical man. The Hendersons had resources; they would be fine. But a little girl; it had changed everything. *There is no one to help her but me.*

When Maddi had the chance, she would learn more...about the girl, where she was hiding, who was threatening her. She would learn who cared so much about dividing Maddi and Henderson that they would be willing to kill a child. She would learn who had reached out to Justice, and the identities of the powerful men he supposedly represented. She would learn it all...when she had the chance. But for now, she needed to go.

She picked up her travel bag and draped it over her shoulder. She walked to the door and grabbed the knob. She put her hand over her mouth; she could barely breathe. *Dear God...what am I doing?* But she had to go; she had no choice. Her departure was the only thing standing between a nameless monster and an innocent little girl. Maddi didn't actually know Lili, but she felt an overpowering need to save her.

But walking out that door would destroy Maddi...that much she knew. She clung to the doorknob. *I...I love you, Henderson.* She began to cough; she thought she might be sick. She pushed against the door. She felt pressure on the other side; someone was trying to come in. She opened it, stunned to see a man she knew so well. Why was he there? He had two agents with him, which meant that the visit was official. Had he somehow been forced to reveal Matt's identity? Maddi stared at him; she wanted to cry. *No, he would never do that...he would never betray me like that.*

With tears in her eyes and an ache in her heart, she said, "I don't know why you're here, Hank, but please, keep him safe. It is now completely up to you."

CHAPTER 41

Edinburgh, Scotland

Hank hadn't been ready for Maddi's greeting. As a matter of fact, it was the last thing he expected. In all his years of knowing her, Hank had never seen Maddi so...broken.

His entourage had arrived at the nursing home with little fanfare. *"We're here on behalf of the United States Government to question your resident, Matt Henderson."* They had been shown to Henderson's room, where a Secret Service agent had verified ID. That was when everything changed. There was Maddi, her eyes red, her face drawn. Had something happened to Henderson? She walked past him, her comment confusing, to say the least. Hank watched in wonder as she continued down the hall to the elevator. The Secret Service agent who was with her gave him a shrug and fell in behind her. *What the hell happened?* He walked into Henderson's room, half-expecting the man to be dying – *no, she wouldn't have left his side* – or maybe even dead. But the opposite seemed to be the case. Not only was he not hovering at the brink of death, he was sitting up, his head in his hands, his monitors reading 'normal' across the board. Maddi had left Henderson's side for some other reason. *There's a rift in the kingdom,* he thought, instantly ashamed of himself. He walked into the room and approached the bed. "Hey Henderson."

Henderson lifted his head slowly. "Hey Hank."

Henderson looked terrible. His eyes were empty; nothing like Hank remembered them. Hank shifted back and forth, awkward about what he had come to do. He took a seat by the bed. "Do you want a glass of water, Matt?"

The man shook his head.

Hank sighed. He didn't want to do this. He cleared his throat. "Um…I need to ask you some questions. Are you up to it?"

"Sure."

Hank looked at one of his agents and nodded. The man switched on a recorder. Hank said, "This is Dr. Hank Clarkson, Deputy Director for Homeland Security, and I'm speaking with Matt Henderson, currently a resident at Sacred Hearts, an extended-stay facility in Edinburgh, Scotland, where he has been in a coma for the past four months." He paused. "Mr. Henderson, I first need to determine that you are of sound mind. Do you happen to know what day it is, and where you were prior to the coma?"

Henderson said nothing.

"Mr. Henderson?"

He looked up. "I can't tell you the day…it's a bad day." He looked away. Hank could barely hear him as he mumbled "I was in Dalgety Bay before I came here."

Hank sighed and cleared his throat. "Good enough. Did you play any role in the terrorist attacks that took place in January, eight months ago, in the cities of Charleston, Columbia, Chicago, LA, and Laredo?"

Henderson stared at him with those empty eyes; they were painful to look at. "What does it matter, Hank?"

Hank frowned. "Well, if you had nothing to do with it, it matters a lot."

"I had nothing to do with it." He paused. "But I did so many awful things, Hank. I deserve whatever happens to me." He looked down at his hands. "Lock me away, kill me…I don't care anymore."

What the hell happened? "Look, Henderson. I'm not sure what just went on here, but keep in mind…sometimes things have a way of working themselves out. Maybe it doesn't seem like it now, but everything might turn around in a few days."

Henderson sighed. "You don't understand. There's no fixing what I've done; who I've been. It's over, Hank. All of it; me and Maddi… everything."

How long had Hank waited to hear those words? For whatever reason, Maddi had cut Henderson loose, and Henderson had just told him it was over. Was it really? Was Maddi finally over Martin Henderson? *It doesn't matter, Hank, you've moved on.* Hank looked at his one-time rival, shook his head, and sighed. "Just answer one question for me, Henderson. Do you know anything about who was behind the terror attacks?"

Henderson didn't move. He looked up and, with eyes that had grown even more empty, he nodded. "I do."

Hank's eyes widened. "So, tell me…who did it?"

"I can't tell you."

"Why not?"

"Because he's mine to deal with."

"What the hell are you talking about?" Hank wanted to hit him. "Do you realize that if you know anything about the attacks and refuse to tell me, I'll have to arrest you?"

"Do it. Arrest me."

Hank shook his head. "I don't want to arrest you. You saved my son's life, for Christ's sake!"

Henderson lowered his head. He said nothing.

Hank frowned. "Don't make me do this, Henderson."

Still nothing. Hank looked at one of his agents and motioned for him to take charge of the man who had just come out of a coma…a man who had been nearly burned alive…a man who had saved countless people at the risk of his own life…a man whose grief seemed to know no bounds. "I'm sorry, Henderson, but I am forced to place you under arrest."

Suddenly the door burst open and Walter Henderson marched in. "You'll do no such thing, Dr. Clarkson."

CHAPTER 42

London, England

Dr. James Samuels took a last sip of scotch as he sat up in his recliner and looked out at the dark night. The last two days had been very productive; Ms. Stone was showing progress with her OCD, and Mr. Sprite was finally starting to open up to him. Samuels grinned. *And Walter Henderson reached out to me in an effort to save his son.*

The call from Walter had been a surprise. Never in a million years had Samuels expected to have help in his quest to save Justice, especially now that Nenita was gone. But to have the support of one of the most illustrious members of American society, well…it didn't get much better than that. It would certainly make things easier. After all, if there was anyone who might be able to open a door or two, it was Walter Henderson.

Samuels had been surprised, however, at the man's genial disposition. He had imagined a man of Walter's station in life to be aloof, maybe even condescending, but Walter was anything but. The two men had discussed how he could entice Justice but not Cobra, and, though Samuels thought it a long shot that Justice himself would be the one to actually show, he did believe it was worth a try. But it was also a risk. As Walter had pointed out, *"…I don't really want to cross paths with Cobra again if I don't have to."*

Nor do I, Samuels thought with a grimace.

He rose from his chair and walked into his bedroom. He slid out of his clothes and was about to put on pajamas, when he heard his cellphone ring in the den. He looked at a clock by his bed and frowned. Almost ten p.m. *Who would call at this time of night?* He threw on the pajamas, grabbed a robe, and ran to get the call. "Hello?" he asked, winded.

A deep chuckle put him on edge, and he fell into his chair. "Is this the esteemed psychiatrist, Dr. James Samuels?"

The voice had power; as if the evil in its bearer was able to cross through the line and grab him by the neck. Samuels hugged the arm of his chair and said as calmly as he could, "Y—yes, it is. May I help you?"

Another laugh, this one a bit more aggressive. "Yes, Doctor, you may. It would appear that my father has reached out to the bothersome Mark Justice. I find that rather annoying, don't you?"

Samuels was beginning to panic. How had Cobra gotten his cellphone number? He flinched. *Justice.* Samuels had left the number with Justice's secretary. If that was the case, then did Cobra realize that the number had been intended for Justice? He sighed; he didn't know. He had yet to determine how much each psyche knew of the other; there hadn't been time. But it would appear that at least a little of what was said or done crossed over. "I…I don't know what you're talking about, sir. I didn't catch your name."

"Don't be coy, Doctor. You know who I am."

Samuels held his breath. Should he acknowledge the killer? *Why not? It isn't like we haven't come face-to-face before.* "Dear me, I'm…I'm guessing this is Cobra. Good evening, sir. How might I help you?"

"As I said, I'm pissed that Daddy has left a message for the insufferable Justice."

"Why should that annoy you, Cobra?"

A longer pause. "Because the two of them are cooking up something, and I need to know what it is. I'm counting on you to tell me, Doctor. Write down this number."

Had Walter actually spoken with Justice? Or had he merely left a message? Either way, Cobra knew of the message, but not its contents. Fascinating. He threw open the top drawer of a nearby desk and grabbed a pen and a pad of paper. "Go ahead."

Cobra rattled off a number. Samuels wrote it down, and was about to ask where Cobra was staying so perhaps the two men could talk face-to-face, but before he could say a word, Cobra said, "Call me once you know what they're up to."

"I don't know—" Samuels heard a click; the call had ended. He looked down at the number on the pad. *Cobra's phone number…dear God, I have Cobra's number.*

His hands were shaking, and he slammed down the receiver. He walked into the living room and poured another glass of scotch. He drank it down in one gulp, all the while trying to think what to do. He should call Scotland Yard and give them the number. Perhaps they could trace it to a location. He shook his head. *No, they can only do that if he's on the line.* His eyes widened. *I could call him, and then maybe they could trace it.*

Suddenly, he thought of Walter. *But first, I need to warn Walter.* Samuels had no idea what plan Walter had put in place to meet with Justice, but he needed to let Walter know that he might be in danger… that Cobra was at least somewhat aware.

He scrolled to Walter's recent phone call and pushed 'send' to call him back. While it was ringing, he tried to think what he would say. *"Hello, Walter…Cobra called and he's irate that you're meeting with Justice. You might want to be on your guard."* But he didn't have a chance to deliver the message; the call went to voicemail. *How much should I say on a recording?* He sighed and, after the beep, said, "Um…Mr. Henderson, this is Dr. Samuels. I have…information…that is vital regarding what we discussed yesterday. Please call me the minute you get this message."

He hung up and stared at his phone. He needed to call the Yard. He had failed to do so the last time around, and it had resulted in the vicious murder of a young woman; a mother. He had felt the guilt of it as if he himself had wielded the blade.

He had met the Yard's acting inspector at Dalgety Bay. *What was his name?* he wondered as he shuffled through a stack of cards on his desk. He found the card. *Ah yes, Perkins.* Two numbers were listed; the first for Scotland Yard, the second for his personal cell. He dialed the second number, disappointed when it, too, went to voicemail. He said, "Perkins, it's Dr. James Samuels. We met in Dalgety Bay. I have vital information related to that incident. Please call the minute you get this." He then dialed the Yard and asked to speak directly with Inspector Perkins, "…regarding a matter of the utmost importance."

"I'm sorry, sir, but 'e's in Boscastle this week…you know, out in Cornwall. 'e's tryin' to help with recovery efforts after last week's flood.

We been havin' trouble with the cellphones, and the landlines are down. But I'll do my best to get a message to 'im."

Samuels sighed. "I understand. Please try to get through to him tonight, son. Let him know that it's Dr. Samuels who is calling, and that it is urgent. Thank you."

He returned to his study and poured a third glass of scotch. Though he might regret it in the morning, he knew there was no way he was getting any sleep tonight, not without some help. As he raised the glass to his lips, he was surprised to see that his hand was still shaking. He gulped down the scotch, leaned back in his chair, and closed his eyes…waiting…waiting for someone to call him back.

CHAPTER 43

Edinburgh, Scotland

Hank had been forced to restrain himself after Walter's stunning pronouncement. He had said nothing, trying to come up with a respectful way of contradicting the powerful and well-connected Henderson icon. Finally, with as much professionalism as he could gather, he looked at Walter and said, "With all due respect, sir, I've been instructed by my director to place this man into custody and return him to the United States for questioning concerning the bioterror attacks which took place in January."

Walter walked over and stood by his son. "I've just spoken with your director, Doctor. He has allowed me to assume responsibility for Matt for the next several days. There is a matter of extreme urgency and Matt's expertise is needed."

Hank was baffled...and angry. "I'm sorry sir, but I'll need something more than just your word."

Walter pulled a faxed communique from his pocket and handed it to Hank. Hank read through the order, which confirmed everything Walter had just said. He noted the familiar Director's signature at the bottom. "Give me a minute." He stepped into the hall, pulled out his phone, and dialed Hanover's private cell.

Hanover answered after the first ring. "Hi Hank. I figured you'd be calling."

"Is Walter Henderson telling me the truth?"

"Yes, I'm afraid so."

Hank flinched. "Matt claims he's innocent, but says he knows who was behind the Lassa fever attacks. Based on your instructions, sir, I should be bringing him back to the States, not turning him over to his fa—his uncle."

"He knows who's behind it? Did he give you any idea who it was?"

"No, and I don't think he plans to…without some…uh… persuasion." He paused. "So, with all due respect to Walter Henderson, I think I should take the man into custody, head for the plane, and get him to America."

Hank heard the man let out a deep sigh. "There will be plenty of time for that, Hank." He paused. "Do you remember the uprising in Latvia in '91?"

"When Latvia gained their independence from Russia?"

"Yes, and do you recall about four years ago when there was another battle in Latvia?"

Hank frowned. "No sir, I can't say that I do."

"Well, in both instances, there were two men who almost single-handedly kept Latvia free and independent against the Russian oppressors."

Hank rolled his eyes. "Let me guess; Walter and Martin Henderson were the magnificent men who somehow saved a nation."

Hanover chuckled. "Yep. They're heroes in Latvia. And now, the Hendersons are needed once again. There has been an attack on Riga."

"By who?"

"Russia. It appears they're trying to take back the Baltic States."

"You're kidding."

"No, I wish I was."

Hank frowned. *Did Hanover somehow learn that Matt is actually Martin?* "So why does *Matt* need to be a part of this push to save a country?"

"Because Martin is dead."

He still doesn't know.

Hanover continued. "Walter insists that he needs an able-bodied Henderson at his side." He paused. "I think – in light of what the family has done for America and for the world over the years – we at least owe him the honoring of his wishes."

This is too damned confusing. "Alright, sir, but I'd hardly call Matt an able-bodied Henderson. He just came out of a coma for Christ's sake!"

There was a pause. "I know. But Walter insists the man will be helpful." He paused. "Apparently, there are secrets among families such as theirs…secrets that will bolster their efforts."

Secrets? You don't know the half of it. "Okay, sir, so, what would you like me to do?"

"Go with them. You and your agents can keep an eye on Matt, support the Latvians as they resist the Russian advance, then return to the States with Matt whenever this thing is over."

Hank shook his head in disbelief. "What if 'this thing' isn't over quickly, Hanover?"

"Then I guess you'll be gone for quite a while, Hank."

CHAPTER 44

Edinburgh, Scotland

Walter had received word of the attack on Riga at 9:35 p.m., UK time, just as he and Dora were walking into their hotel suite. He had immediately called the head of Riga's militia, who had confirmed it. Walter had then called his good friend, James Wilcox, who just happened to be the President of the United States, to find out what the U.S. response was going to be. The President had been somber. *"Latvia's a part of NATO, so, of course, we'll support them. However, in an effort to keep this from becoming an all-out war, I wonder, Walter, if you would be willing to go to Latvia and maybe work some magic with your diplomacy."*

Walter had put in a call to his Latvian Security officer, and had waited impatiently for a call back. Would he need to fly over there? If so, could he take Martin with him? He and his son had weathered many assaults on their adopted country; he hoped Martin would be up to the challenge. But he had just come out of a coma; he was too weak to be of much use in battle. But he could help in other ways. No one was better at a game of chess than Martin, and, if Russia was involved, then chess was what it would be.

At 9:40, just five minutes later, Walter had been given a heads-up about Clarkson's trip to London. A good friend of his in the State Department had called, letting him know that a deputy from Homeland Security would soon arrive in Edinburgh to question Matt about his role in the bioterror attacks. To Walter's knowledge, 'Matt' didn't even exist at the time those attacks were carried out. And there was no way Martin would have been involved in such a thing. Regardless, Martin was in no shape to undergo a rigorous interrogation. The assault on Riga – though

253

horrifying – had given Walter an excuse to ask Homeland's Director to put off the interrogation. In the meantime, Walter could investigate the allegations against Matt, and come up with a plan to either clear his name or keep him away from America…permanently, if necessary. He wasn't going to let anyone – not even the United States government – take his son away from him. *I will die first.*

Fortunately, he was well-acquainted with Homeland's Director, Jason Hanover. The two had met soon after the hotel blast that had nearly ended his son's life. Hanover had just begun a stint at the Justice Department and the explosion, which smacked of domestic terrorism, had placed him instantly on the case. It had been Hanover who had delivered the bad news to Walter soon after he and Dora had arrived in DC…

"Um, it's nice to meet you, Mr. Henderson."

"Call me Walter. This is Dora."

Hanover nodded. "I appreciate you coming here today. We've gone through the debris several times, looking for anything that could confirm that your son was still in the building when it went up in flames. There was little that survived. However, in spite of the fact that we found no…ugh…remains, we did find…this um…this wallet." Hanover pulled a charred leather wallet from his pocket and handed it to Walter.

Walter took the wallet and touched the leather tenderly. He had given the wallet to Martin the year before, as a celebration of the success of his company, Marker Health Insurance. He had had it engraved, and, as he took it from Hanover, he brushed his fingers over the initials, MH. Dora was doing her best not to cry; he pulled her close and looked at Hanover. His voice broke as he said, "What about hospitals, urgent cares?"

"There's been no sign of him, sir."

"And the…the morgue? No one's found his…body…maybe far-removed from the scene…maybe mistaking him for a victim of a robbery or an assault?"

"No sir; we've been monitoring hospitals, urgent cares, and morgues over a fifty-mile radius for the past month. There's no sign of him, sir." There was only silence. Hanover added, "We'll continue to look for him, sir…"

And they had…for two more months. Finally, after the third month, they had added Martin's name to the list of victims and had proceeded with a memorial service in honor of all who had died. Hanover had stood with Walter and Dora through the entire ceremony.

The minute Walter had heard that the Deputy Director was coming to take Matt back to America, he had called his friend at the State Department, had gotten Hanover's private cellphone number, and had given the man a call. *"Is this Jason Hanover?"*

"Yes, it is. May I ask who's calling?"

"It's Walter Henderson. We met four years ago…in DC."

"Um, yes sir, I remember. What can I do for you, sir?"

"I understand you've sent your deputy over here to question my nephew?"

"Yes sir. I assure you; he'll be afforded every legal protection. We're willing to provide him an attorney, but something tells me you'll cover that."

"I certainly will; after all, the poor man's been through hell and back."

Silence. *"Yes sir. I'm so sorry to do this."*

"What exactly is Matthew being accused of?"

"Your nephew's name was listed on a document found in a property search of a former Pentagon employee." He paused. *"The information suggests that he played a supportive role in January's bioterror attacks."*

"Forgive me for saying this, Director, but 'suggests' isn't admissible in a court of law. Is there something more significant that ties my nephew to the attacks?"

There was a pause. *"No sir. But we're compelled to follow up on all leads. Our liaison on the case — an official from the Pentagon — has looked through the paperwork, and insists that we at least question your nephew."*

"And who might that be?"

"I'm not at liberty to say, sir."

"I see. Well, I have one request to make, Director."

"I'll do anything I can, sir."

"The Hendersons have been vested in the safety of Latvia for nearly a century now. And, though we like to keep our presence there low-key, suffice it to say, we care deeply about the country."

"I understand, sir. I'm aware of your intervention in '91, and again in 2000."

Walter sighed. *"You will learn soon that Latvia is once again under attack."*

There was a pause. *"I wasn't aware, sir."*

"I only just found out myself. My grandfather made a promise to the prior owner of our castle, as well as to Dwight Eisenhower, that the Hendersons would look out for Latvia and do our best to keep it out of the hands of Russian invaders.

Our family has honored that pledge ever since. I'll need my nephew to help me with this, Director."

"With all due respect, sir, your nephew has just awakened from a five-month coma. I can't imagine that he'll be of much use."

Walter had to bite his tongue. "With all due respect sir, the value of a soldier is not only seen on the battlefield."

Silence. "That is a good point, sir."

"I need him at my side to fight this battle. Then, I swear to you, I'll return him to America myself to face your interrogators regarding crimes I know he didn't commit."

Silence. "Sir, I—"

"Before you decide, keep this in mind: The integrity of the Henderson name means more to me than even my own life. Though we may not have always made honorable choices, we have lived honorably for both Latvia and the United States. I would not sully that honor by lying to you now."

A pause. "I'll need to send my deputy and his agents with you."

"That's fine."

"Okay then. Mr. Henderson, I'll release your nephew to the shared custody of you and Dr. Clarkson. I have nothing but the highest regard for you and your family and all you've been through." He paused. "But let me say this: If, for some reason, you back away from your promise, I will use the full force of the United States military to hunt down both you and your nephew. Are we clear?"

"Yes, Director Hanover, we are."

But now, as Walter stared at his son, he was left to wonder if Martin could even survive the trip to Latvia. Though he had seemingly recovered from the coma, something had changed in the hour since he had last seen him. He looked terrible…lifeless. *What happened from the time we left to the time we came back? And where is Maddi?*

Maybe he should wait…talk to Maddi. At least let her know they were leaving. He stared at his son. Clarkson was hovering over the man, still trying to get him to talk. *The sooner I get him on a plane to Latvia, the better.* He could call Maddi on the way and have her meet them at the plane.

He checked his watch. A few minutes after ten. By now, his private jet should be waiting at the airport. The journey to Latvia would take about two-and-a-half hours. With the time-change, that would have them landing outside the compound just before three a.m. It would be quiet then; or at least it should be. *Another reason why we would be wise to leave now.*

But he was transporting his ailing son into a war zone. Was that wise?

He looked at Hank and frowned. Hank represented America; America wanted his son. Walter didn't know why; that would come later. For now, all he knew was that he needed to get Martin out of there… and soon. *I'll sort out the rest later.*

CHAPTER 45

Edinburgh, Scotland

Hank stood by as Matt was loaded on a stretcher and carried out of the room. But it wasn't Hank's medics from America who were overseeing the transfer. Apparently, Walter had pulled in a team of doctors from London's prestigious University Hospital. Hank instructed his own team to find lodging in Edinburgh, with an understanding that they would stay on call for the eventual trip back to the States. His two agents would continue on with him to Latvia.

He moved closer to Walter, who was walking with the stretcher. "I spoke with Hanover. I'm to go with you to Latvia, Mr. Henderson."

"Yes, Jason told me as much. And please, call me Walter." He paused. "I hope I'm not inconveniencing you too greatly."

Inconvenienced isn't the word I'd use. "Not at all, sir. Where are we going and how may I be of service?"

"To our home outside Uzava."

Hank nodded, fighting a grin as Walter casually said the word "home." The castle near Uzava sat on an estate that was over 100 acres, and was fortified with a full army, a small battalion of ships, and the finest security available. *Home indeed.*

Hank looked down at the man who now called himself Matt. *Does Walter know who you are?* Hank had learned of the switch five months ago, just after the Dalgety Bay attack. And the news had been a shock, to say the least. Martin's appearance had somehow been dramatically altered. Though the hair could have easily been dyed, the structural changes of the face and the removal of the scars had to have involved a technologically advanced surgery. *Where did he have that done?*

The fact that so few were aware of Martin's new identity was nothing short of a miracle. Maddi had done all she could to keep the secret, and, as far as he knew, not even her brother Andrew was aware. And, if Andrew didn't know, no one did. *Except me.* Why had she told Hank? To spare him the agony of thinking she had fallen for another man? Or was there more to it? *She needs me to help her keep his identity protected.*

Which was evidenced by her parting comment. *"Keep him safe, Hank…it is now completely up to you."* Hank flinched. *No big deal…I'm just sole caretaker for this man's identity…for his entire wellbeing.* For whatever reason, Maddi had forfeited the job.

And Hank was fully aware of the consequences should he fail. Martin Henderson was the Phoenix, and the Phoenix was wanted for the bioterror attacks. If Henderson was ever identified as Phoenix, he would likely go to prison for life, or maybe even be executed as a traitor. *Let alone the shame and disgrace it would bring to the Henderson name.*

Hank winced. *The Henderson name…like it is its own commodity.* And it was; every bit as much as grain or gold or natural gas. The revelation that the man responsible for killing scores of Americans had been a Henderson – a notable one, at that – would cause markets to fall, indexes to crumble, and Latvia to suffer. *How odd,* he thought, *to think that a surname could carry so much weight.*

He watched as Walter guided the entourage toward the elevator. He looked at him, so protective over the man on the stretcher. It was hard to think that he and Dora, the guy's own parents, weren't aware that Matt was really their son. *I'll bet they know.* But he would say nothing until he was sure.

Henderson's eyes were closed, his agony still evident in his tightly drawn features. *What happened to you?* The only thing Hank had been told about Henderson's last several months was that he had been in a coma since leaving Dalgety Bay, and that Maddi hadn't left his side…until now.

Had she known Hank was coming? Maybe she thought he had flown overseas to say thank you to the man who had saved Roger's life, or to follow up on the incident at Dalgety Bay. Should he call her and let her know that Henderson was being taken away? What if she was unaware that 'Matt' was being questioned about the terror attacks? What if she had merely stepped out for coffee or a bite to eat? What if her ominous *"...keep him safe, Hank,"* was nothing more than a weak comment by a tired woman? He shook his head. It was far more than that. He had *felt* her anguish...she was truly leaving Henderson behind.

As he looked down at the man being wheeled silently down the hall, he suddenly felt sorry for him. *Ha!* Martin Henderson had been born into wealth, had created a mammoth insurance company from the ground up, had survived two raging fires, both of which should have killed him, and had won Maddi's heart. Nonetheless, Hank felt sorry for him. The man was sick and sad, and it was clear that something terrible had happened between him and Maddi. *They're finally over...after years of wanting it to be, it finally is.*

He thought of Jenny and felt a sudden stab of guilt. *I'll go with Matt to Latvia so he and his father can save a country...then I'll load him onto the DC 9 medical transport plane and get him back to Washington...so I can be with Jenny, the woman I love.*

He stepped closer to the gurney. His agents were nearby, so he had to be careful what he said. Why? *Because Maddi asked me to.* "Well, Matt, I guess it's you and me, together again."

Henderson said nothing as he looked up at him, the empty eyes so tragic that Hank was forced to turn away. He couldn't wait for this assignment to end. He would call Jenny the minute they got down to the street and tell her that he loved her and would come home as soon as he could.

They reached the elevator and Walter said, "I have an unmarked ambulance outside. We have to hurry." He paused. "Oh, and Hank, other than updates to your Director, I ask that you speak to no one until this thing is resolved. Not a single soul."

CHAPTER 46

Philadelphia, Pennsylvania

The sun had sunk low in the sky by the time Todd Jackson pulled up to Jack Steinke's house on North Street in Philadelphia. He parked two blocks away and did his best to seem casual as he strolled along a tree-lined street in the old German community. The fading sunlight sent shadows through the trees, and he smiled as he breathed in the night air. It was refreshing…revitalizing in some strange sort of way. He reached house number 2136 and jogged up the steps to the porch. He knocked twice on a dark gray door that looked like it had been recently painted. It was opened by an older woman who was attractive in spite of her age; likely Steinke's wife. Steinke wasn't the best-looking man; Todd was surprised he had such a good-looking wife.

"Good evening, ma'am. My name is Todd Jackson."

The woman smiled, making her even more attractive. Todd winked and shifted his stance as she opened the door wider. "Why, come on in Mr. Jackson. The boys are downstairs." She showed him to the door of the basement, and he suddenly felt like he was twelve years old, visiting the neighbor boy, Johnny Banks, at his home in Evansville, Indiana. Johnny's mom, who had also been a looker, had always said the same thing. *"Come on in, Todd…the boys are downstairs."*

Todd went down the steps, bending his head a bit to avoid the low ceiling. When he reached the bottom step, he saw seven men gathered around a table. They had poker chips and a pair of dice lying on the table. But the deck of cards hadn't been touched; there was no poker game being played tonight. The men's faces were stern, impassive. This was the Blue Brotherhood, and people lived and died based on what these seven – now eight – men decided.

There was an open chair beside Jack Steinke and Todd sat down. Jack was a big man with thick features and a bulging nose. His eyes were light blue, almost gray, and his hair, still lots of it, had turned white. He reminded Todd of a character from Lord of the Rings. He looked at Todd and smiled. "Welcome." Jack said to the others, "Todd and I are both Indiana boys." He patted him on the back. "You want a soda or some chips?"

Todd's hands were sweating; he rubbed them on his lap. "No, I'm good, thanks."

"Okay. Let's get started. First of all, great work, Todd, on taking care of that Malone character. One less asshole to pollute the Philadelphia streets." He shifted and his chair squeaked. "Now, onto new business. We've got a problem with a guy on death row that just got his sentence overturned on final appeal. There's some 'new evidence' that throws doubt on his conviction, and they've actually let the guy walk." He sighed. "Now, I'm not saying the guy wasn't maybe innocent of the crime they were getting ready to fry him for, but he was definitely guilty of at least three other murders over the course of the last twenty years. His name is Peter Jacobs. Anybody wanna' look into it?"

A man across the table said, "I'll take care of it. He lives near me… or at least he did before he went to prison. I'll find him."

Steinke nodded. "Good. The next, um, *situation,* is going to take two of you." He paused. "There's these brothers, Tom and Tim Molotov, that have been terrorizing South Philly for the last six months. Four days ago, the guys in the tenth precinct collared them for breaking and entering, and found a knife on one of them that had been used in a murder the day before." He paused. "Before the boys could get the assholes to turn on each other, some do-gooder lawyer came in and started bullshitting about their rights being violated. Next thing you know, the discovery of the knife is inadmissible because the arrest wasn't right." He pounded the table, causing the poker chips to shake and a few of the men to flinch. "Damned lawyers!" There were nods of agreement. "Anyway, the Molotov brothers have been released, the charges dismissed." He bristled. "It's horse shit, that's what it is." He shook his head. "So, which two of you want to handle it?"

The cop on the other side of Steinke spoke up. "Larry and I will take it." He punched his partner affectionately. "Gladly, right bro?" Larry nodded.

Steinke nodded. "Good."

He spent another twenty minutes assigning cases to the men in the room. Todd was given the name of a man who had killed a butcher just as he was opening his shop for the day. The killer had walked after it was discovered that he met the qualifications for being 'learning disabled.' *"What the hell does that have to do with anything?"* Todd had asked. The men had all nodded, and Todd had agreed to take care of it.

As eight o'clock rolled around, Steinke leaned back, put his hands behind his head, and said, "Now, is there any other filth out there that needs cleaned off the streets?"

Todd cleared his throat. He had to be careful how he broached the subject of the man with the devil tattoo; the boys gathered around that table weren't going to have a lot of sympathy for the hookers on the corner of Christian and Vine. "Have any of you ever seen or heard of a guy with a devil tattoo on his face?"

There were a few subtle nods, and Todd sensed a sudden undercurrent in the room. He continued, somewhat awkwardly. "I...I think he might be a pretty bad guy. I think he's a rapist...and who knows what else."

Silence. Finally, the cop named Larry said, "The guy's Special Forces. They call him Lucifer on the street. He was a good man at one time, but he saw too much shit overseas and kinda' went nuts."

More silence. Every man at that table respected Special Forces. Those were the guys who gave up everything to make themselves the best. And many of them had paid the ultimate price, either with their lives or their sanity. "Lucifer" sounded like just one more casualty of war.

Todd looked around the room. Did that mean that the man was off limits? Even for the "justice makers" gathered at the table? Did Lucifer get a free pass just because he was a crazy ex-marine? That didn't seem right, but Todd didn't want to ruffle feathers his first night in the Brotherhood. He remained silent and nodded.

Steinke glanced at him and said, "I'll look into it." He scanned the room. "Is that it, then?" He waited and no one said anything. "Okay, if there's nothing more, I got only one other piece of business." He turned to Todd. "Jackson, I happen to know that your daddy was a cop."

Todd nodded. "Yes sir, he was."

Steinke continued. "And do you know how he died, son?"

Todd shifted uncomfortably. "Yes sir. He was taken down by the same kind of scum we're dealing with around this table."

Steinke nodded as he stared at Todd and said evenly, "There's more to the story."

Todd narrowed his eyes. *What the hell does that mean?* He waited while Steinke wiped his forehead with a handkerchief, folded it, then slid it into a pants pocket. "I don't know what went down the night your dad was killed, but I know one thing," he flinched as he looked around the room, "...it wasn't a couple of punks that killed Evan Jackson."

Todd cleared his throat; he was having trouble catching his breath. "Excuse me sir, but what exactly are you saying?"

Steinke sighed. "All I'm sayin' is this: you are now part of the Blue Brotherhood, and we have one purpose and one purpose only: To carry out justice when the system fails to do so. I think your dad's murder may be one of those situations. I was a beat cop in a nearby precinct at the time, and the bust never seemed quite right," he paused, "...too many things that didn't add up." He let out a deep sigh. "Anyway, it wouldn't be right to bring you into this organization without lookin' into it, don't you agree?"

Todd's leg was shaking. He put his hand on his knee to stop it, but it continued to shake. *What the hell is he talking about?* Todd had heard the story of his father's death a thousand times; first from his mother when he was little, then from the boys on the force as he entered the ranks. And, though Evan had died in Evansville, Indiana, and Todd lived and worked in Philadelphia, the cops knew about their own. So, from the Police Academy all the way through his training as a beat cop, Todd had heard about the murder of his father, the brave Evan Jackson. His mother's words stayed in his mind, just as fresh as when she had told him the story so many years ago...

"There is only one thing you need to know about your father, Todd. He was a brave man who died protecting the people of this town."

"What happened, Mom?"

"It doesn't matter what happened; just know that he died a hero."

"But I want to know what happened."

His mother narrowed her eyes, taking forever to respond. "I'll tell you these details once, and only once, Todd, then we'll never mention it again. Got it?"

Todd nodded.

She took a deep breath. "There was a gang of men holding up a liquor store. Your daddy, a captain by then, was covering street patrol for a cop who was out with surgery. His partner was at the courthouse and was on his way back to the station when the call came in. Your father went to the scene alone—which he wasn't supposed to do – and saw the men running from the store. He jumped out of his cruiser and raised his gun to try to stop them. Two men threw down their guns and put up their hands. A third man aimed his pistol directly at your father, and pulled the trigger... six times." She flinched. "Six times!" She sighed. "Your daddy died instantly. Only the first two men were captured. They swore they had nothin' to do with killin' a cop, and that they didn't know the third man, the shooter, but the police thought they knew plenty. They were convicted of the robbery, and aidin' and abettin' a capital crime. But those two men – to this day – deny knowin' anything about the murder or the man who did it."

Todd frowned. "Where was the partner?"

"Still on his way to the scene."

"Then how do you know?"

His mother's eyes flashed. "How do I know what?"

"So many details. That it was the third guy that fired the shots...that dad died instantly...that kind of stuff."

She frowned. Through clenched teeth she said, "There must've been a witness..."

But now he wondered if maybe there hadn't been. Maybe she had simply been told that story to give her comfort after his death. Something else had happened to his father; something that had been kept secret for over twenty years. He cleared his throat. "Did you say anything at the time? Did anybody look into it?"

Steinke frowned. "No, I didn't have enough clout at the time. But I don't know why nobody else did." He sighed. "Maybe that's why I want to look into it now." He cleared his throat. "Anyway, now that you're one of us, I'll get the boys in Evansville to pull the file. I've heard rumors, but I'm not gonna' share no rumors. I'll let you know what they find when we meet next month."

He stood, indicating an end to the meeting. Todd sat glued to his seat. The other men filed up the stairs and Steinke looked down at Todd. "You let me look into it, son. I promise I'll let you know what I find." He paused and put his hand on Todd's shoulder. "The whole point of this organization is to make things right without getting caught. So, don't you go looking into this. If we find out what happened and we...handle it...I don't want them to have any reason to come looking for you. Do you understand?"

Todd was seething, but what Steinke said made sense. He nodded and stood up slowly. "Yes sir. I understand."

"Good, now let's go upstairs."

Todd followed big Jack Steinke up the stairs, watching as Jack bumped his head on the low ceiling. Under different circumstances, it might have been funny. But there was nothing funny about what had gone on in that basement. The eight men gathered around that table were prepared to do anything – even murder – to make things better for the people they were sworn to protect.

As he left the Steinke residence and walked the two blocks to his car, he knew that something else – something even bigger – had happened in that basement. Todd had learned that his father's death may not have gone down the way he had been told for the past twenty years. He reached his car and slid behind the wheel, unable to shake the question that suddenly consumed him: *What really happened to my father that night?*

CHAPTER 47

Edinburgh, Scotland

Maddi's feet were moving, but she didn't know how. It felt like the sidewalk was crumbling beneath her as she stumbled down Easter Road. It was dark; she knew it was late, but she had no idea what time it was. She didn't care. Dense fog had come in, followed by misty rain, but she hardly noticed. She felt nothing; not fear, not the rain, nothing. Her bodyguards were with her, but she barely saw them. They were practically running to keep up with her. The bigger of the two, Cravens, was out of breath. "Senator, please. You need to stop. We've been walking for over three hours, and we need to get you to a protected area. We can't continue to keep you safe out on the streets like this."

Then don't protect me.

She fell into a sprint. The leaner agent, Cross, dashed in front of her. He, too, was breathing heavily as he said, "Madam, with all due respect, this is not acceptable." He grabbed her by the arm and walked her to a bench that sat back from the road. She looked at him and frowned. *So…what now?* She guessed they had called for a car to take her somewhere…but where? Henderson's room had been her room. *Where will I stay now?*

There was nothing they could do; there was nothing anyone could do. Though she had concluded that the only way to keep Lili safe was to leave Henderson, she hadn't expected it to hurt so badly. And, though the realization that he had shot one of her dearest friends should have made it easier, the opposite was true. It was as if the horror of what he had done had become some strange bond between them. She had seen it in his eyes; his shame over the murder of Al-Gharsi. She knew a

267

similar shame. And she could see that he regretted it. Though he said that he had felt nothing, she could tell it was a lie.

She frowned. *Why would he lie about such a thing?* The question had been haunting her. It was almost as if he had been *encouraging* her to go. Why? She didn't know. All she knew was that she longed to go back to him, let him know that it didn't matter what he had done, then stay with him forever.

But the threat to Lili had changed everything. Maddi hadn't questioned the validity of the text that had threatened the girl's life… she had dealt with enough powerful men to know that they rarely made idle threats. So, in spite of all she was about to lose – her love for Henderson that had literally been her lifeblood for the past four years – she had had no choice; she had needed to let him go.

But the pain was unbearable. Her heart, her head…every part of her felt the ache of what she had done. She was struggling to breathe; it felt like she was smothering. The walking helped her think, but it didn't help with the pain. And it was clear that her agents had had enough; they weren't going to let her wander the streets of Edinburgh any longer.

Somehow, in the midst of it all, she had managed to respond to the text from the driver; the man who had been sent by the U.S. President to take her and the Hendersons to a foreign transport plane. It had come through soon after she had walked out of the nursing home. *"I'm here,"* was all it said.

"Mission has been cancelled," she had texted in reply. She hoped it was enough.

A black sedan pulled up. Cross walked over, spoke to the driver, then waved for Cravens. Cross climbed in front as Cravens led Maddi to the back. He slid in beside her and they drove off. It was late; the traffic was light. They moved quickly through town.

They slowed to a stop as a man crossed in front of them. Maddi watched him; an older man with a shuffling gait, a raincoat hanging loosely from his stooped frame. She fought tears, curious where the man could be going so late at night…alone.

They continued on, driving past the castle and along the Royal Mile. She saw it all, but she saw nothing. She thought of Hank showing up out of nowhere. Why him, and why was he taking Henderson to America? Though he knew the truth about Henderson, Maddi felt certain he hadn't told anyone. He had promised her that he wouldn't, and one thing about Hank, he always kept his promises. Which meant that, for whatever reason, Homeland Security was taking a non-citizen – who had just come out of a coma – back to America. Why? What did they know? What did they *think* they knew? And why had Hank flown all the way to Scotland without at least telling Maddi he was coming?

They were all good questions…reasonable questions. *I should call him,* she thought, fighting another round of tears. Just to hear his voice would be comforting; Hank had always been comforting. She could ask the motive for his trip, and get a sense of what was known by those back home. She could also ask him about the War-on-Terror committee, and at least find out if he was aware that nearly all of its members were dead.

She pulled out her phone; her hand was shaking so much she could barely even hold it. She was about to dial when she stopped. Depending on his answers, the call might require more privacy than she had in that town car. Besides, it was possible he was on his way back to America. She shoved the phone in her purse. *I'll call him later.*

The car slowed at a turnoff that led to a tree-lined drive. As they made the turn, she recognized the hotel she had stayed in before they moved Henderson to the nursing home. They stopped at the front door. A doorman was standing ready, braving the rain as he reached out and opened Maddi's car door.

Cross slid out of the front seat and offered Maddi his hand. She took it and they hurried inside. She fought a renewed round of tears when she spotted the concierge. He had gone through that first month right along with her…when Henderson was still in the hospital. The last time she had seen him – about four months ago – she and Henderson were still very much in love. Seeing him now, knowing so much had changed, well, it was killing her. She put on a smile as best she could and gave him a quick wave.

He came from behind his desk. "Welcome back, Madam. I hope all is well with your Mr. Henderson?"

She wanted to say, *"He's no longer my Mr. Henderson,"* but instead she nodded and said, "He's doing a bit better, I think."

He clapped his hands. "That is wonderful to hear, Madam."

He looked like he was going to ask another question, when Cravens said quickly, "Is the suite secure?"

The concierge nodded. "Yes sir. I oversaw the vetting myself, along with one of Inspector Perkins' top aides."

Cravens nodded and practically dragged Maddi to the elevator. The three of them stepped inside, and no one said a word. It was as if someone had died.

They reached their floor and stepped into the hall. Maddi's phone vibrated and she answered with a dull, "Hello."

"Good evening, Senator…it's Phil."

"Hel—Hello Phil." She cleared her throat. "So good to hear from you."

"I know it's late there, but I tried earlier and wasn't able to reach you." He paused. "Claire Porter called again. She said that it was urgent that she talk to you."

Maddi closed her eyes. She had completely forgotten about calling Claire. She had written the number on a sheet of paper, but it was back at the nursing home. "I…I don't have her number with me, Phil. Could you give it to me again?"

"Certainly, Senator. Do you have a pen?"

Maddi looked at Cravens. He was pulling a pen from his pocket, along with a crumpled receipt he had gotten somewhere. He held the receipt in his hand with the pen ready and nodded. Maddi said, "I'm Ready, Phil."

He read off the number, she repeated it so Cravens could write it down, then she thanked him. She was about to hang up, when he said, "Are you doing okay, Senator?"

No…not at all. "I'm fine, Phil. Thanks for asking. Are things going well there?"

"Yes…but you are missed. Hurry home, Senator."

Maddi's eyes began to water; she rubbed them. "I…I will." She hung up, refusing to look at Cravens, knowing she would burst into tears if she did. "Let's go."

He nodded, and they walked down the hall to the suite. He unlocked the door and had Cross stay outside with Maddi while he did a quick inspection. A minute later, he waved them in and handed Maddi the paper with Claire's number. She shoved it in her pocket. She went straight to the bedroom and closed the door. She leaned against it, a torrent of tears forcing her to the floor. She sat there alone in the dark for a good ten minutes, crying silently as she mourned the loss of the man that she loved.

Finally, she wiped her eyes and looked at the darkness surrounding her. *Get up, Maddi.* She took a deep breath, then stood and turned on a lamp. She pulled Claire's number from her pocket and stared at the number, unsettled as she tried to imagine what Claire might need to tell her that was so urgent that she would call Maddi's secretary twice in a matter of days. She checked the time. *1:15 a.m....8:15 at night back home.*

She held her breath and dialed.

The call was answered quickly, with a cautious, "Hello?"

"Claire, it's Maddi."

There was a pause. "Maddi...it is so good to hear your voice."

Maddi closed her eyes, comforted by the soothing voice of the therapist. "Yours, too. Is everything okay?"

"No, Maddi." Claire's voice had changed. It was more...distant. "I have a bit of a dilemma...a problem, if you will."

"A problem?"

"Yes. I had hoped to talk to you before...before I took care of it, but, when I didn't hear from you, I went ahead with it."

"Went ahead with what?"

A pause. "I'd...I'd like to tell you face to face. Are you coming home soon?"

Maddi frowned. That was the second time that someone had mentioned her coming home. Home suddenly sounded like an excellent idea. There was nothing holding her in Scotland; not anymore. "You know Claire...I think I might. As a matter of fact, I'll look into flights first thing in the morning. I have a few loose ends to tie up here, but I could be back in DC by Friday; Saturday at the latest. Does that work?"

"I'm afraid Friday will be too late."

Maddi frowned. "What do you mean, 'too late'?"

There was another pause. Maddi thought Claire might have hung up. "Claire?"

"I really need to tell you face to face, Maddi."

"What are you talking about?" Maddi felt weak; she was suddenly aware of how exhausted she was. She walked to a Queen Anne chair in the corner of the room and fell into it. "Claire...just tell me. We'll both feel better."

"I doubt it." Claire's voice was barely a whisper. "Maddi, I have this requirement...this obligation as a therapist."

Maddi's hands had again begun to shake. She held the phone tighter. "Go on."

"Well, I'm supposed to tell the authorities...whenever I learn of a...a crime."

Maddi's head was spinning. "I...I don't understand."

Claire's voice was shaky. "I...I should have said something before you told me...your story. I didn't expect it...and then we just kept going with it...because I knew that was what you needed...but now I feel so terrible—"

"Claire, what are you trying to say?" Claire sounded like she was crying. Maddi rubbed her forehead, doing her best to soften her tone. "It's okay, Claire. Just say it."

"No Maddi, it's not okay. Earlier today I spoke with...the Assistant Prosecutor for Vanderburgh County."

For the second time that night, Maddi felt like she was going to be sick.

When Claire spoke again, her voice sounded different... detached...almost cold. "I'm flying to Indiana Thursday afternoon... to meet with him and let him know about...a shooting that took place twenty-two years ago in an alley in downtown Evansville."

CHAPTER 48

Philadelphia, Pennslyvania

Todd got home just after eight-thirty. He immediately called his mother. The call was a short one. She let him know – in no uncertain terms – that she wanted nothing to do with digging up memories of that time in their lives. *"It was awful, Todd. Just let sleeping dogs lie."*

He had ended the call without a goodbye. The next call would be to a friend of his, Blake Williams. The two had gone to the academy together. Todd was from Evansville, and Blake was from Indianapolis. Blake had always been a bit of a cutup and the two had become friends. Todd's hope was that Blake had joined the city's police force. He was pleased when he found Blake's name listed in their ranks. He checked the time. Eight-forty p.m. Would Blake be there that late? Todd nodded. He himself was often at the Philly precinct after hours, either doing paper work or preparing to go to trial for the DA. The odds were good that Blake did the same. Todd dialed the precinct, crossing his fingers as he asked for Blake Williams.

After a minute, a deep voice came on the line. "This is Officer Williams."

"Blake? Blake Williams. It's Todd Jackson. You remember, from the Academy?"

There was a pause. "Yeah, how could I forget? Remember the time when—"

"Blake, I don't have much time. I need a favor."

A pause. "Sure, Jackson. Just name it."

"Do you remember how I told you that my dad was a cop? And I think I also told you that he was gunned down during a robbery in

Evansville in '82. The murder was attributed to three assholes and my dad has always been regarded as a hero."

"As he should be."

Todd sighed. "You're right about that. Anyway, there's a group of cops here in Philly who've taken an interest in dad's murder."

"Why?"

Todd frowned. Should he tell Blake that there was a question surrounding his father's death? *No, the fewer who know, the better.* "I think it's routine. Somethin' to do with cops killed in the line of duty, and the fact that my dad was one of 'em."

"Okay. So, do you want me to gather up what I can for them?"

"No. I'd kinda like to do my own digging…behind the scenes, if you know what I mean."

There was a pause. "What time frame are we talking?"

"Twenty-two years ago."

"Okay. That'll be on micro phish. I'll see what I can find."

"That would be great."

"Just one thing, Jackson."

"What's that?"

"Sometimes when we go 'phishing,' we don't always like what we catch." Blake burst out laughing. "That's a pretty good one, isn't it?"

Todd forced a laugh. "Yeah, that's really funny. Just let me know what you find, okay?"

"Sure, no problem."

Todd hesitated. "Hey, Blake."

"Yeah?"

"Keep this between us, okay? You know, Academy brother to Academy brother?"

Another pause. "Sure. What's your cellphone number?"

Todd gave him the number and hung up. What would it mean if his father's murder hadn't gone down the way that he had been told for the past twenty years? More importantly, why would someone create a lie to hide it? A rather elaborate lie, as it turned out. Todd certainly didn't *care* if the men convicted of killing his father had been falsely condemned; they were probably scumbags anyway. *But why the lie?*

He stared through a pair of dingy curtains and watched as the last rays of sunlight lit up the sky. A lone sparrow flew past, and Todd watched it as it disappeared beyond a row of tall maples. He shook his head. He had been told to leave the matter alone. *"Let the Brotherhood handle it, Todd."* One thing was certain; he wasn't about to leave it alone. There was more to it, and he was determined to find out what it was.

He walked back to the couch and turned on the TV. As he stared at a rerun of "Home Improvement," Blake's words kept running through his mind: *"Sometimes when we go 'phishing,' we don't always like what we catch."*

CHAPTER 49

Edinburgh, Scotland

Maddi hadn't moved from the Queen Anne chair. Claire's words had been like a punch to the gut; Maddi felt completely blindsided. Her trusted therapist, the person who knew more about her than anyone, had called to let her know that she was reporting her crime – *the sordid history of my past* – to the police. It was unfathomable. When Maddi had finally found her voice, all she had managed to say was *"Why?"*

"I did everything I could to avoid this, Maddi. I talked to a lawyer friend; I spoke with the local DA…I even went so far as to talk to a DC circuit judge. All of them said the same thing…I'm obligated to report a capital crime, regardless how old, if it occurred in one of several specific states, which includes Indiana."

"But Claire, nothing will change. There will be nothing that will come of it… other than the effect it will have on my life and on the lives of those who love me."

"I know, Maddi. And I'm sorry…sorrier than you could ever know. I wanted you to have a chance to prepare."

Maddi had had to fight to control her anger…and her disbelief. *"I get a whole day-and-a-half – overseas – to prepare myself, my friends, and my family for the utter destruction of my reputation and my life? Thanks, Claire."*

Then, in that way that only Claire could, she had said, *"I know it doesn't feel like it now, Maddi, but you'll be glad I did this. You'll find comfort in what I'm about to do."*

"Claire, I think that's something you're telling yourself to justify this. What about that whole 'doctor-patient confidentiality' issue?"

"It doesn't apply…not with capital cases." There had been a pause. *"Maddi, I know you're angry. I get it; I wish it could be different. But what I'll tell*

the Prosecutor is pretty much what you told me. The officer was coming at you, and you had no choice but to defend yourself. I'm confident there will be no repercussions."

Maddi had wanted to scream *"No repercussions? Are you kidding?"* But instead, for whatever reason, she had let it go. After all, Claire was just doing her job. What Claire didn't know…what Maddi had never told her…were the details…the specific, very illegal steps that Maddi's grandfather had taken to make the entire matter disappear. There would definitely be repercussions for that. *The life I knew is over.*

Then, suddenly realizing that her life was about to change dramatically, she had added, *"Claire, I need a favor. A very good friend of mine, Hank Clarkson, is on his way back to the States. It's quite possible, in light of what you've just told me, that I won't get a chance to talk to him. Will you give him a message for me?"*

There had been a pause. *"I…I will, but…why me?"*

"Because, it involves something I wouldn't want anyone else in DC to know. You're good at keeping a secret…well, most secrets." She had paused. *"Anyway, just tell him to watch his back. Tell him it has something to do with a secret committee that he was on…and that several of the members…have died."* Maddi had paused, so flustered she could barely speak. *"It's…it's probably nothing. Just let him know that a terrible man, Morningstar—"* she had stopped herself. *"I'm sure it's nothing…unless someone shoots a high-ranking Secret Service agent in the next day or two,"* she had forced a laugh. *"Please, just tell Hank to…to watch his back."*

She could hear Claire scribbling. *"I…I will, Maddi. I'll deliver the message."*

"Thanks, Claire."

She had then heard what sounded like a sob. *"I'm…I'm so sorry, Maddi."*

Maddi had ended with, *"I understand, Claire. I really do,"* which had likely reinforced – far more than angry words – that she didn't understand at all.

She looked over at a grandfather clock. It was late and the room was dark. As the hands inched toward two a.m., Maddi tried to think of the steps she would need to take to prepare her loved ones for the news. Her mother and Andrew already knew what had taken place in that dark alley twenty-two years ago. And, though Hank didn't know the details, he was aware that something bad had happened. *But what about Tonna?*

What will it do to her to learn that her biological mother gunned down her biological father? Just thinking of it made Maddi sick.

Hopefully, no one would need to know about Tonna. After all, the pregnancy had little to do with what had happened, right? Maddi sighed. *No, it had everything to do with it.* Evan had humiliated Maddi over that pregnancy; he had threatened to end it for her if she didn't end it herself. *Which is why I killed him.* But had she done it out of spite…from a position of anger and hate? Or had she actually felt threatened? Did it matter? She sighed. *Yes, one is a crime of passion; the other is self-defense.*

Regardless, she needed to talk to Tonna before the story broke. Whether or not Claire included Tonna in her relaying of events, the poor girl would still have to confront the fact that her mother killed her father. Maddi shook her head. *I did the only thing I could…with the situation I had been handed.*

She thought of Henderson and her heart broke. Though she still didn't know *why* he had killed Al-Gharsi, she guessed that he, too, had done the only thing he could with the situation he had been handed. She closed her eyes. It was killing her inside to not know…to have no idea what had happened to the good man she had fallen in love with.

Her eyes fell on her purse. It was still where she had dropped it when she walked into the room. She could see the corner of Henderson's journal next to a novel she would likely never read. *That journal might tell me…it might explain why he did what he did.*

She choked back a sob as she stood, walked over, and grabbed the black leather journal from her purse. She returned to her chair and set it in her lap. She stared at it, then touched the cover gently, her fingers trembling as they brushed against the soft leather. Henderson had written it during the dark days, those four long years when the world thought he was dead. But he hadn't been dead; he had been very much alive, doing what?

Killing people.

She opened the cover and looked again at the first entry.

> *Saturday, November 11ᵗʰ, 2000.*
> *Who am I? A simple question…no simple answer.*
> *I hurt…all the time, I hurt.*

But not just where my skin was burned. I hurt inside...in my heart.
No...even deeper.
In my soul. There. That's where I hurt.
Maddi, where are you?

She cleared her throat. If she was going to do this, she had to be ready. She read the next two entries; words she had already read...words that had disturbed her so much that she had vowed that she would go no further until he was with her.

Tuesday, November 14th, 2000
Stop! It needs to stop! I can't do this.
It's up to me...I can stop it.
So why don't I?
I'm weak...afraid.
Not for me, though.
Maddi, I miss you.

Sunday, November 19th, 2000.
Today, I learned how to kill a man with my bare hands.
I was surprisingly good at it.
A part of me even liked it.
What's happening to me?
Don't leave me, Maddi.

She braced herself to turn the page. Whatever she read from here forward would be new to her, and likely difficult to handle. She closed her eyes. Did she really want to know what had happened to the man who had changed so much that he had been able to gun down a good man – a peacemaker – in a New York City restaurant? *And to do it so well that he didn't even get caught?* She took a deep breath and nodded. *I have to know.*

She turned the page, and with a forced resolve, began to read...

Thursday, November 23rd, 2000

Thanksgiving.
Nothing to be thankful for...except Maddi.
But I can't have her.
All I have is pain...inside and out.
And I will do anything to make it stop.

Friday, December 1ˢᵗ, 2000
It's snowing again.
I used to love the snow.
Now, it's just snow.
I will learn to shoot like a sniper today.
Maddi, I miss you.

And so it went, entry after entry. Pain, anger, despair. Were Maddi to have read such words in a novel, she would have likely put down the book. The emotion was too real; it was as if *she* was feeling it, not him... not Henderson, the man who had been through so much...too much.

But read it she did...word after horrifying word. Pain so real she felt the ache of it in every part of her body. When she had gotten about halfway through, she stopped, so exhausted she had to fight to go on. *One more entry, then I'll try to sleep.*

She turned the page...

Sunday, December 24ᵗʰ, 2000
Christmas Eve.
I heard from Lili today. Not in person;
In my dreams.
But her voice was so real...
As if we were back at the castle getting ready to go sledding
I miss you, Lili

Maddi's eyes widened. *Lili! Dear God...she's in his journal!* He knew that girl well...he knew her personally...*they went sledding together!* No wonder he could hear her when no one else could.

Except for me. Why had Maddi been able to hear her?

She read on, suddenly desperate to understand how an innocent little girl could find herself on the pages of a journal written by a desperate man who had lost his way...

Monday, January 1ˢᵗ, 2001
My overseer knows of Lili.

Maddi stopped. She reread the line. His overseer...who was that? And what did it mean that the man – or woman – knew of Lili? She started to shake. She read on...

He knows who she is and where she lives.
He told me this to scare me...I think.
I'm not worried. No one would hurt an innocent child.
But I need to prepare.

Maddi wiped tears from her eyes as she stared at the words. *"...I need to prepare." Dear god...prepare for what?* What had Henderson thought his overseer would do to Lili? Her eyes narrowed. *Was that why he did it...was that why Henderson killed Al-Gharsi?* Had someone threatened Lili's life, just as someone had done hours ago in a text to Maddi, leaving Henderson no choice but to kill?

Maddi laid the journal on the arm of her chair, then stood and walked to the window, her fatigue suddenly forgotten. Was Lili the answer to all of it? Had Henderson been forced to kill out of fear for the safety of a little girl? The same girl who Maddi was trying to save by leaving the only man she would ever love? Would Henderson have actually sacrificed Middle East peace to save a single child? Maddi stared out at the darkness and sighed. *Yes...if he knew her...if he had gone sledding with her.*

Chapter 50

Indianapolis, Indiana

Blake Williams had been on the night shift for the past three months, and, though it really messed with his sleep, he liked the fact that the police station was quieter at night. Tonight was no exception, and, as he said goodnight to the last of the day-shifters, he sat at his desk, combed his fingers through his hair, and pulled his computer in front of him. He adjusted his glasses and stared at the screen. He was curious about Todd Jackson's request. *Why dig up something that happened over twenty years ago?* He frowned. *Especially when the assholes who did it are already doin' time.*

He would start by looking through the scanned-in micro phish. Even though Todd's father, Evan, had died while serving with the Evansville police department, all records from that era had been centralized to Indianapolis in 1999, and Blake found the summary of events with only a few clicks. He read through the report, but saw nothing out of the ordinary. It had taken place in December of 1982. Evan Jackson had been heading back to the station when there had been a disturbance at a nearby convenience store. He had gone – alone – to investigate, and had been overtaken by three thugs as they had been leaving the store. One got away, but the other two had been apprehended and were doing time in a nearby penitentiary. *Seems straightforward enough.*

Blake went to the next report; it was a separate summary written by a reporter who had arrived at the scene soon after the murder. Blake read it through and frowned. He scrolled back to the first report. There was an inconsistency. The first report had mentioned three robbers, while the second mentioned only two. Only two men had served time for the crime, so Blake decided that the first report had simply stated three in error. He read it again, this time to the end, stunned when he saw the name of the third suspect; Spooks Rally. Blake had heard of him; he was a witness in a federal trial that had been going on for the past three years. One of Blake's buddies was working with the Feds to try to find the kingpin of an international drug ring rumored to have a command center in Indianapolis. Blake had heard his friend mention Spooks' name time and time again in conjunction with the case. It was curious that that same criminal had been tied with the two punks involved in Evan's murder twenty-two years ago. What happened to him? Had he ever been arrested for the crime? *Was Spooks the shooter? It doesn't make any sense.*

He could find no current location for Spooks and wondered if he had been placed in witness-protection. He could only get that info from the Feds. *Or maybe the guy's dead.* Either way, he wasn't going to be able to question Spooks Rally any time soon.

Curious, he pulled up another site, which listed the state's prisons. He needed to find out what had happened to the other two crooks. He read through the names until he found the two that had been convicted of killing Evan Jackson. From what he could tell, one of them had died in Indianapolis State Prison about a year ago. The other was doing time in Pendleton Maximum Security, about forty minutes northeast of Indianapolis.

Blake was curious and a little unsettled, both by the inconsistency in the number of robbers at the scene, and by the mention of Spooks Rally, with no follow-up on what had happened to him. Though the murder had taken place over twenty years ago, he wondered if the prisoner at Pendleton could maybe fill in the gaps.

Blake checked his watch. *Nine-forty...likely 'lights out' at the penitentiary.* He wondered if his friend, Josh Ervine was still working the night shift there. Maybe Josh could question the prisoner. He looked up the number and dialed. "This is Officer Blake Williams, downtown Indy precinct. Does Josh Ervine still cover your night shift?"

There was a pause. "Yes, Officer. Do you need to speak to him?"

"Yes."

"I'll get word to him to call you. It shouldn't take long."

"Great. Thank you." Blake gave her the number and hung up. He stared at a stack of files on his desk and sighed. He had been putting off paperwork all evening; he pulled the stack in front of him. *Might as well get these papers filled out while I'm waiting.*

He stood and got a refill on his coffee. He returned to his desk, set his cup beside him, then took a file from the top of the stack. The first item was routine, done every six months on behalf of a grant he had received when he joined the Academy. The grant had made it possible for him to attend the highly-respected Indianapolis Police Academy and, though he hated the paperwork, he filed it willingly, knowing he couldn't have become a cop without help from the foundation. He looked at the questionnaire and sighed; every six months it was the same: Where are you serving? In what capacity? Do you feel your life choice to have been a good one? *Yeah, yeah, yeah…and who the hell cares?*

He leaned forward and filled in his answers. When he was finished, he slid the paper in an envelope, sealed it, and addressed it. As he put it on a stack of outgoing mail, he nodded and thought, *Thanks again, Madison Foundation.*

CHAPTER 51

Washington, DC

It worked! Morningstar thought as he stared at the champagne in his glass. *The bitch left him!* Janet had gotten word just minutes ago that the French transport plane that had been requested to take Cynthia Madison and three others to an 'undisclosed location" had been cancelled. Not only that; Morningstar had given Levi the task of monitoring all Edinburgh hotels. Madison's name had popped up on the list sometime between 12:30 and 1:00 a.m. Edinburgh time. She and her agents had apparently checked into a hotel for the night. *Which means she isn't coming back with him.*

He laughed as he emptied the glass. He reached for the bottle; it was empty. He had drunk nearly all of it. Janet had had just half a glass. *"Gotta make sure li'l Benjamin is healthy,"* she had told Morningstar as she had declined his offer for another glass. At first it had angered him. *"If I tell you to have another glass of champagne, then, by God, you will, woman...do you understand me?"* Those words hadn't actually left his mouth, however. He had recalled all too well the last time he had tried to bully Janet. It hadn't gone well; not at all. He sneered. No one was going to bully Janet; not even Morningstar.

She had gone to bed soon after the call from her contact at the State Department, leaving Morningstar alone in the sitting room of the Starlight Hotel suite. He was glad to be alone. He had a lot to think about. As Sherlock Holmes had said on countless occasions, *"The game is afoot,"* ...and so it was with Morningstar. The chess match had begun, and there were a considerable number of pieces in play.

The last Morningstar had heard, Hank Clarkson had arrived in Edinburgh sometime after nine p.m. Edinburgh time, which meant that he was likely on his way back to America with Henderson...*and without Madison*. If they left by midnight, the seven-hour flight should have them landing at Andrews Airforce Base at around two a.m. He had instructed Levi to monitor landings throughout the night, and to call him the minute Henderson's plane set down. He patted his phone. *Just a few more hours until you're home again, son.*

Clearly, his decision to spare Clarkson's life had been a good one. But soon, he, too, would need to go. *He has served his purpose.* It wouldn't be long before Clarkson realized that nearly all of the members of the War on Terror committee were dead. Morningstar narrowed his eyes. He would need to come up with an especially clever way to kill the man. He laughed. *My specialty...killing people without leaving a trace.*

He had heard from nearly all of his sons; everything was going as planned. Pocks was in London awaiting his next mission, Gad was in Latvia maneuvering to get inside the Henderson encampment, Simeon and Naphtali were still hunting for the warship, and Judah had taken Morningstar's advice and was staying in DC as the President began his late summer campaign push across America.

That left just Dan – Cobra – whose intriguing psychopathology had thrown a bit of a wrench into Morningstar's plans. When the man had answered the phone as Justice, Morningstar had been forced to quickly recalibrate. But as it turns out, the new plan was even better than the original one. Rather than have Cobra threaten Madison with the revelation of her secret if she didn't leave Henderson, he was able to persuade the gullible Justice to "save" the poor woman and the man she loved by having him warn her about a powerful group of men who had learned a Henderson secret...a secret that, if it got out, would ruin not only Matt Henderson, but his entire family. And, though it hadn't worked as planned – Madison had been willing to defy the threat – it had allowed Morningstar to send her an important message. *There are powerful men who know all about your precious Henderson.*

Justice had asked for nothing in return; only that the mystery agent *'...keep his word.'* Morningstar had vowed to do so. Had he meant it? Of course not, but he would wait to use what he knew about the Hendersons until it was needed. The revelation that both Phoenix and

Cobra were Walter Henderson's biological sons would set the world on fire.

So much of what he was about to do would set the world on fire. That had been his purpose all along. The fact that he continued to find willing dupes to help him was a clear testament to his favor in the eyes of God. Actually, he had concluded that he had pretty much become an equal with God. He laughed. *God will soon be coming to me for advice.*

He gulped down the last of the champagne, then set the empty glass on the table. He walked to the liquor cabinet and was about to pull out a bottle of Basil Hayden, when his private cellphone rang. He ran back and grabbed it from the desk. "Yes?"

The minute he heard the deep laugh on the other end of the line he knew exactly who it was. "Hello, Morningstar."

"Hello, Dan. Long time, no talk to."

Another laugh; this one was more of a smirk. "It appears that you have been talking to the annoying Mark Justice."

Morningstar's eyes widened. *How does this work? Does he know what I said?*

As if in answer, Cobra added, "You should probably consult me before you reach out to that bastard…regardless of what you want to discuss."

Morningstar's mind was going a mile a minute. How could he take advantage of this situation? He cleared his throat. "I…I was actually looking for you, Dan."

"I'm not Dan, you dumbass." A pause. "Why were you looking for me?"

Think, Morningstar…think! "Um…well…uh, I have a little job for you."

Another pause. "Did you offer this same job to Justice?"

"No. I was actually quite disappointed with my chat with Justice."

"I see. And why was that?"

"Because I had hoped that he would be clever…like you…but he didn't even come close." Morningstar grinned. "Actually, I found Justice to be somewhat of a bore."

Genuine laughter this time. "Yes, he is that. What is this *job* you want me to do?"

Morningstar chuckled. "I need you to kill someone."

"My specialty."

"Yes, but it has to look like an accident."

"I see. And who am I killing this time?"

Morningstar poured the Basel Hayden into a glass and drank it down in one gulp. He smacked his lips and set the glass on the counter. "Dr. Hank Clarkson. I believe that you know his son, Roger."

There was a pause. "I do. I actually know Hank, as well. I had the opportunity to spend a brief bit of time with him in a cave underneath Paris…but I digress." A pause. "So, where is this Hank?"

"On his way from Scotland to America as we speak."

"America? You want me to travel across the ocean to kill him?"

"Yes, Dan. I'll make the arrangements. Be near your phone."

Another pause. "And what do I get in return?"

Morningstar flinched; Cobra always wanted something in return. "Isn't it enough that you're killing Roger's daddy?"

"No. I have big plans for Roger, and they don't involve Hank."

Morningstar swallowed. He needed to come up with something quick. Suddenly, he grinned. "Don't worry, Cobra, once Hank is dead, I'll give you something that you've always wanted."

"Yeah…and what's that?"

"Revenge…on your father and your brother and everything they stand for."

"You know that I can kill them any time I want to."

"This is better than killing them."

"What could be better than killing them?"

It was Morningstar's turn to laugh. "The pain of loss, Dan. Once I know that Hank is dead, I'll show you a blueprint that will allow you to take everything from the Hendersons *without* killing them." He waited. Would Cobra bite?

After a long pause, he heard Cobra sigh. "This better be good, Morningstar."

Morningstar wanted to say, *'Or what?'* but he refrained, deciding that he didn't want to know the answer. "Oh, it will be good. You have my word, Dan."

He heard a "humph" and the line went dead. He stared at the phone. He poured another glass of bourbon and, again, downed it in one gulp. With a simple phone call, he had just solved two very thorny problems. If things went as planned, not only would he destroy Henderson and his annoying family, but he would kill off another member of his secret War on Terror committee. He picked up his empty glass and threw it against the wall. It shattered into pieces, and he laughed. "Yes, God, You gave me Cobra, but never forget, 'tis I who comes up with the plans."

CHAPTER 52

Edinburgh, Scotland

Never had Gina looked more beautiful. And he, Corporal James Calvin, had never felt so much love for one person. He was to be shipped off that afternoon for another tour in Iraq, but, this time, it was harder to leave. The first three tours had been easy; the locations were away from the gunfire, and the majority of the world supported what the coalition forces were trying to do. But things had heated up since then. Iraq had become not only a hotbed of insurgency, but a hotbed of political warfare, as well. Calvin cared nothing about the politics, but he did care about the Iraqi people. Though the insurgents made it seem as though America wasn't wanted there, he knew better. The Iraqis he had gotten to know cherished their brief experiment with democracy. And it was their love of freedom that would allow Calvin to somehow leave behind the beautiful woman he had just made love with.

"Call me, will you Jimmy...every day?"

Her long brown hair was mussed from sleep and she looked more beautiful than she ever had. He leaned over and kissed her. "I will, babe. Every day...I promise."

He stood and walked to the door. It was time to go; time to say goodbye to the love of his life. He was grateful for what they had... he knew it would carry him through the worst firefight. As he looked back at her, he thought, 'even if I never see her again... I've left a part of me with her, and she now owns my soul...'

Henderson awoke in a sea of sweat. The Calvin memory – a relic of the face transplant that had somehow left him with the memories and emotions of the man whose face he now wore – had left him feeling even more depressed. He was on a stretcher in a plane, and the IV he longed to shed had come with him. But he was still sick; he could feel it. His half-brother, Cobra, had made sure of it. Even though Henderson had come out of the coma, he continued to suffer from the strange illness that would take him for a while, then release him, then take him again. *What did that bastard do to me?*

The plane had yet to move; something about the fog. His father was sitting on one side of him, his mother on the other, and they each held a hand. Their expressions were protective, like when he had had pneumonia as a child. They had protected him his whole life, and it felt good to have them with him. Then he remembered: *Maddi has left me.* He closed his eyes and turned his head, doing his best to bury it in the pillow. Though her departure had been necessary, not only to keep her secrets but to rid her of the stain that he had become, her absence had left a hole in his heart he felt certain would never mend.

Henderson had longed to die many times over the course of the last four years, but never had he wanted it more than now. He looked at the monitors surrounding him and the IV in his arm and frowned. *How will I die with all this keeping me alive?* He wanted to reach over and strip it all away, but he knew…*that won't kill me.* It was as if Cobra had known; as if he had purposely made sure that Henderson wouldn't die, but would be sickened forever by whatever Cobra had given him. Had that been his plan? To force Henderson to be forever ill, weak and defeated as he came face to face with the terrible things he had done? If so, he had succeeded. And now, on top of it, Henderson had lost the only woman he would ever love. *Why couldn't it have ended like Calvin and Gina?*

James Calvin, a corporal in the U.S. Army, had died bravely on an Iraqi battlefield soon after that afternoon when he had left Gina in their bed. He had then unknowingly donated his face to Henderson's reconstruction. But Henderson hadn't only gotten the man's solid jaw and smooth skin; he had also gotten his psyche. By some bizarre quirk of fate, he was aware of Calvin's thoughts and feelings, and had been forced to experience them many times since the transformation in March. *And now I get to suffer as I feel his love for – and from – his beautiful Gina.*

Calvin's death had given Henderson a new chance at life, an opportunity to start over…not only with the new face, but with a new direction, away from the killing he had done for four years; away from

Morningstar. But, without Maddi, none of it mattered. She had been his heartbeat for four long years, and now…it was as if he was dead.

He coughed and Dora leaned closer, patting his forehead with a damp cloth, soothing him with gentle words of reassurance. He closed his eyes; he couldn't look at her. *She has no idea who she's comforting.*

He began to shake. He had been through too much; suffered too greatly…*and for what?* There he lay; physically broken, emotionally dead. His reconstructed face meant nothing; Calvin's contribution had been a waste.

He waited, hoping that another image from Calvin's past might offer guidance. That's what had always happened before. Calvin had become his guide through the darkness, a wise voice as he navigated a world of unparalleled suffering. *So, why am I being tortured by a memory of undying love from his wife, Gina, when I have turned away the only woman that I will ever care for?* It was as if even Calvin was mocking him; as if he, too, had turned his back on him. Calvin had died knowing his lover's heart belonged to him. But not Henderson. No, Maddi had left him, not only with sorrow, but with disillusionment…*and just a little bit of fear.* He had seen it in her eyes, and it had hurt him far more than her physical absence. *Maddi is afraid of me.*

He couldn't take it; he knew he couldn't live with it, and, out of nowhere, he reached up and jerked the IV from his arm. "I just want to die! Why is that so hard to understand?"

Dora stared at him, stunned, as tears came to her eyes. Henderson turned away. *She doesn't understand. She still thinks Martin's alive; that he's living inside this broken body.* But Walter got it, probably Hank, too; Martin was dead. And it was time that Dora faced the same truth: the bitter man lying next to her longing for death, hating himself wasn't Martin; he was a stranger. The sooner she came to grips with it, the better.

Though he had faced the worst pain possible, it had been tolerable because of two driving forces: his love for Maddi and his hatred for Morningstar. Maddi was gone and he was left with nothing but his deep hatred for his enemy. Was it enough? Was his desire for vengeance enough to make him want to live? Did his need to make Morningstar pay for what he'd done to him – for what he'd taken from him – give him the will to carry on? *Take over the world, Morningstar. What do I care? Lili's dead…and Maddi's gone.*

A medic replaced the IV as Walter leaned in and whispered sternly in his ear, "Look, son, I don't know what happened in the time from when we left to when we came back," he rubbed his eyes; Henderson could see the hurt, "…but you can't do this to your mother. She…lost you once and it nearly…killed her." He sighed. "To hear you be so hateful…so empty, well…it's killing her all over again."

Henderson closed his eyes and turned his head. *Is this some cruel joke, God? You let me live…You let me grasp for a brief moment the people I used to know and love, and then You rip them from me. Why? What have I done that makes You feel the need to punish me? Yes, I did awful things as the Phoenix, but I didn't ask for that role…it was forced on me by a madman. And yet it is I who am being blamed for the atrocities of the world, it is I who am suffering this loss of love, and it is I who must try to put on a brave face for a mother and father who have suffered greatly as a result of the choices that I have been forced to make.* He tightened his jaw. He would cry out no longer; he would spare Dora that. But, at the first opportunity, he would most certainly find a way to die.

CHAPTER 53

Edinburgh, Scotland

Maddi had no idea how long she had stood at that window. She felt numb; paralyzed by all that had happened and all she had learned… about Henderson, about Lili, about herself. She pulled back the curtain and looked out at the night. It was still raining; there was no moon, no stars. The few lampposts scattered here and there weren't enough to push back the darkness. And she felt it…every inch of that black wet night. She had learned just hours ago that she was about to be turned in for a crime she had committed over two decades ago, and that the man she loved more than life itself had murdered her dear friend, Al-Gharsi. And she had figured out just minutes ago that Henderson may have carried out that horrid act for the love of a child.

She closed her eyes. *Like me.* She absently put her hand to her belly…to the memory of her own child hiding inside her, needing her protection.

We both killed a man…to save a child.

Again, she began to shake. Soon she was shaking so badly she was forced to return to the chair. She closed her eyes and took several deep breaths. *Both of us…did a very bad thing…for all the right reasons.* She frowned. *So, why did I leave him?* She sighed. Also, for all the right reasons. *To save a little girl's life.*

But she felt like she was dying inside. If leaving him was for all the right reasons, then why did it hurt so bad. She struggled to swallow, and began to choke. *Calm down, Maddi… you have to calm down.* But she couldn't; too much had gone wrong. Regardless of why Henderson had killed a man, he had done it, and sooner or later the world would learn of it, and his life would be over. Regardless of why Maddi had killed a man, she had done it, and the world would soon learn of it, and her life would be over. But her life felt as if it had already ended; in a nursing home just miles from where she sat. She stared at the wall, too numb to even cry. She had lost everything…absolutely everything.

Then she heard it; the voice; the same voice she had heard at the nursing home, in Dalgety Bay, and at her home in DC. It was Lili. *"Remember the saying."*

Maddi scanned the room, looking for Lili. She stood and checked behind the bed, then walked to the closet. She opened the door and looked inside. No one. She checked the bathroom and pulled aside the shower curtain, her hands shaking as she waited to see the ghost – the young child – who kept speaking to her from…where? There was no one. *Again, just my imagination…it has to be.* She returned to the chair; she was still shaking.

"Remember the saying…that your mom used to tell you when things got tough."
Maddi closed her eyes and covered her ears. *You're losing it, girl.*

"I'll remind you," said the voice. *"The barn's burnt down, now I see the moon."*

Maddi opened her eyes. "What did you say?"

"The barn's burnt down, now I see the moon."

Tears filled Maddi's eyes as she again looked around the room. Her mother *had* said that…on several occasions, not the least of which was the day that Maddi told her she was pregnant. *But how does this girl, this Lili, who I can never see, know that?*

"Where are you?" Maddi whispered.

Silence.

"Where are you, Lili?" she said again, a bit louder. "Are you safe?"

The voice was fading. *"I can't tell you where I am, but I'm safe…for now."*

Maddi held her breath and waited. But she could feel it; the girl, Lili, was gone. And with her was gone the comfort…the pure goodness that the child seemed to convey.

Maddi walked to the window. Lili was safe, *"…for now."* What did that even mean? As Maddi stared again at a malevolent night, she pondered the unlikelihood of the same girl – the same *ghost* – talking to her again and again, across time and space…*and then being used as a threat to get me to leave Henderson.* The man who had texted her also knew Lili.

Was it possible that he was behind it all…that the vile man who had texted Maddi was also the 'overseer' Henderson had spoken of in his journal? It made far more sense than thinking they were different. But if it was the same man, then who was he? And why was it so important to him that Maddi say goodbye to Henderson…forever?

She stumbled to the bed, digesting the implausibility of it all; a ghost child who was real, but talked to her from a place far away…a despicable man who was willing to use that child to get what he wanted, not only from Henderson, but from her.

But strangest of all was the fact that the child seemed to *know* Maddi…she had known exactly what to say; exactly what her mother had said to her so many years ago.

Maddi sighed. It didn't really matter. There was no moon to see… not for her, anyway. Henderson was gone…this time, forever. Even if she were to try to go back to him, he was now in the custody of the United States Government. He was out of her life…for good.

She began to cry…silent, unrelenting tears. Soon, the tears became sobs as she thought, *Dear God…what have I done?* How could she have left him? And now, for whatever reason, he was being questioned by the U.S. government. Yes, it was Hank who was asking the questions, but he hadn't come there on a mission of kindness; she had seen it in his eyes.

If only I had taken all four of us to that transport plane…then, at least Henderson would be safe. She shook her head and sighed. *But Lili wouldn't.* She nodded. *I had to do it…I had no other choice but to leave him behind.*

Suddenly, she frowned. *But I could've gone away by myself.* She could have taken that plane to some exotic island where the challenges of the world couldn't touch her. Not only the pain from her loss of Henderson, but the reality of what her trusted therapist was about to do. Claire would soon tell a prosecutor, who would tell the world that Senator Cynthia Madison shot a cop in a back alley twenty-two years ago and covered it up. Her political enemies would have a field day. *My career is over.*

Maddi had been a senator, first in the Statehouse, then in the Capitol, for over a decade; there wasn't a day that went by that she didn't feel that she had ended up exactly where she was supposed to. *What will I do now?* She sighed. *I suppose it depends on whether I go to jail.* She wondered how long the Prosecutor would sit on the news. *Not long, I'm sure.* Which meant that her arrival home would be eventful, to say the least.

There was nothing she could do about it. The die had been cast. Her political enemies would run with the story, regardless of what Maddi said or did. But those who mattered – those few she truly cared about – would understand. *But what about Tonna?* She sat up and sighed. *I need to talk to Tonna…soon.*

She slid from the bed and walked to a mirror. She combed her fingers through her hair, stunned at the woman looking back at her. Even in the dim lamplight, she could see the gray circles under her eyes, the paleness of her skin. She turned away, unwilling to look at herself a second longer. She took a step toward the door. Her legs buckled, and she fell against the wall. She took a deep breath, gathered her strength, and walked to the door. She gripped the knob, doing her best to steady her hand as she turned it and opened the door.

Cravens was sitting on the couch with a field manual draped on his lap. He looked up and frowned. "Everything okay, Senator?"

She cleared her throat. "I…I need to talk to Tonna Kauffold…as soon as possible." She paused. "And then we need to book a flight… for home."

He laid his manual on the table and looked up at her. "Are you sure, Senator?"

She nodded. Again, her knees felt weak, and she stumbled to a chair.

He stood to help her. "Are you sure you're okay, Senator?"

Maddi looked up at him and sighed. *Dear Cravens.* "No, I can't say that I am." She offered a weak smile, as she added, "The barn's burning down, Cravens…let's hope I see the moon."

CHAPTER 54

Philadelphia, Pennsylvania

Todd was antsy. It had been nearly three hours since he had called Blake, and he hadn't left his apartment. He was currently drumming the table with his fingers, having done his best to try to relax on his oversized blue couch; the couch his mom had given him. He grinned as he thought of his mother. Though she was a weak woman, she had been good to him. She was small and a bit mousy, but she had managed to take care of him and raise him up right. She had even gotten him through the prestigious – and high-priced – Indianapolis Police Academy with nothing more than the meager earnings of a Safeway employee. *And a little help from some sort of foundation.* But the foundation's role had been minimal, he was sure. His mother had simply managed her funds well. *Like my daddy musta taught her before he died.* His phone vibrated and he jumped.

"Hey Todd, it's Blake."

"Finally!"

"Sorry, but I wanted to check things out before I called you." He lowered his voice. "I'm in the back of the precinct and I'm using my cellphone. I just got off the phone with a guard at Pendleton. I had him question one of the guys accused of killing your dad. The other guy's dead."

"Were there only two? I thought there were three."

"Yeah, well, that's the problem. There's a discrepancy. It's why I called my friend."

Todd leaned forward. "Okay…so what did the scumbag prisoner have to say?"

There was a pause. "He said the third guy was only added to bolster the case."

Todd frowned. "What the hell does that mean?"

"I don't know. The prisoner I talked to, Denzel Banks, admits to the robbery, but he swears that he and his buddy had nothing to do with killing a cop."

"They were never convicted of it, right?"

"No, just the robbery. But the prison guards have made his life a living hell because they think he had something to do with killin' a cop. He swears he's innocent."

"Don't they all?"

"Yeah, but this is different. He swears there was a cover-up of some sort."

"What's he mean…a cover-up?"

"He told the guard that powerful people made the truth disappear. He and his friend took the fall and they never should have."

"Isn't Banks guilty of about thirteen robberies?"

"Yeah, and the heist in Evansville woulda put him away for life, regardless; 'three strikes' and all that. But even now, twenty years later, the thing that pisses him off the most is that they think he killed a cop."

"What do you think? Is there any truth to his story?"

"I didn't think so at first, but then I reread the reports." Todd could hear papers rustling in the background. "Like I said, they're inconsistent; one says there were three guys, another says two. But then I saw that there was a report missing; a first-responders' report. They would have had to have called EMS. I looked for it everywhere; it's not there. And the murder weapon…it was never found, either." He paused. "Jackson, someone killed your father twenty-two years ago, but I don't think it went down the way they said."

Todd's mind felt muddled. "Are you sure about the prisoner? I mean, was he maybe givin' you something just so he could beg for an early release?"

"I don't think so. He's in for life, no matter what. Besides, he's right about the discrepancies. Somethin' doesn't add up about the whole thing."

"Three crooks versus two, no first-responder's report, and no murder weapon...right?"

"Right."

Todd frowned. "I wonder why they didn't work harder to find answers." He paused. "I'm kinda pissed off, if ya' wanna' know the truth."

"I get it. The whole thing smells if you ask me." Blake hesitated. "Listen, I know you're gonna' try to look into this. I'll give you a link and the passwords that'll let you access the records, but," there was a pause, "...Jackson, you can't tell a soul that I gave you any of this, okay?"

"Sure thing, Blake." Todd took down the information and hung up the phone.

He left the apartment and jumped in his car. He drove to the station, determined to learn more about what had happened in a lonely alley twenty-two years ago. He was certain now that someone had covered it up, and he was hell-bent on learning who and why. He knew the Blue Brotherhood was looking into it; maybe he should just let them handle it. One thing was certain; if they found out who killed his daddy, they would make things right. *But it's my job; I should be the one who evens the score.*

He reached the station and ran inside, nodding at two night-beat cops. He went into the records room and pulled out the scrap of paper where he had jotted down the passwords. He logged onto the computer and went to the link that Blake had mentioned. He plugged in the first password, which opened all files prior to 1999. He then used the second password, which gave him access to specific files. He started by opening the section which catalogued members of the police force. Every person who had ever served was listed, along with every detail, award, or punishment they had ever received. Todd's mother had told him that they had moved to Evansville because of a promotion. Todd found the transfer papers and was filled with pride. *"This selection comes as no surprise, considering the fine work that Evan Jackson has done for the people of McCordsville."*

Todd was only a baby at the time; he remembered nothing of McCordsville, and his mother had never bothered to share much about it. As a matter of fact, his mom had shared little of his childhood, and even less about his father…she seemed content to remember him only as a brave police officer; nothing more. There were no family photos; it was as if the past was nothing more than the life of a cop who died in the line of duty. Why? Todd had assumed it was because of the violent way he had died. *It hurt Mom too bad to even think about those days.* But maybe there was more to it. Maybe something bad had happened in McCordsville, and they had left town to escape. Maybe his father had pissed somebody off and that was why he had moved the family to Evansville. And then, maybe that person had followed him to Evansville and had taken care of business. Maybe Evan's partner at the time could shed some light. *If he's still alive.*

Todd scanned the file for the name of his dad's partner.

He found a list of cops and their partners on the McCordsville police force during the time when his father was there. He skimmed the list and saw the name Stewart Madison listed beside his father's. He clicked to Madison's file and read it through. He stopped when he got to the end, surprised to see that Madison had been gunned down during a jewelry heist. Both men had been killed in pretty much the same way. A coincidence?

He rubbed his chin as he leaned back in the chair. *I need to go at this from a different angle.* Maybe if he could find out what happened to the missing EMS report, he could get some insight into what happened that day. *There has to be a reason why it was removed from the record.* He clicked on a link that took him to old newspaper articles concerning gang busts, bank heists, and other police business. He was hoping to find an article about the murder…maybe an interview with one of the paramedics at the scene. He started with a section titled "Officers Killed in the Line of Duty," but there was nothing. *Why not?* He finally found an article from an Evansville paper archived under the heading "Robberies." It told of the robbery at the convenience store, and the subsequent murder of his father. He read it through and found no surprises. There were the names of the two robbery suspects, the store they had been trying to rob, and a mention of a third man, '…*who somehow managed to escape the police.*' There was a brief paragraph about Evan Jackson's bravery. The more Todd read, the madder he got, and just as he was about to click off, he noted a small blurb at the end. "Another officer at the scene declined to offer any information. The officer, Gerome Mitchell, would say only that the matter would be handled internally."

Todd's eyes widened. *Gerome Mitchell...what the hell? The man's my captain!*

He checked his watch. *Ten-forty-five.* Mitchell often stayed late, swearing it was the only time he got any work done.

Todd ran from the archive room to the back of the station. He burst into the captain's office. Mitchell looked up from a half-raised cup of coffee. "Can I help you, Jackson?"

"You were there!"

The captain, a middle-aged man with much older eyes, set down the coffee and looked at Todd over a pair of cheap reading glasses. He said calmly, "I was where?"

"At the scene when my dad was killed."

Mitchell sat back and removed the glasses. He laid them on the desk and breathed a heavy sigh. "I wasn't exactly at the scene, Todd." He paused. "I came along about three minutes later. My partner and I saw two thugs running from that direction, and we collared them. With nothing else to go on, they became the only suspects." He paused. "And they swore they knew nothing about it."

Todd's eye was twitching. "But why were you in Evansville?"

"I had family in nearby Spurgeon, and I spent about six months in Evansville. I was asked to come to Philly soon after that incident with your father."

Todd could barely contain himself. "Didn't you find that odd?"

Mitchell shook his head and sighed. "Naw, cops were being encouraged to move to big cities all the time. *That's where the crime is'* they would always tell us."

Todd was bristling. "So, tell me about that night. Is there something that might suggest that those thugs weren't telling the truth?"

"What's this about, Todd?"

"Let's just say I've gotten some information that suggests that someone else was responsible for my dad's murder. Like maybe it had nothing to do with the crooks who robbed that store. The first responder's report is missing. And no weapon was found."

Mitchell rubbed his eyes and leaned forward, rustling papers on his desk. "Maybe you should just let sleeping dogs lie."

Todd glared at the man. "You sound like my mom. Now come on, Captain. If there's something more, I deserve to know what it is!"

Mitchell rubbed his forehead. His voice was quiet as he said, "There is something."

Todd was pacing in front of the desk. "What?"

The captain's voice grew quieter still. "What I'm about to tell you hasn't been told to anyone, not even my superior officer at the time." He stood, walked to the door, and closed it. He returned to his seat and eased into it slowly. He leaned back and crossed his arms over his chest. "Something did happen about that time, Todd, which might've had an impact on the case."

Todd fell into a chair in front of the desk. He rubbed his hands on his thighs to try to calm down. "I'm listening."

Mitchell sighed. "There was a woman. Well, actually, a girl, that your daddy must have gotten hooked up with somehow."

Todd's eyes widened. "A girl? What's a damn skirt got to do with anything?"

"I think your daddy might've had a fling with this girl, and then I think he left her high and dry. She was pretty upset about it."

"Big deal, Chief. Love 'em and leave 'em... what's it matter?"

"Well, in this case it mattered a lot. The girl was pregnant."

Todd's eyes widened even further. "Did she have the kid?"

Mitchell shook his head. "I don't know. Your dad accused her of sleeping around and said the kid wasn't his, but she swore it was. She was sure pissed off when your daddy didn't want anything to do with her."

Todd frowned. "Who was it? Who was the girl?"

Mitchell shook his head and sighed. He looked long and hard at Todd. "Well, at the time she was a nobody. But she's turned out to be a pretty big deal."

"Who is she?"

Mitchell shifted in his seat. "Her dad and your dad had been partners back in McCordsville."

"My dad knocked up *his partner's daughter?*" Todd grimaced. He tried to remember the name. He closed his eyes and visualized the page. "Madison."

Mitchell nodded. "Yeah, a pretty ugly thing at the time. But Stewart Madison had been dead for years, and I guess your dad thought enough time had passed."

Todd frowned. "So, what's this Madison bitch doing now?"

Mitchell chuckled. "She's the Majority Whip of the United States Senate."

THE END OF PART I

ABOUT THE AUTHOR

Dr. Jill Vosler is a family physician whose medical studies took her abroad to the University of Edinburgh in Scotland and on to extensive travel throughout the UK and Europe. Her love for these places has flavored her novels, along with the many years spent as a deputy coroner under the guidance of her father, who was the county coroner well into his eighties. She has a keen interest in geopolitics and a passion for music, but most enjoys traveling the world with family and friends.

NewAtlantianLibrary.com or
AbsolutelyAmazingEbooks.com
or AA-eBooks.com

Thank you for reading. Please review this book. Reviews help others find Absolutely Amazing eBooks and inspire us to keep providing these marvelous tales.

If you would like to be put on our email list to receive updates on new releases, contests, and promotions, please go to AbsolutelyAmazingEbooks.com and sign up.

For sales, editorial information, subsidiary rights information
or a catalog, please write or phone or e-mail

AbsolutelyAmazingEbooks
Manhanset House
Shelter Island Hts., New York 11965, US
Tel: 212-427-7139
www.AbsolutelyAmazingEbooks.com
bricktower@aol.com
www.IngramContent.com

For sales in the UK and Europe please contact our distributor,
Gazelle Book Services
White Cross Mills
Lancaster, LA1 4XS, UK
Tel: (01524) 68765 Fax: (01524) 63232
email: jacky@gazellebooks.co.uk

Printed in the USA
CPSIA information can be obtained
at www.ICGtesting.com
LVHW051911031123
763018LV00019B/66